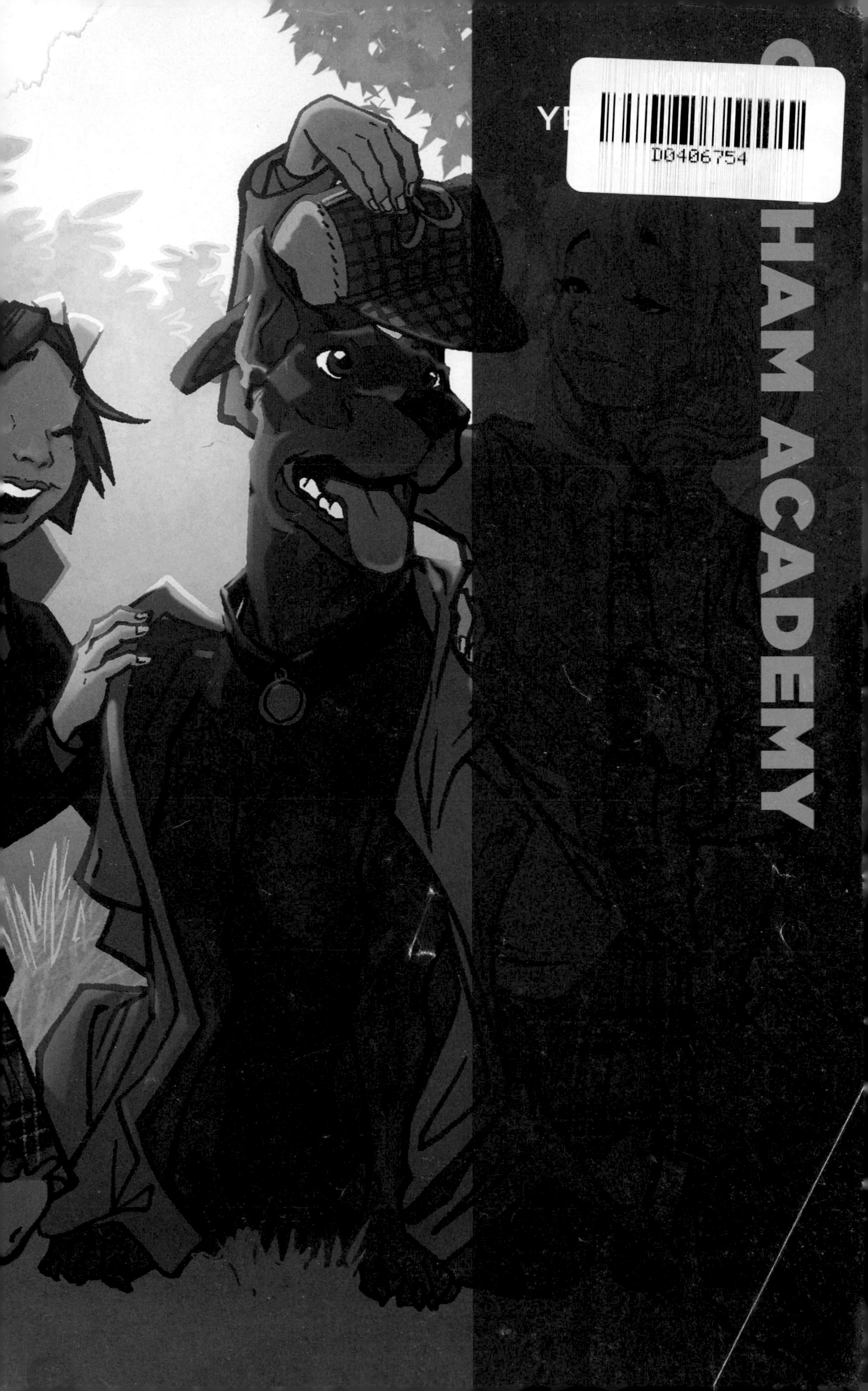
HAM ACADEMY

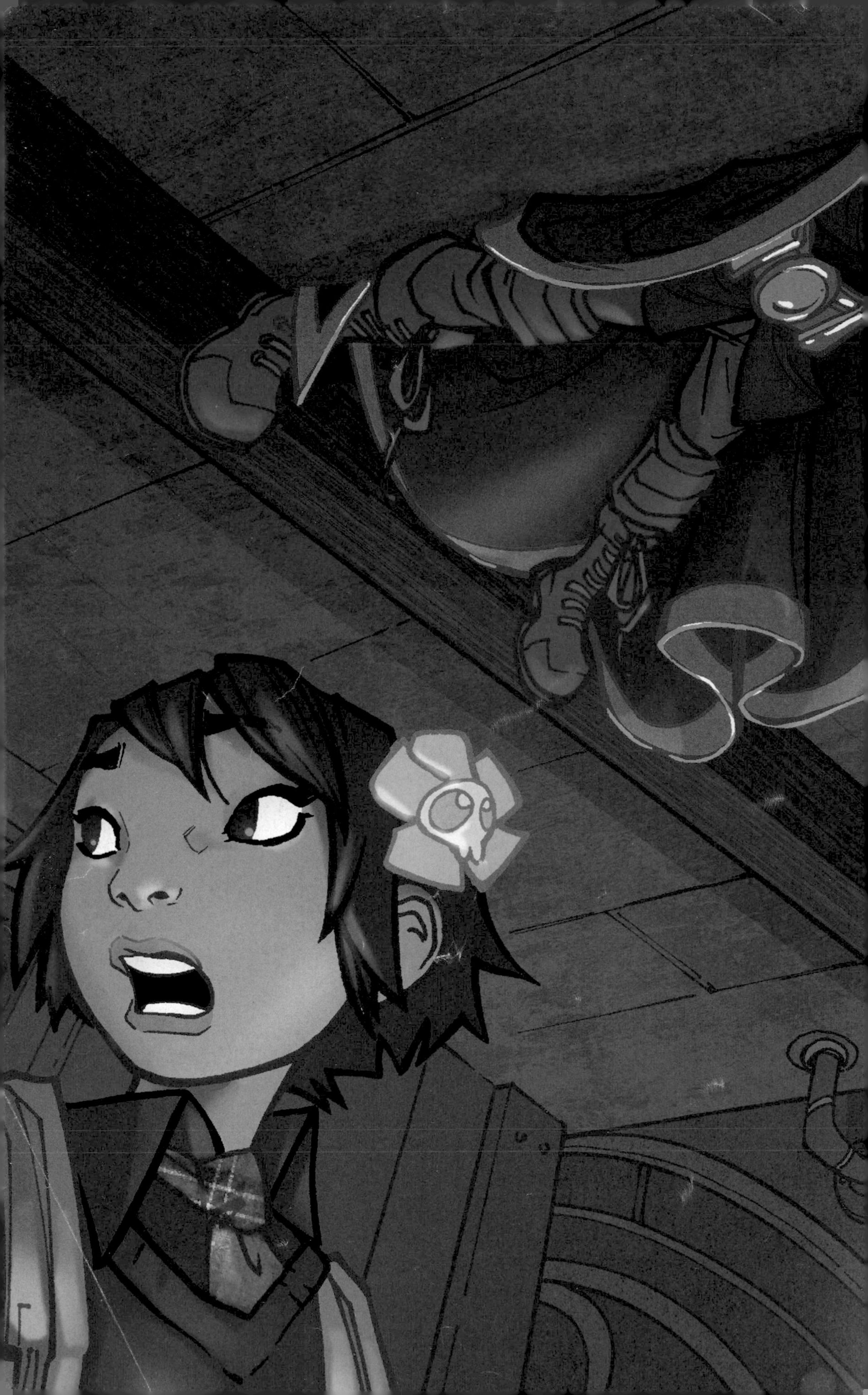

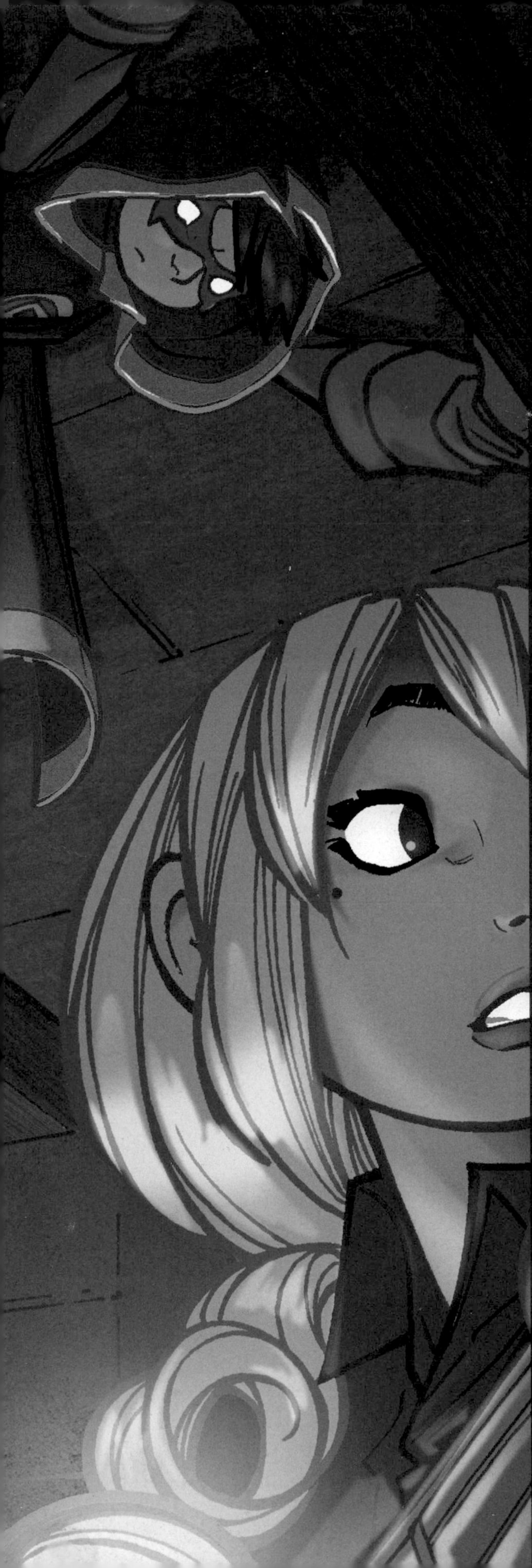

GOTHAM ACADEMY

VOLUME 3
YEARBOOK

WRITTEN BY
BRENDEN FLETCHER

PENCILS BY
ADAM ARCHER

INKS BY
SANDRA HOPE

COLOR BY
ADAM ARCHER
SERGE LaPOINTE

LETTERS BY
STEVE WANDS

FEATURING SHORT STORIES BY
DEREK FRIDOLFS
DUSTIN NGUYEN
KATIE COOK
HOPE LARSON
KRIS MUKAI
ZAC GORMAN
EDUARDO MEDEIROS
RAFAEL ALBUQUERQUE
DAVE McCAIG
MINGJUE HELEN CHEN
JAMES TYNION IV
CHRISTIAN WILDGOOSE
KEN NIIMURA
ANNIE WU
MICHAEL DIALYNAS
DAVID PETERSEN
MORITAT
STEVE ORLANDO
MINKYU JUNG
NATASHA ALTERICI
FAITH ERIN HICKS
BECKY CLOONAN
MSASSYK
ROB HAYNES
COLLEEN COOVER

COLLECTION COVER ART BY
MINGJUE HELEN CHEN

REBECCA TAYLOR Editor – Original Series
JEB WOODARD Group Editor – Collected Editions
ROBIN WILDMAN Editor – Collected Edition
STEVE COOK Design Director – Books
DAMIAN RYLAND Publication Design

BOB HARRAS Senior VP – Editor-in-Chief, DC Comics

DIANE NELSON President
DAN DiDIO and JIM LEE Co-Publishers
GEOFF JOHNS Chief Creative Officer
AMIT DESAI Senior VP – Marketing & Global Franchise Management
NAIRI GARDINER Senior VP – Finance
SAM ADES VP – Digital Marketing
BOBBIE CHASE VP – Talent Development
MARK CHIARELLO Senior VP – Art, Design & Collected Editions
JOHN CUNNINGHAM VP – Content Strategy
ANNE DePIES VP – Strategy Planning & Reporting
DON FALLETTI VP – Manufacturing Operations
LAWRENCE GANEM VP – Editorial Administration & Talent Relations
ALISON GILL Senior VP – Manufacturing & Operations
HANK KANALZ Senior VP – Editorial Strategy & Administration
JAY KOGAN VP – Legal Affairs
DEREK MADDALENA Senior VP – Sales & Business Development
JACK MAHAN VP – Business Affairs
DAN MIRON VP – Sales Planning & Trade Development
NICK NAPOLITANO VP – Manufacturing Administration
CAROL ROEDER VP – Marketing
EDDIE SCANNELL VP – Mass Account & Digital Sales
COURTNEY SIMMONS Senior VP – Publicity & Communications
JIM (SKI) SOKOLOWSKI VP – Comic Book Specialty & Newsstand Sales
SANDY YI Senior VP – Global Franchise Management

GOTHAM ACADEMY VOLUME 3: YEARBOOK

Published by DC Comics. Compilation and all new material Copyright © 2016 DC Comics. All Rights Reserved.
Originally published in single magazine form in GOTHAM ACADEMY 13-18, GOTHAM ACADEMY ANNUAL 1.
Copyright © 2016 DC Comics. All Rights Reserved. All characters, their distinctive likenesses and related elements
featured in this publication are trademarks of DC Comics. The stories, characters and incidents featured in this publication
are entirely fictional. DC Comics does not read or accept unsolicited submissions of ideas, stories or artwork.

DC Comics, 2900 West Alameda Avenue, Burbank, CA 91505
Printed by RR Donnelley, Salem, VA, USA. 9/30/16. First Printing.
ISBN: 978-1-4012-6478-9

Library of Congress Cataloging-in-Publication Data is available.

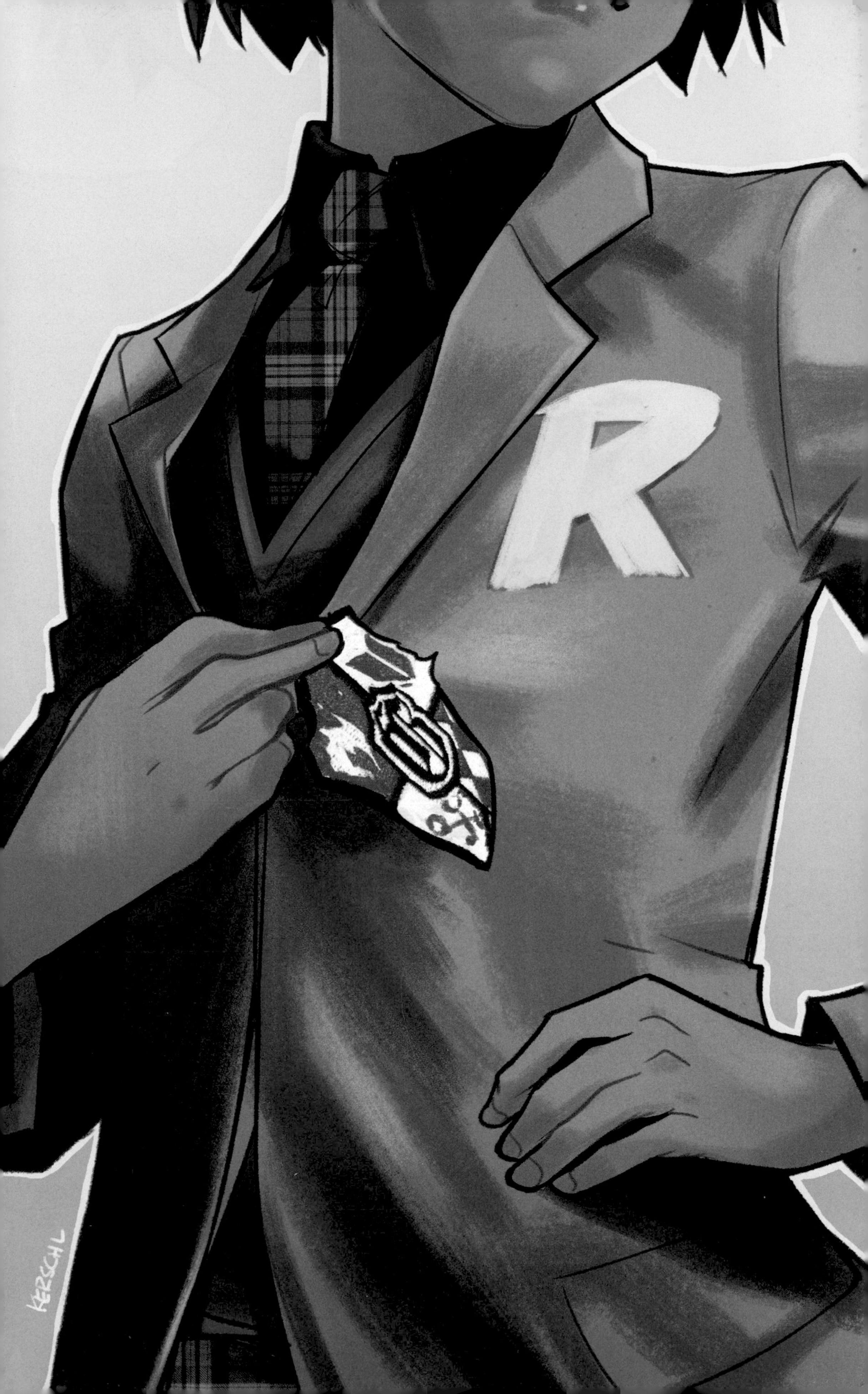
KERSCHL

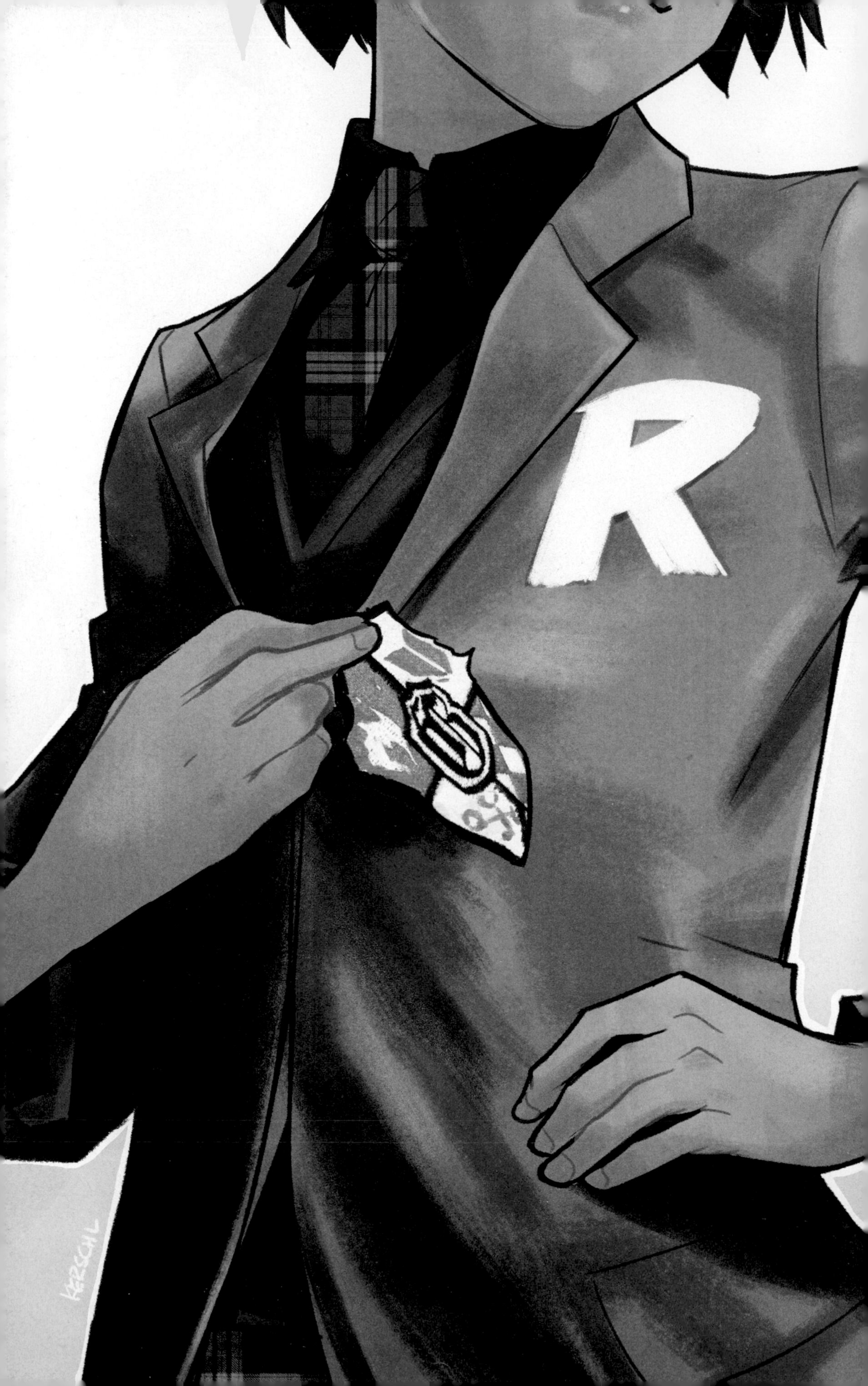

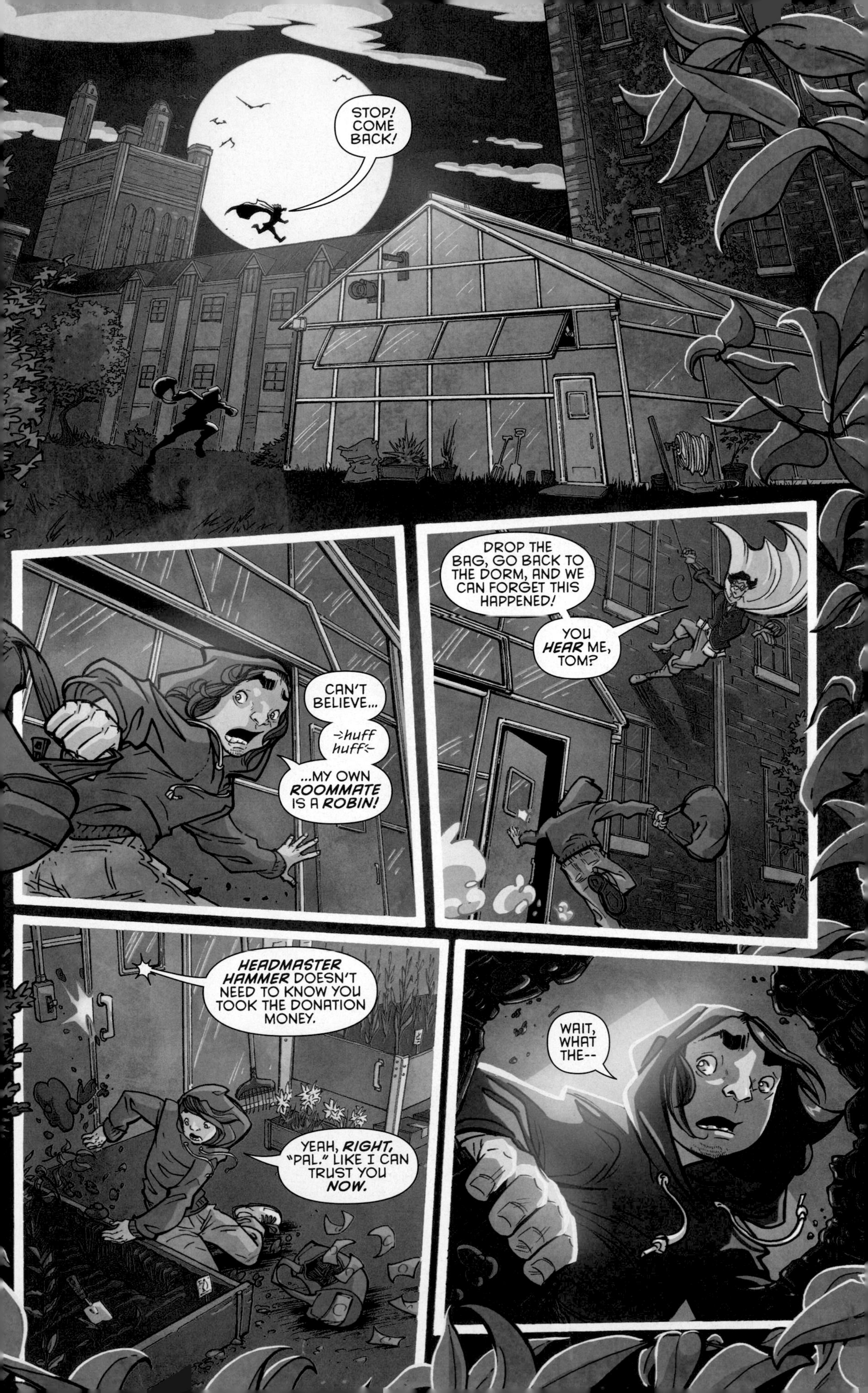
STOP! COME BACK!
CAN'T BELIEVE...
huff huff
...MY OWN ROOMMATE IS A ROBIN!
DROP THE BAG, GO BACK TO THE DORM, AND WE CAN FORGET THIS HAPPENED!
YOU HEAR ME, TOM?
HEADMASTER HAMMER DOESN'T NEED TO KNOW YOU TOOK THE DONATION MONEY.
YEAH, RIGHT, "PAL." LIKE I CAN TRUST YOU NOW.
WAIT, WHAT THE--

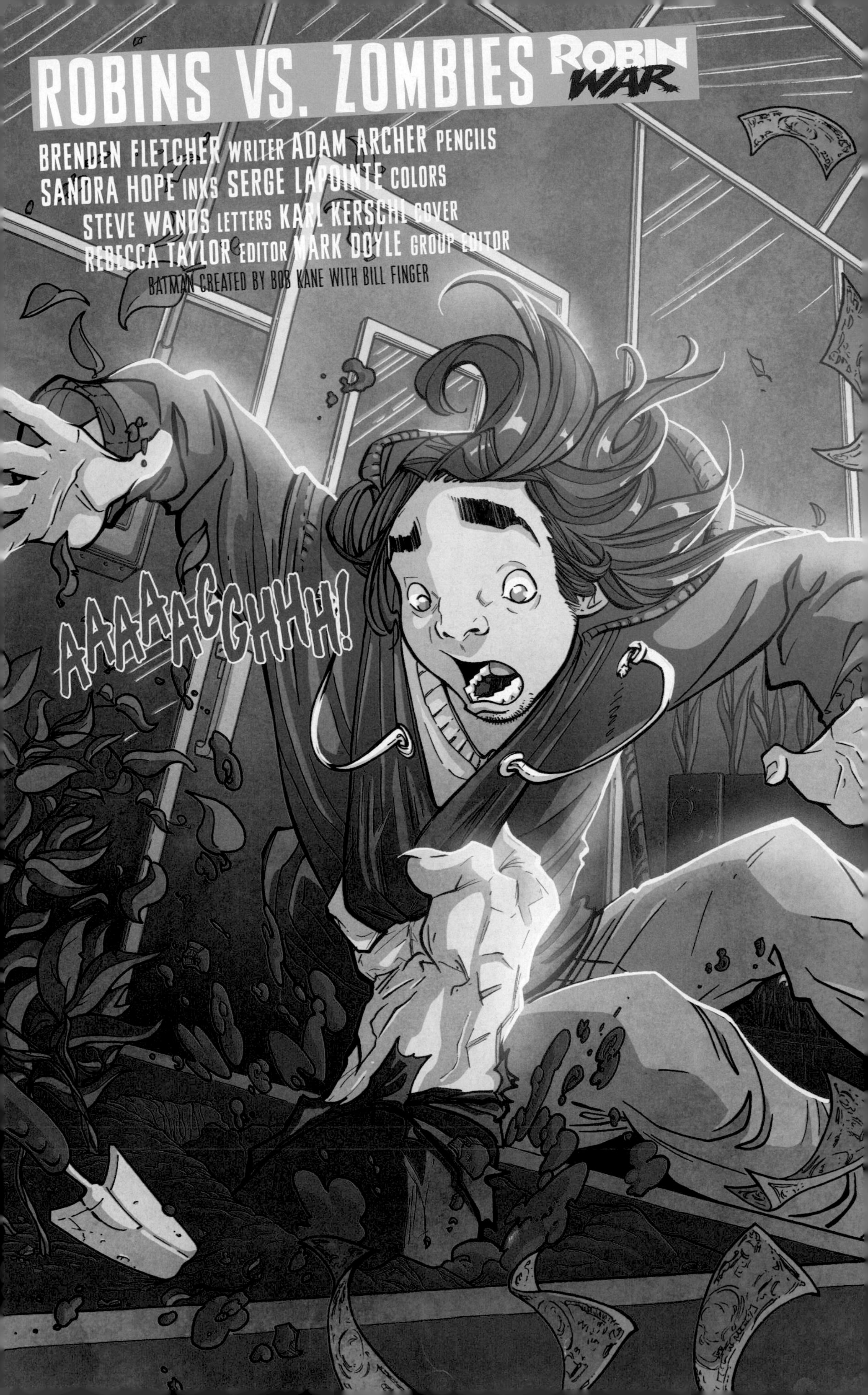
ROBINS VS. ZOMBIES
ROBIN WAR
BRENDEN FLETCHER WRITER ADAM ARCHER PENCILS
SANDRA HOPE INKS SERGE LAPOINTE COLORS
STEVE WANDS LETTERS KARL KERSCHL COVER
REBECCA TAYLOR EDITOR MARK DOYLE GROUP EDITOR
BATMAN CREATED BY BOB KANE WITH BILL FINGER
AAAAAGHHH!

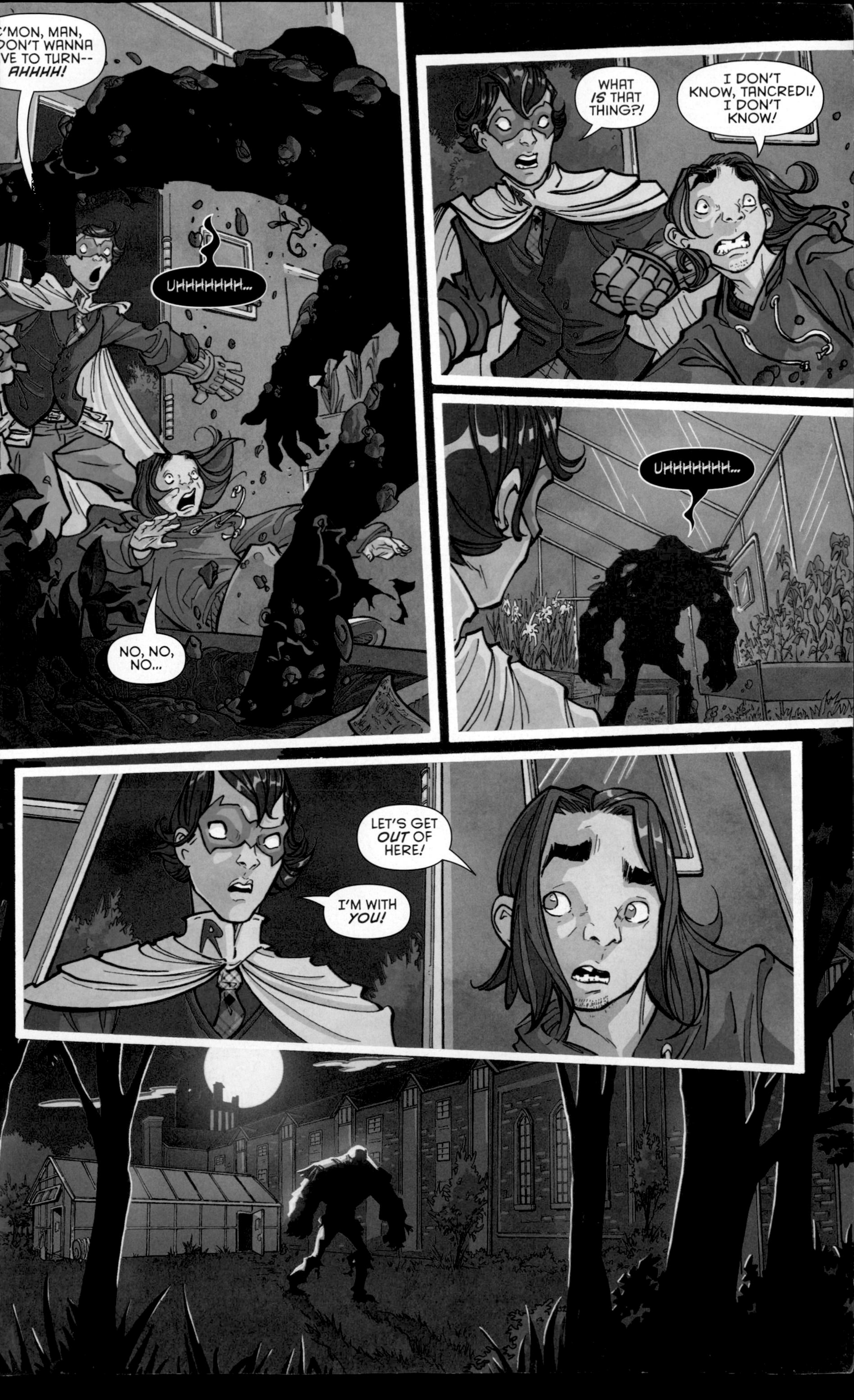
C'MON, MAN, DON'T WANNA VE TO TURN-- AHHHH!
UHHHHHHH...
NO, NO, NO...
WHAT IS THAT THING?!
I DON'T KNOW, TANCREDI! I DON'T KNOW!
UHHHHHHH...
LET'S GET OUT OF HERE!
I'M WITH YOU!

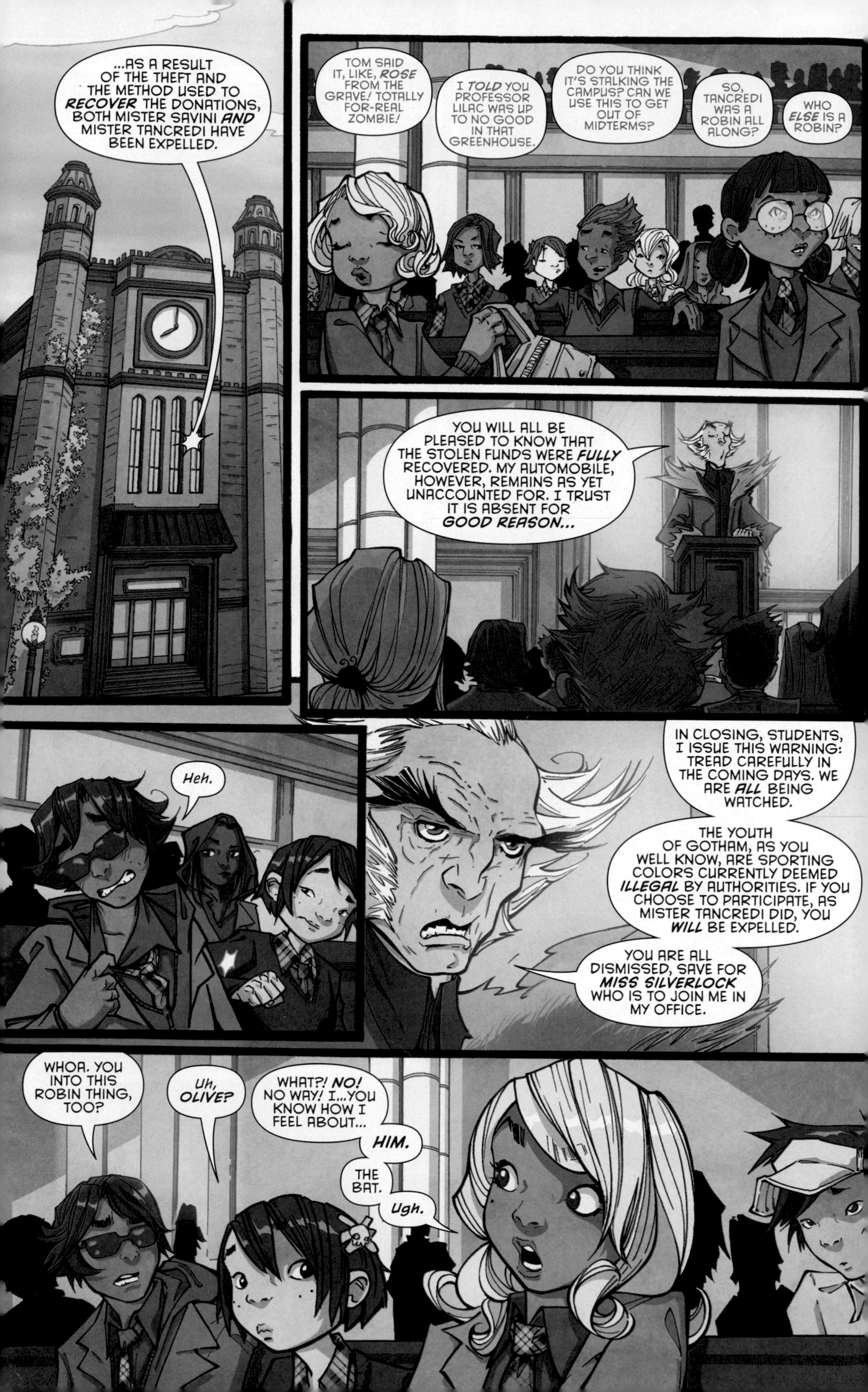
...AS A RESULT OF THE THEFT AND THE METHOD USED TO RECOVER THE DONATIONS, BOTH MISTER SAVINI AND MISTER TANCREDI HAVE BEEN EXPELLED.
TOM SAID IT, LIKE, ROSE FROM THE GRAVE! TOTALLY FOR-REAL ZOMBIE!
I TOLD YOU PROFESSOR LILAC WAS UP TO NO GOOD IN THAT GREENHOUSE.
DO YOU THINK IT'S STALKING THE CAMPUS? CAN WE USE THIS TO GET OUT OF MIDTERMS?
SO, TANCREDI WAS A ROBIN ALL ALONG?
WHO ELSE IS A ROBIN?
YOU WILL ALL BE PLEASED TO KNOW THAT THE STOLEN FUNDS WERE FULLY RECOVERED. MY AUTOMOBILE, HOWEVER, REMAINS AS YET UNACCOUNTED FOR. I TRUST IT IS ABSENT FOR GOOD REASON...
Heh.
IN CLOSING, STUDENTS, I ISSUE THIS WARNING: TREAD CAREFULLY IN THE COMING DAYS. WE ARE ALL BEING WATCHED.
THE YOUTH OF GOTHAM, AS YOU WELL KNOW, ARE SPORTING COLORS CURRENTLY DEEMED ILLEGAL BY AUTHORITIES. IF YOU CHOOSE TO PARTICIPATE, AS MISTER TANCREDI DID, YOU WILL BE EXPELLED.
YOU ARE ALL DISMISSED, SAVE FOR MISS SILVERLOCK WHO IS TO JOIN ME IN MY OFFICE.
WHOA. YOU INTO THIS ROBIN THING, TOO?
Uh, OLIVE?
WHAT?! NO! NO WAY! I...YOU KNOW HOW I FEEL ABOUT...
HIM.
THE BAT.
Ugh.

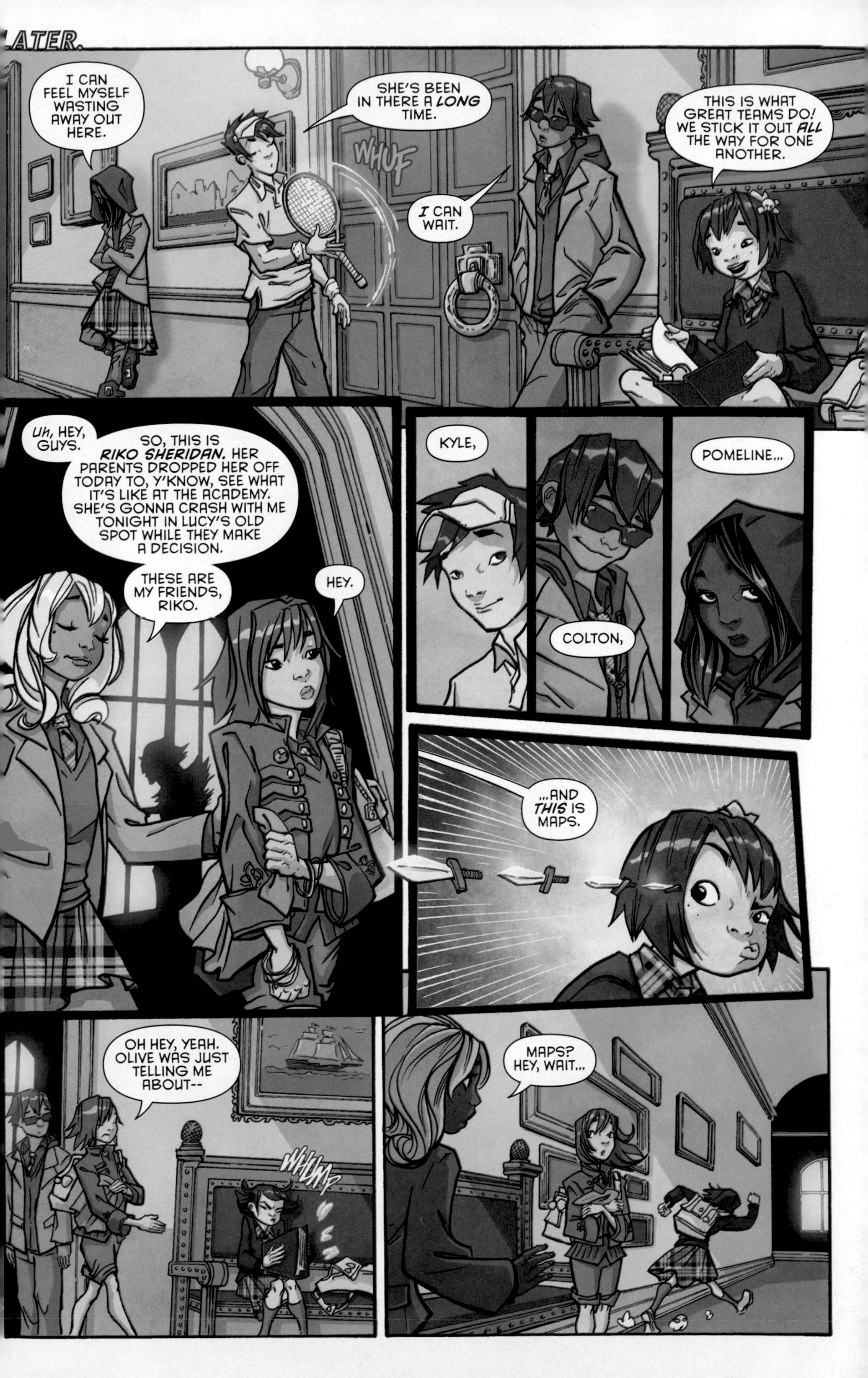
LATER.
I CAN FEEL MYSELF WASTING AWAY OUT HERE.
SHE'S BEEN IN THERE A LONG TIME.
WHUF
I CAN WAIT.
THIS IS WHAT GREAT TEAMS DO! WE STICK IT OUT ALL THE WAY FOR ONE ANOTHER.
Uh, HEY, GUYS.
SO, THIS IS RIKO SHERIDAN. HER PARENTS DROPPED HER OFF TODAY TO, Y'KNOW, SEE WHAT IT'S LIKE AT THE ACADEMY. SHE'S GONNA CRASH WITH ME TONIGHT IN LUCY'S OLD SPOT WHILE THEY MAKE A DECISION.
THESE ARE MY FRIENDS, RIKO.
HEY.
KYLE,
COLTON,
POMELINE...
...AND THIS IS MAPS.
OH HEY, YEAH. OLIVE WAS JUST TELLING ME ABOUT--
WHUMP
MAPS? HEY, WAIT...

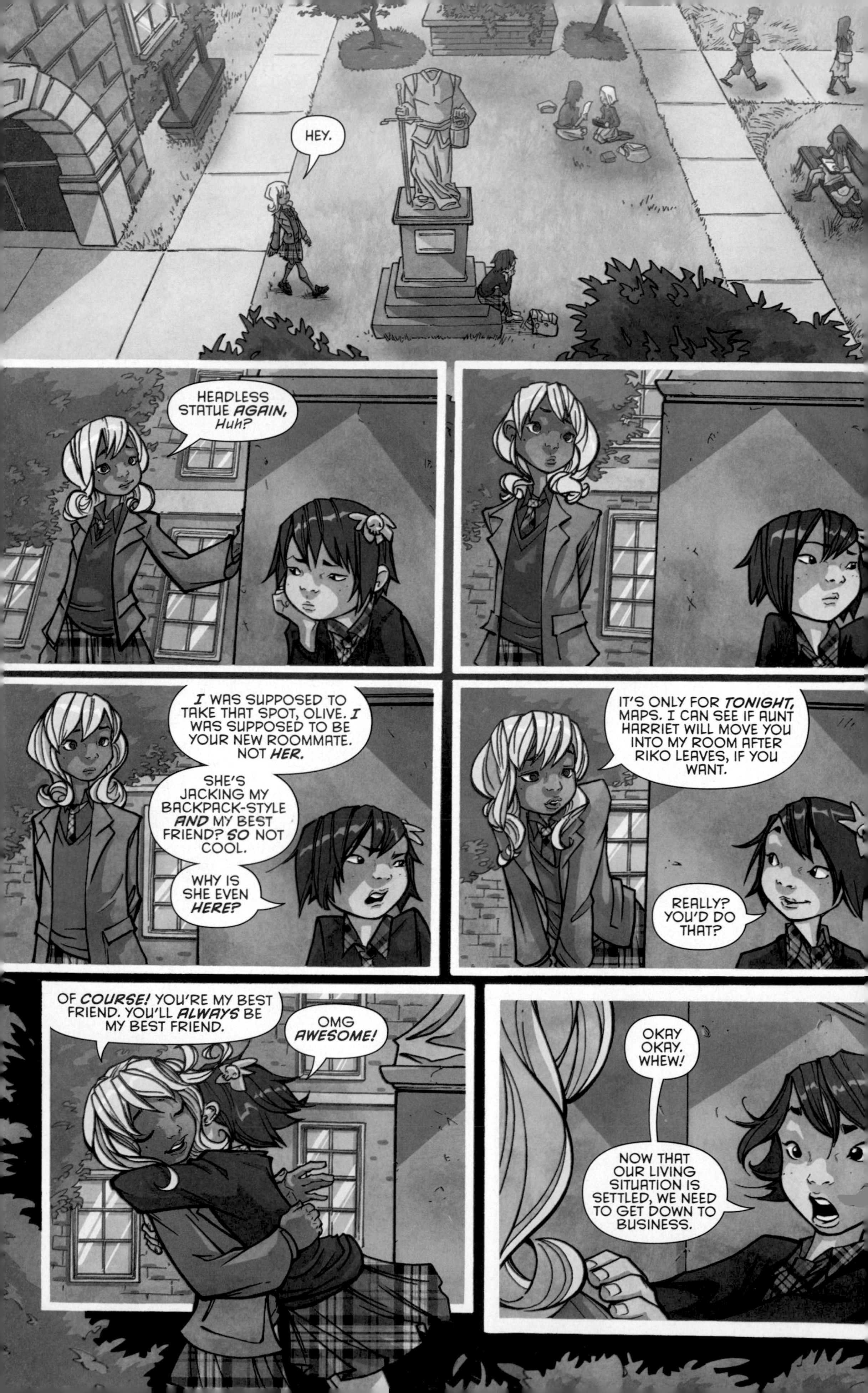
HEY.
HEADLESS STATUE AGAIN, Huh?
I WAS SUPPOSED TO TAKE THAT SPOT, OLIVE. I WAS SUPPOSED TO BE YOUR NEW ROOMMATE. NOT HER.
SHE'S JACKING MY BACKPACK-STYLE AND MY BEST FRIEND? SO NOT COOL.
WHY IS SHE EVEN HERE?
IT'S ONLY FOR TONIGHT, MAPS. I CAN SEE IF AUNT HARRIET WILL MOVE YOU INTO MY ROOM AFTER RIKO LEAVES, IF YOU WANT.
REALLY? YOU'D DO THAT?
OF COURSE! YOU'RE MY BEST FRIEND. YOU'LL ALWAYS BE MY BEST FRIEND.
OMG AWESOME!
OKAY OKAY. WHEW!
NOW THAT OUR LIVING SITUATION IS SETTLED, WE NEED TO GET DOWN TO BUSINESS.

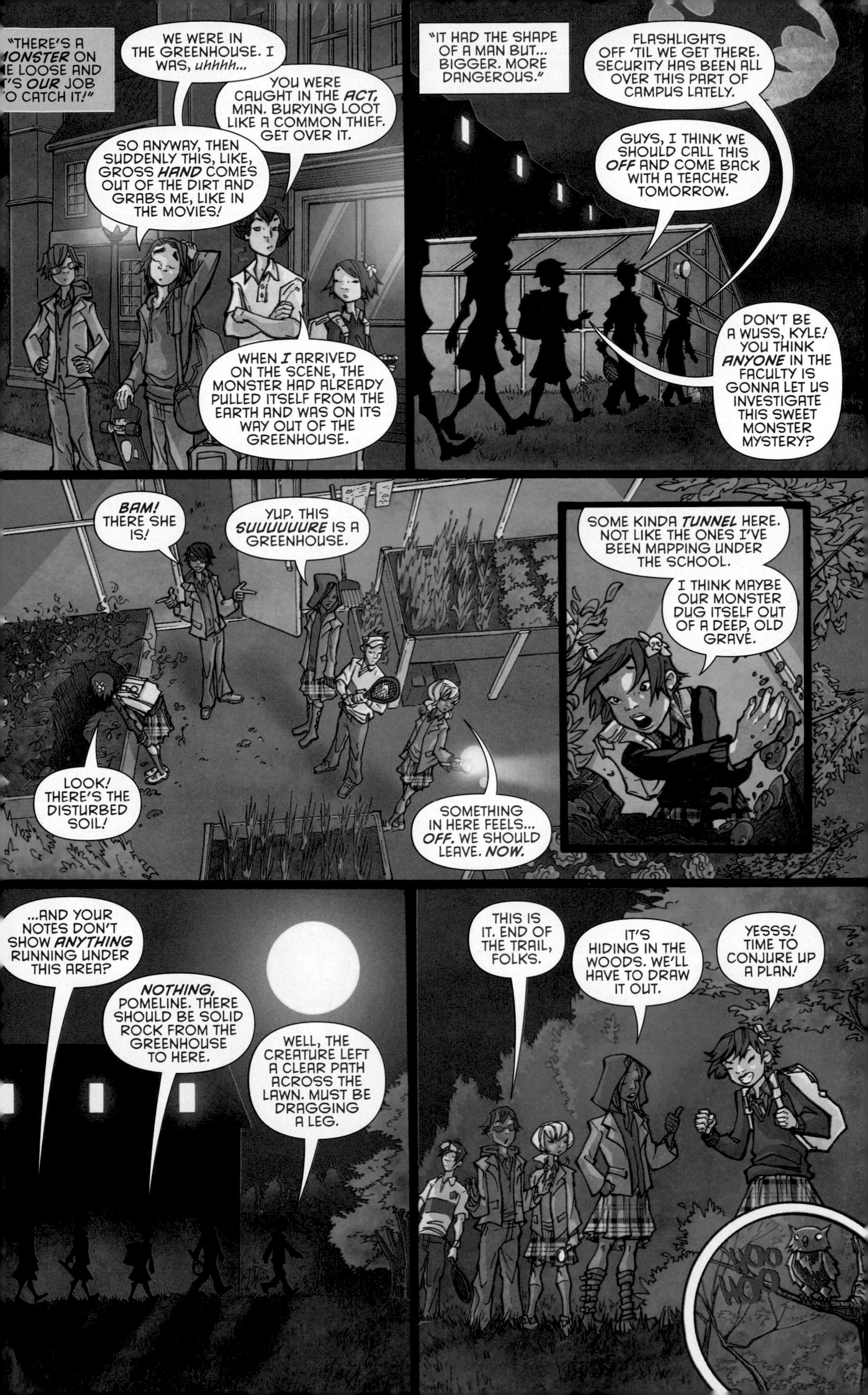
"THERE'S A MONSTER ON THE LOOSE AND IT'S OUR JOB TO CATCH IT!"
WE WERE IN THE GREENHOUSE. I WAS, uhhhh...
YOU WERE CAUGHT IN THE ACT, MAN. BURYING LOOT LIKE A COMMON THIEF. GET OVER IT.
SO ANYWAY, THEN SUDDENLY THIS, LIKE, GROSS HAND COMES OUT OF THE DIRT AND GRABS ME, LIKE IN THE MOVIES!
WHEN I ARRIVED ON THE SCENE, THE MONSTER HAD ALREADY PULLED ITSELF FROM THE EARTH AND WAS ON ITS WAY OUT OF THE GREENHOUSE.
"IT HAD THE SHAPE OF A MAN BUT... BIGGER. MORE DANGEROUS."
FLASHLIGHTS OFF 'TIL WE GET THERE. SECURITY HAS BEEN ALL OVER THIS PART OF CAMPUS LATELY.
GUYS, I THINK WE SHOULD CALL THIS OFF AND COME BACK WITH A TEACHER TOMORROW.
DON'T BE A WUSS, KYLE! YOU THINK ANYONE IN THE FACULTY IS GONNA LET US INVESTIGATE THIS SWEET MONSTER MYSTERY?
BAM! THERE SHE IS!
YUP. THIS SUUUUUURE IS A GREENHOUSE.
LOOK! THERE'S THE DISTURBED SOIL!
SOMETHING IN HERE FEELS... OFF. WE SHOULD LEAVE. NOW.
SOME KINDA TUNNEL HERE. NOT LIKE THE ONES I'VE BEEN MAPPING UNDER THE SCHOOL.
I THINK MAYBE OUR MONSTER DUG ITSELF OUT OF A DEEP, OLD GRAVE.
...AND YOUR NOTES DON'T SHOW ANYTHING RUNNING UNDER THIS AREA?
NOTHING, POMELINE. THERE SHOULD BE SOLID ROCK FROM THE GREENHOUSE TO HERE.
WELL, THE CREATURE LEFT A CLEAR PATH ACROSS THE LAWN. MUST BE DRAGGING A LEG.
THIS IS IT. END OF THE TRAIL, FOLKS.
IT'S HIDING IN THE WOODS. WE'LL HAVE TO DRAW IT OUT.
YESSS! TIME TO CONJURE UP A PLAN!
HOO HOO

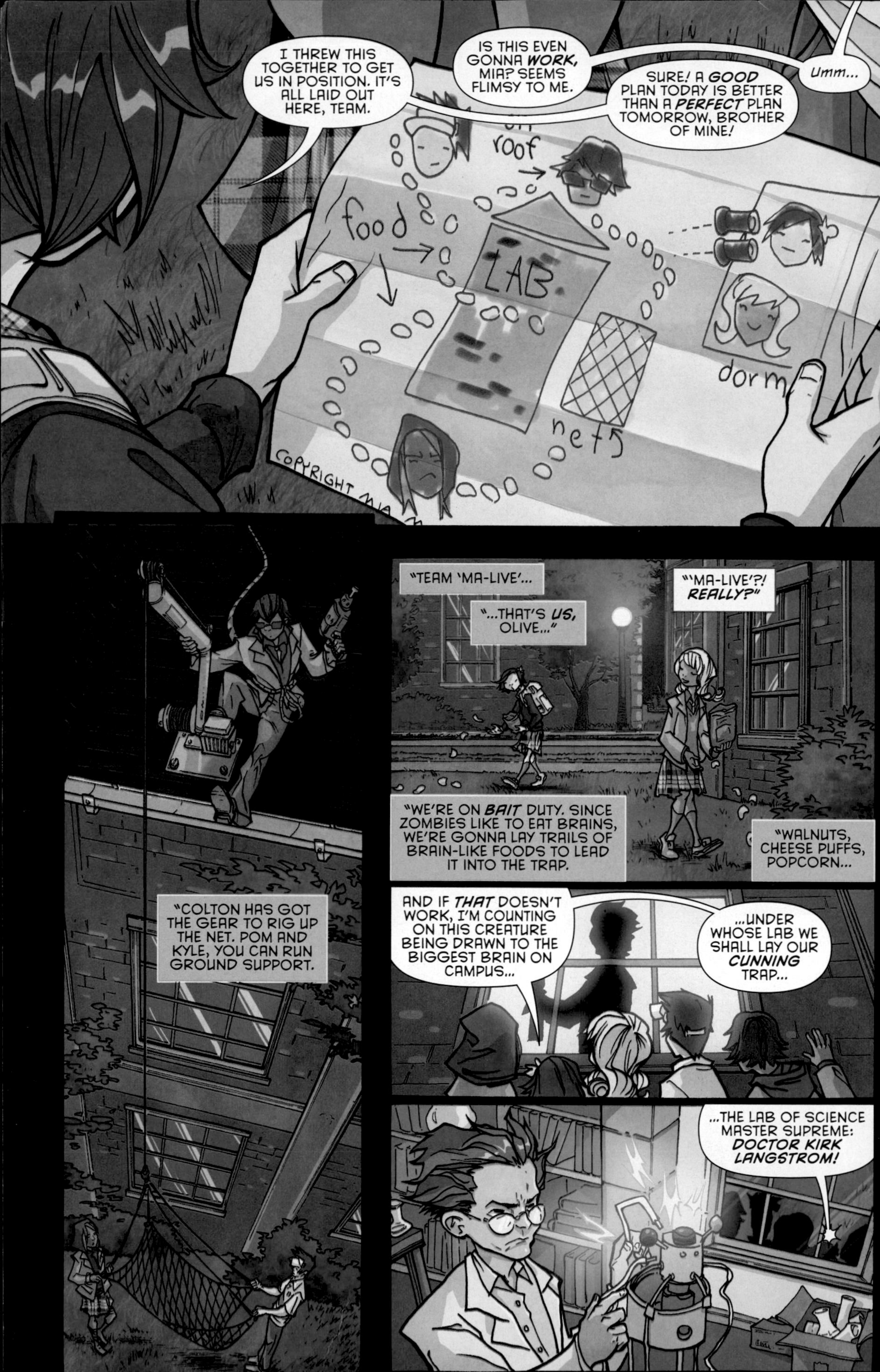
I THREW THIS TOGETHER TO GET US IN POSITION. IT'S ALL LAID OUT HERE, TEAM.
IS THIS EVEN GONNA WORK, MIA? SEEMS FLIMSY TO ME.
Umm...
SURE! A GOOD PLAN TODAY IS BETTER THAN A PERFECT PLAN TOMORROW, BROTHER OF MINE!
roof
food
LAB.
dorm
nets
"TEAM 'MA-LIVE'...
"...THAT'S US, OLIVE..."
"'MA-LIVE'?! REALLY?"
"WE'RE ON BAIT DUTY. SINCE ZOMBIES LIKE TO EAT BRAINS, WE'RE GONNA LAY TRAILS OF BRAIN-LIKE FOODS TO LEAD IT INTO THE TRAP.
"WALNUTS, CHEESE PUFFS, POPCORN...
"COLTON HAS GOT THE GEAR TO RIG UP THE NET. POM AND KYLE, YOU CAN RUN GROUND SUPPORT.
AND IF THAT DOESN'T WORK, I'M COUNTING ON THIS CREATURE BEING DRAWN TO THE BIGGEST BRAIN ON CAMPUS...
...UNDER WHOSE LAB WE SHALL LAY OUR CUNNING TRAP...
...THE LAB OF SCIENCE MASTER SUPREME: DOCTOR KIRK LANGSTROM!

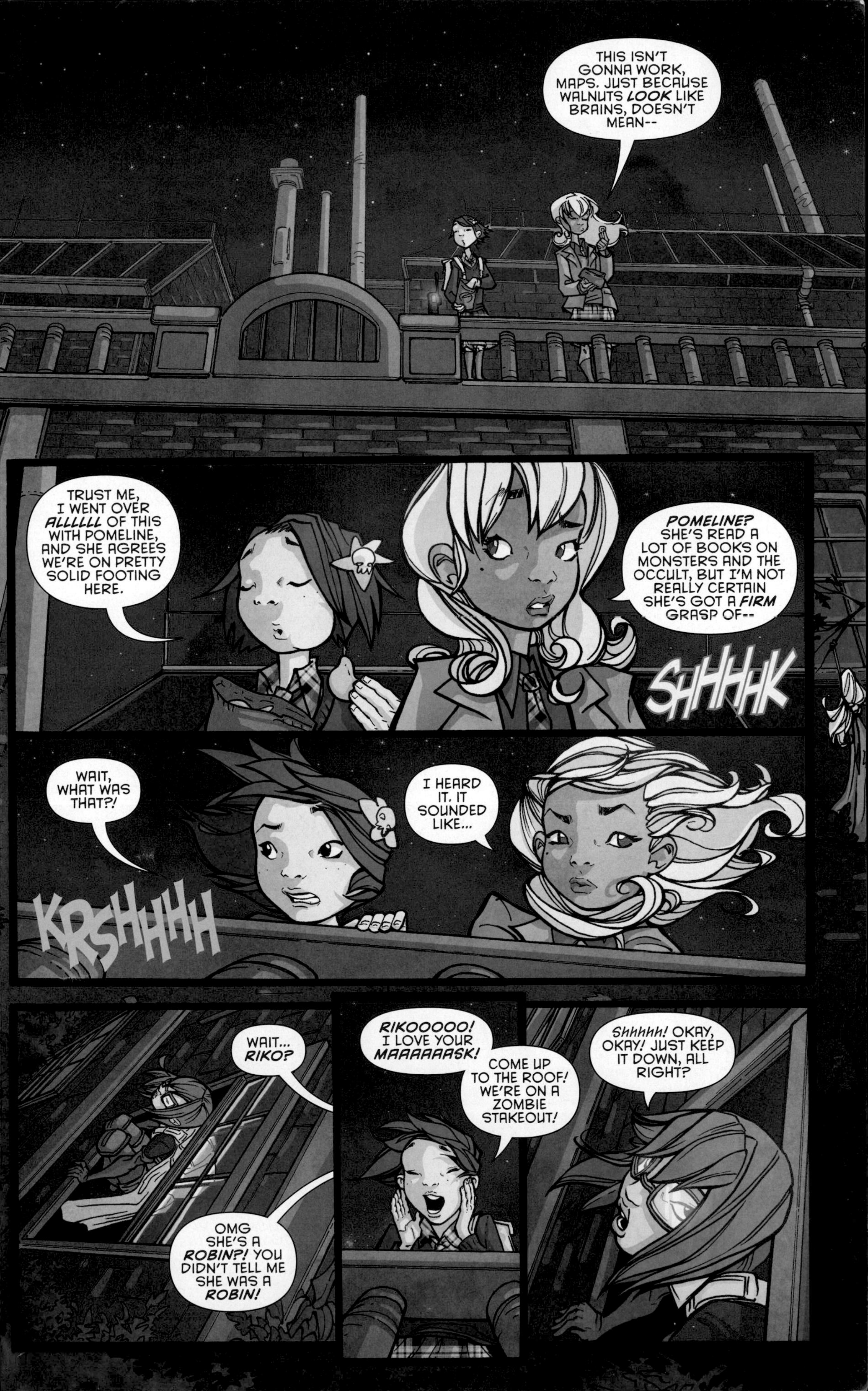
THIS ISN'T GONNA WORK, MAPS. JUST BECAUSE WALNUTS LOOK LIKE BRAINS, DOESN'T MEAN--
TRUST ME, I WENT OVER ALLLLLL OF THIS WITH POMELINE, AND SHE AGREES WE'RE ON PRETTY SOLID FOOTING HERE.
POMELINE? SHE'S READ A LOT OF BOOKS ON MONSTERS AND THE OCCULT, BUT I'M NOT REALLY CERTAIN SHE'S GOT A FIRM GRASP OF--
SHHHHK
WAIT, WHAT WAS THAT?!
I HEARD IT. IT SOUNDED LIKE...
KRSHHHH
WAIT... RIKO?
OMG SHE'S A ROBIN?! YOU DIDN'T TELL ME SHE WAS A ROBIN!
RIKOOOOO! I LOVE YOUR MAAAAAASK!
COME UP TO THE ROOF! WE'RE ON A ZOMBIE STAKEOUT!
Shhhhh! OKAY, OKAY! JUST KEEP IT DOWN, ALL RIGHT?

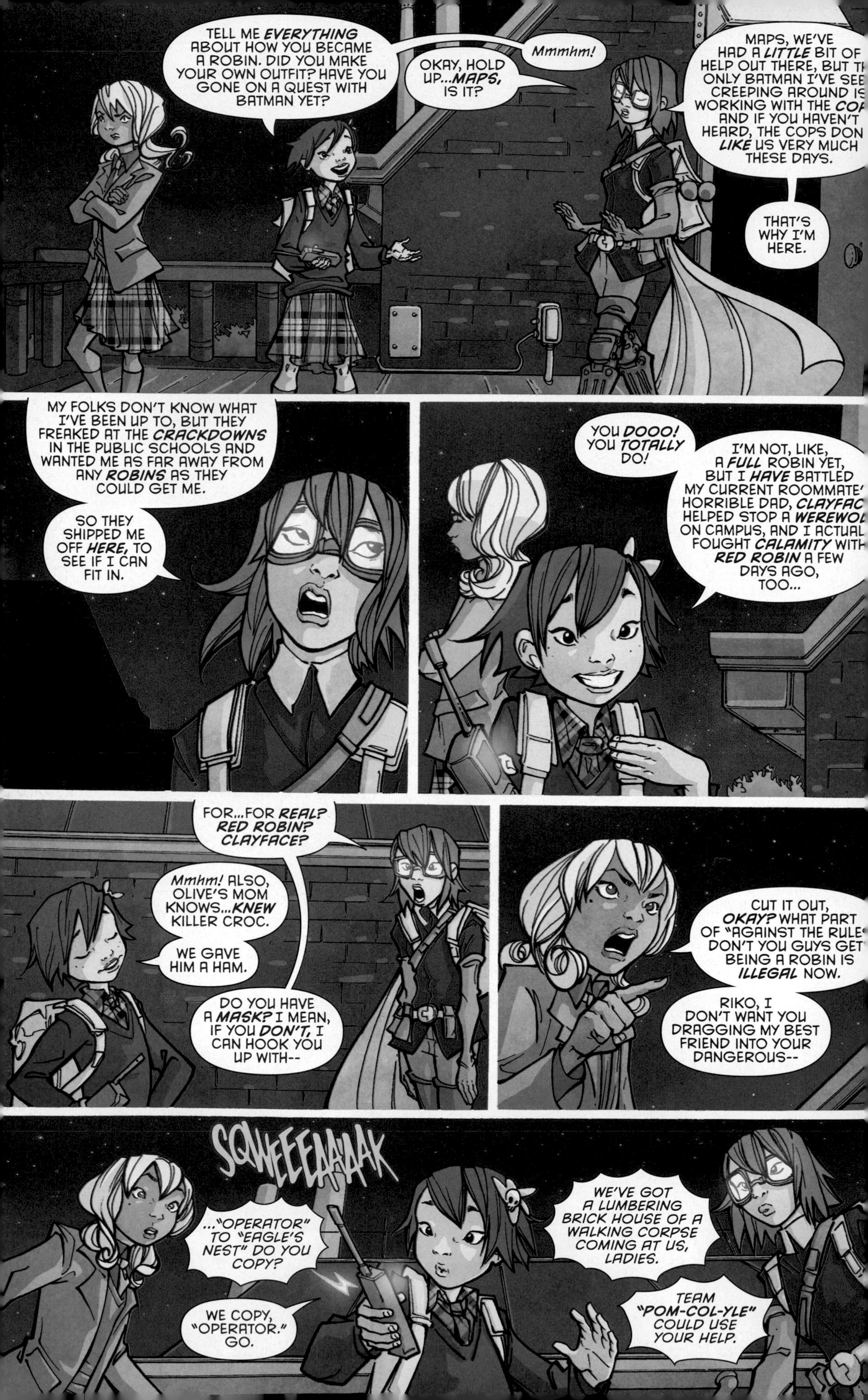
TELL ME EVERYTHING ABOUT HOW YOU BECAME A ROBIN. DID YOU MAKE YOUR OWN OUTFIT? HAVE YOU GONE ON A QUEST WITH BATMAN YET?
Mmmhm!
OKAY, HOLD UP...MAPS, IS IT?
MAPS, WE'VE HAD A LITTLE BIT OF HELP OUT THERE, BUT TH ONLY BATMAN I'VE SEE CREEPING AROUND IS WORKING WITH THE COP AND IF YOU HAVEN'T HEARD, THE COPS DON LIKE US VERY MUCH THESE DAYS.
THAT'S WHY I'M HERE.
MY FOLKS DON'T KNOW WHAT I'VE BEEN UP TO, BUT THEY FREAKED AT THE CRACKDOWNS IN THE PUBLIC SCHOOLS AND WANTED ME AS FAR AWAY FROM ANY ROBINS AS THEY COULD GET ME.
SO THEY SHIPPED ME OFF HERE, TO SEE IF I CAN FIT IN.
YOU DOOO! YOU TOTALLY DO!
I'M NOT, LIKE, A FULL ROBIN YET, BUT I HAVE BATTLED MY CURRENT ROOMMATE' HORRIBLE DAD, CLAYFAC HELPED STOP A WEREWOL ON CAMPUS, AND I ACTUAL FOUGHT CALAMITY WITH RED ROBIN A FEW DAYS AGO, TOO...
FOR...FOR REAL? RED ROBIN? CLAYFACE?
Mmhm! ALSO, OLIVE'S MOM KNOWS...KNEW KILLER CROC.
WE GAVE HIM A HAM.
DO YOU HAVE A MASK? I MEAN, IF YOU DON'T, I CAN HOOK YOU UP WITH--
CUT IT OUT, OKAY? WHAT PART OF "AGAINST THE RULE DON'T YOU GUYS GET BEING A ROBIN IS ILLEGAL NOW.
RIKO, I DON'T WANT YOU DRAGGING MY BEST FRIEND INTO YOUR DANGEROUS--
SQWEEEAAAK
..."OPERATOR" TO "EAGLE'S NEST" DO YOU COPY?
WE COPY, "OPERATOR." GO.
WE'VE GOT A LUMBERING BRICK HOUSE OF A WALKING CORPSE COMING AT US, LADIES.
TEAM "POM-COL-YLE" COULD USE YOUR HELP.

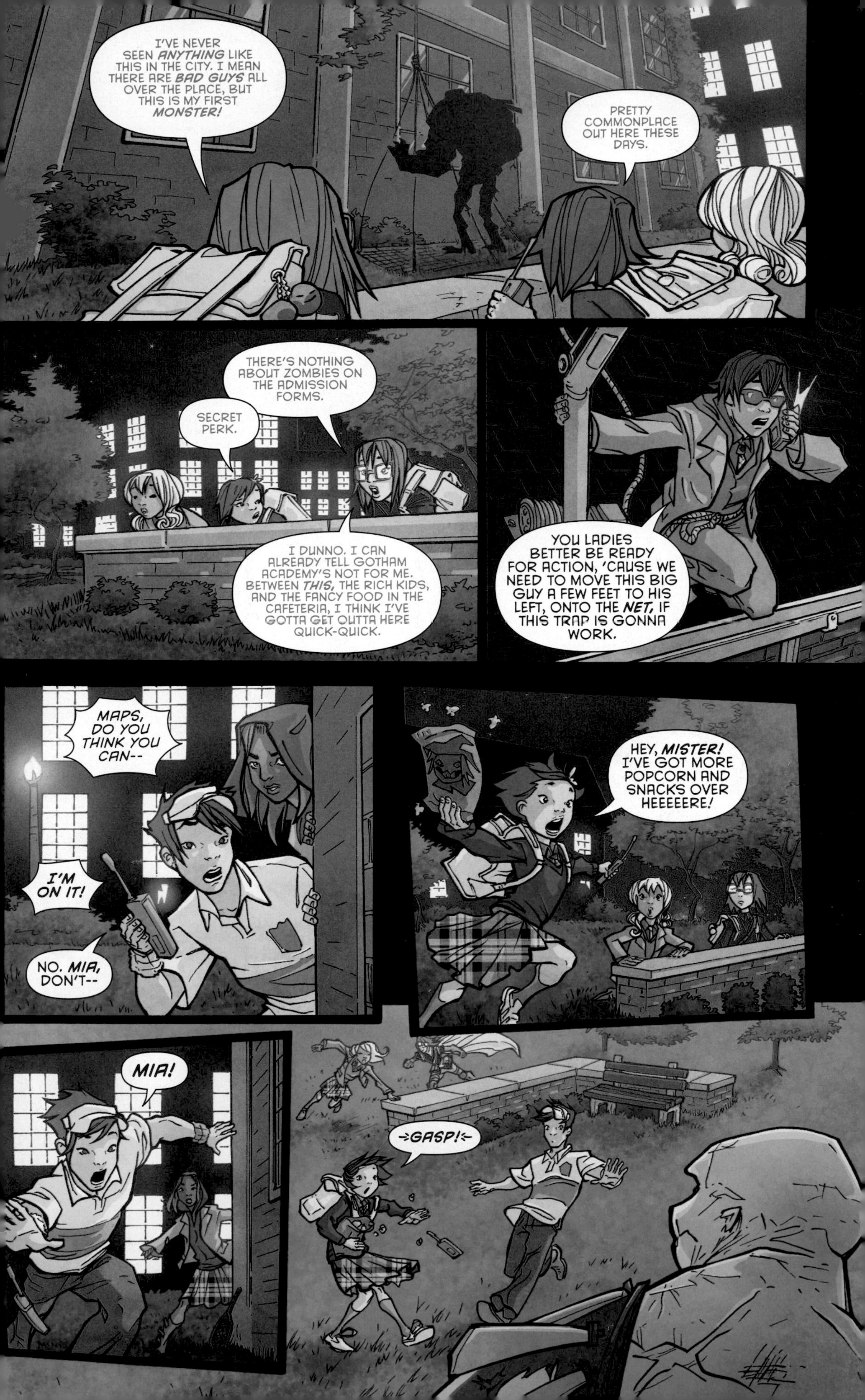
I'VE NEVER SEEN ANYTHING LIKE THIS IN THE CITY. I MEAN THERE ARE BAD GUYS ALL OVER THE PLACE, BUT THIS IS MY FIRST MONSTER!
PRETTY COMMONPLACE OUT HERE THESE DAYS.
THERE'S NOTHING ABOUT ZOMBIES ON THE ADMISSION FORMS.
SECRET PERK.
I DUNNO. I CAN ALREADY TELL GOTHAM ACADEMY'S NOT FOR ME. BETWEEN THIS, THE RICH KIDS, AND THE FANCY FOOD IN THE CAFETERIA, I THINK I'VE GOTTA GET OUTTA HERE QUICK-QUICK.
YOU LADIES BETTER BE READY FOR ACTION, 'CAUSE WE NEED TO MOVE THIS BIG GUY A FEW FEET TO HIS LEFT, ONTO THE NET, IF THIS TRAP IS GONNA WORK.
MAPS, DO YOU THINK YOU CAN--
I'M ON IT!
NO. MIA, DON'T--
HEY, MISTER! I'VE GOT MORE POPCORN AND SNACKS OVER HEEEEERE!
MIA!
GASP!

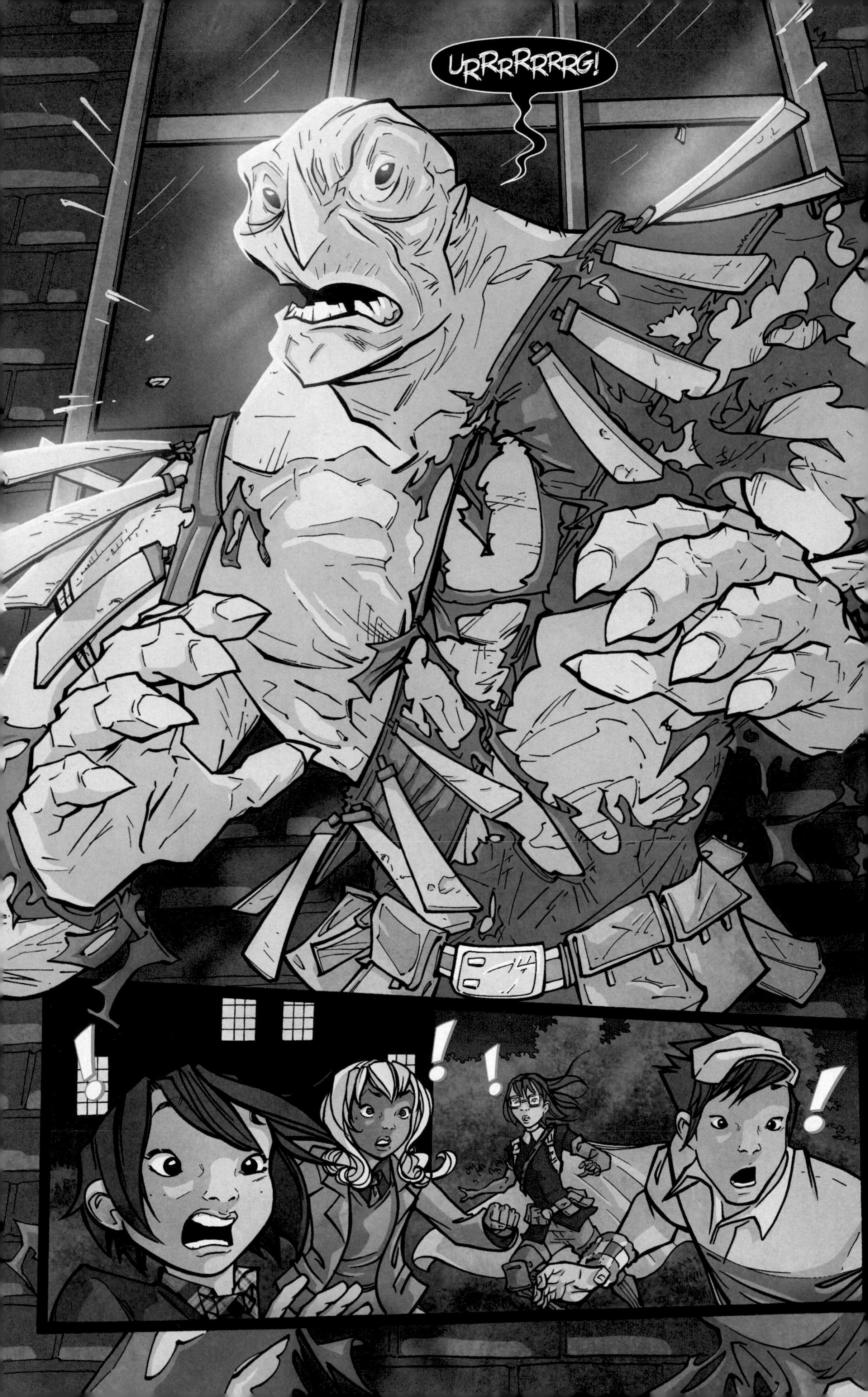
URRRRRRRG!
!
!
!
!

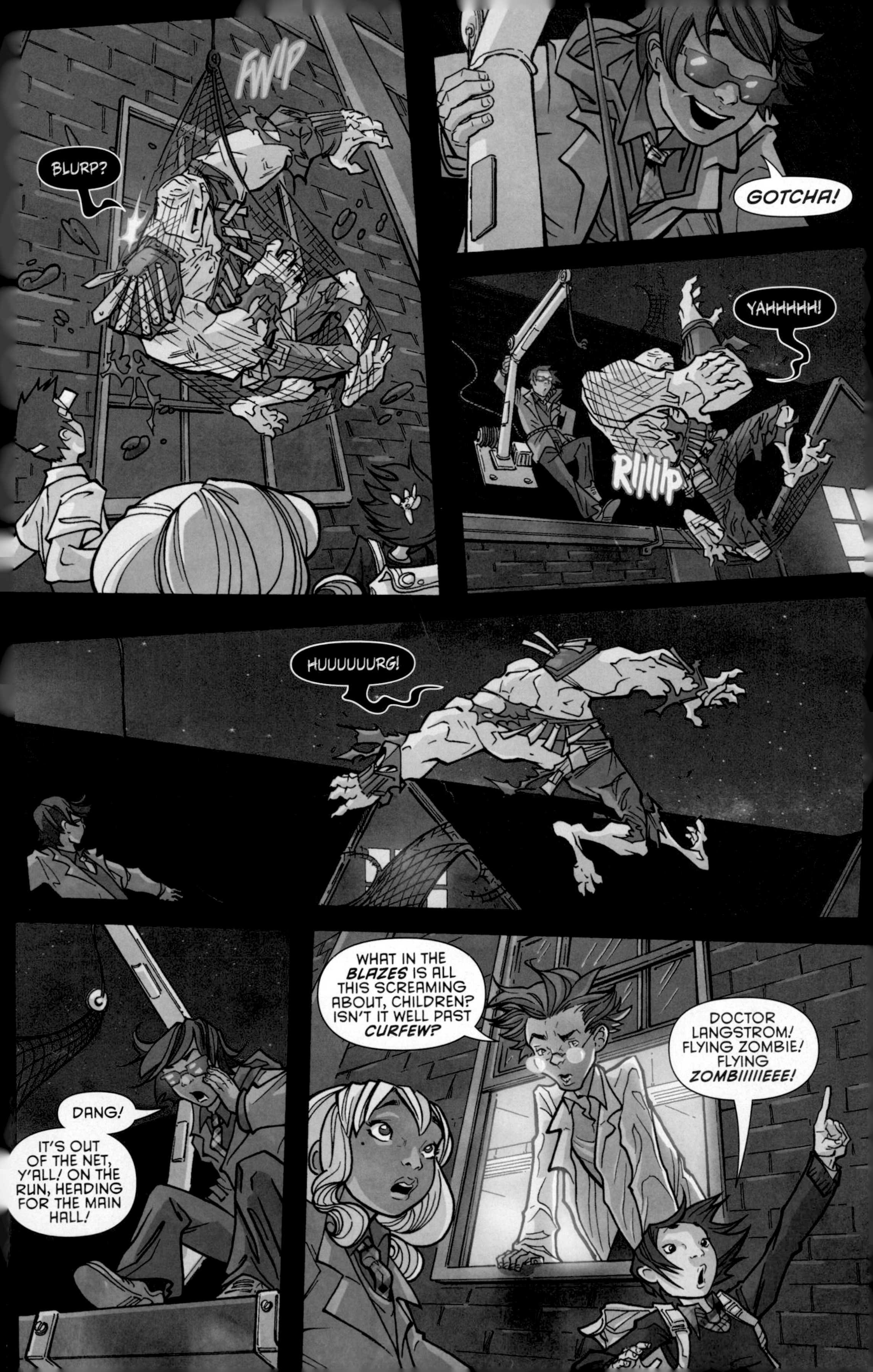
FWIP
BLURP?
GOTCHA!
YAHHHHH!
RIIIIIP
HUUUUUURG!
DANG!
IT'S OUT OF THE NET, Y'ALL! ON THE RUN, HEADING FOR THE MAIN HALL!
WHAT IN THE BLAZES IS ALL THIS SCREAMING ABOUT, CHILDREN? ISN'T IT WELL PAST CURFEW?
DOCTOR LANGSTROM! FLYING ZOMBIE! FLYING ZOMBIIIIIIEEE!

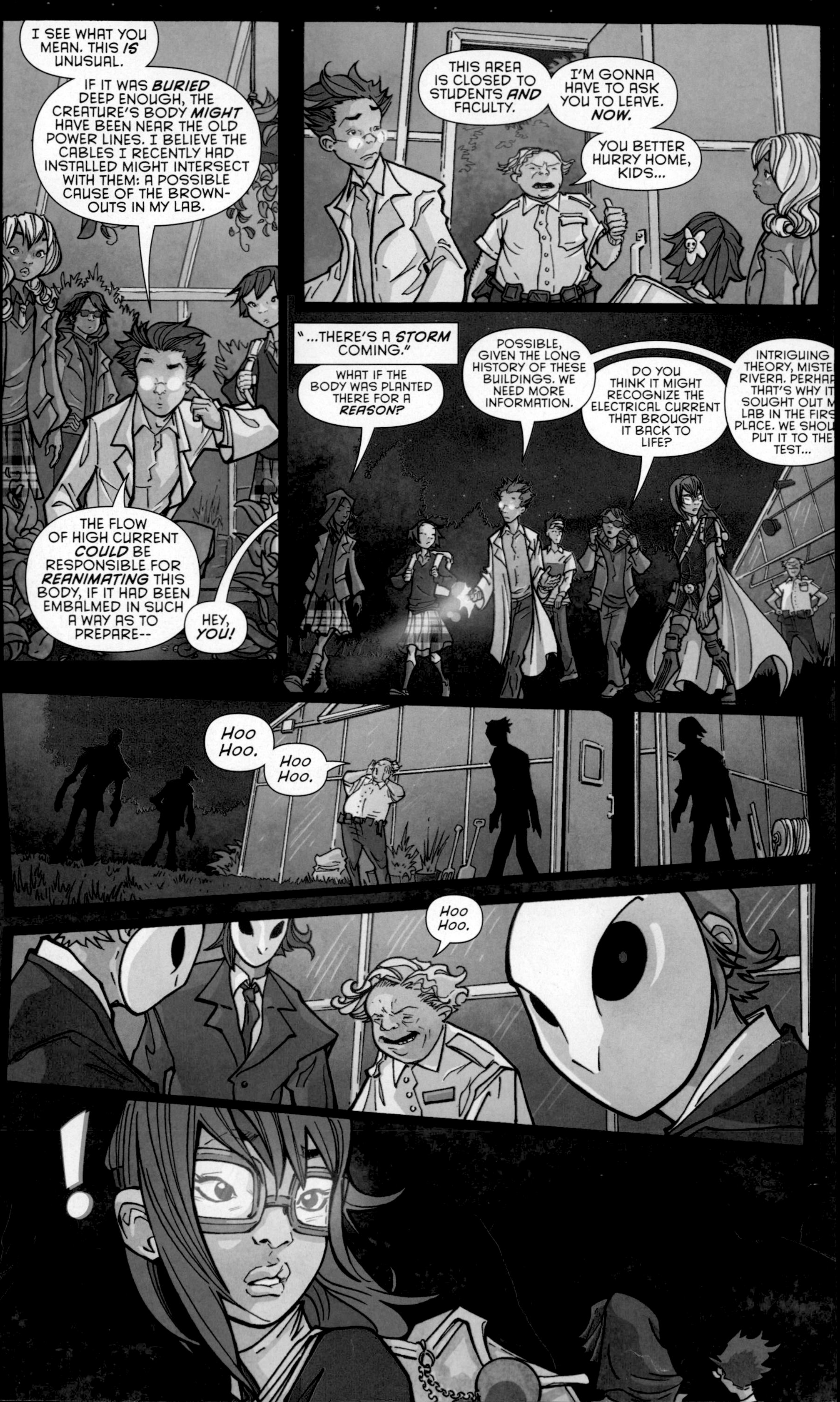
I SEE WHAT YOU MEAN. THIS *IS* UNUSUAL.
IF IT WAS *BURIED* DEEP ENOUGH, THE CREATURE'S BODY *MIGHT* HAVE BEEN NEAR THE OLD POWER LINES. I BELIEVE THE CABLES I RECENTLY HAD INSTALLED MIGHT INTERSECT WITH THEM: A POSSIBLE CAUSE OF THE BROWN-OUTS IN MY LAB.
THE FLOW OF HIGH CURRENT *COULD* BE RESPONSIBLE FOR *REANIMATING* THIS BODY, IF IT HAD BEEN EMBALMED IN SUCH A WAY AS TO PREPARE--
HEY, *YOU!*
THIS AREA IS CLOSED TO STUDENTS *AND* FACULTY.
I'M GONNA HAVE TO ASK YOU TO LEAVE. *NOW.*
YOU BETTER HURRY HOME, KIDS...
"...THERE'S A *STORM* COMING."
WHAT IF THE BODY WAS PLANTED THERE FOR A *REASON?*
POSSIBLE, GIVEN THE LONG HISTORY OF THESE BUILDINGS. WE NEED MORE INFORMATION.
DO YOU THINK IT MIGHT RECOGNIZE THE ELECTRICAL CURRENT THAT BROUGHT IT BACK TO LIFE?
INTRIGUING THEORY, MISTE RIVERA. PERHAP THAT'S WHY IT SOUGHT OUT M LAB IN THE FIRS PLACE. WE SHOU PUT IT TO THE TEST...
Hoo Hoo.
Hoo Hoo.
Hoo Hoo.
!

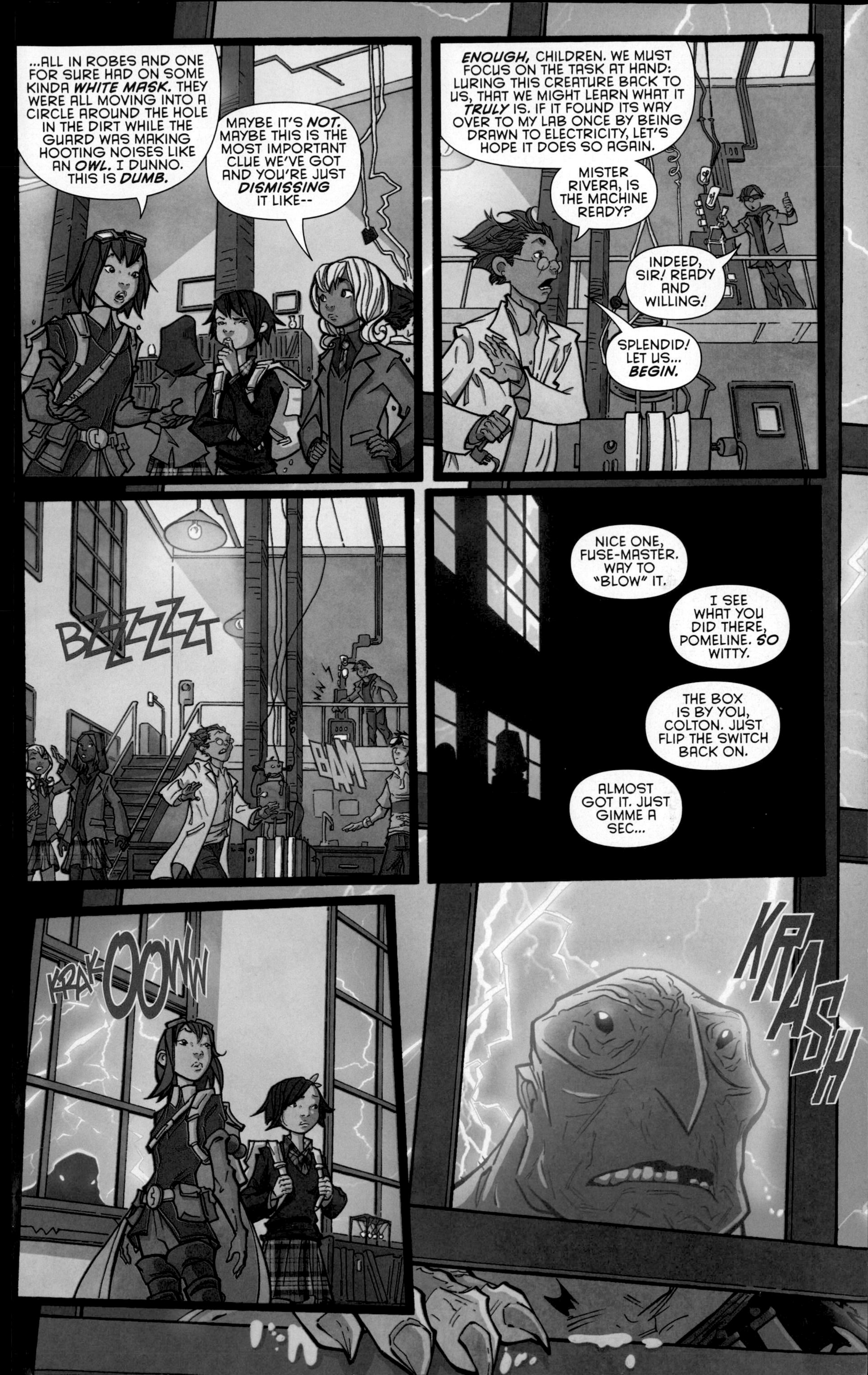

...ALL IN ROBES AND ONE FOR SURE HAD ON SOME KINDA *WHITE MASK.* THEY WERE ALL MOVING INTO A CIRCLE AROUND THE HOLE IN THE DIRT WHILE THE GUARD WAS MAKING HOOTING NOISES LIKE AN *OWL.* I DUNNO. THIS IS *DUMB.*
MAYBE IT'S *NOT.* MAYBE THIS IS THE MOST IMPORTANT CLUE WE'VE GOT AND YOU'RE JUST *DISMISSING* IT LIKE--
ENOUGH, CHILDREN. WE MUST FOCUS ON THE TASK AT HAND: LURING THIS CREATURE BACK TO US, THAT WE MIGHT LEARN WHAT IT *TRULY* IS. IF IT FOUND ITS WAY OVER TO MY LAB ONCE BY BEING DRAWN TO ELECTRICITY, LET'S HOPE IT DOES SO AGAIN.
MISTER RIVERA, IS THE MACHINE READY?
INDEED, SIR! READY AND WILLING!
SPLENDID! LET US... *BEGIN.*
BZZZZZZT
BAM
NICE ONE, FUSE-MASTER. WAY TO "BLOW" IT.
I SEE WHAT YOU DID THERE, POMELINE. *SO* WITTY.
THE BOX IS BY YOU, COLTON. JUST FLIP THE SWITCH BACK ON.
ALMOST GOT IT. JUST GIMME A SEC...
KRAK-OOOWW
KRASH

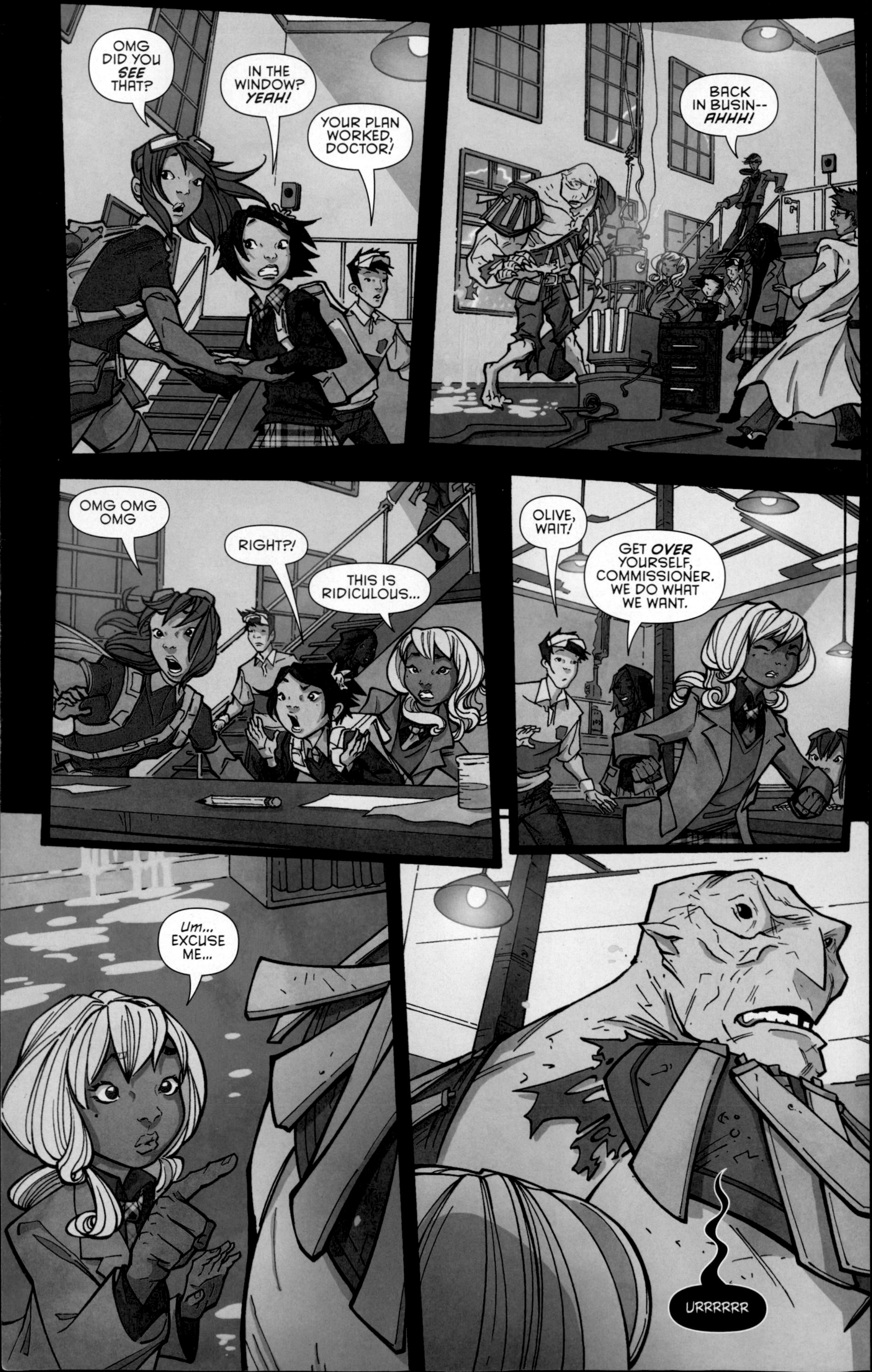
OMG DID YOU SEE THAT?
IN THE WINDOW? YEAH!
YOUR PLAN WORKED, DOCTOR!
BACK IN BUSIN-- AHHH!
OMG OMG OMG
RIGHT?!
THIS IS RIDICULOUS...
OLIVE, WAIT!
GET OVER YOURSELF, COMMISSIONER. WE DO WHAT WE WANT.
Um... EXCUSE ME...
URRRRRR

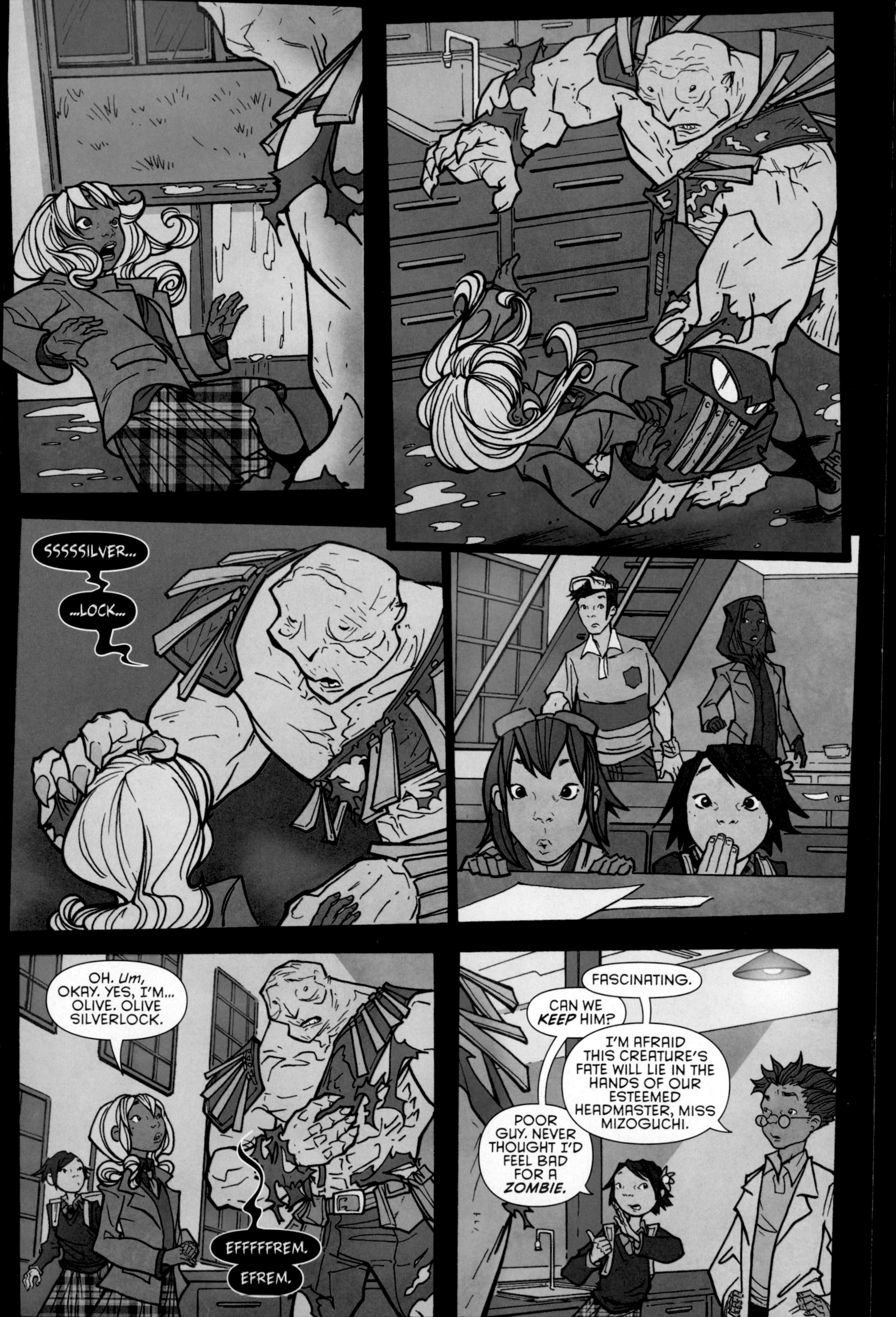
SSSSSILVER...
...LOCK...
OH. Um, OKAY. YES, I'M... OLIVE. OLIVE SILVERLOCK.
EFFFFFREM.
EFREM.
FASCINATING.
CAN WE KEEP HIM?
I'M AFRAID THIS CREATURE'S FATE WILL LIE IN THE HANDS OF OUR ESTEEMED HEADMASTER, MISS MIZOGUCHI.
POOR GUY. NEVER THOUGHT I'D FEEL BAD FOR A ZOMBIE.

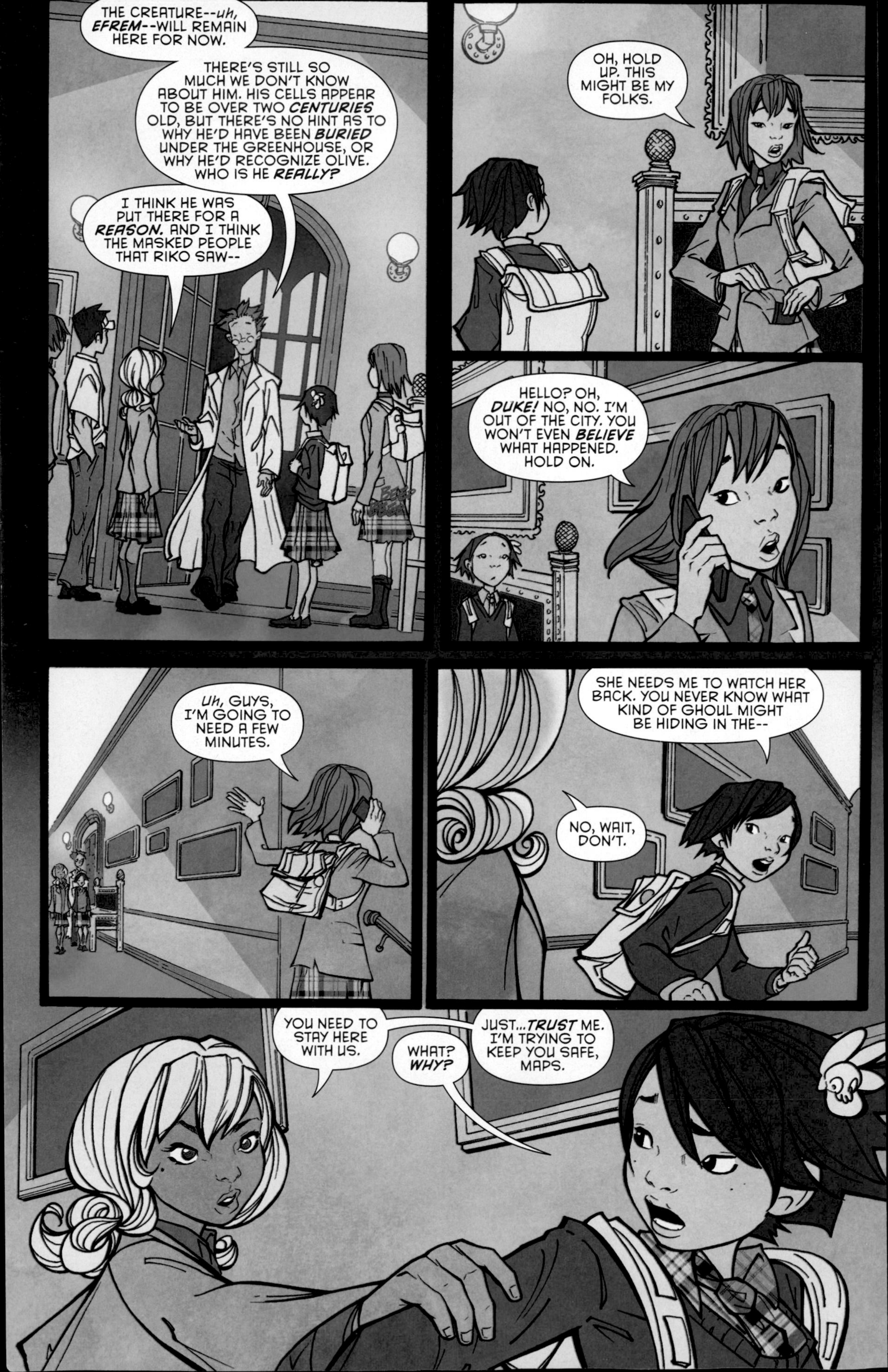
THE CREATURE--*uh, EFREM*--WILL REMAIN HERE FOR NOW.
THERE'S STILL SO MUCH WE DON'T KNOW ABOUT HIM. HIS CELLS APPEAR TO BE OVER TWO *CENTURIES* OLD, BUT THERE'S NO HINT AS TO WHY HE'D HAVE BEEN *BURIED* UNDER THE GREENHOUSE, OR WHY HE'D RECOGNIZE OLIVE. WHO IS HE *REALLY?*
I THINK HE WAS PUT THERE FOR A *REASON.* AND I THINK THE MASKED PEOPLE THAT RIKO SAW--
OH, HOLD UP. THIS MIGHT BE MY FOLKS.
HELLO? OH, *DUKE!* NO, NO. I'M OUT OF THE CITY. YOU WON'T EVEN *BELIEVE* WHAT HAPPENED. HOLD ON.
Uh, GUYS, I'M GOING TO NEED A FEW MINUTES.
SHE NEEDS ME TO WATCH HER BACK. YOU NEVER KNOW WHAT KIND OF GHOUL MIGHT BE HIDING IN THE--
NO, WAIT, DON'T.
YOU NEED TO STAY HERE WITH US.
WHAT? *WHY?*
JUST...*TRUST* ME. I'M TRYING TO KEEP YOU SAFE, MAPS.

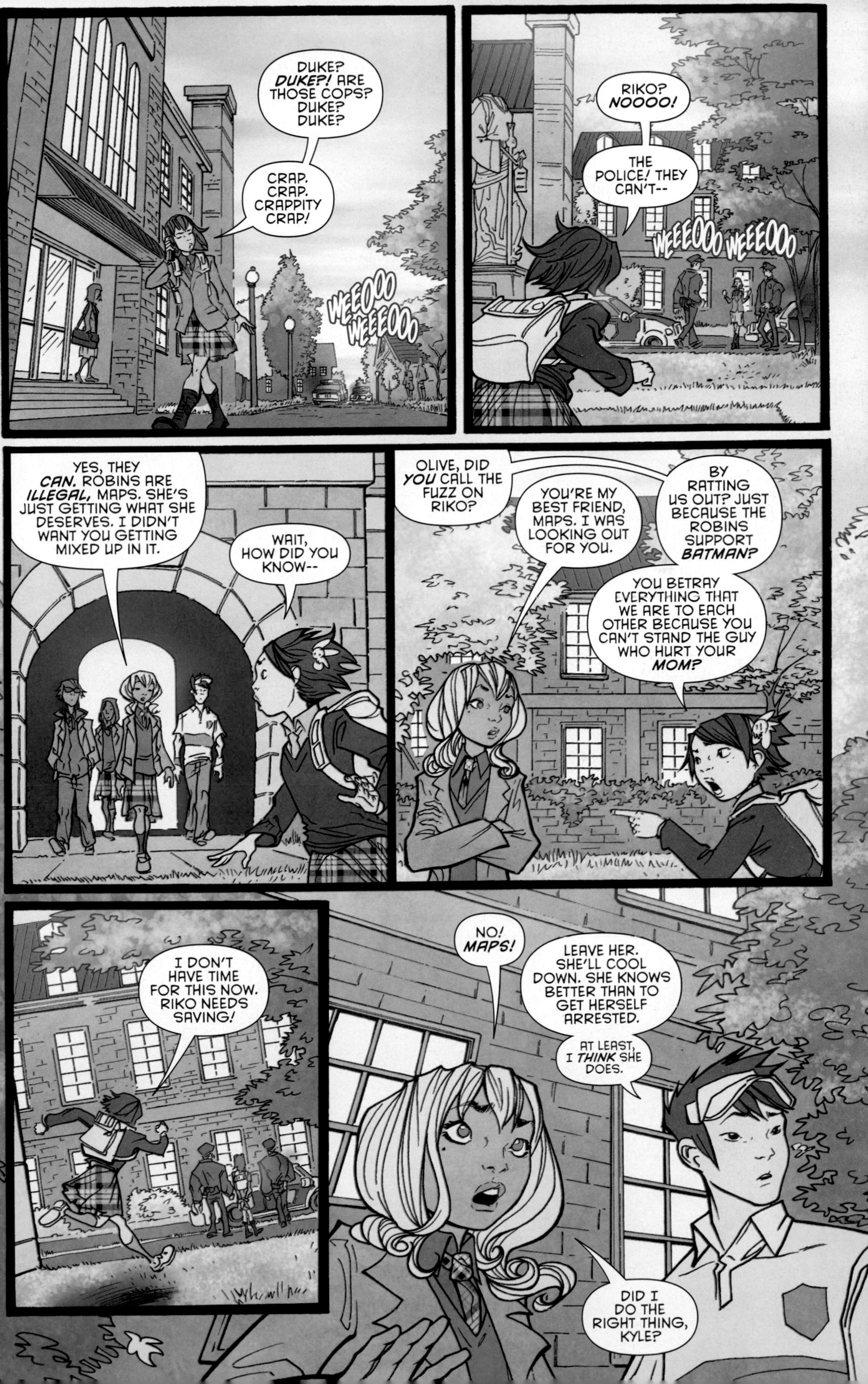
DUKE? DUKE?! ARE THOSE COPS? DUKE? DUKE?
CRAP. CRAP. CRAPPITY CRAP!
WEEOOO WEEEOOO
RIKO? NOOOO!
THE POLICE! THEY CAN'T--
WEEEOOO WEEEOOO
YES, THEY CAN. ROBINS ARE ILLEGAL, MAPS. SHE'S JUST GETTING WHAT SHE DESERVES. I DIDN'T WANT YOU GETTING MIXED UP IN IT.
WAIT, HOW DID YOU KNOW--
OLIVE, DID YOU CALL THE FUZZ ON RIKO?
BY RATTING US OUT? JUST BECAUSE THE ROBINS SUPPORT BATMAN?
YOU'RE MY BEST FRIEND, MAPS. I WAS LOOKING OUT FOR YOU.
YOU BETRAY EVERYTHING THAT WE ARE TO EACH OTHER BECAUSE YOU CAN'T STAND THE GUY WHO HURT YOUR MOM?
I DON'T HAVE TIME FOR THIS NOW. RIKO NEEDS SAVING!
NO! MAPS!
LEAVE HER. SHE'LL COOL DOWN. SHE KNOWS BETTER THAN TO GET HERSELF ARRESTED.
AT LEAST, I THINK SHE DOES.
DID I DO THE RIGHT THING, KYLE?

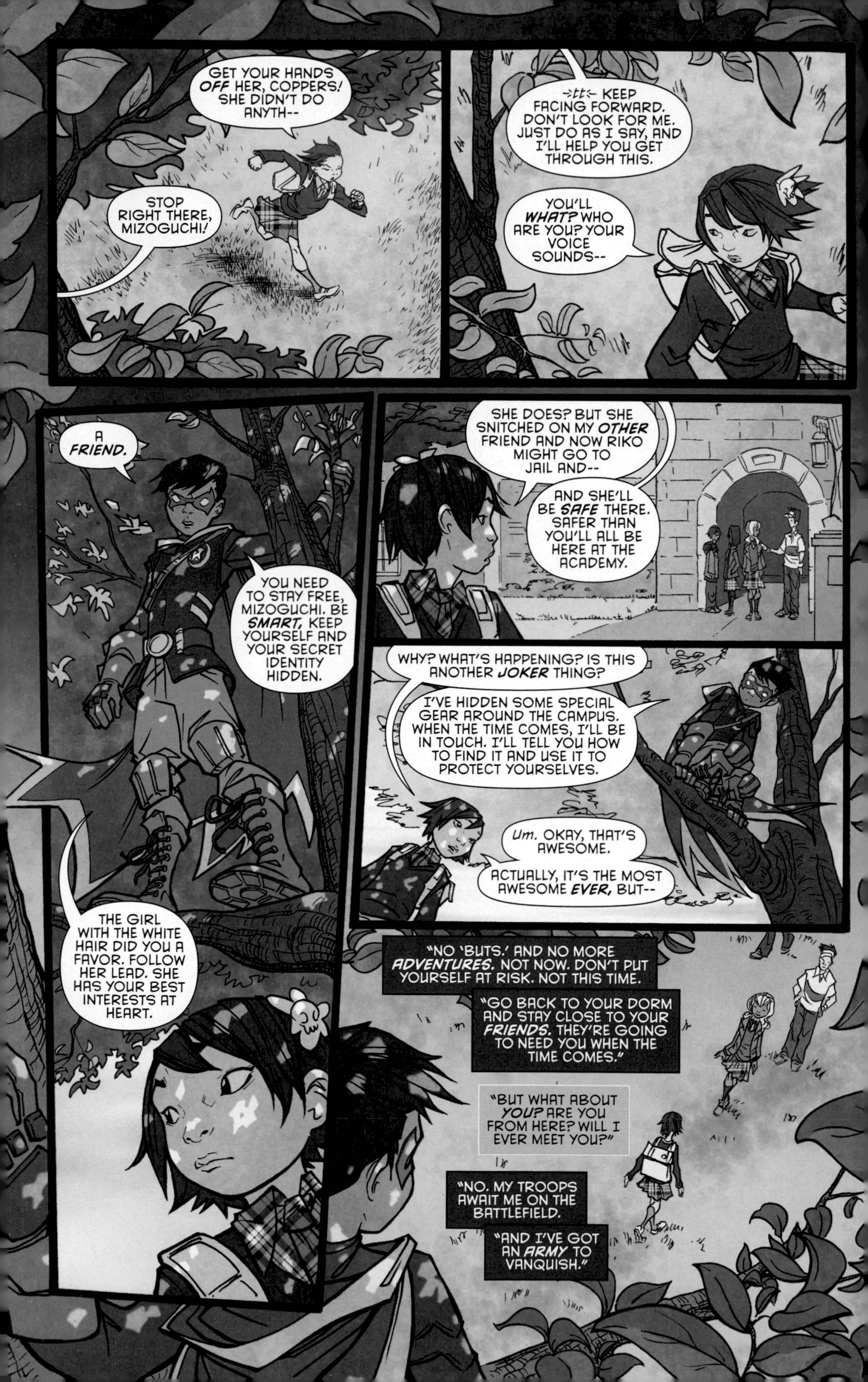
GET YOUR HANDS OFF HER, COPPERS! SHE DIDN'T DO ANYTH--
STOP RIGHT THERE, MIZOGUCHI!
-tt- KEEP FACING FORWARD. DON'T LOOK FOR ME. JUST DO AS I SAY, AND I'LL HELP YOU GET THROUGH THIS.
YOU'LL WHAT? WHO ARE YOU? YOUR VOICE SOUNDS--
A FRIEND.
YOU NEED TO STAY FREE, MIZOGUCHI. BE SMART, KEEP YOURSELF AND YOUR SECRET IDENTITY HIDDEN.
THE GIRL WITH THE WHITE HAIR DID YOU A FAVOR. FOLLOW HER LEAD. SHE HAS YOUR BEST INTERESTS AT HEART.
SHE DOES? BUT SHE SNITCHED ON MY OTHER FRIEND AND NOW RIKO MIGHT GO TO JAIL AND--
AND SHE'LL BE SAFE THERE. SAFER THAN YOU'LL ALL BE HERE AT THE ACADEMY.
WHY? WHAT'S HAPPENING? IS THIS ANOTHER JOKER THING?
I'VE HIDDEN SOME SPECIAL GEAR AROUND THE CAMPUS. WHEN THE TIME COMES, I'LL BE IN TOUCH. I'LL TELL YOU HOW TO FIND IT AND USE IT TO PROTECT YOURSELVES.
Um. OKAY, THAT'S AWESOME.
ACTUALLY, IT'S THE MOST AWESOME EVER, BUT--
"NO 'BUTS.' AND NO MORE ADVENTURES. NOT NOW. DON'T PUT YOURSELF AT RISK. NOT THIS TIME.
"GO BACK TO YOUR DORM AND STAY CLOSE TO YOUR FRIENDS. THEY'RE GOING TO NEED YOU WHEN THE TIME COMES."
"BUT WHAT ABOUT YOU? ARE YOU FROM HERE? WILL I EVER MEET YOU?"
"NO. MY TROOPS AWAIT ME ON THE BATTLEFIELD.
"AND I'VE GOT AN ARMY TO VANQUISH."

ANG   SUSAN TRENT   ALEXANDER LI   WILLIAM LANG   RAD SE

SON   MISSY RODGERS   TRISTAN GREY   HAM   RYAN

HALL   COLTON RIVERA   OLIVE SILVERLOCK   MIA MIZOGUCHI   BETSY

ATUE   KYLE MIZOGUCHI   POMELINE FRITCH   PIZZA CLUB   LINDA

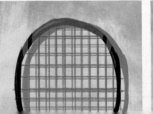

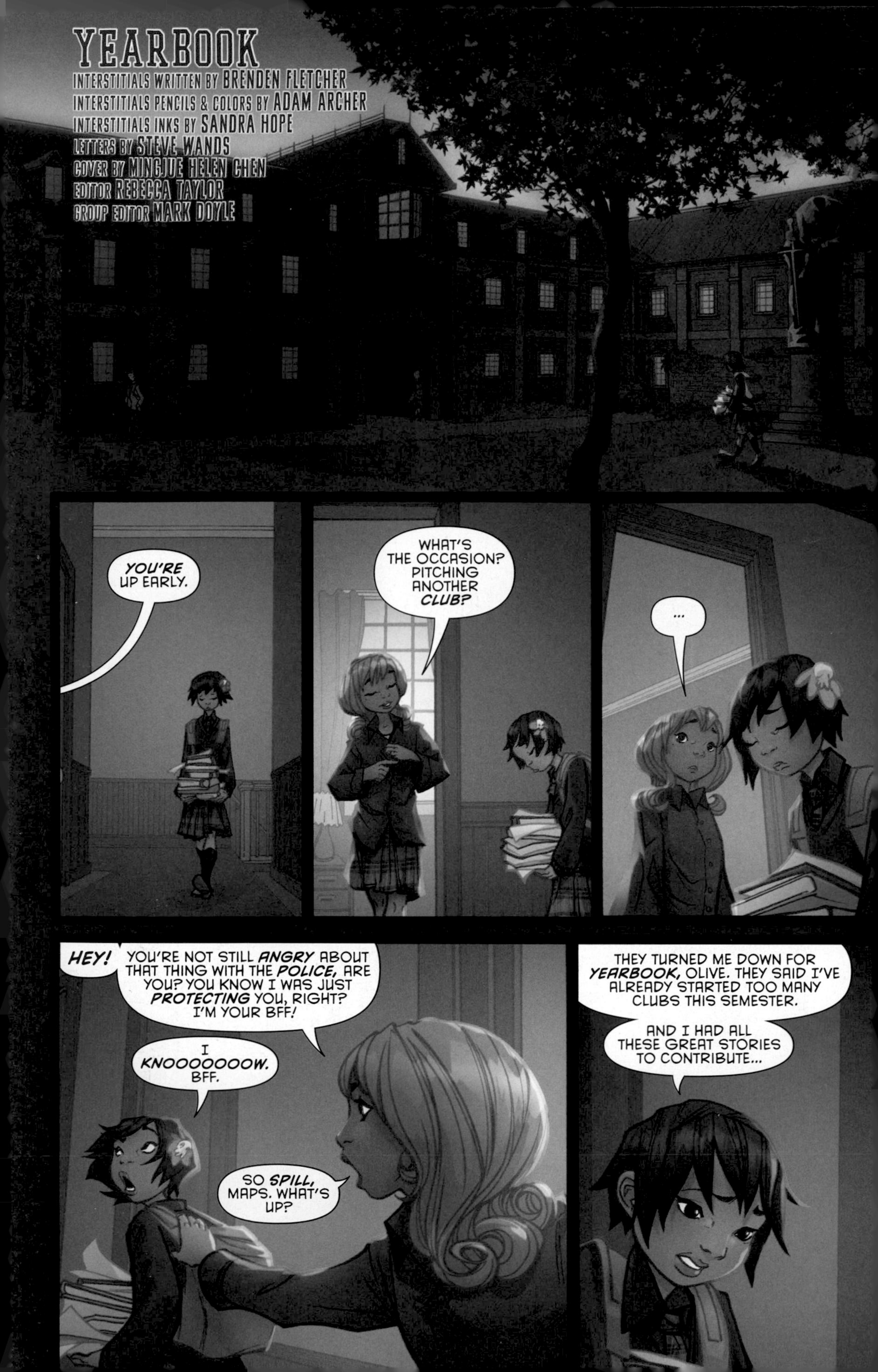
YEARBOOK
INTERSTITIALS WRITTEN BY BRENDEN FLETCHER
INTERSTITIALS PENCILS & COLORS BY ADAM ARCHER
INTERSTITIALS INKS BY SANDRA HOPE
LETTERS BY STEVE WANDS
COVER BY MINGJUE HELEN CHEN
EDITOR REBECCA TAYLOR
GROUP EDITOR MARK DOYLE
YOU'RE UP EARLY.
WHAT'S THE OCCASION? PITCHING ANOTHER CLUB?
...
HEY!
YOU'RE NOT STILL ANGRY ABOUT THAT THING WITH THE POLICE, ARE YOU? YOU KNOW I WAS JUST PROTECTING YOU, RIGHT? I'M YOUR BFF!
I KNOOOOOOOW. BFF.
SO SPILL, MAPS. WHAT'S UP?
THEY TURNED ME DOWN FOR YEARBOOK, OLIVE. THEY SAID I'VE ALREADY STARTED TOO MANY CLUBS THIS SEMESTER.
AND I HAD ALL THESE GREAT STORIES TO CONTRIBUTE...

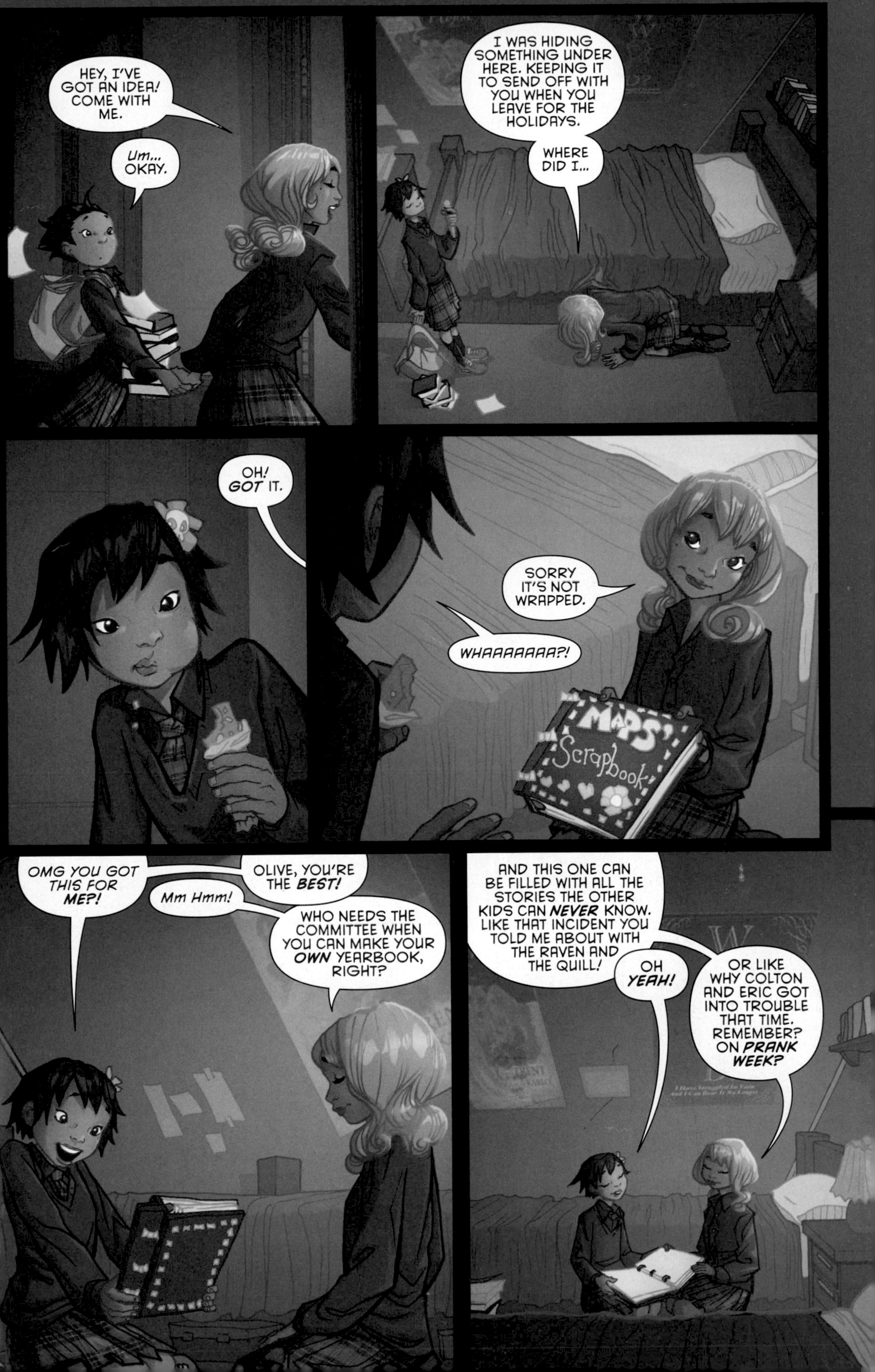
HEY, I'VE GOT AN IDEA! COME WITH ME.
Um... OKAY.
I WAS HIDING SOMETHING UNDER HERE. KEEPING IT TO SEND OFF WITH YOU WHEN YOU LEAVE FOR THE HOLIDAYS.
WHERE DID I...
OH! GOT IT.
SORRY IT'S NOT WRAPPED.
WHAAAAAAA?!
MAPS' Scrapbook
OMG YOU GOT THIS FOR ME?!
OLIVE, YOU'RE THE BEST!
Mm Hmm!
WHO NEEDS THE COMMITTEE WHEN YOU CAN MAKE YOUR OWN YEARBOOK, RIGHT?
AND THIS ONE CAN BE FILLED WITH ALL THE STORIES THE OTHER KIDS CAN NEVER KNOW. LIKE THAT INCIDENT YOU TOLD ME ABOUT WITH THE RAVEN AND THE QUILL!
OH YEAH!
OR LIKE WHY COLTON AND ERIC GOT INTO TROUBLE THAT TIME. REMEMBER? ON PRANK WEEK?

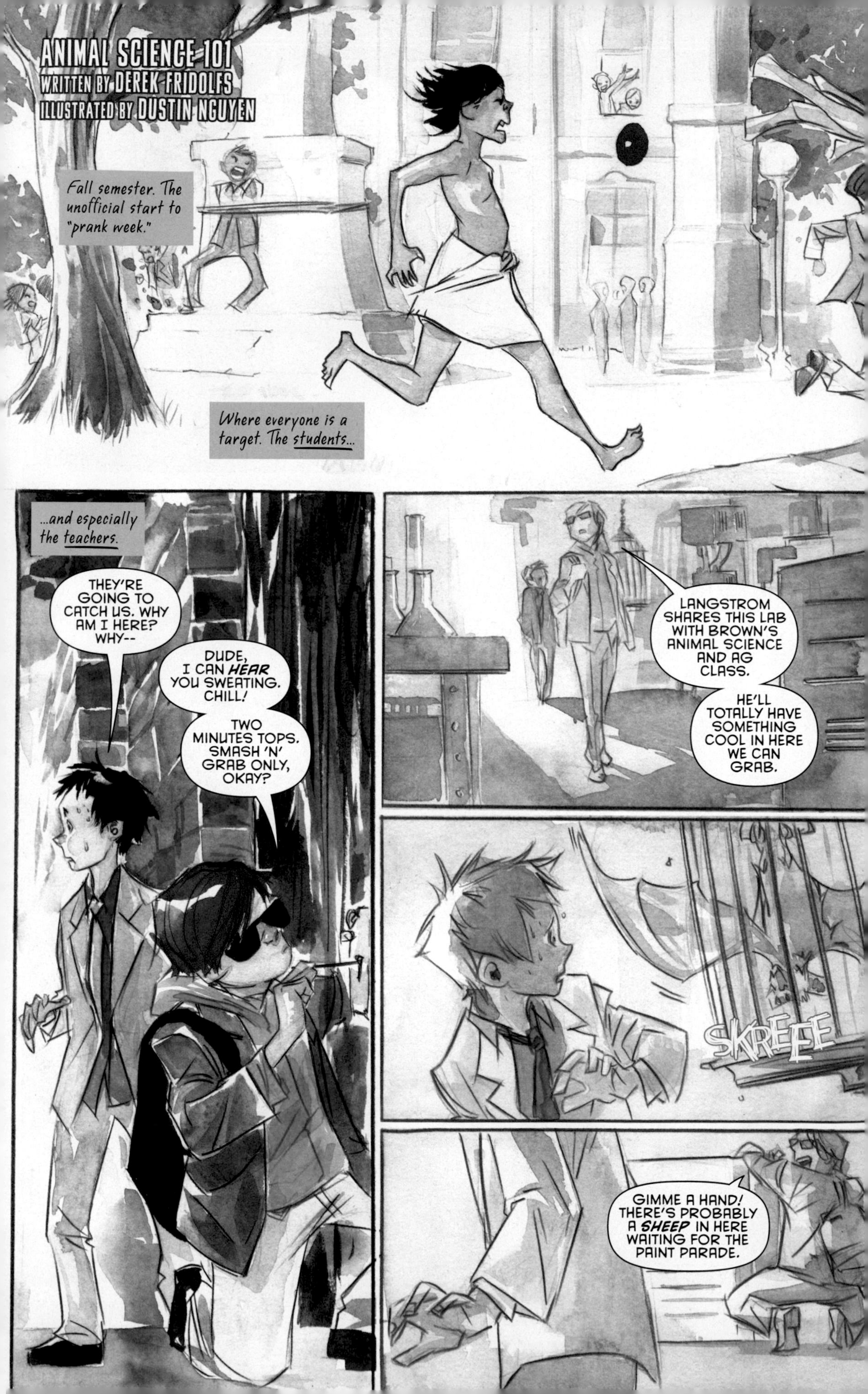

ANIMAL SCIENCE 101
WRITTEN BY DEREK FRIDOLFS
ILLUSTRATED BY DUSTIN NGUYEN
Fall semester. The unofficial start to "prank week."
Where everyone is a target. The students...
...and especially the teachers.
THEY'RE GOING TO CATCH US. WHY AM I HERE? WHY--
DUDE, I CAN HEAR YOU SWEATING. CHILL!
TWO MINUTES TOPS. SMASH 'N' GRAB ONLY, OKAY?
LANGSTROM SHARES THIS LAB WITH BROWN'S ANIMAL SCIENCE AND AG CLASS.
HE'LL TOTALLY HAVE SOMETHING COOL IN HERE WE CAN GRAB.
SKREEE
GIMME A HAND! THERE'S PROBABLY A SHEEP IN HERE WAITING FOR THE PAINT PARADE.

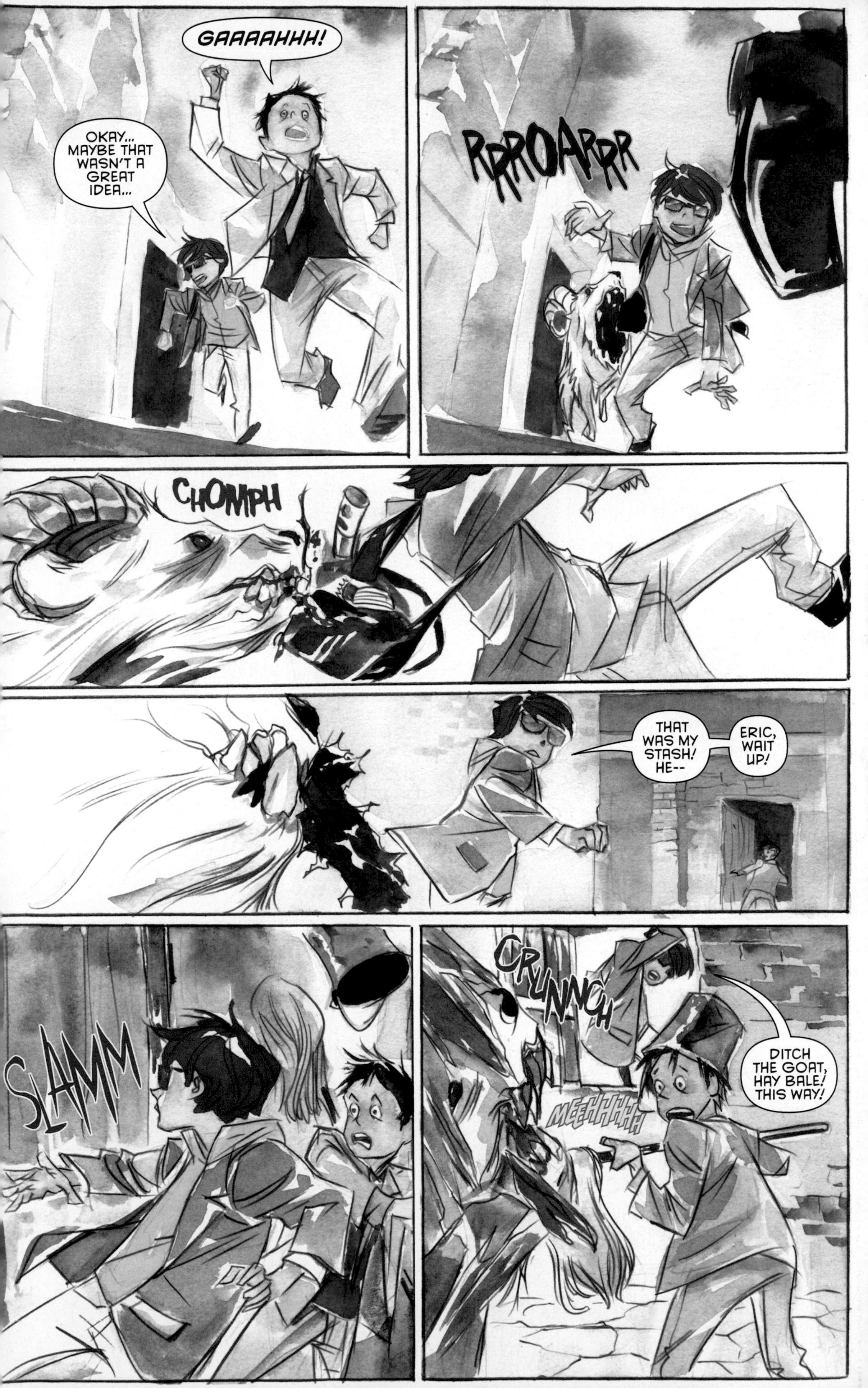
GAAAAHHH!
OKAY... MAYBE THAT WASN'T A GREAT IDEA...
RRROARRR
CHOMPH
THAT WAS MY STASH! HE--
ERIC, WAIT UP!
SLAMM
CRUNNCH
MEEHHHHH
DITCH THE GOAT, HAY BALE! THIS WAY!

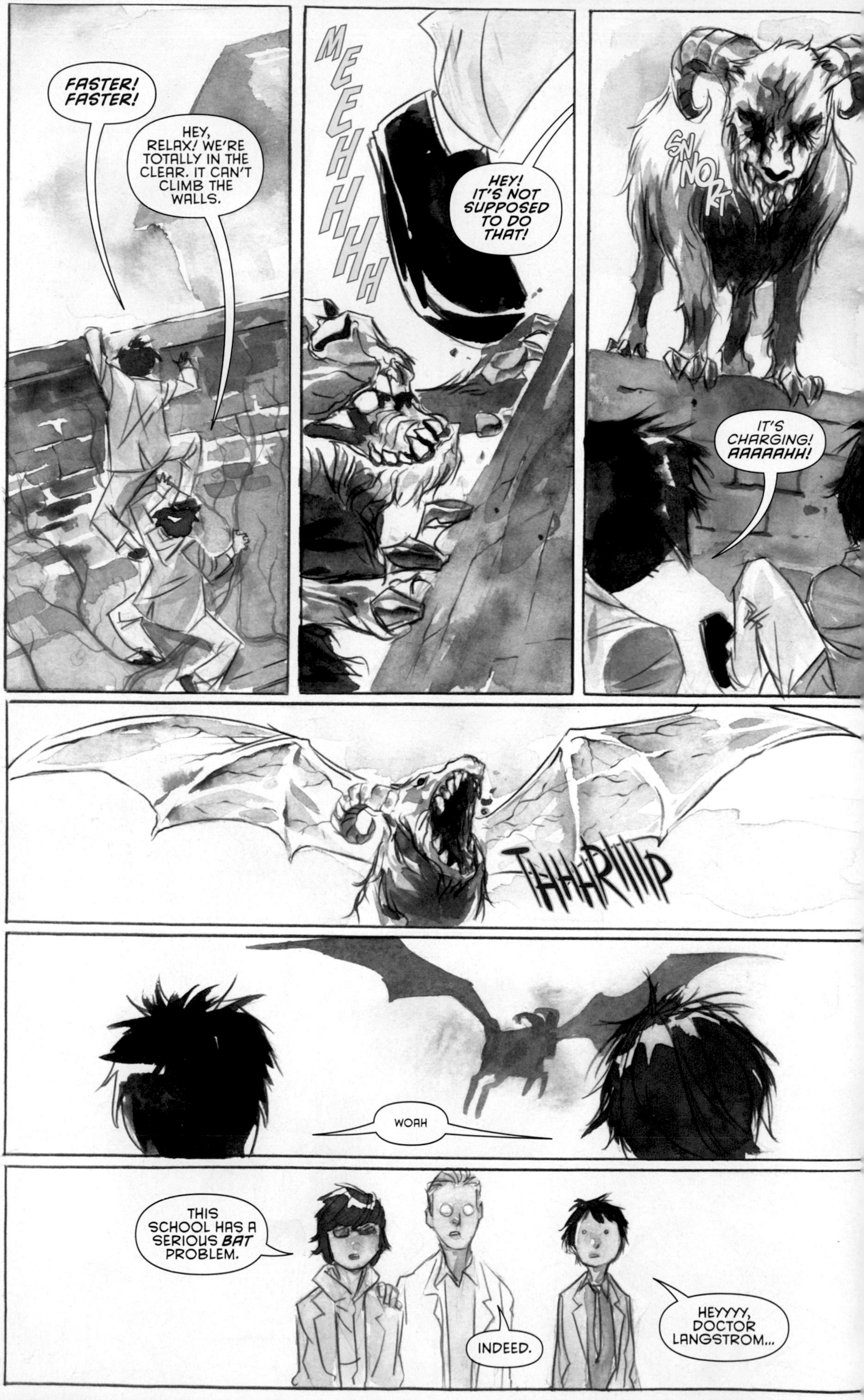
FASTER! FASTER!
HEY, RELAX! WE'RE TOTALLY IN THE CLEAR. IT CAN'T CLIMB THE WALLS.
MEEHHHHH
HEY! IT'S NOT SUPPOSED TO DO THAT!
SNNORT
IT'S CHARGING! AAAAAHH!
THHRIIIP
WOAH
THIS SCHOOL HAS A SERIOUS BAT PROBLEM.
INDEED.
HEYYYY, DOCTOR LANGSTROM...

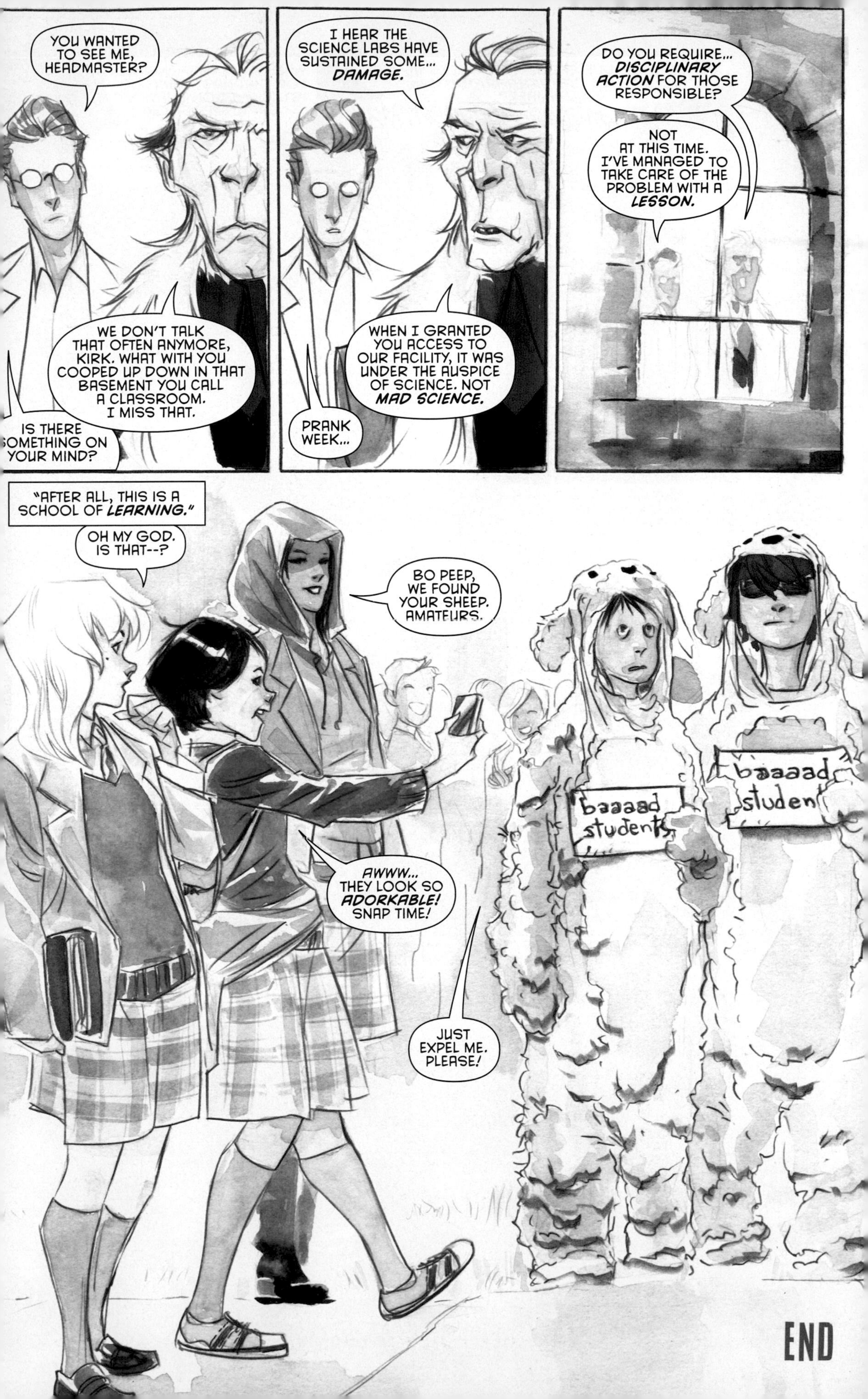
YOU WANTED TO SEE ME, HEADMASTER?
WE DON'T TALK THAT OFTEN ANYMORE, KIRK. WHAT WITH YOU COOPED UP DOWN IN THAT BASEMENT YOU CALL A CLASSROOM. I MISS THAT.
IS THERE SOMETHING ON YOUR MIND?
I HEAR THE SCIENCE LABS HAVE SUSTAINED SOME... DAMAGE.
WHEN I GRANTED YOU ACCESS TO OUR FACILITY, IT WAS UNDER THE AUSPICE OF SCIENCE. NOT MAD SCIENCE.
PRANK WEEK...
DO YOU REQUIRE... DISCIPLINARY ACTION FOR THOSE RESPONSIBLE?
NOT AT THIS TIME. I'VE MANAGED TO TAKE CARE OF THE PROBLEM WITH A LESSON.
"AFTER ALL, THIS IS A SCHOOL OF LEARNING."
OH MY GOD. IS THAT--?
BO PEEP, WE FOUND YOUR SHEEP. AMATEURS.
baaaad students
baaaad studen
AWWW... THEY LOOK SO ADORKABLE! SNAP TIME!
JUST EXPEL ME. PLEASE!
END

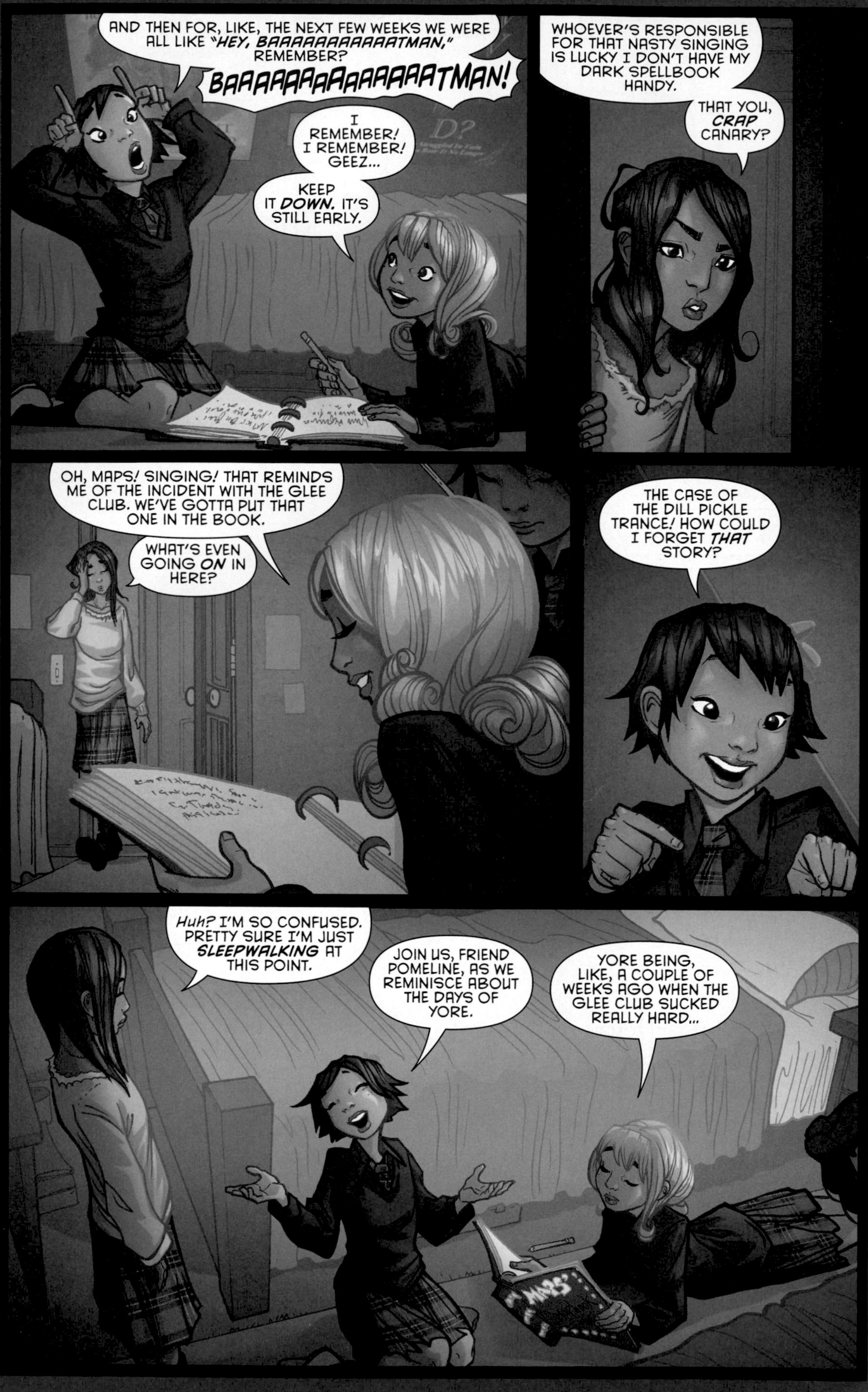
AND THEN FOR, LIKE, THE NEXT FEW WEEKS WE WERE ALL LIKE "*HEY, BAAAAAAAAAAAATMAN,*" REMEMBER?
BAAAAAAAAAAAAAAATMAN!
I REMEMBER! I REMEMBER! GEEZ...
KEEP IT **DOWN.** IT'S STILL EARLY.
WHOEVER'S RESPONSIBLE FOR THAT NASTY SINGING IS LUCKY I DON'T HAVE MY DARK SPELLBOOK HANDY.
THAT YOU, ***CRAP*** CANARY?
OH, MAPS! SINGING! THAT REMINDS ME OF THE INCIDENT WITH THE GLEE CLUB. WE'VE GOTTA PUT THAT ONE IN THE BOOK.
WHAT'S EVEN GOING ***ON*** IN HERE?
THE CASE OF THE DILL PICKLE TRANCE! HOW COULD I FORGET ***THAT*** STORY?
Huh? I'M SO CONFUSED. PRETTY SURE I'M JUST ***SLEEPWALKING*** AT THIS POINT.
JOIN US, FRIEND POMELINE, AS WE REMINISCE ABOUT THE DAYS OF YORE.
YORE BEING, LIKE, A COUPLE OF WEEKS AGO WHEN THE GLEE CLUB SUCKED REALLY HARD...
MAPS

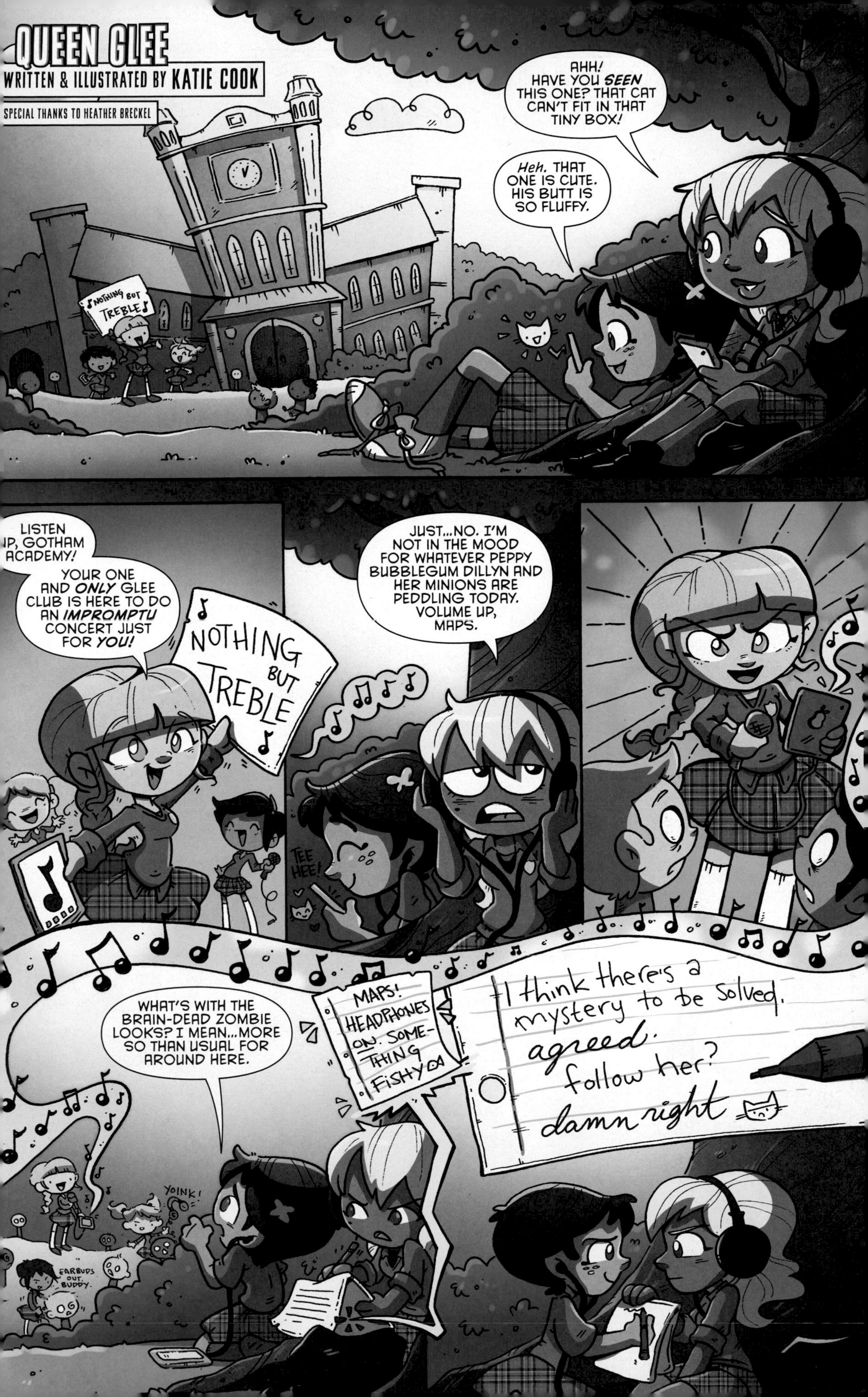
QUEEN GLEE
WRITTEN & ILLUSTRATED BY KATIE COOK
SPECIAL THANKS TO HEATHER BRECKEL
NOTHING BUT TREBLE
AHH! HAVE YOU SEEN THIS ONE? THAT CAT CAN'T FIT IN THAT TINY BOX!
Heh. THAT ONE IS CUTE. HIS BUTT IS SO FLUFFY.
LISTEN UP, GOTHAM ACADEMY!
YOUR ONE AND ONLY GLEE CLUB IS HERE TO DO AN IMPROMPTU CONCERT JUST FOR YOU!
NOTHING BUT TREBLE
JUST...NO. I'M NOT IN THE MOOD FOR WHATEVER PEPPY BUBBLEGUM DILLYN AND HER MINIONS ARE PEDDLING TODAY. VOLUME UP, MAPS.
TEE HEE!
WHAT'S WITH THE BRAIN-DEAD ZOMBIE LOOKS? I MEAN...MORE SO THAN USUAL FOR AROUND HERE.
MAPS! HEADPHONES ON. SOMETHING FISHY
I think there's a mystery to be solved.
agreed.
follow her?
damn right
YOINK!
EARBUDS OUT, BUDDY.

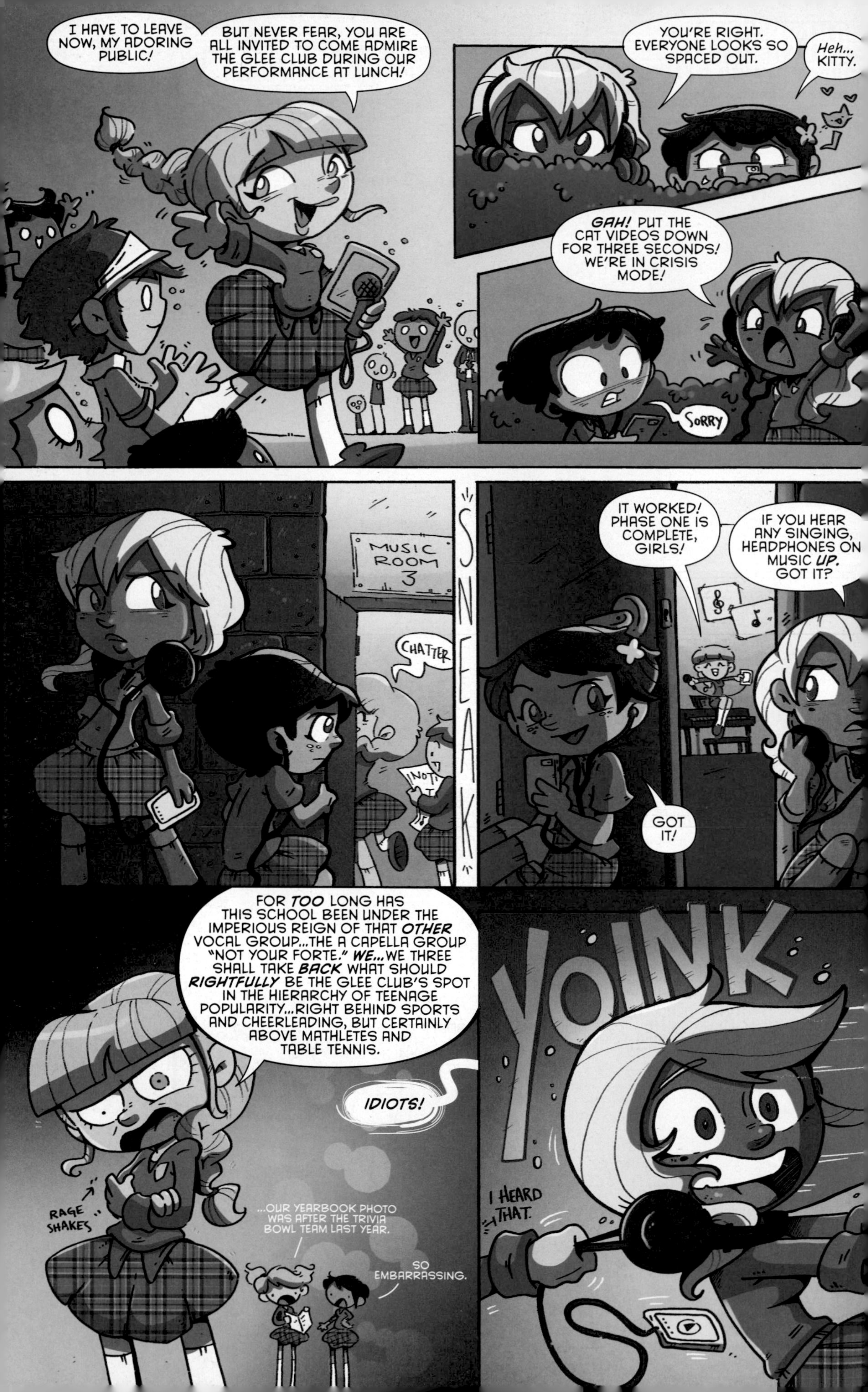
I HAVE TO LEAVE NOW, MY ADORING PUBLIC!
BUT NEVER FEAR, YOU ARE ALL INVITED TO COME ADMIRE THE GLEE CLUB DURING OUR PERFORMANCE AT LUNCH!
YOU'RE RIGHT. EVERYONE LOOKS SO SPACED OUT.
Heh... KITTY.
GAH! PUT THE CAT VIDEOS DOWN FOR THREE SECONDS! WE'RE IN CRISIS MODE!
SORRY
MUSIC ROOM 3
CHATTER
NOT
SNEAK
IT WORKED! PHASE ONE IS COMPLETE, GIRLS!
IF YOU HEAR ANY SINGING, HEADPHONES ON MUSIC UP. GOT IT?
GOT IT!
FOR TOO LONG HAS THIS SCHOOL BEEN UNDER THE IMPERIOUS REIGN OF THAT OTHER VOCAL GROUP...THE A CAPELLA GROUP "NOT YOUR FORTE." WE...WE THREE SHALL TAKE BACK WHAT SHOULD RIGHTFULLY BE THE GLEE CLUB'S SPOT IN THE HIERARCHY OF TEENAGE POPULARITY...RIGHT BEHIND SPORTS AND CHEERLEADING, BUT CERTAINLY ABOVE MATHLETES AND TABLE TENNIS.
IDIOTS!
RAGE SHAKES
...OUR YEARBOOK PHOTO WAS AFTER THE TRIVIA BOWL TEAM LAST YEAR.
SO EMBARRASSING.
YOINK
I HEARD THAT.

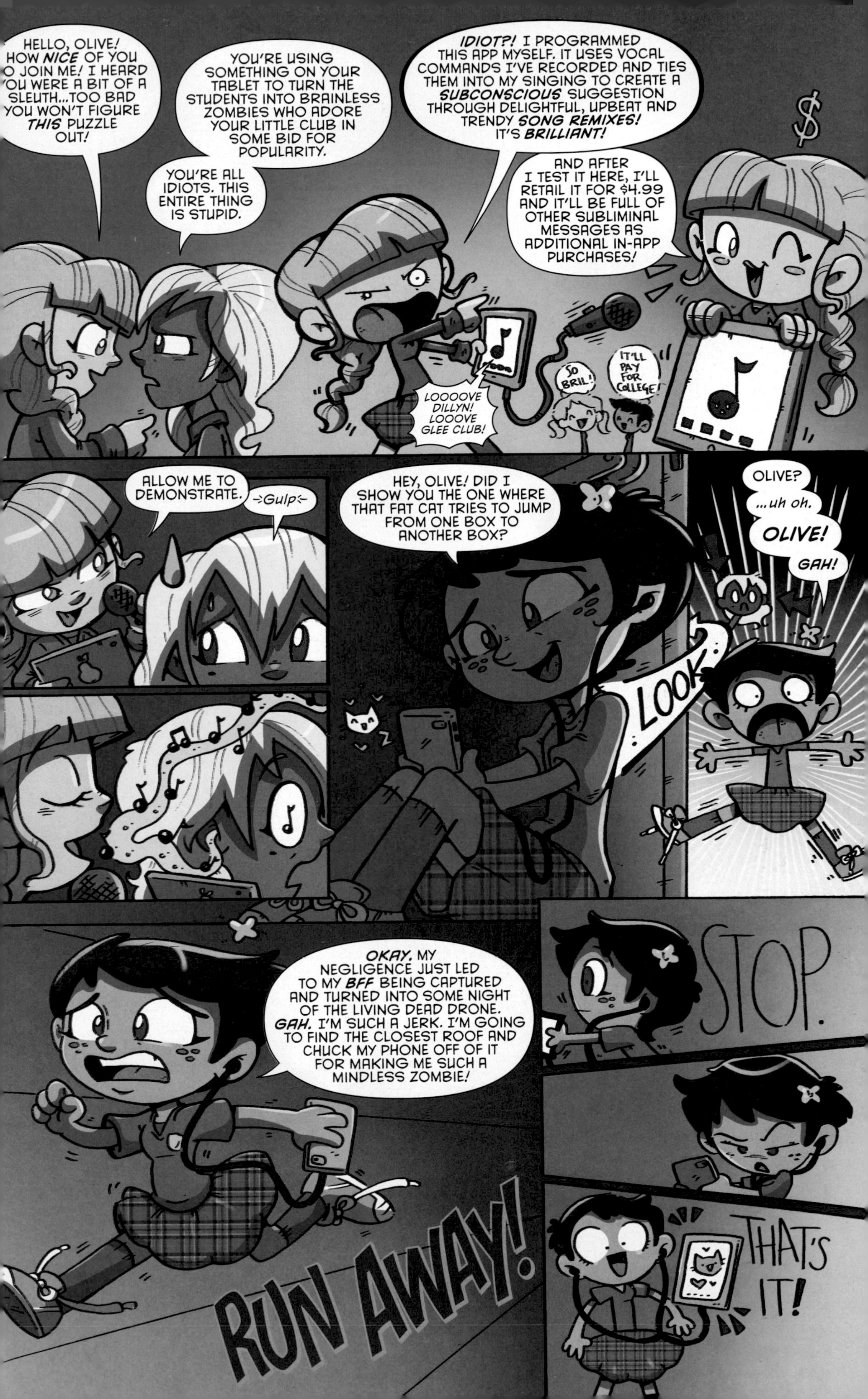
HELLO, OLIVE! HOW NICE OF YOU TO JOIN ME! I HEARD YOU WERE A BIT OF A SLEUTH...TOO BAD YOU WON'T FIGURE THIS PUZZLE OUT!
YOU'RE USING SOMETHING ON YOUR TABLET TO TURN THE STUDENTS INTO BRAINLESS ZOMBIES WHO ADORE YOUR LITTLE CLUB IN SOME BID FOR POPULARITY.
YOU'RE ALL IDIOTS. THIS ENTIRE THING IS STUPID.
IDIOT?! I PROGRAMMED THIS APP MYSELF. IT USES VOCAL COMMANDS I'VE RECORDED AND TIES THEM INTO MY SINGING TO CREATE A SUBCONSCIOUS SUGGESTION THROUGH DELIGHTFUL, UPBEAT AND TRENDY SONG REMIXES! IT'S BRILLIANT!
LOOOOVE DILLYN! LOOOVE GLEE CLUB!
SO BRIL!
IT'LL PAY FOR COLLEGE!
AND AFTER I TEST IT HERE, I'LL RETAIL IT FOR $4.99 AND IT'LL BE FULL OF OTHER SUBLIMINAL MESSAGES AS ADDITIONAL IN-APP PURCHASES!
$
ALLOW ME TO DEMONSTRATE.
Gulp
HEY, OLIVE! DID I SHOW YOU THE ONE WHERE THAT FAT CAT TRIES TO JUMP FROM ONE BOX TO ANOTHER BOX?
OLIVE?
...uh oh.
OLIVE!
GAH!
LOOK
OKAY. MY NEGLIGENCE JUST LED TO MY BFF BEING CAPTURED AND TURNED INTO SOME NIGHT OF THE LIVING DEAD DRONE. GAH. I'M SUCH A JERK. I'M GOING TO FIND THE CLOSEST ROOF AND CHUCK MY PHONE OFF OF IT FOR MAKING ME SUCH A MINDLESS ZOMBIE!
RUN AWAY!
STOP.
THAT'S IT!

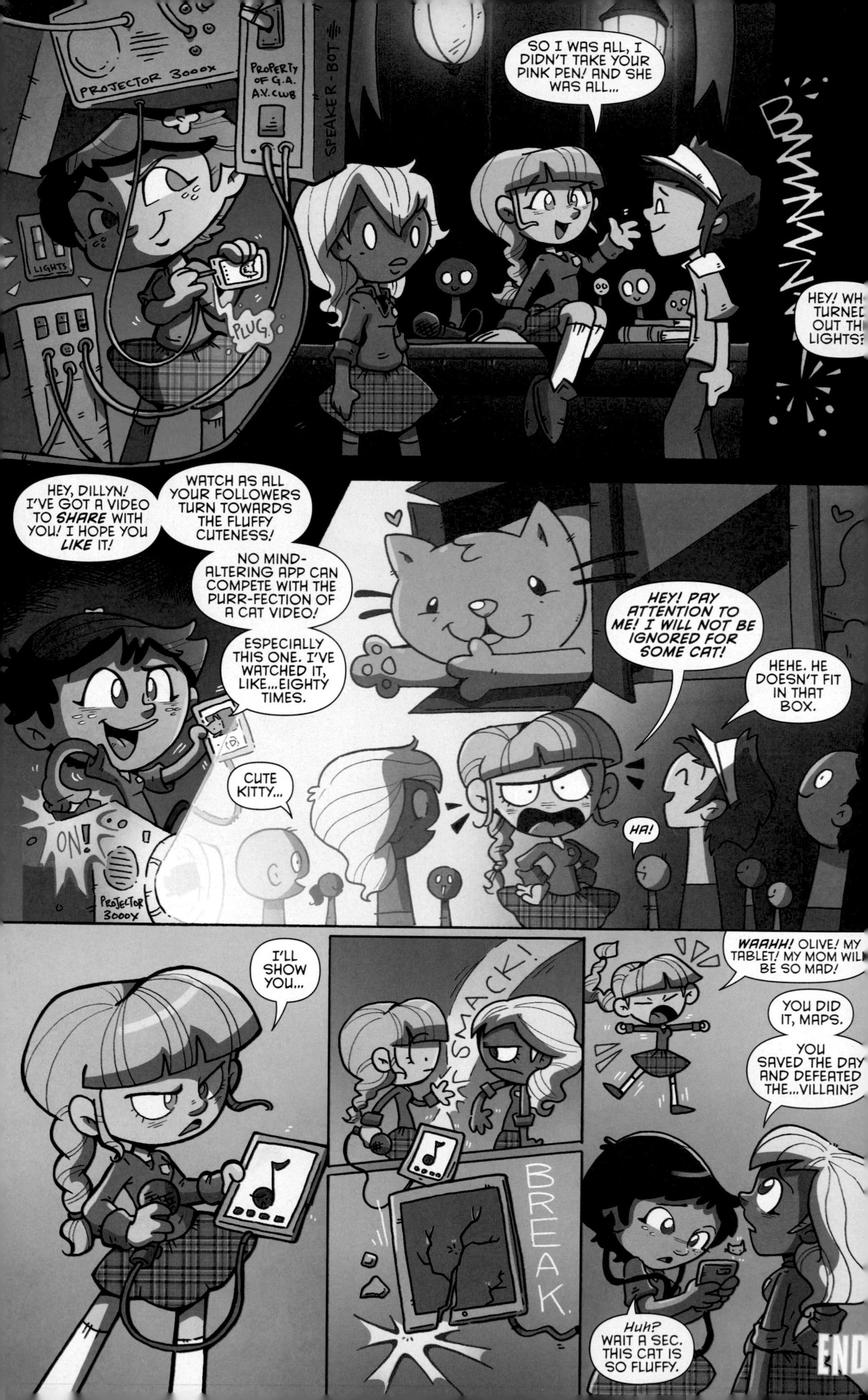

PROJECTOR 3000X
PROPERTY OF G.A. A.V. CLUB
SPEAKER-BOT
LIGHTS
PLUG.
SO I WAS ALL, I DIDN'T TAKE YOUR PINK PEN! AND SHE WAS ALL...
BWWMMMMN
HEY! WH TURNED OUT TH LIGHTS?
HEY, DILLYN! I'VE GOT A VIDEO TO SHARE WITH YOU! I HOPE YOU LIKE IT!
WATCH AS ALL YOUR FOLLOWERS TURN TOWARDS THE FLUFFY CUTENESS!
NO MIND-ALTERING APP CAN COMPETE WITH THE PURR-FECTION OF A CAT VIDEO!
ESPECIALLY THIS ONE. I'VE WATCHED IT, LIKE...EIGHTY TIMES.
ON!
PROJECTOR 3000X
CUTE KITTY...
HEY! PAY ATTENTION TO ME! I WILL NOT BE IGNORED FOR SOME CAT!
HEHE. HE DOESN'T FIT IN THAT BOX.
HA!
I'LL SHOW YOU...
SMACK!
BREAK.
WAAHH! OLIVE! MY TABLET! MY MOM WIL BE SO MAD!
YOU DID IT, MAPS.
YOU SAVED THE DAY AND DEFEATED THE...VILLAIN?
Huh? WAIT A SEC. THIS CAT IS SO FLUFFY.
END

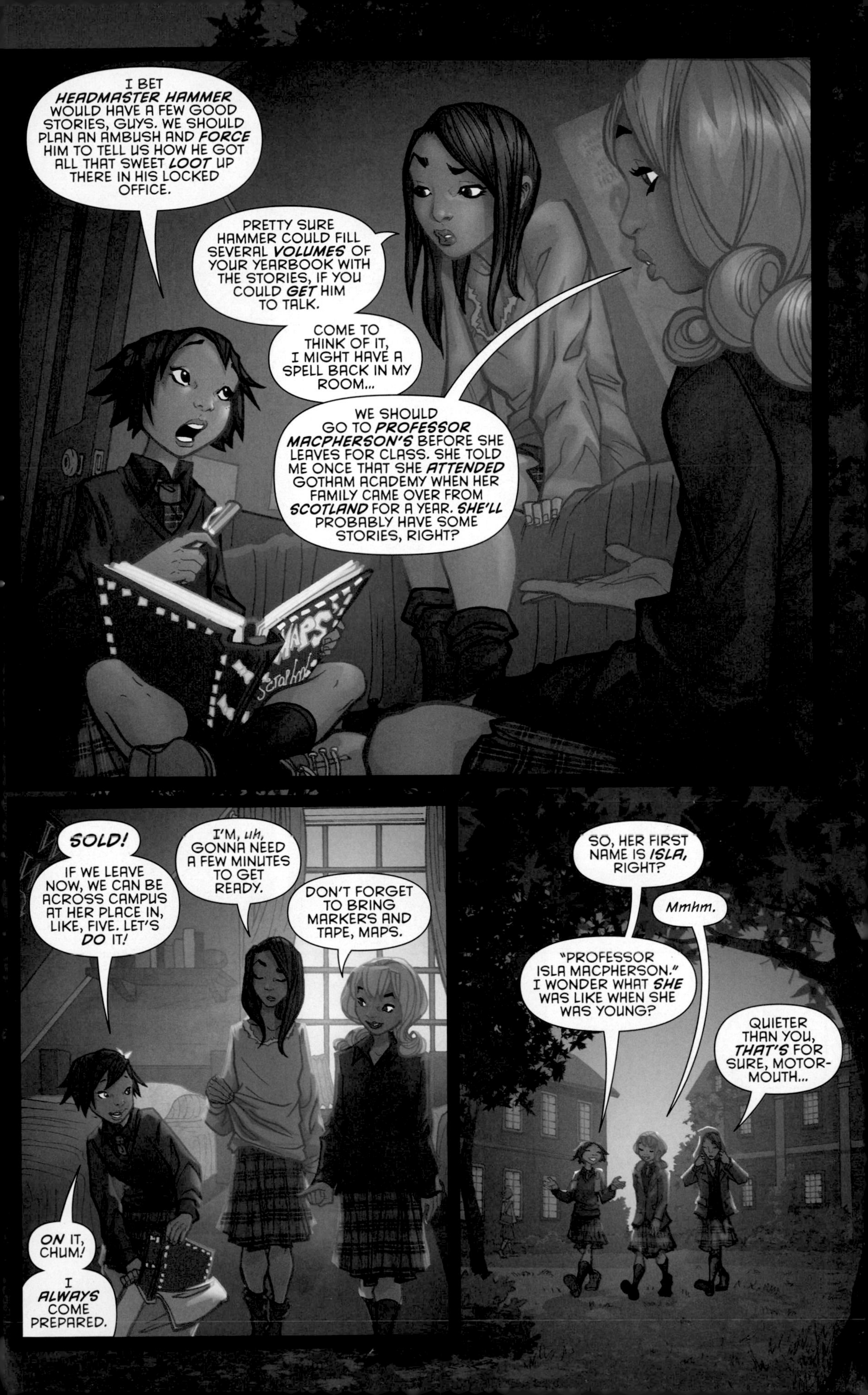
I BET HEADMASTER HAMMER WOULD HAVE A FEW GOOD STORIES, GUYS. WE SHOULD PLAN AN AMBUSH AND FORCE HIM TO TELL US HOW HE GOT ALL THAT SWEET LOOT UP THERE IN HIS LOCKED OFFICE.
PRETTY SURE HAMMER COULD FILL SEVERAL VOLUMES OF YOUR YEARBOOK WITH THE STORIES, IF YOU COULD GET HIM TO TALK.
COME TO THINK OF IT, I MIGHT HAVE A SPELL BACK IN MY ROOM...
WE SHOULD GO TO PROFESSOR MACPHERSON'S BEFORE SHE LEAVES FOR CLASS. SHE TOLD ME ONCE THAT SHE ATTENDED GOTHAM ACADEMY WHEN HER FAMILY CAME OVER FROM SCOTLAND FOR A YEAR. SHE'LL PROBABLY HAVE SOME STORIES, RIGHT?
MAPS
Scrapbook
SOLD!
IF WE LEAVE NOW, WE CAN BE ACROSS CAMPUS AT HER PLACE IN, LIKE, FIVE. LET'S DO IT!
I'M, uh, GONNA NEED A FEW MINUTES TO GET READY.
DON'T FORGET TO BRING MARKERS AND TAPE, MAPS.
ON IT, CHUM!
I ALWAYS COME PREPARED.
SO, HER FIRST NAME IS ISLA, RIGHT?
Mmhm.
"PROFESSOR ISLA MACPHERSON." I WONDER WHAT SHE WAS LIKE WHEN SHE WAS YOUNG?
QUIETER THAN YOU, THAT'S FOR SURE, MOTOR-MOUTH...

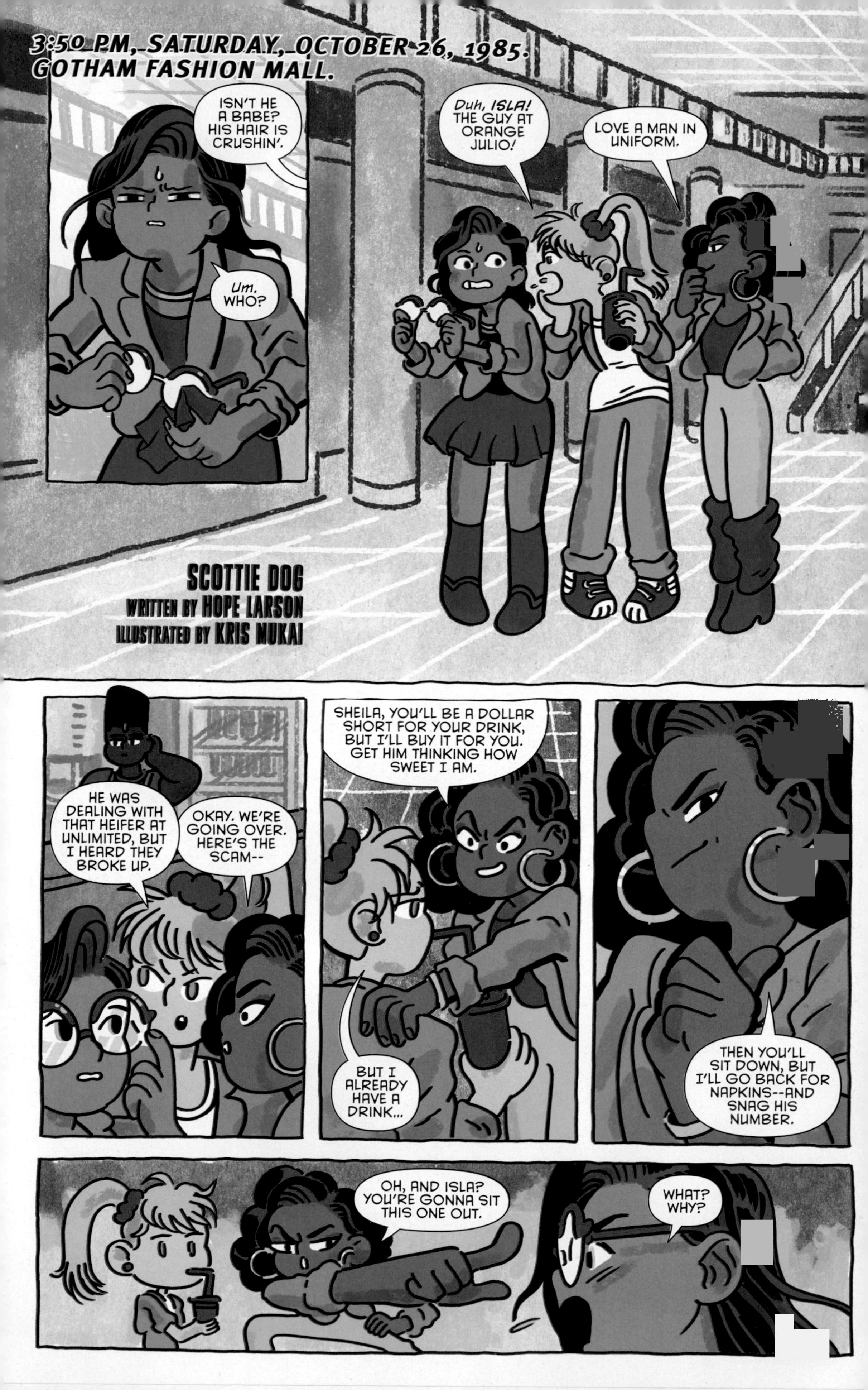
3:50 PM, SATURDAY, OCTOBER 26, 1985.
GOTHAM FASHION MALL.
ISN'T HE A BABE? HIS HAIR IS CRUSHIN'.
Um. WHO?
Duh, ISLA! THE GUY AT ORANGE JULIO!
LOVE A MAN IN UNIFORM.
SCOTTIE DOG
WRITTEN BY HOPE LARSON
ILLUSTRATED BY KRIS MUKAI
HE WAS DEALING WITH THAT HEIFER AT UNLIMITED, BUT I HEARD THEY BROKE UP.
OKAY. WE'RE GOING OVER. HERE'S THE SCAM--
SHEILA, YOU'LL BE A DOLLAR SHORT FOR YOUR DRINK, BUT I'LL BUY IT FOR YOU. GET HIM THINKING HOW SWEET I AM.
BUT I ALREADY HAVE A DRINK...
THEN YOU'LL SIT DOWN, BUT I'LL GO BACK FOR NAPKINS--AND SNAG HIS NUMBER.
OH, AND ISLA? YOU'RE GONNA SIT THIS ONE OUT.
WHAT? WHY?

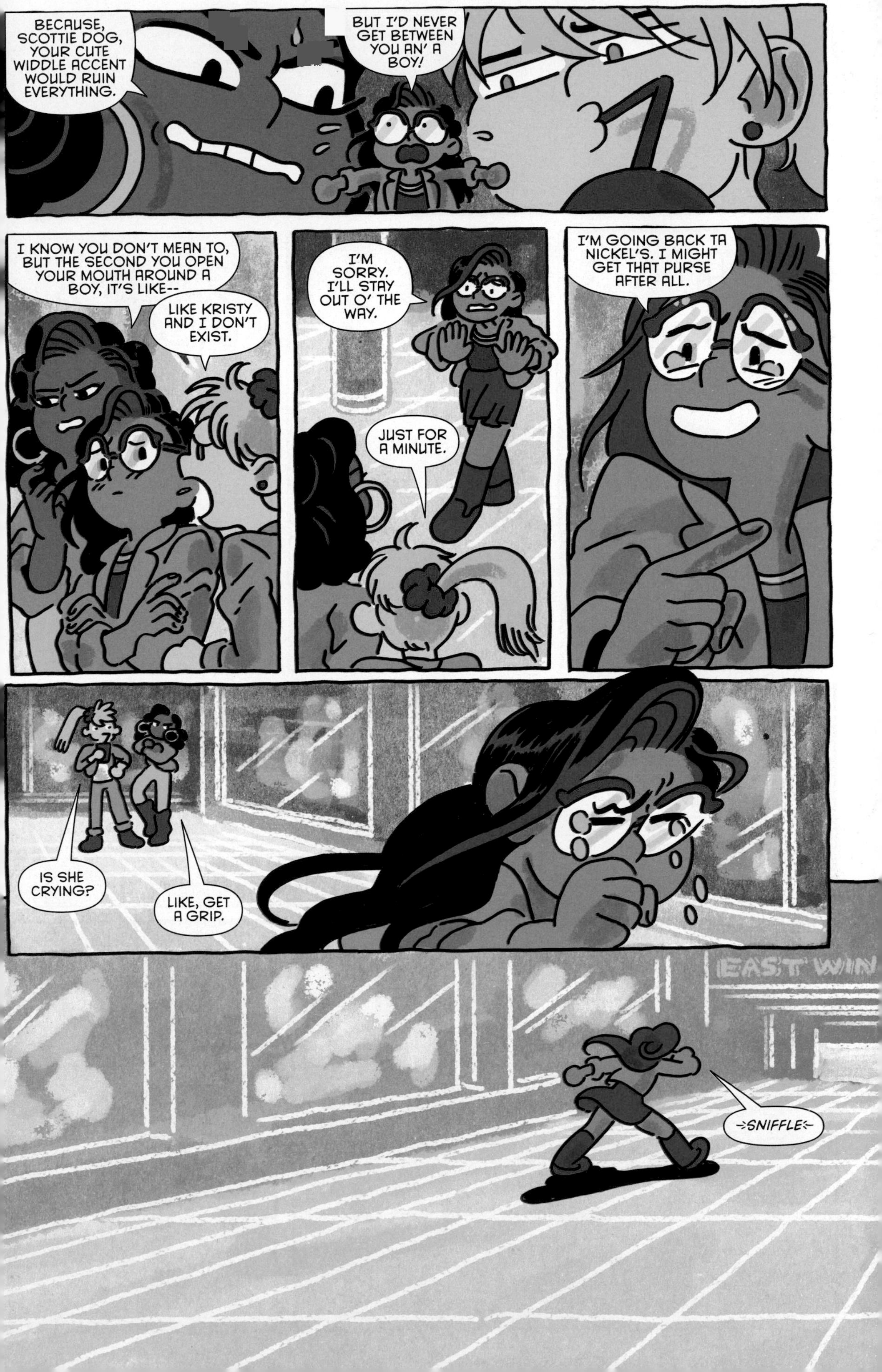
BECAUSE, SCOTTIE DOG, YOUR CUTE WIDDLE ACCENT WOULD RUIN EVERYTHING.
BUT I'D NEVER GET BETWEEN YOU AN' A BOY!
I KNOW YOU DON'T MEAN TO, BUT THE SECOND YOU OPEN YOUR MOUTH AROUND A BOY, IT'S LIKE--
LIKE KRISTY AND I DON'T EXIST.
I'M SORRY. I'LL STAY OUT O' THE WAY.
JUST FOR A MINUTE.
I'M GOING BACK TA NICKEL'S. I MIGHT GET THAT PURSE AFTER ALL.
IS SHE CRYING?
LIKE, GET A GRIP.
EAST WIN
SNIFFLE

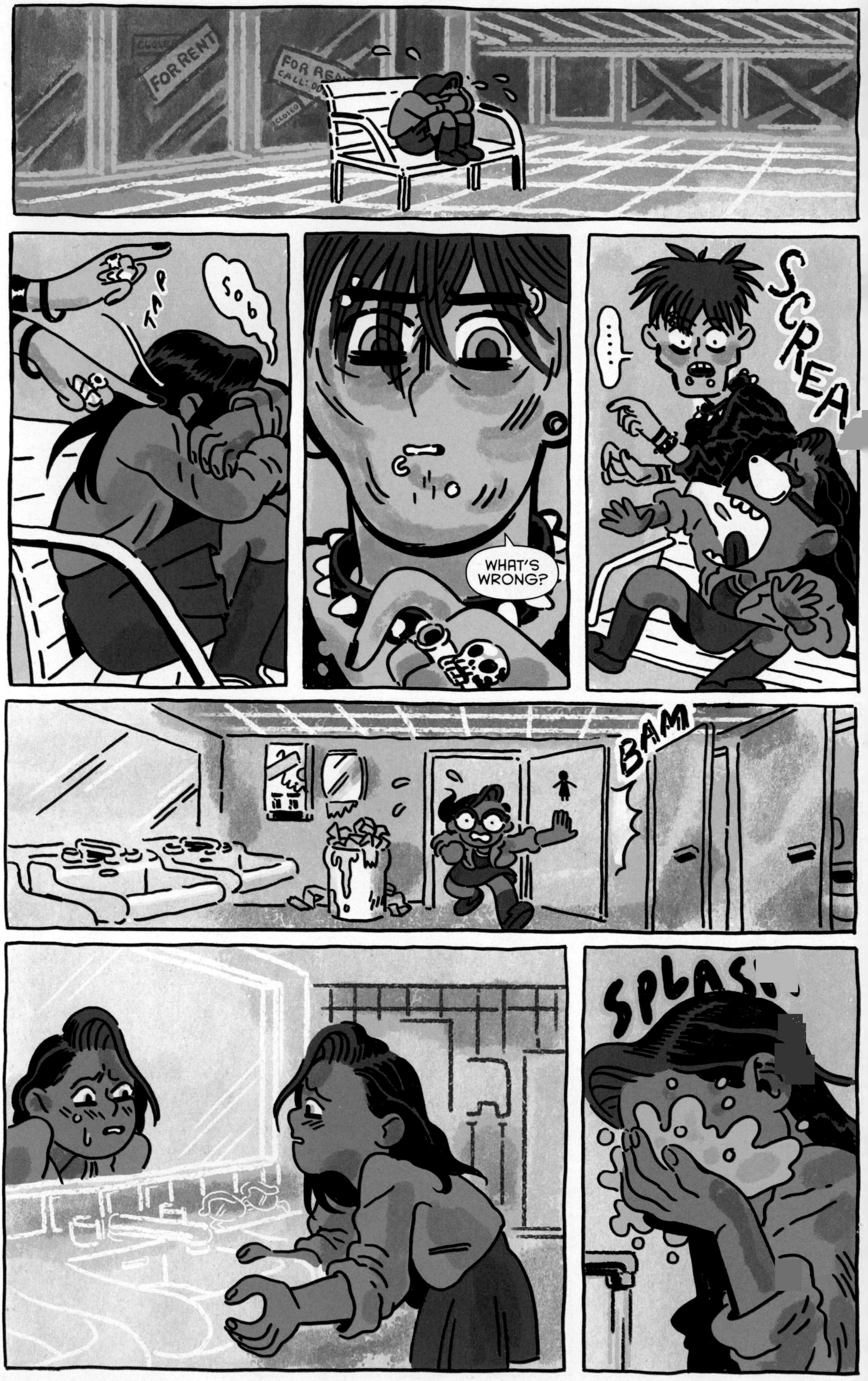
FOR RENT
FOR RENT CALL:
CLOSED
CLOSED
TAP
Sob
WHAT'S WRONG?
. . . . .
SCREA
BAM
SPLAS

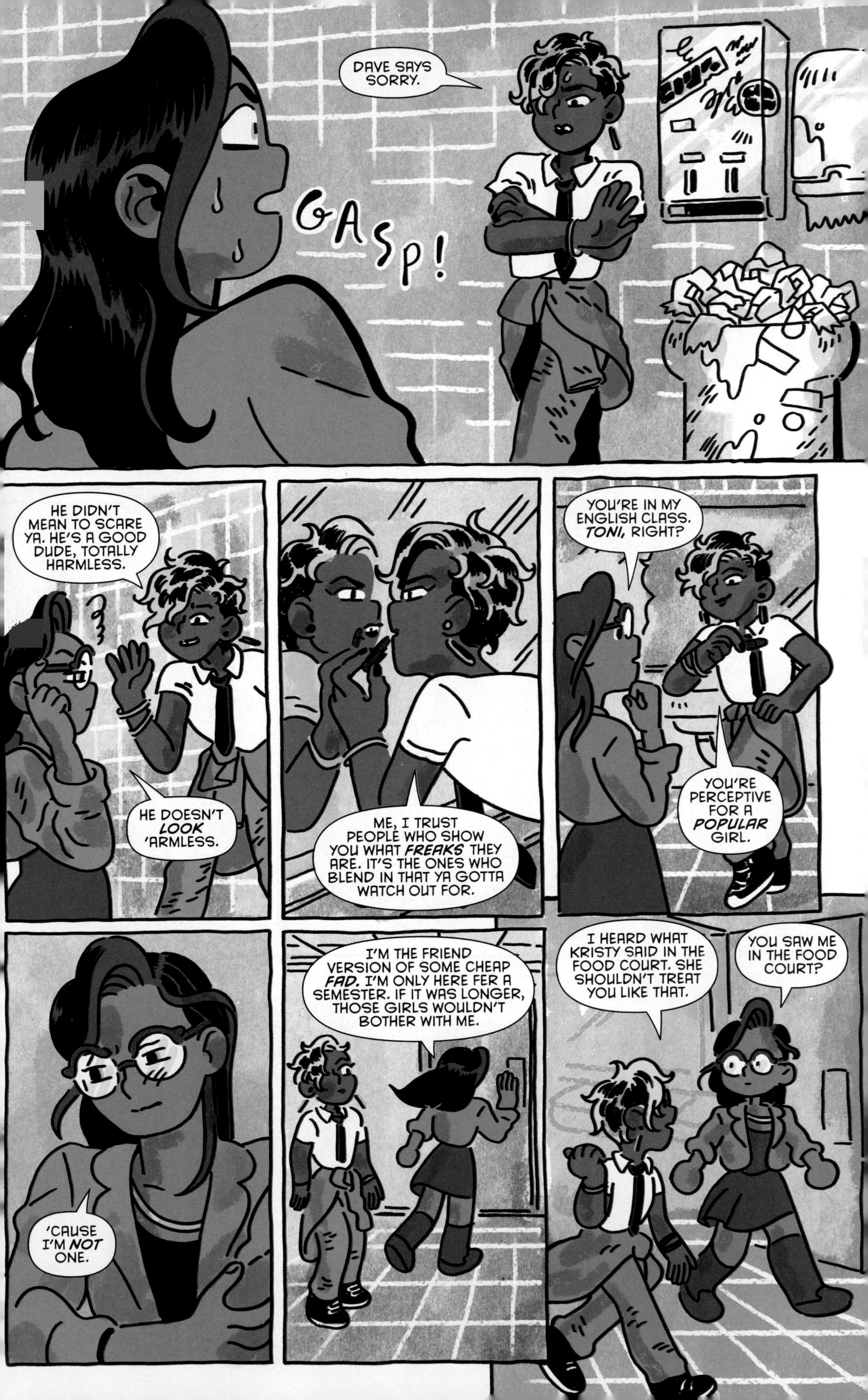
DAVE SAYS SORRY.
GASP!
HE DIDN'T MEAN TO SCARE YA. HE'S A GOOD DUDE, TOTALLY HARMLESS.
HE DOESN'T LOOK 'ARMLESS.
ME, I TRUST PEOPLE WHO SHOW YOU WHAT FREAKS THEY ARE. IT'S THE ONES WHO BLEND IN THAT YA GOTTA WATCH OUT FOR.
YOU'RE IN MY ENGLISH CLASS. TONI, RIGHT?
YOU'RE PERCEPTIVE FOR A POPULAR GIRL.
'CAUSE I'M NOT ONE.
I'M THE FRIEND VERSION OF SOME CHEAP FAD. I'M ONLY HERE FER A SEMESTER. IF IT WAS LONGER, THOSE GIRLS WOULDN'T BOTHER WITH ME.
I HEARD WHAT KRISTY SAID IN THE FOOD COURT. SHE SHOULDN'T TREAT YOU LIKE THAT.
YOU SAW ME IN THE FOOD COURT?

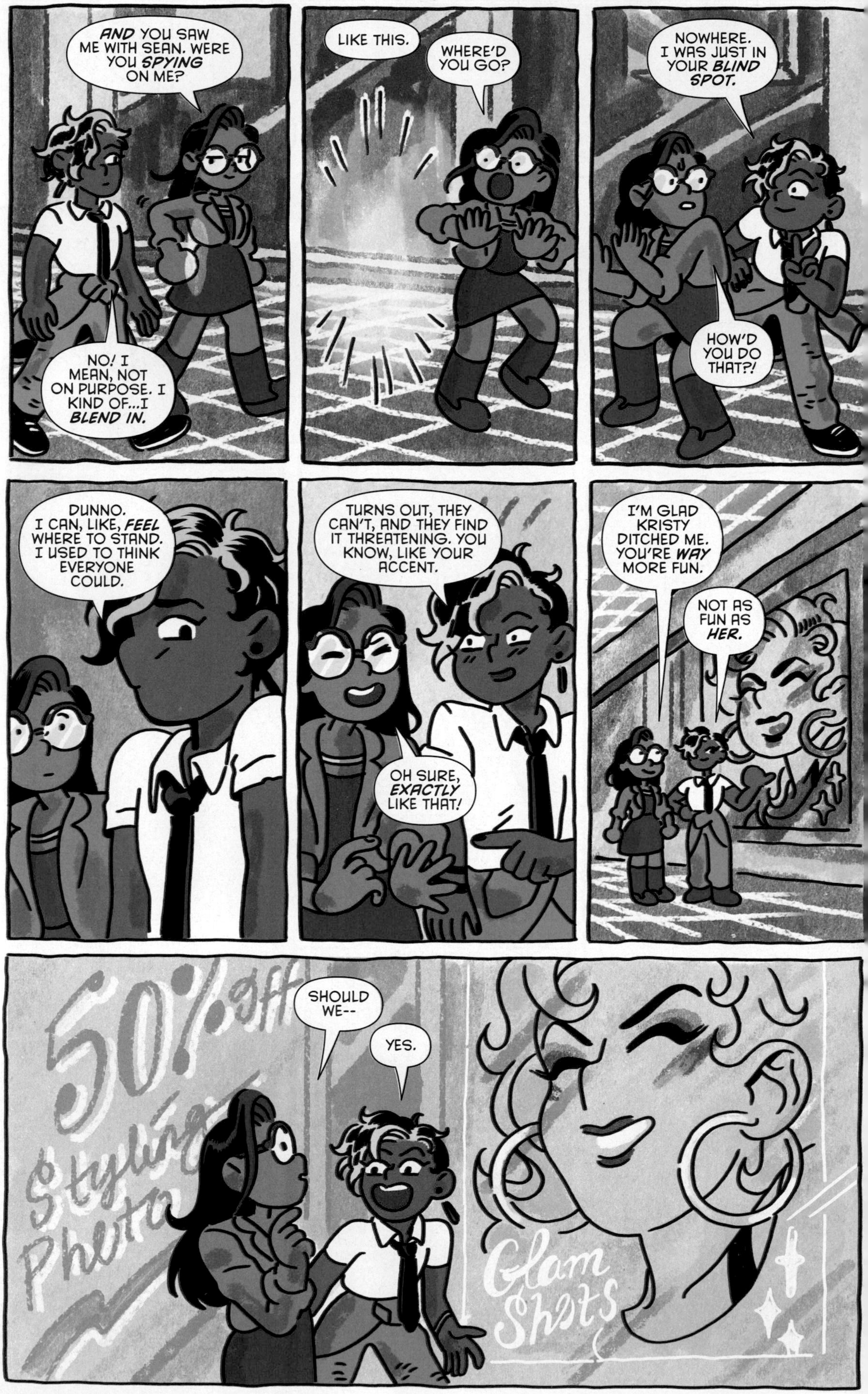
AND YOU SAW ME WITH SEAN. WERE YOU SPYING ON ME?
NO! I MEAN, NOT ON PURPOSE. I KIND OF...I BLEND IN.
LIKE THIS.
WHERE'D YOU GO?
NOWHERE. I WAS JUST IN YOUR BLIND SPOT.
HOW'D YOU DO THAT?!
DUNNO. I CAN, LIKE, FEEL WHERE TO STAND. I USED TO THINK EVERYONE COULD.
TURNS OUT, THEY CAN'T, AND THEY FIND IT THREATENING. YOU KNOW, LIKE YOUR ACCENT.
OH SURE, EXACTLY LIKE THAT!
I'M GLAD KRISTY DITCHED ME. YOU'RE WAY MORE FUN.
NOT AS FUN AS HER.
50% off
Styling
Photo
SHOULD WE--
YES.
Glam Shots

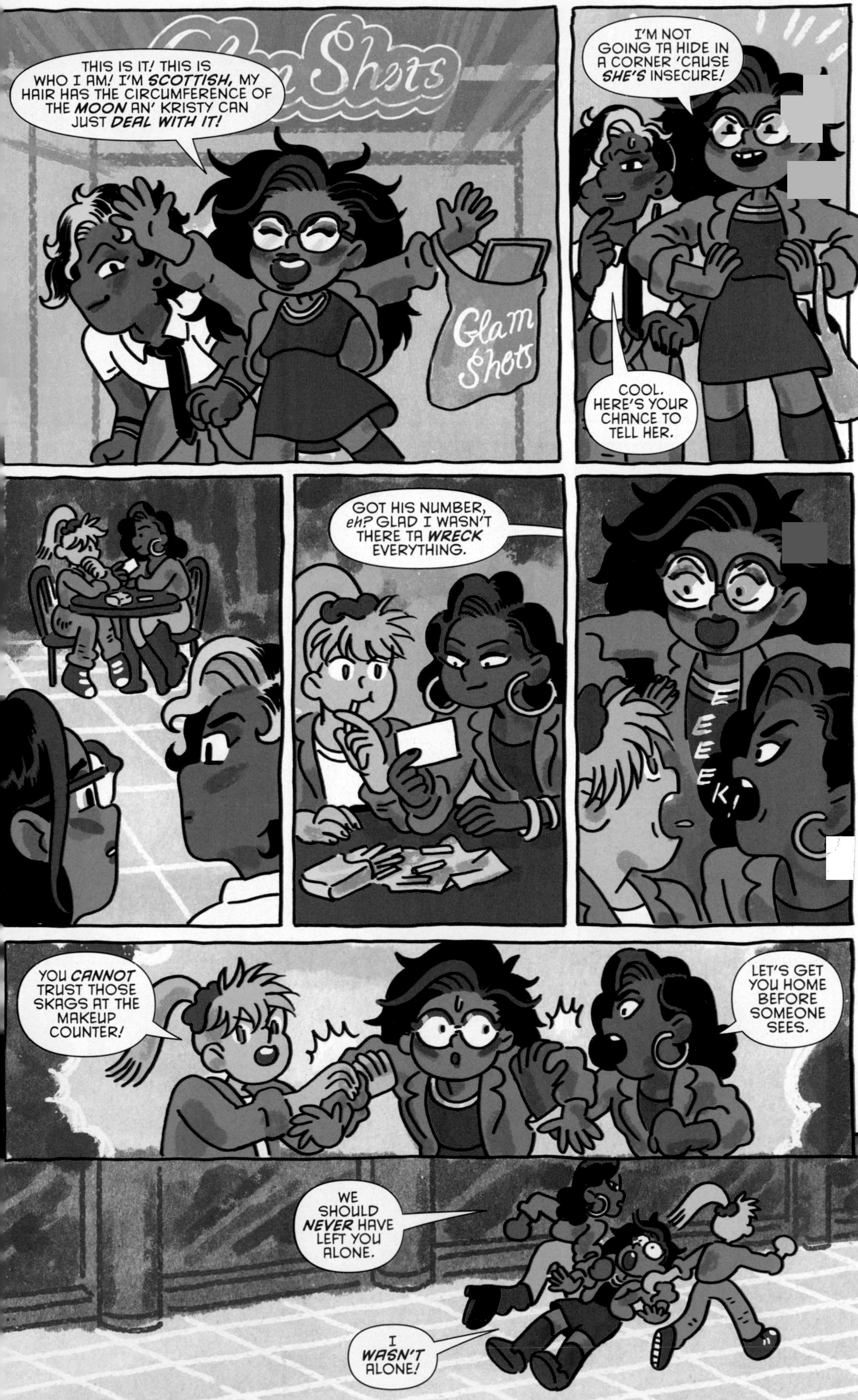
THIS IS IT! THIS IS WHO I AM! I'M SCOTTISH, MY HAIR HAS THE CIRCUMFERENCE OF THE MOON AN' KRISTY CAN JUST DEAL WITH IT!
Glam Shots
I'M NOT GOING TA HIDE IN A CORNER 'CAUSE SHE'S INSECURE!
COOL. HERE'S YOUR CHANCE TO TELL HER.
GOT HIS NUMBER, eh? GLAD I WASN'T THERE TA WRECK EVERYTHING.
EEEEK!
YOU CANNOT TRUST THOSE SKAGS AT THE MAKEUP COUNTER!
LET'S GET YOU HOME BEFORE SOMEONE SEES.
WE SHOULD NEVER HAVE LEFT YOU ALONE.
I WASN'T ALONE!

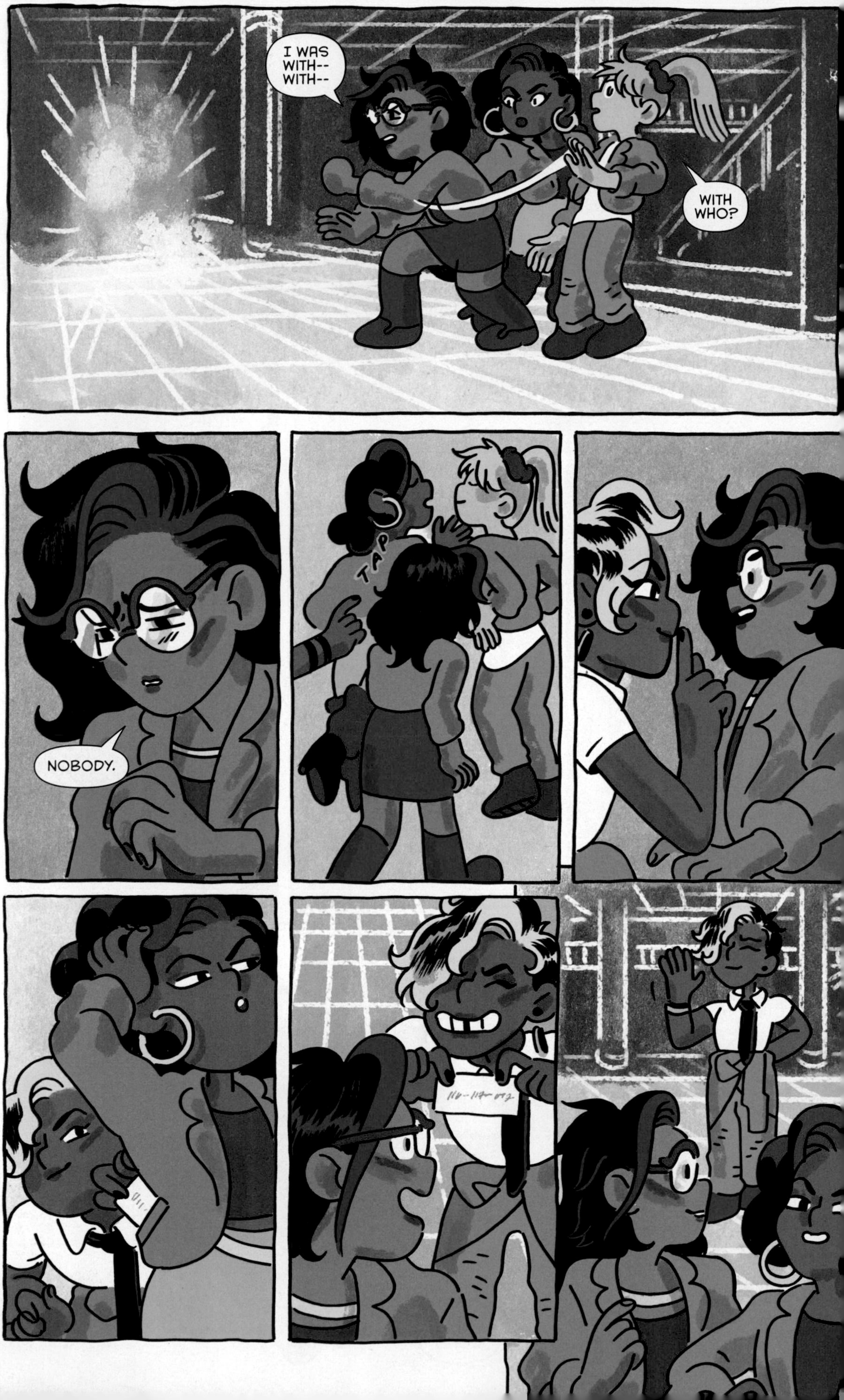
I WAS WITH-- WITH--
WITH WHO?
NOBODY.
TAP

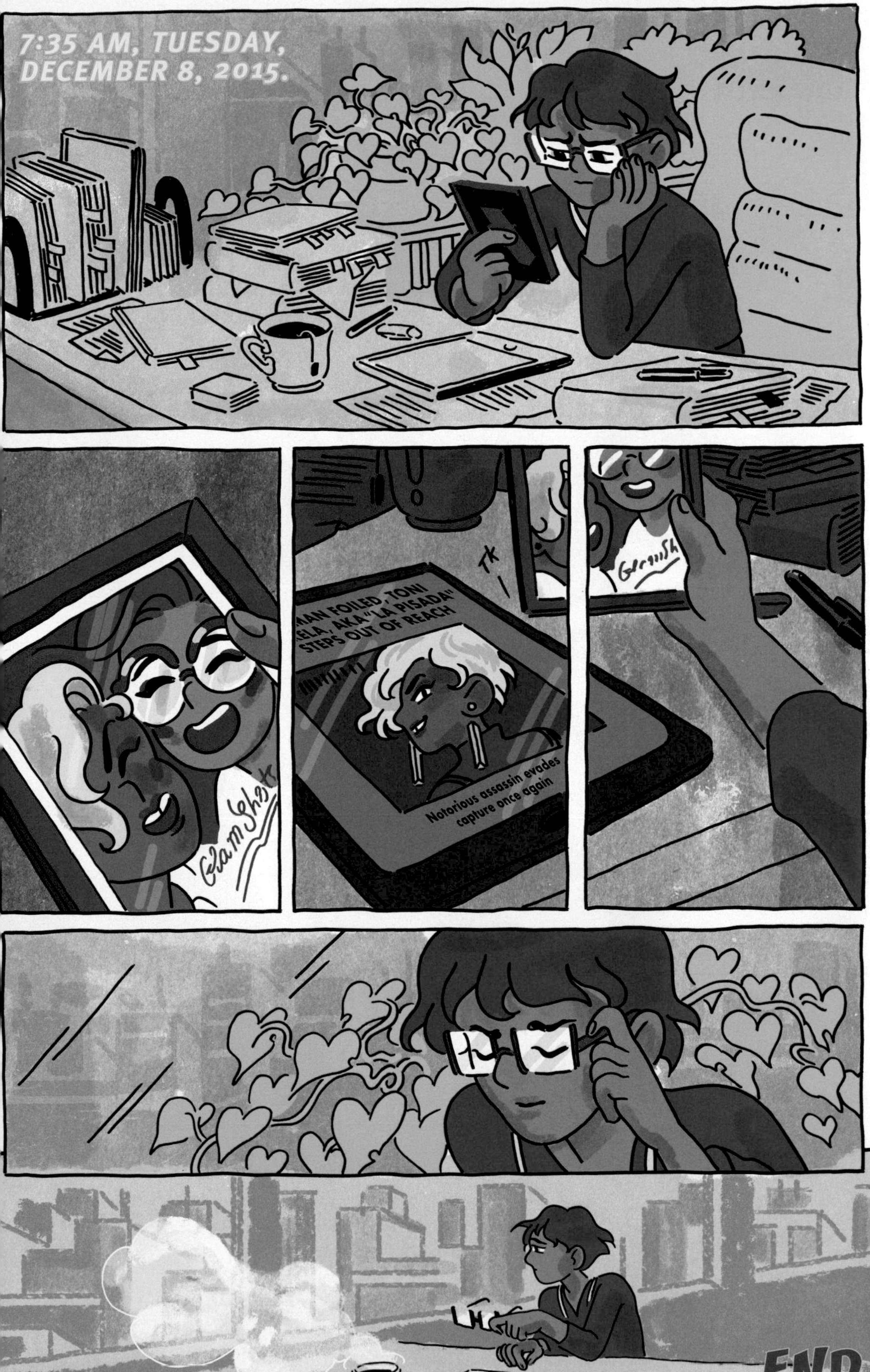
7:35 AM, TUESDAY, DECEMBER 8, 2015.
MAN FOILED, TONI
ELA, AKA "LA PISADA"
STEPS OUT OF REACH
Notorious assassin evades capture once again
TK
END

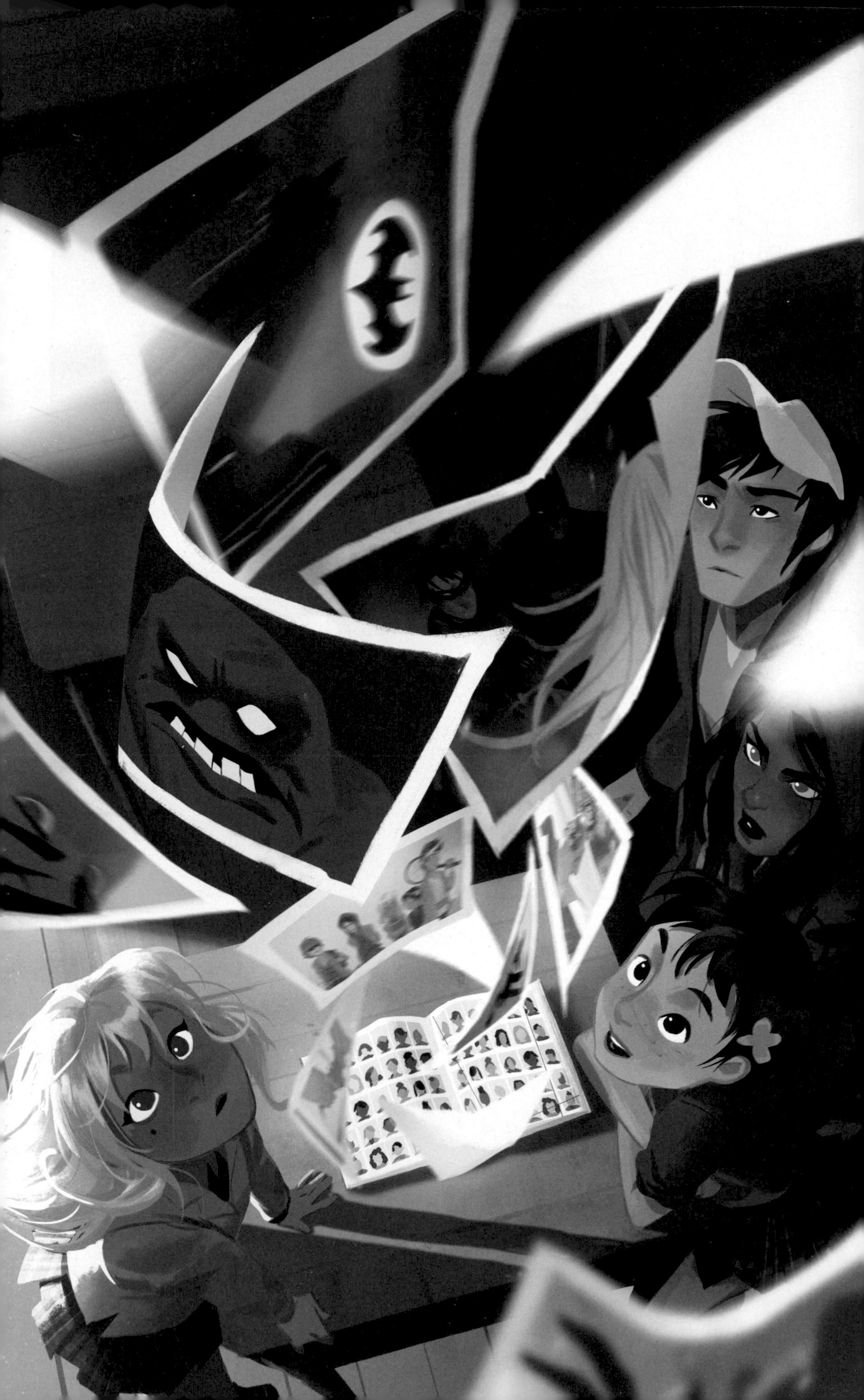

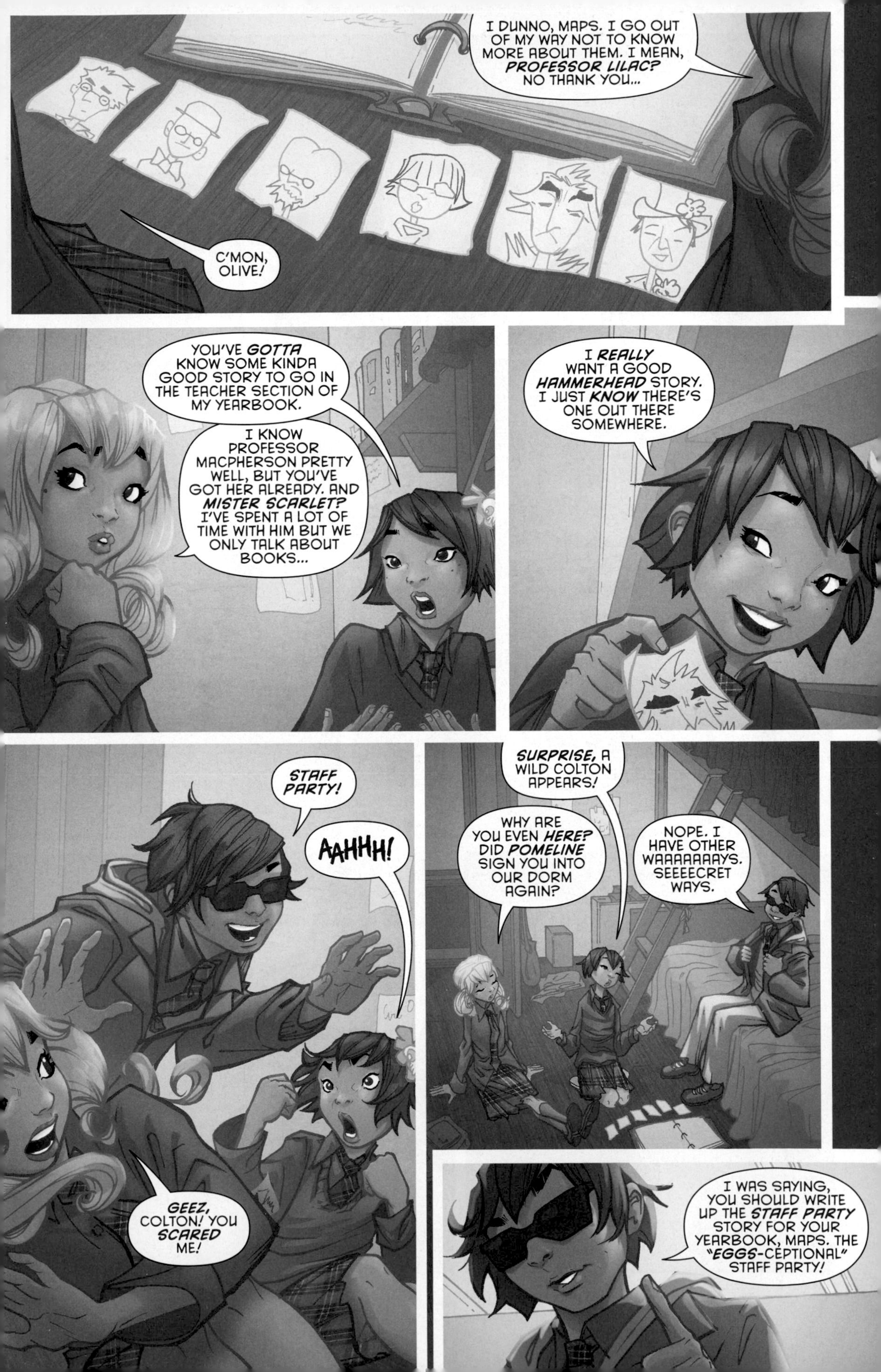
I DUNNO, MAPS. I GO OUT OF MY WAY NOT TO KNOW MORE ABOUT THEM. I MEAN, PROFESSOR LILAC? NO THANK YOU...
C'MON, OLIVE!
YOU'VE GOTTA KNOW SOME KINDA GOOD STORY TO GO IN THE TEACHER SECTION OF MY YEARBOOK.
I KNOW PROFESSOR MACPHERSON PRETTY WELL, BUT YOU'VE GOT HER ALREADY. AND MISTER SCARLET? I'VE SPENT A LOT OF TIME WITH HIM BUT WE ONLY TALK ABOUT BOOKS...
I REALLY WANT A GOOD HAMMERHEAD STORY. I JUST KNOW THERE'S ONE OUT THERE SOMEWHERE.
STAFF PARTY!
AAHHH!
GEEZ, COLTON! YOU SCARED ME!
SURPRISE, A WILD COLTON APPEARS!
WHY ARE YOU EVEN HERE? DID POMELINE SIGN YOU INTO OUR DORM AGAIN?
NOPE. I HAVE OTHER WAAAAAAAYS. SEEEECRET WAYS.
I WAS SAYING, YOU SHOULD WRITE UP THE STAFF PARTY STORY FOR YOUR YEARBOOK, MAPS. THE "EGGS-CEPTIONAL" STAFF PARTY!

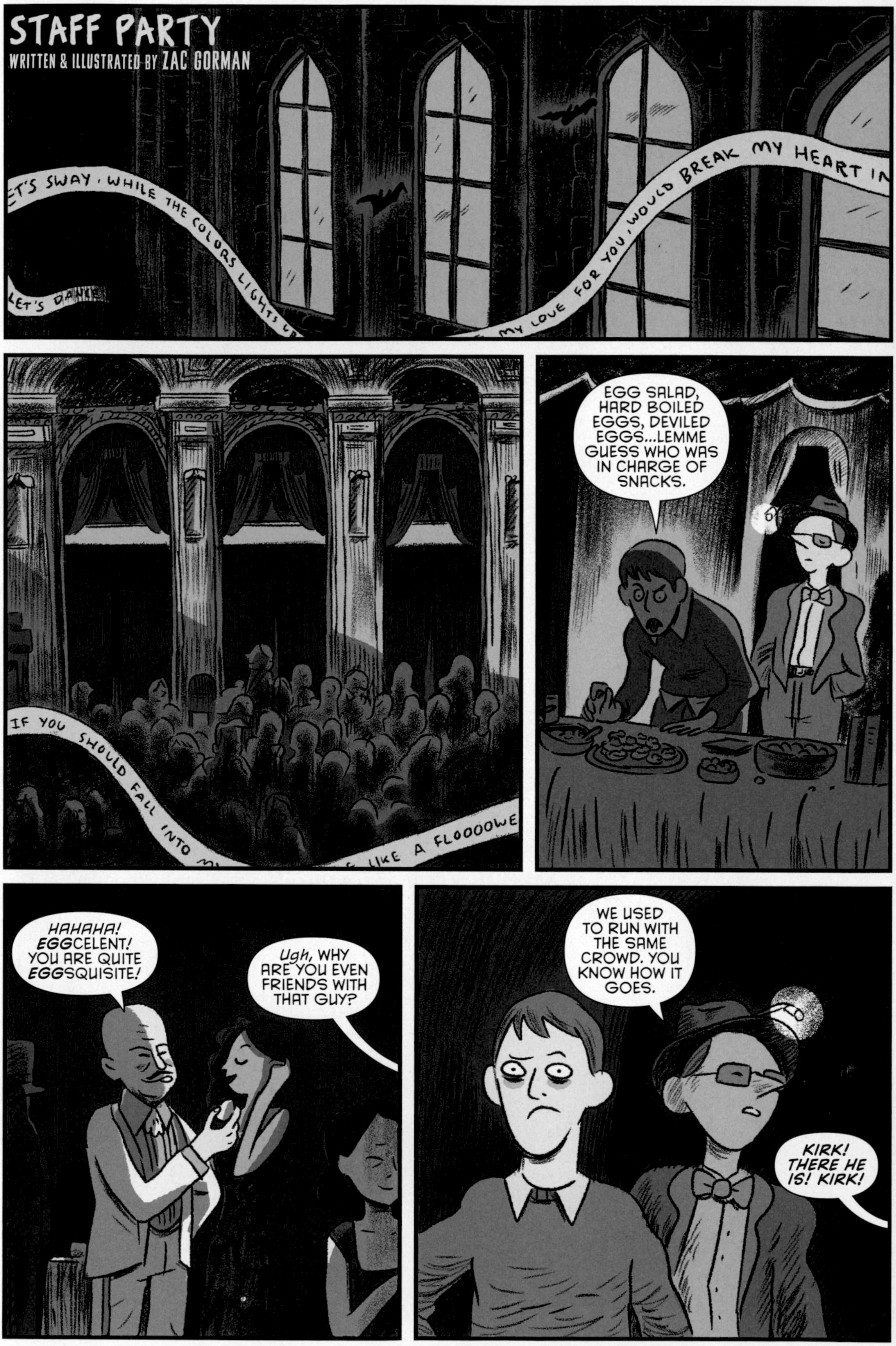
STAFF PARTY
WRITTEN & ILLUSTRATED BY ZAC GORMAN
LET'S DAN
ET'S SWAY, WHILE THE COLORS LIGHTS U
MY LOVE FOR YOU, WOULD BREAK MY HEART IN
IF YOU SHOULD FALL INTO M
LIKE A FLOOOOWE
EGG SALAD, HARD BOILED EGGS, DEVILED EGGS...LEMME GUESS WHO WAS IN CHARGE OF SNACKS.
HAHAHA! EGGCELENT! YOU ARE QUITE EGGSQUISITE!
Ugh, WHY ARE YOU EVEN FRIENDS WITH THAT GUY?
WE USED TO RUN WITH THE SAME CROWD. YOU KNOW HOW IT GOES.
KIRK! THERE HE IS! KIRK!

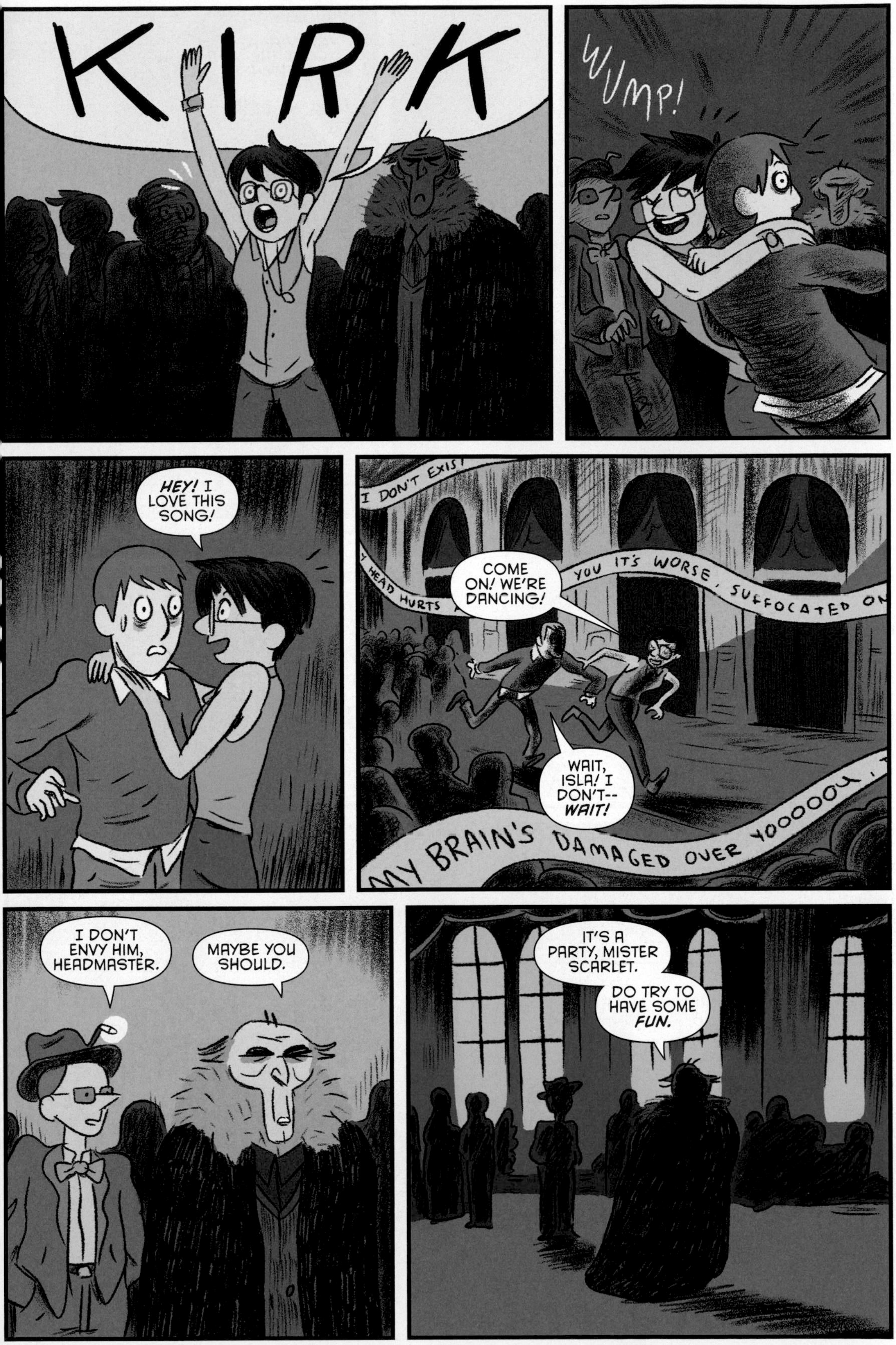
KIRK
WUMP!
HEY! I LOVE THIS SONG!
I DON'T EXIS
HEAD HURTS
YOU IT'S WORSE, SUFFOCATED ON
COME ON! WE'RE DANCING!
WAIT, ISLA! I DON'T-- WAIT!
MY BRAIN'S DAMAGED OVER YOOOOOU,
I DON'T ENVY HIM, HEADMASTER.
MAYBE YOU SHOULD.
IT'S A PARTY, MISTER SCARLET.
DO TRY TO HAVE SOME FUN.

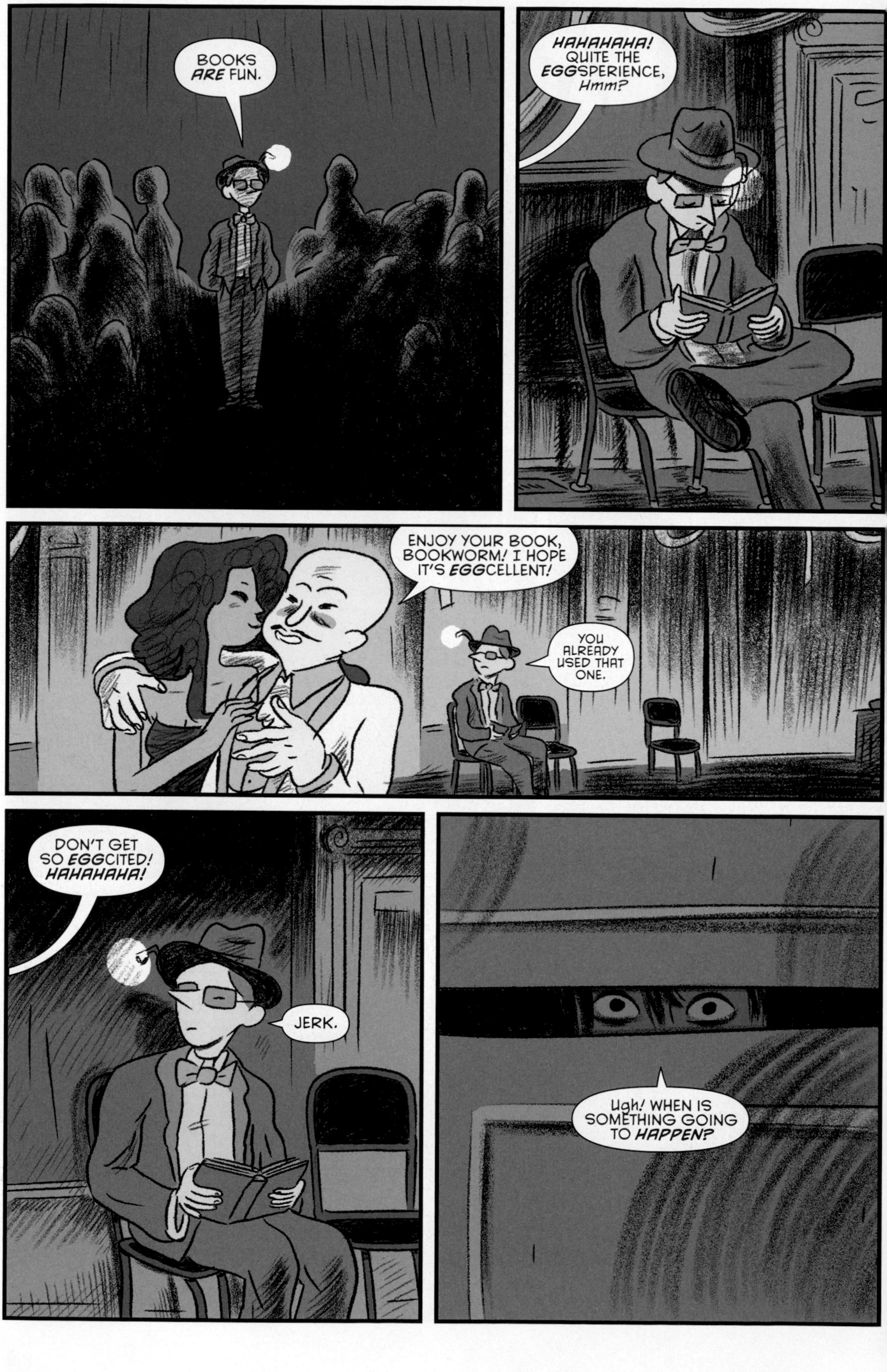
BOOKS ARE FUN.
HAHAHAHA! QUITE THE EGGSPERIENCE, Hmm?
ENJOY YOUR BOOK, BOOKWORM! I HOPE IT'S EGGCELLENT!
YOU ALREADY USED THAT ONE.
DON'T GET SO EGGCITED! HAHAHAHA!
JERK.
Ugh! WHEN IS SOMETHING GOING TO HAPPEN?

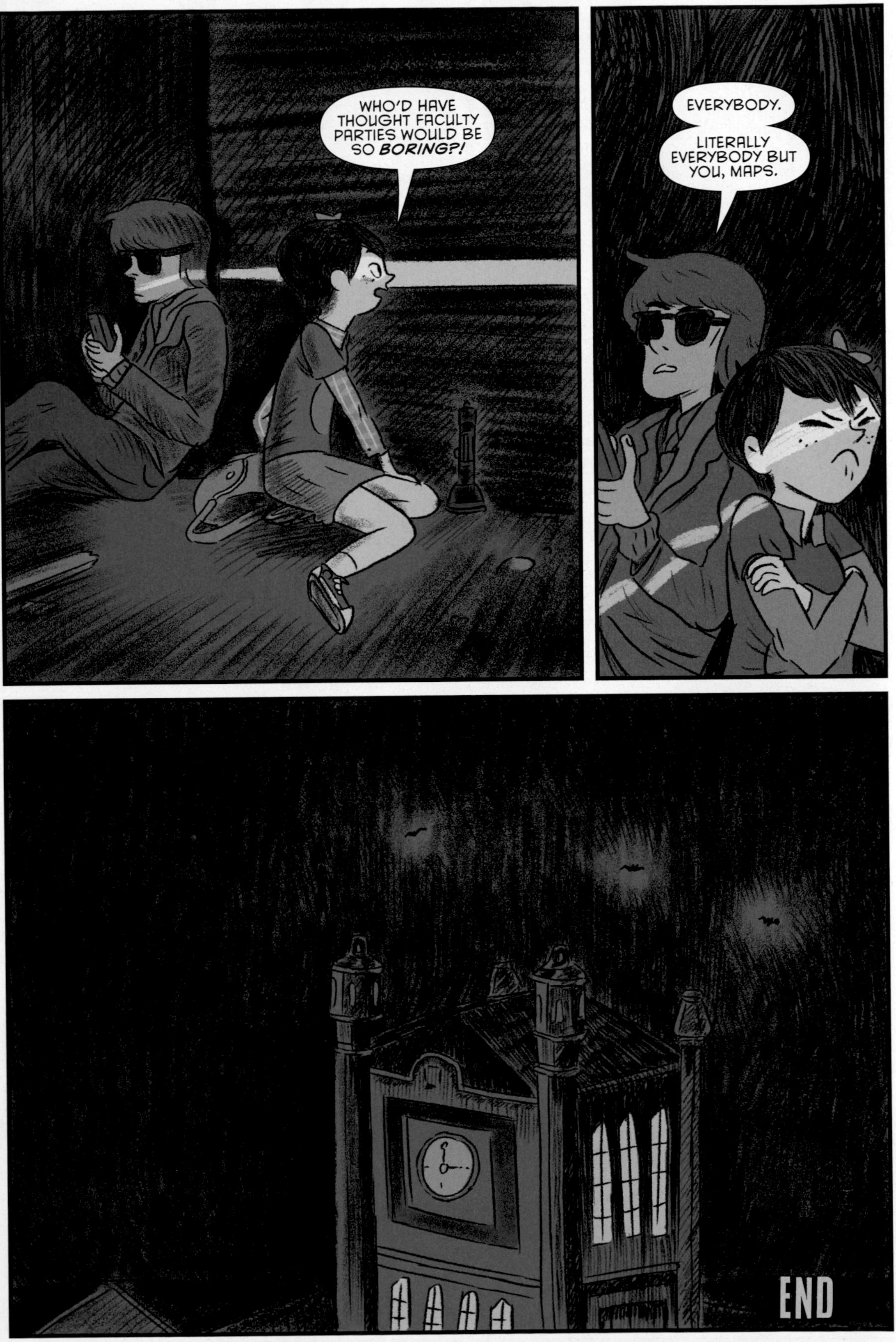
WHO'D HAVE THOUGHT FACULTY PARTIES WOULD BE SO *BORING?!*
EVERYBODY.
LITERALLY EVERYBODY BUT YOU, MAPS.
END

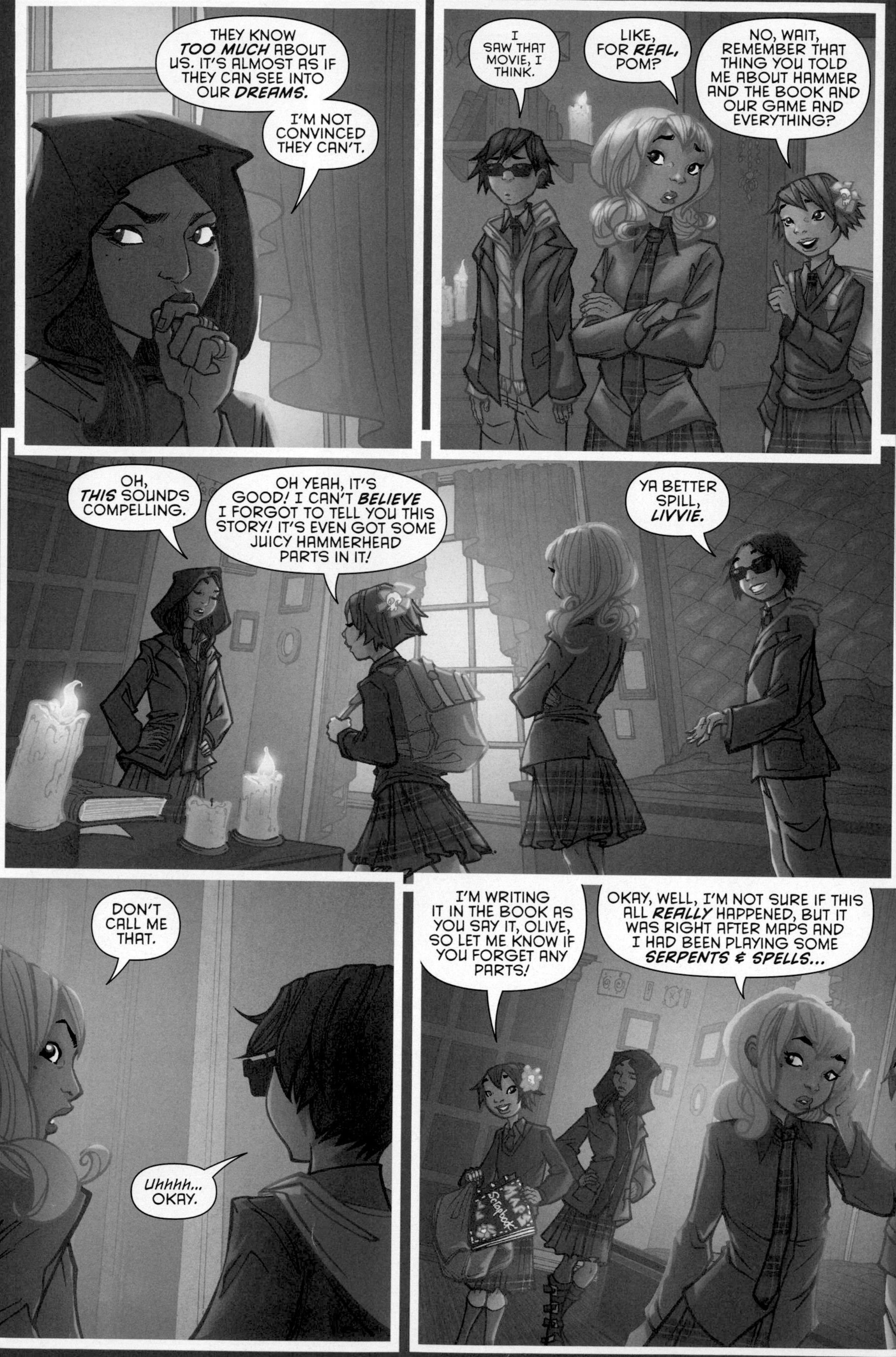
THEY KNOW TOO MUCH ABOUT US. IT'S ALMOST AS IF THEY CAN SEE INTO OUR DREAMS.
I'M NOT CONVINCED THEY CAN'T.
I SAW THAT MOVIE, I THINK.
LIKE, FOR REAL, POM?
NO, WAIT, REMEMBER THAT THING YOU TOLD ME ABOUT HAMMER AND THE BOOK AND OUR GAME AND EVERYTHING?
OH, THIS SOUNDS COMPELLING.
OH YEAH, IT'S GOOD! I CAN'T BELIEVE I FORGOT TO TELL YOU THIS STORY! IT'S EVEN GOT SOME JUICY HAMMERHEAD PARTS IN IT!
YA BETTER SPILL, LIVVIE.
DON'T CALL ME THAT.
Uhhhh... OKAY.
I'M WRITING IT IN THE BOOK AS YOU SAY IT, OLIVE, SO LET ME KNOW IF YOU FORGET ANY PARTS!
OKAY, WELL, I'M NOT SURE IF THIS ALL REALLY HAPPENED, BUT IT WAS RIGHT AFTER MAPS AND I HAD BEEN PLAYING SOME SERPENTS & SPELLS...
MAPS Scrapbook

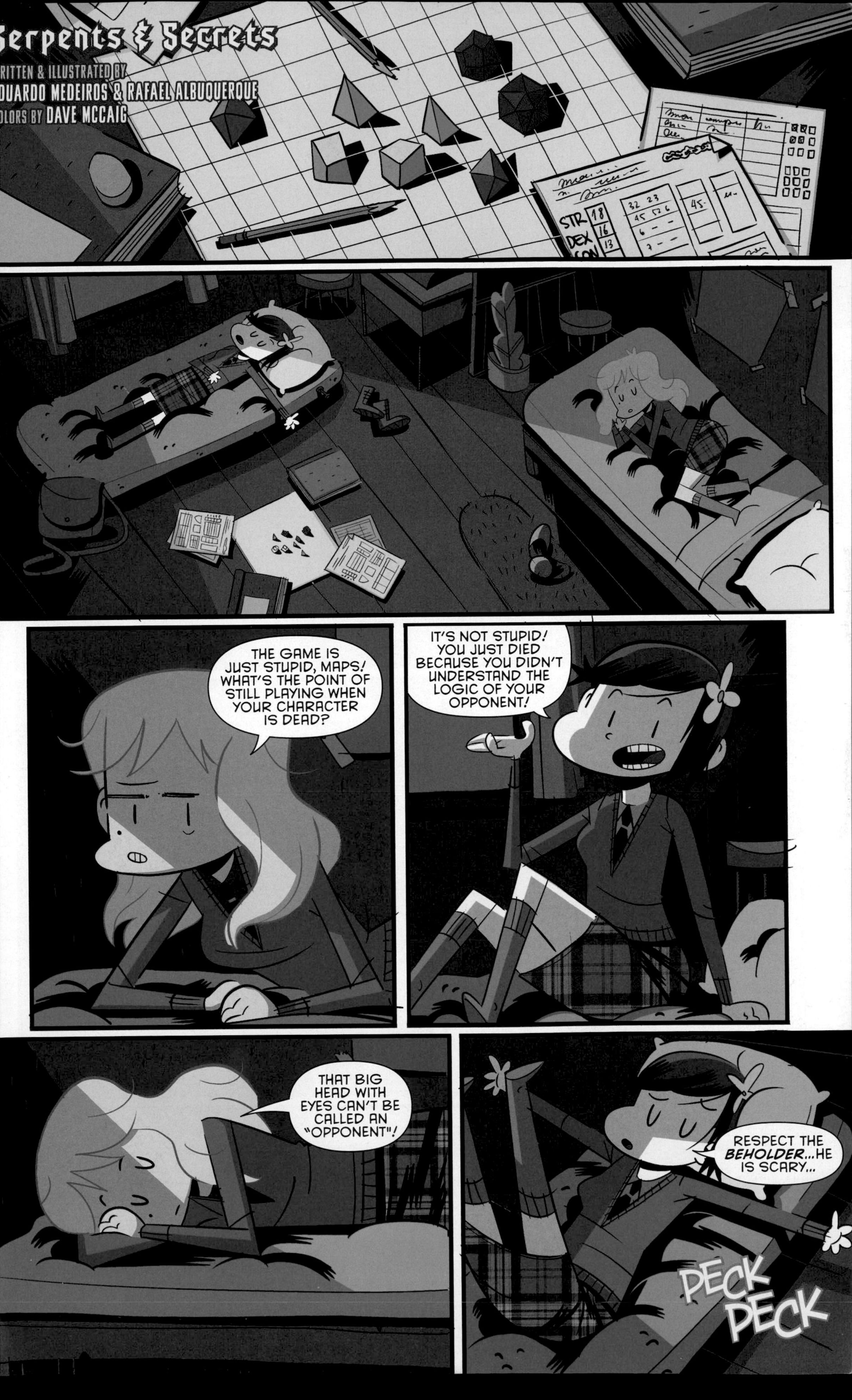

Serpents & Secrets
RITTEN & ILLUSTRATED BY
DUARDO MEDEIROS & RAFAEL ALBUQUERQUE
OLORS BY DAVE MCCAIG
STR 18
DEX 16
CON 13
THE GAME IS JUST STUPID, MAPS! WHAT'S THE POINT OF STILL PLAYING WHEN YOUR CHARACTER IS DEAD?
IT'S NOT STUPID! YOU JUST DIED BECAUSE YOU DIDN'T UNDERSTAND THE LOGIC OF YOUR OPPONENT!
THAT BIG HEAD WITH EYES CAN'T BE CALLED AN "OPPONENT"!
RESPECT THE *BEHOLDER*...HE IS SCARY...
PECK PECK

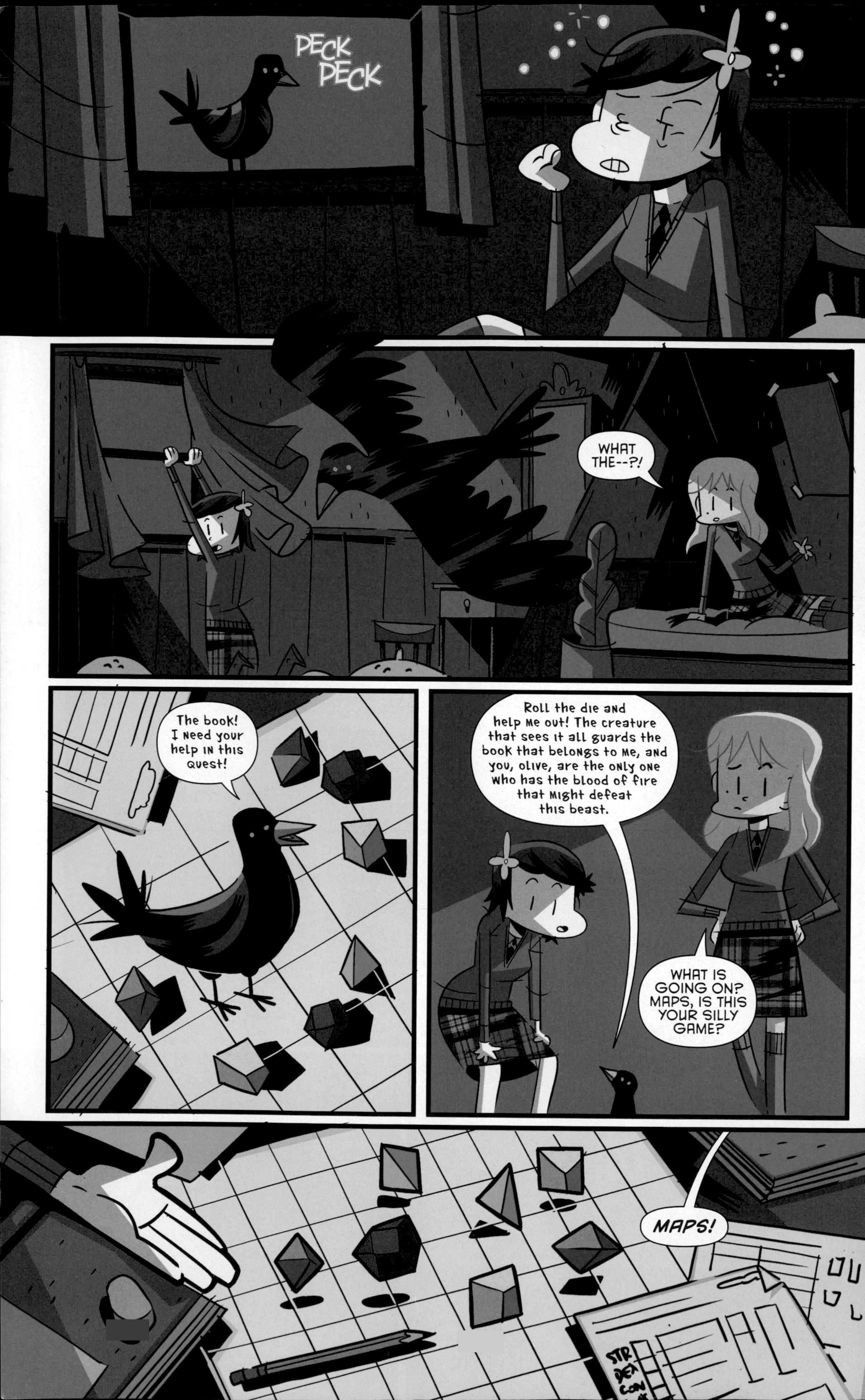
PECK PECK
WHAT THE--?!
The book! I need your help in this quest!
Roll the die and help me out! The creature that sees it all guards the book that belongs to me, and you, olive, are the only one who has the blood of fire that might defeat this beast.
WHAT IS GOING ON? MAPS, IS THIS YOUR SILLY GAME?
MAPS!
STR
DEX
CON

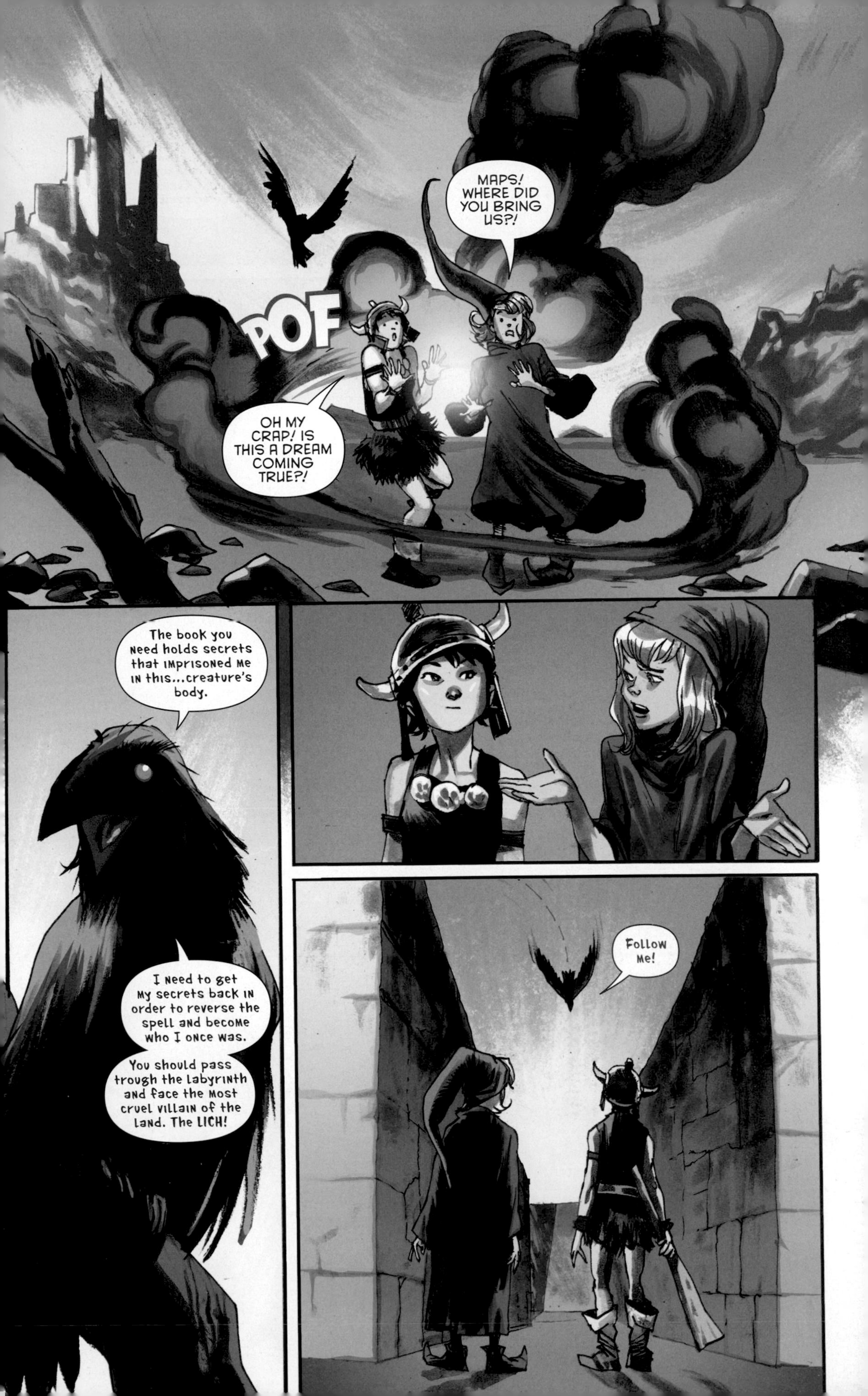
POF
MAPS! WHERE DID YOU BRING US?!
OH MY CRAP! IS THIS A DREAM COMING TRUE?!
The book you need holds secrets that imprisoned me in this...creature's body.
I need to get my secrets back in order to reverse the spell and become who I once was.
You should pass trough the labyrinth and face the most cruel villain of the land. The LICH!
Follow me!

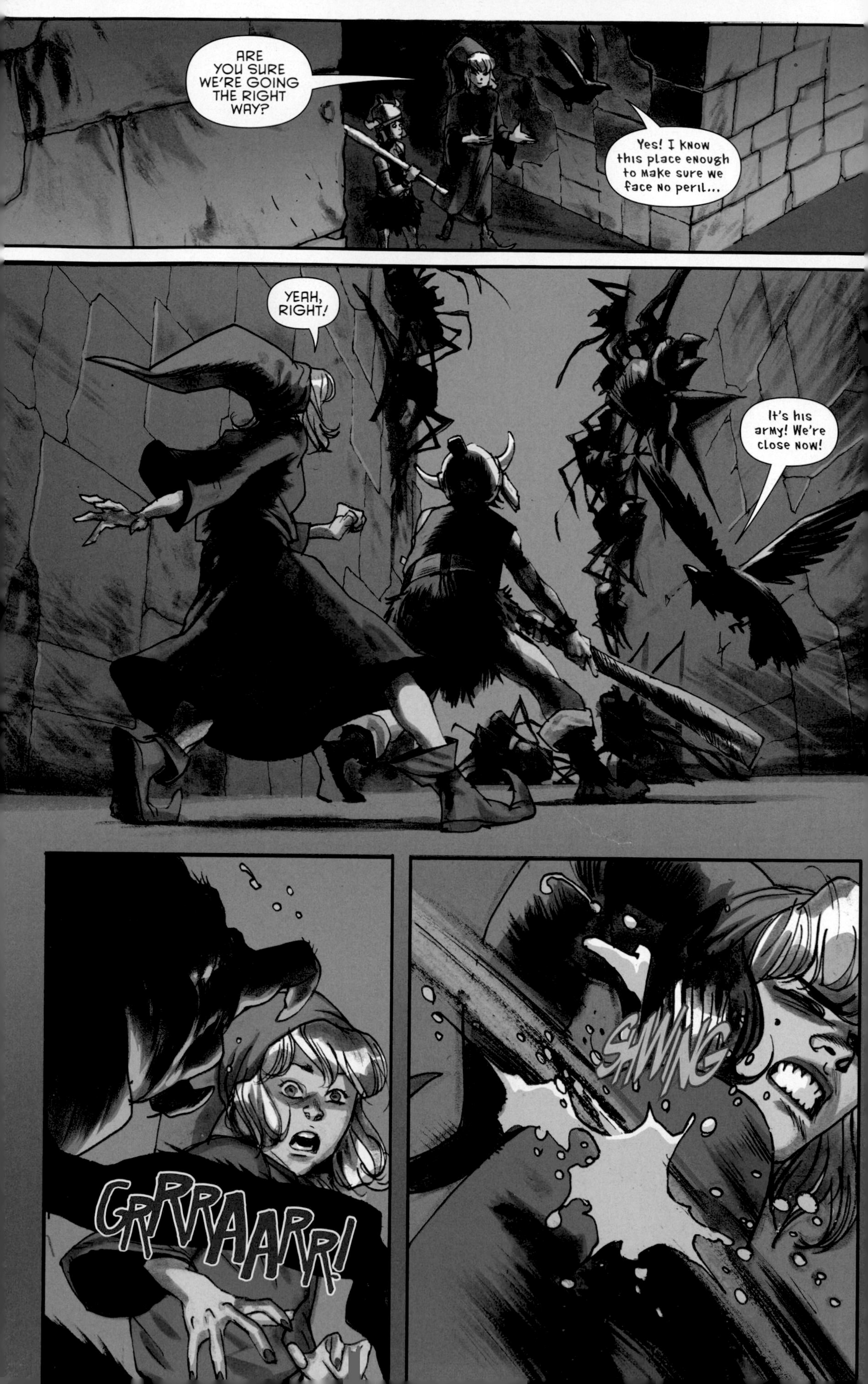
ARE YOU SURE WE'RE GOING THE RIGHT WAY?
Yes! I know this place enough to make sure we face no peril...
YEAH, RIGHT!
It's his army! We're close now!
GRRRAARR!
SHWING

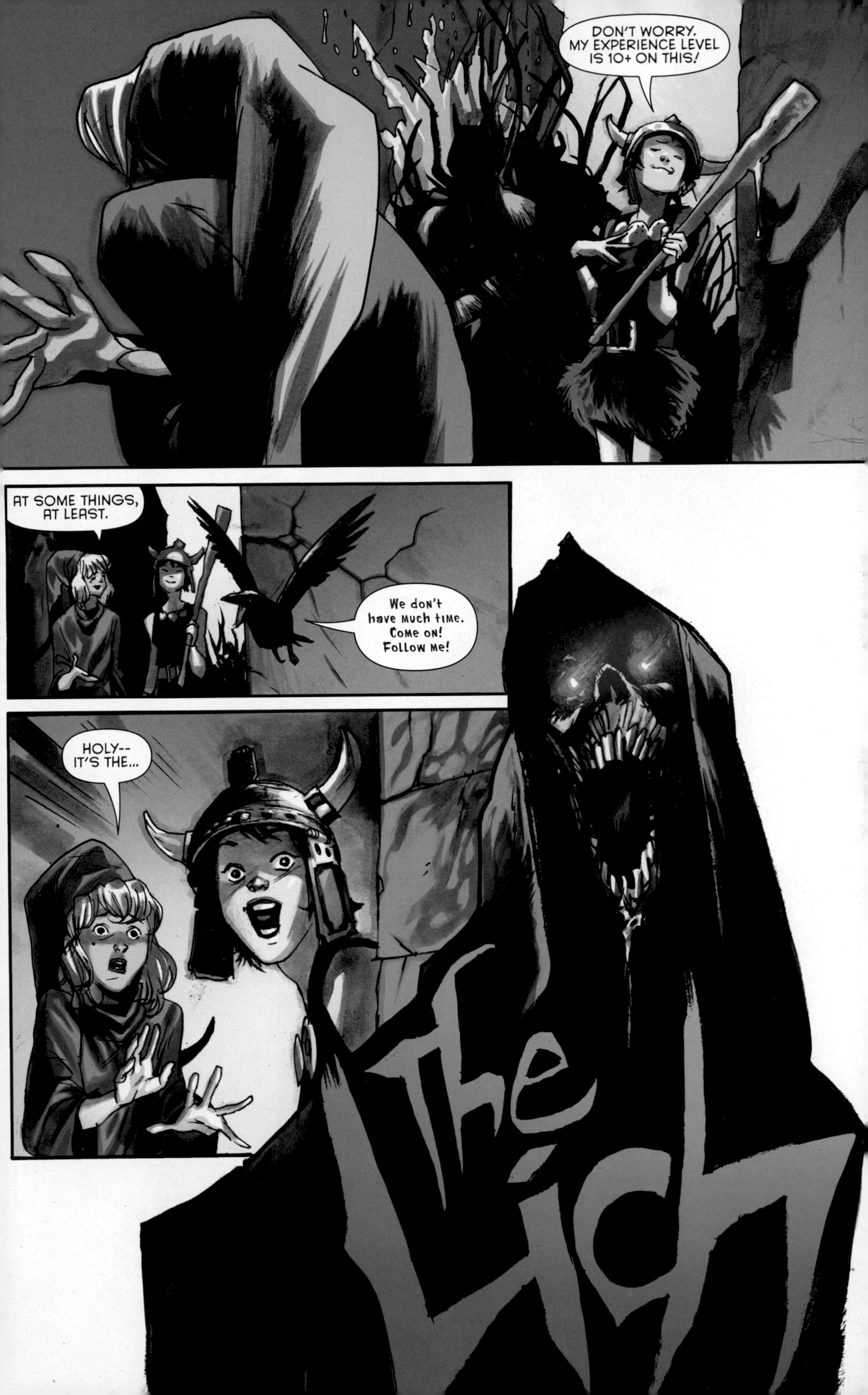
DON'T WORRY. MY EXPERIENCE LEVEL IS 10+ ON THIS!
AT SOME THINGS, AT LEAST.
We don't have much time. Come on! Follow me!
HOLY-- IT'S THE...
The Lich

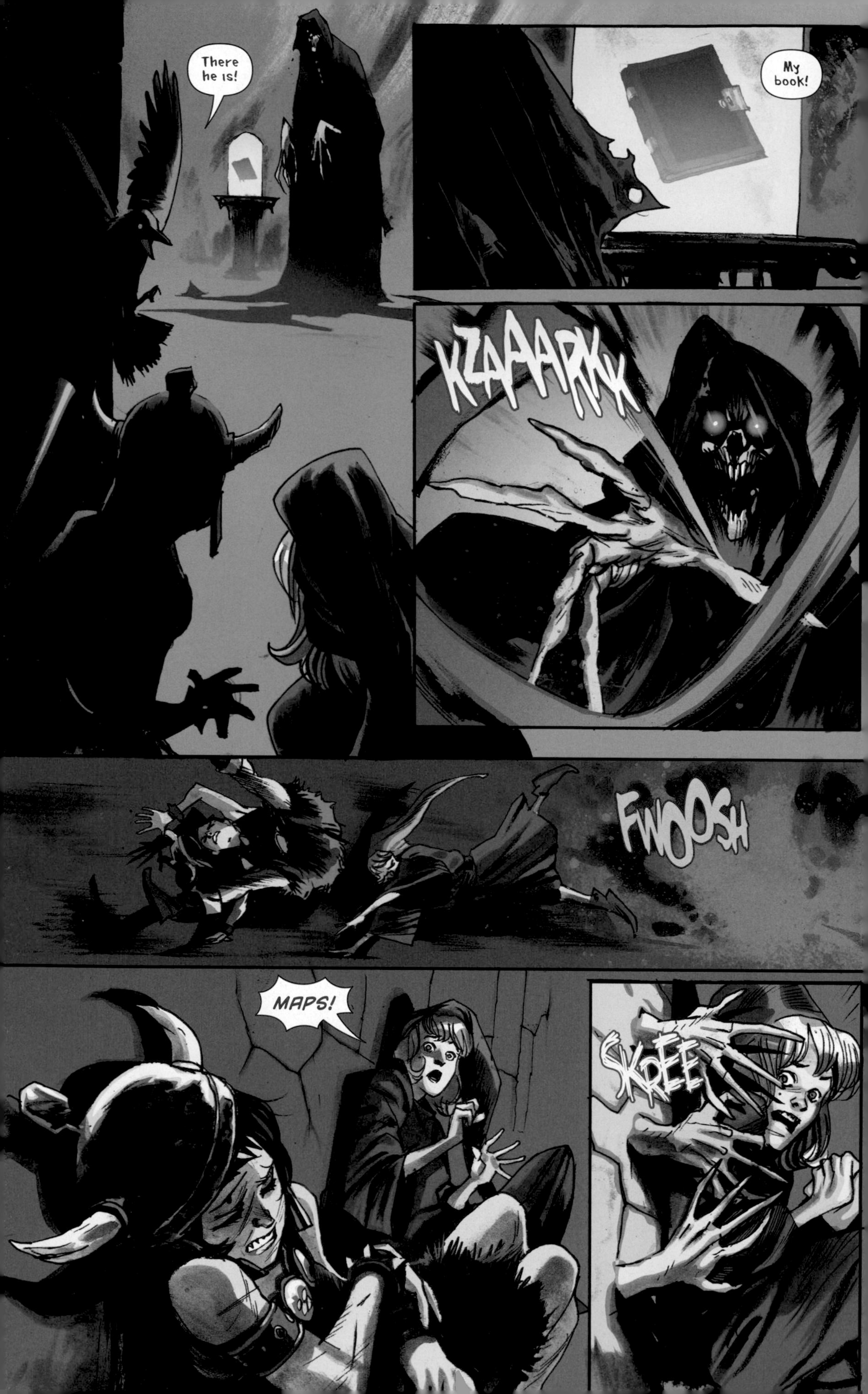
There he is!
My book!
KZAAARKK
FWOOSH
MAPS!
SKREE

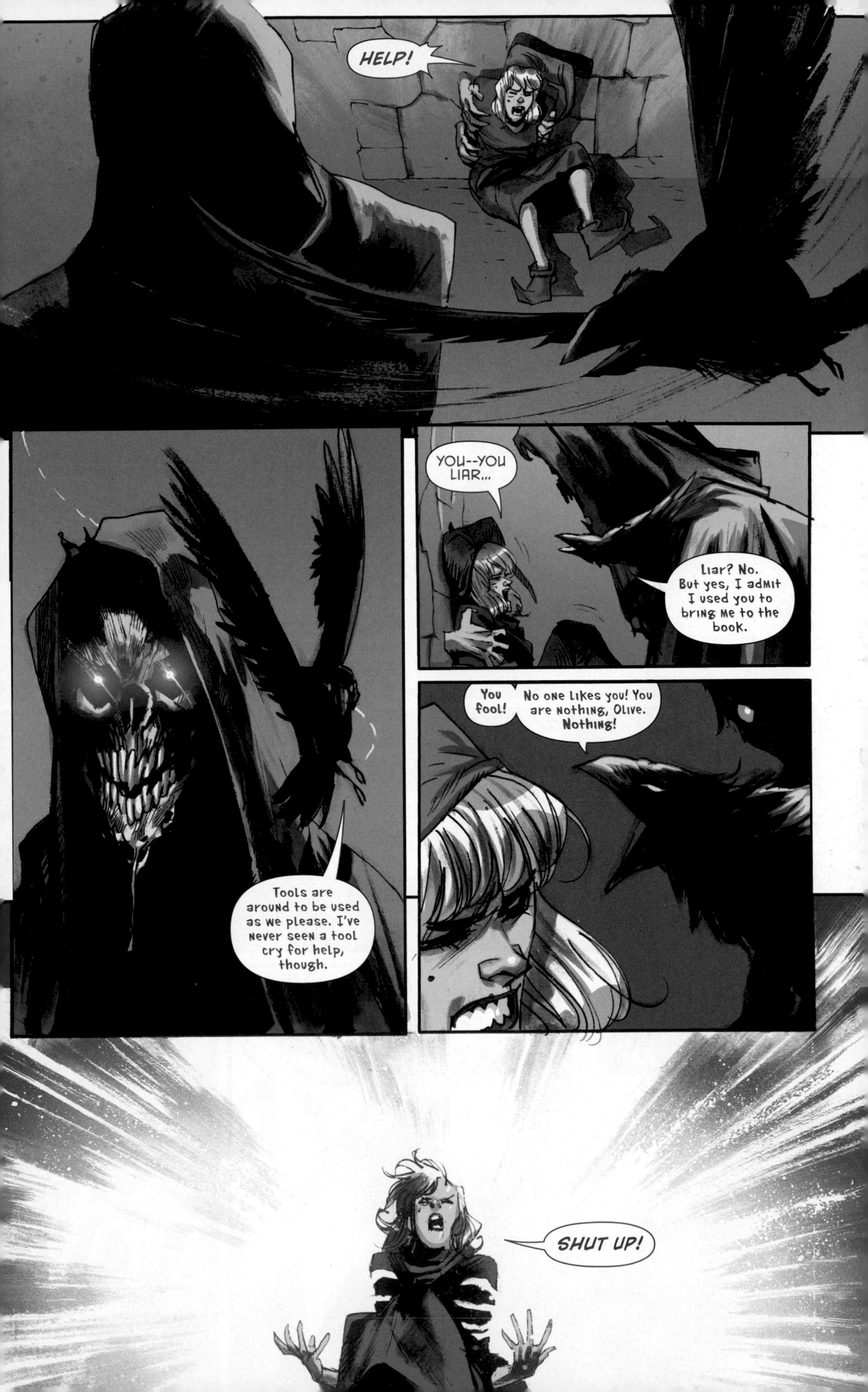
HELP!
YOU--YOU LIAR...
Liar? No. But yes, I admit I used you to bring me to the book.
Tools are around to be used as we please. I've never seen a tool cry for help, though.
You fool!
No one likes you! You are nothing, Olive. Nothing!
SHUT UP!

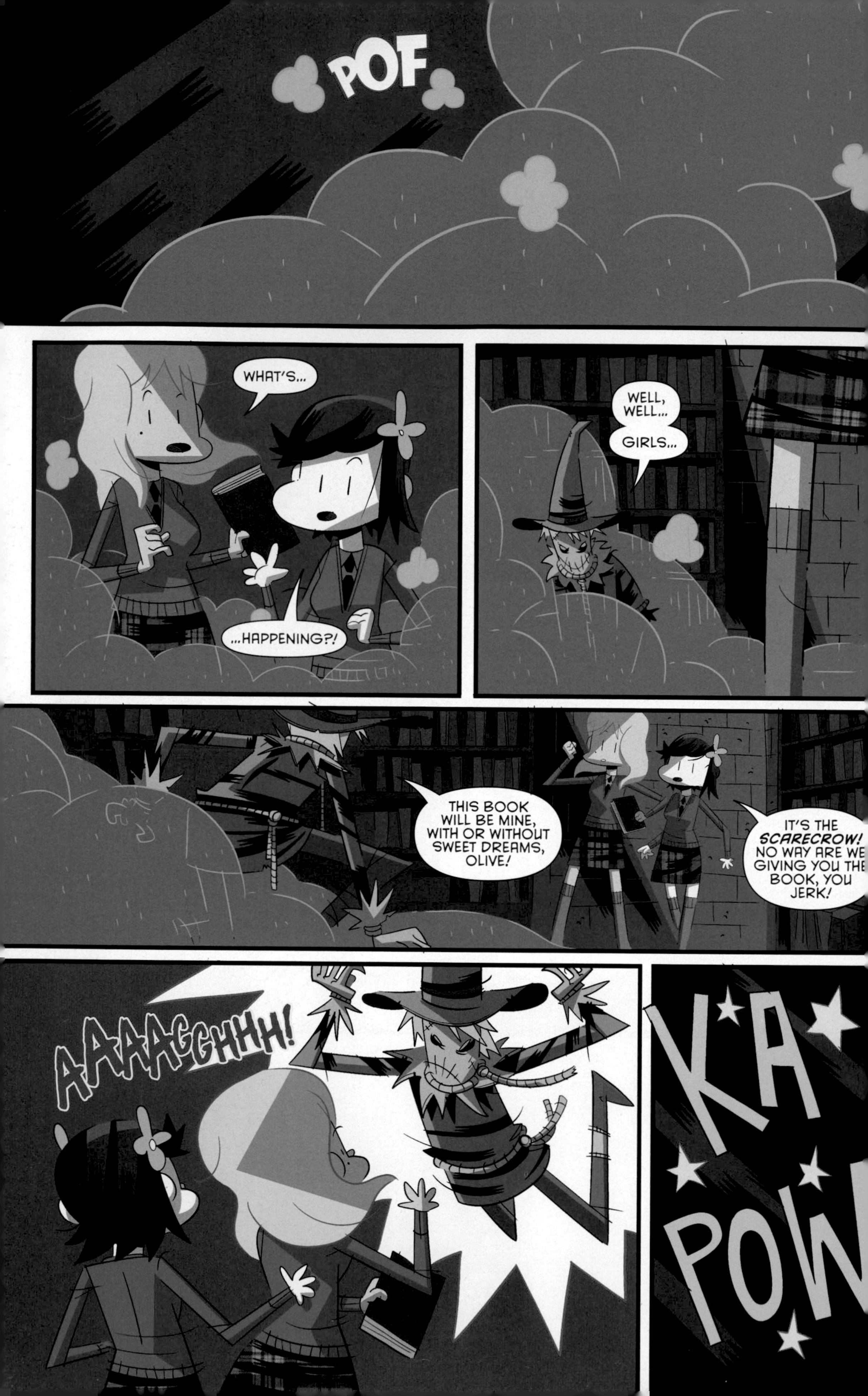
POF
WHAT'S...
...HAPPENING?!
WELL, WELL...
GIRLS...
THIS BOOK WILL BE MINE, WITH OR WITHOUT SWEET DREAMS, OLIVE!
IT'S THE SCARECROW! NO WAY ARE WE GIVING YOU THE BOOK, YOU JERK!
AAAAGHHH!
KA POW

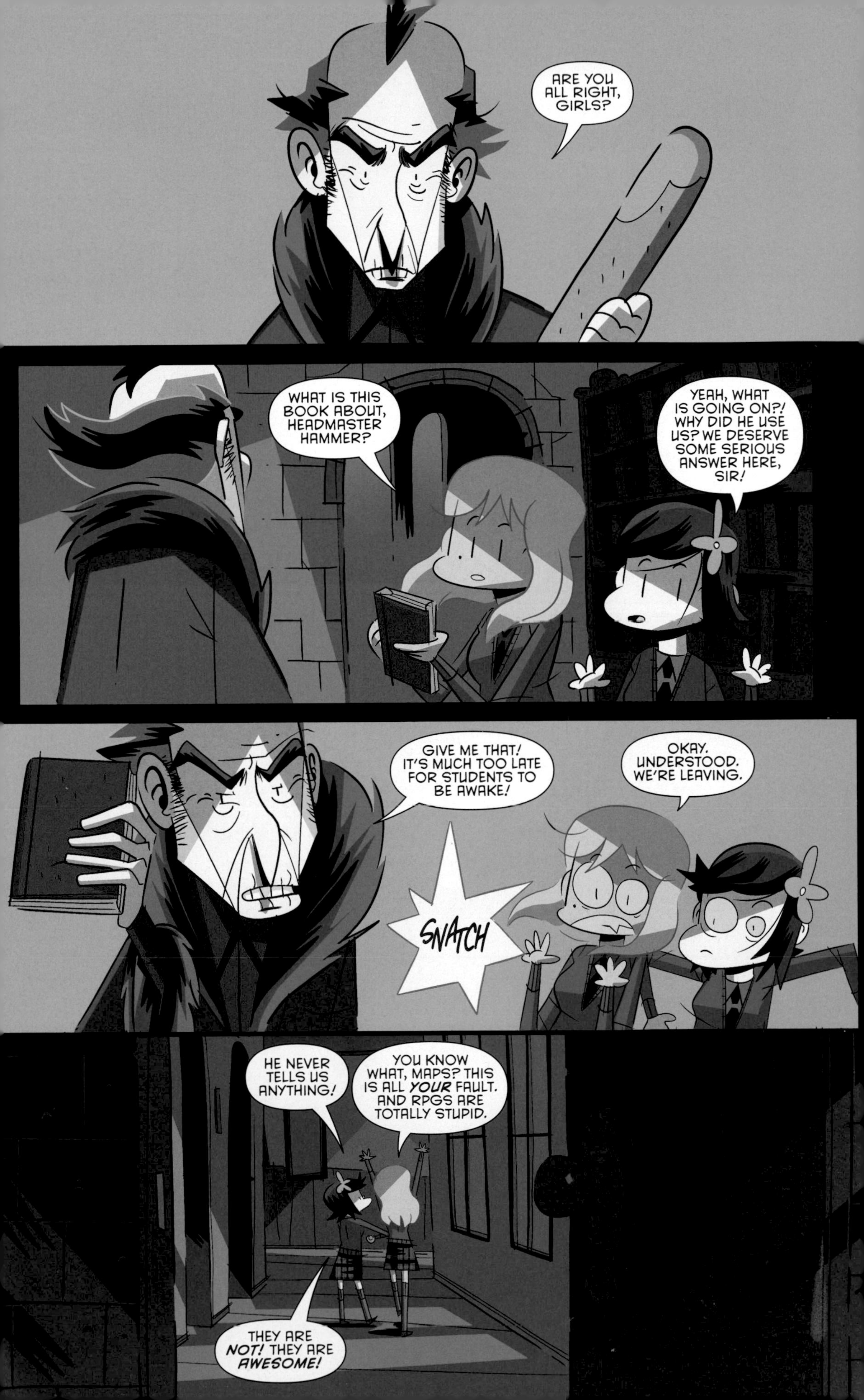
ARE YOU ALL RIGHT, GIRLS?
WHAT IS THIS BOOK ABOUT, HEADMASTER HAMMER?
YEAH, WHAT IS GOING ON?! WHY DID HE USE US? WE DESERVE SOME SERIOUS ANSWER HERE, SIR!
GIVE ME THAT! IT'S MUCH TOO LATE FOR STUDENTS TO BE AWAKE!
OKAY. UNDERSTOOD. WE'RE LEAVING.
SNATCH
HE NEVER TELLS US ANYTHING!
YOU KNOW WHAT, MAPS? THIS IS ALL YOUR FAULT. AND RPGS ARE TOTALLY STUPID.
THEY ARE NOT! THEY ARE AWESOME!

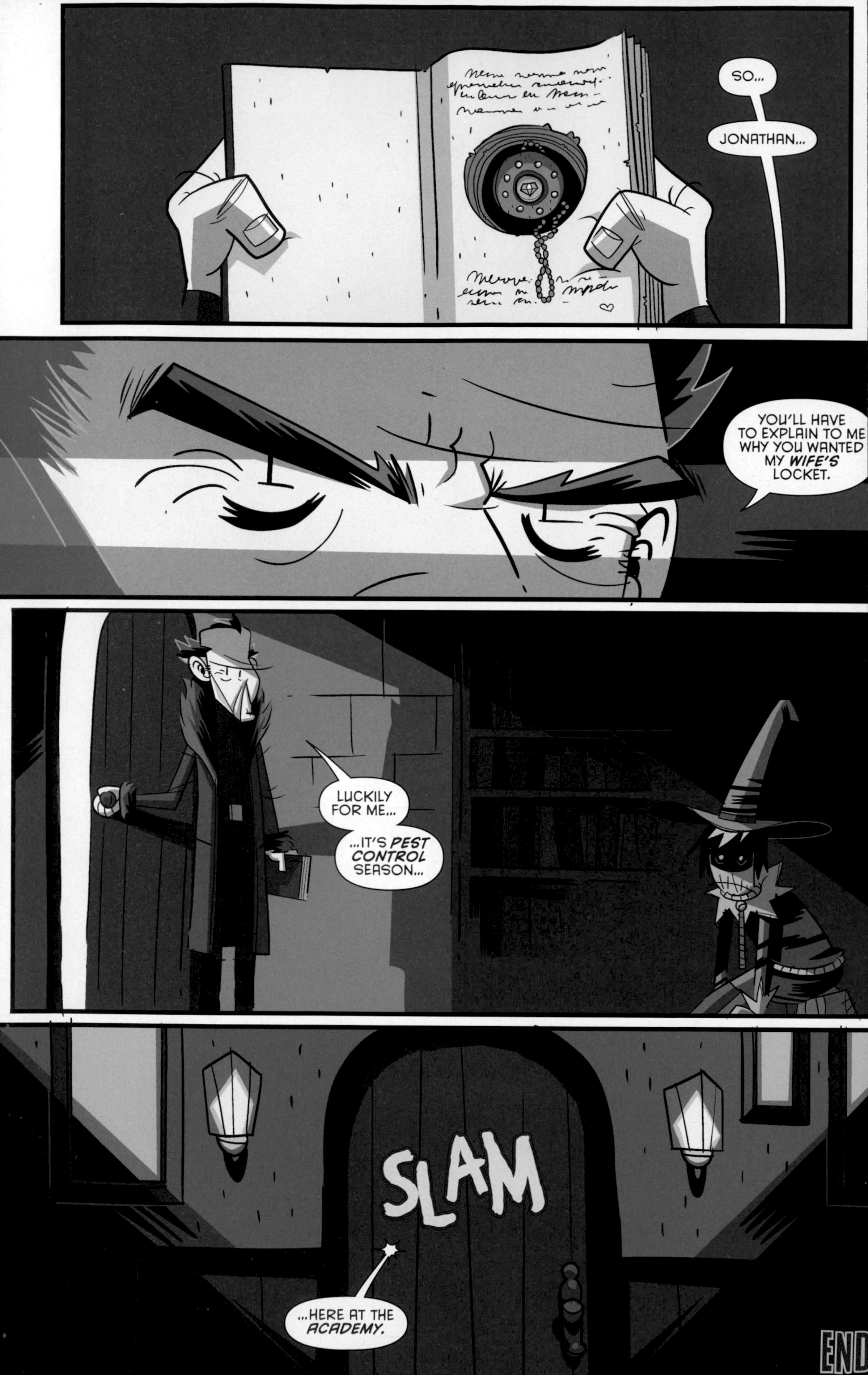
SO...
JONATHAN...
YOU'LL HAVE TO EXPLAIN TO ME WHY YOU WANTED MY WIFE'S LOCKET.
LUCKILY FOR ME...
...IT'S PEST CONTROL SEASON...
SLAM
...HERE AT THE ACADEMY.
END

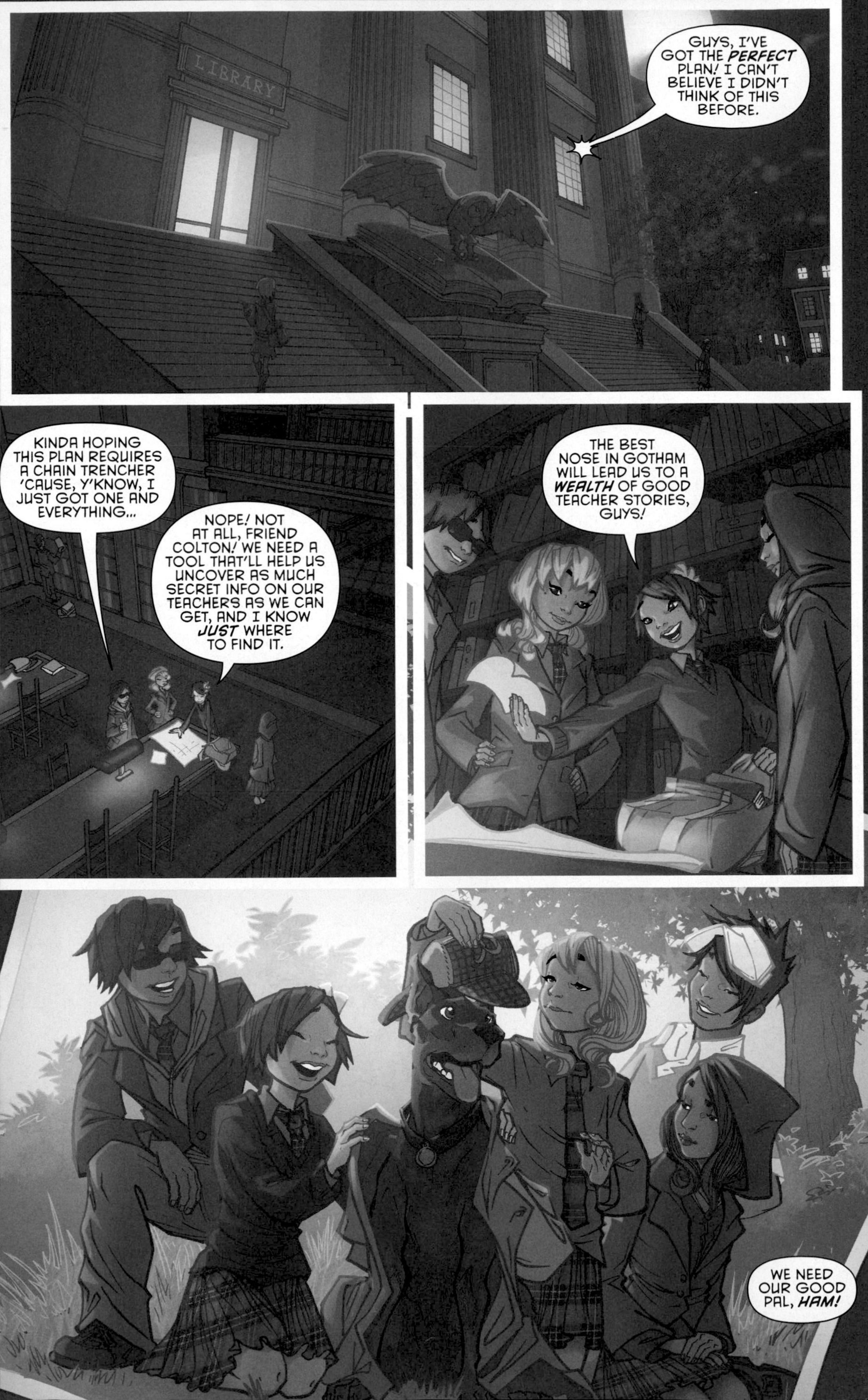
LIBRARY
GUYS, I'VE GOT THE *PERFECT* PLAN! I CAN'T BELIEVE I DIDN'T THINK OF THIS BEFORE.
KINDA HOPING THIS PLAN REQUIRES A CHAIN TRENCHER 'CAUSE, Y'KNOW, I JUST GOT ONE AND EVERYTHING...
NOPE! NOT AT ALL, FRIEND COLTON! WE NEED A TOOL THAT'LL HELP US UNCOVER AS MUCH SECRET INFO ON OUR TEACHERS AS WE CAN GET, AND I KNOW *JUST* WHERE TO FIND IT.
THE BEST NOSE IN GOTHAM WILL LEAD US TO A *WEALTH* OF GOOD TEACHER STORIES, GUYS!
WE NEED OUR GOOD PAL, *HAM!*

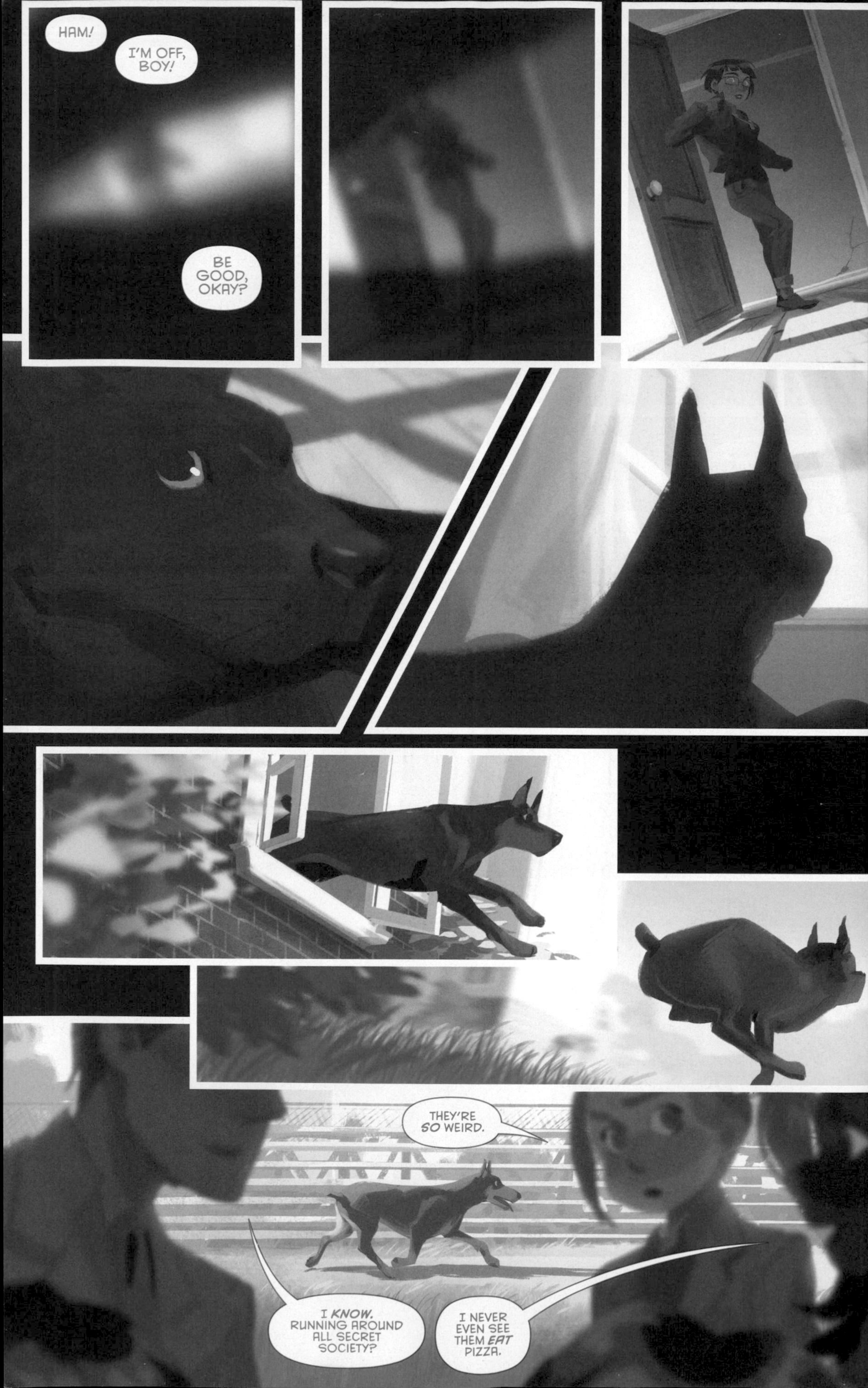
HAM!
I'M OFF, BOY!
BE GOOD, OKAY?
THEY'RE *SO* WEIRD.
I *KNOW.* RUNNING AROUND ALL SECRET SOCIETY?
I NEVER EVEN SEE THEM *EAT* PIZZA.

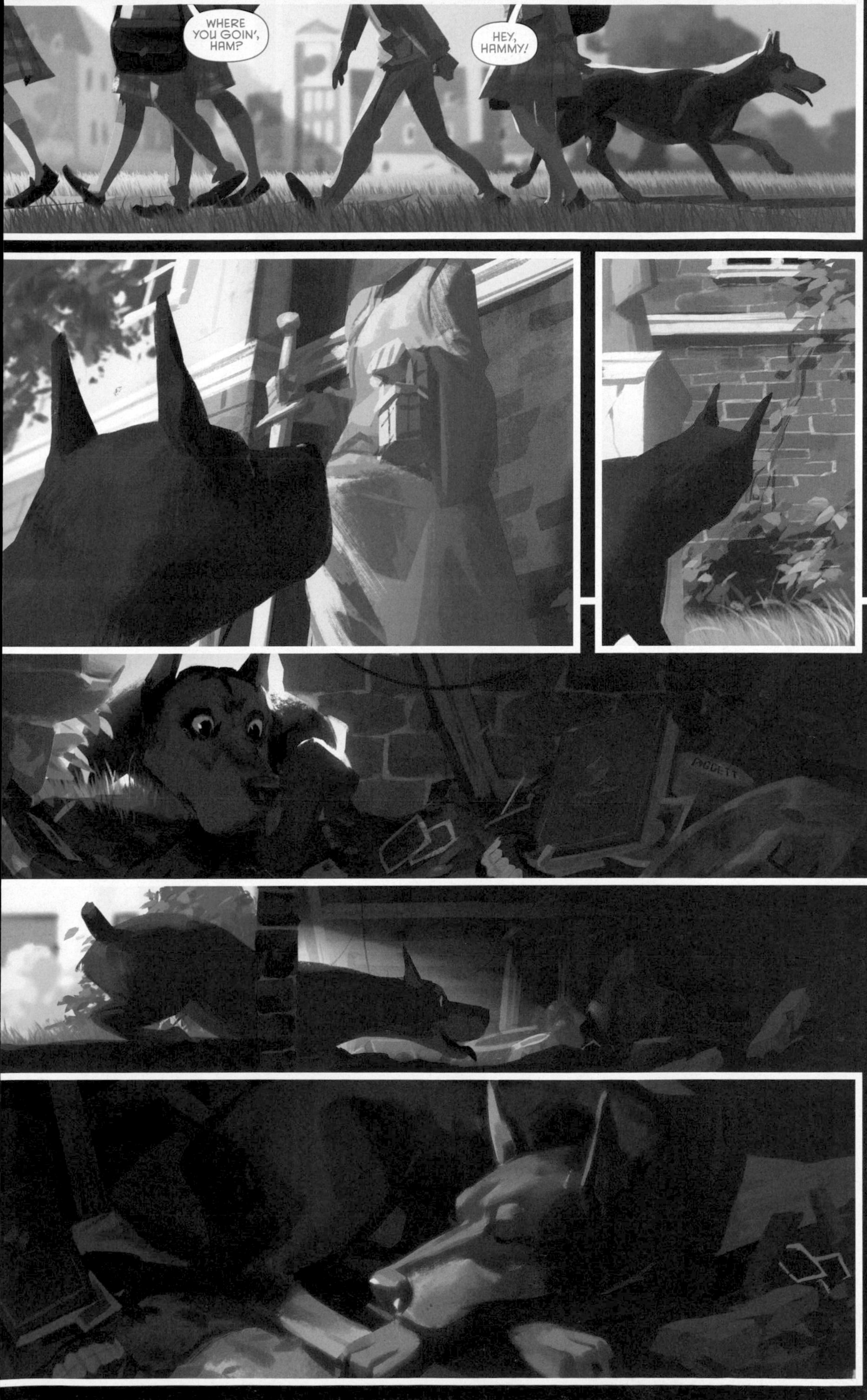
WHERE YOU GOIN', HAM?
HEY, HAMMY!

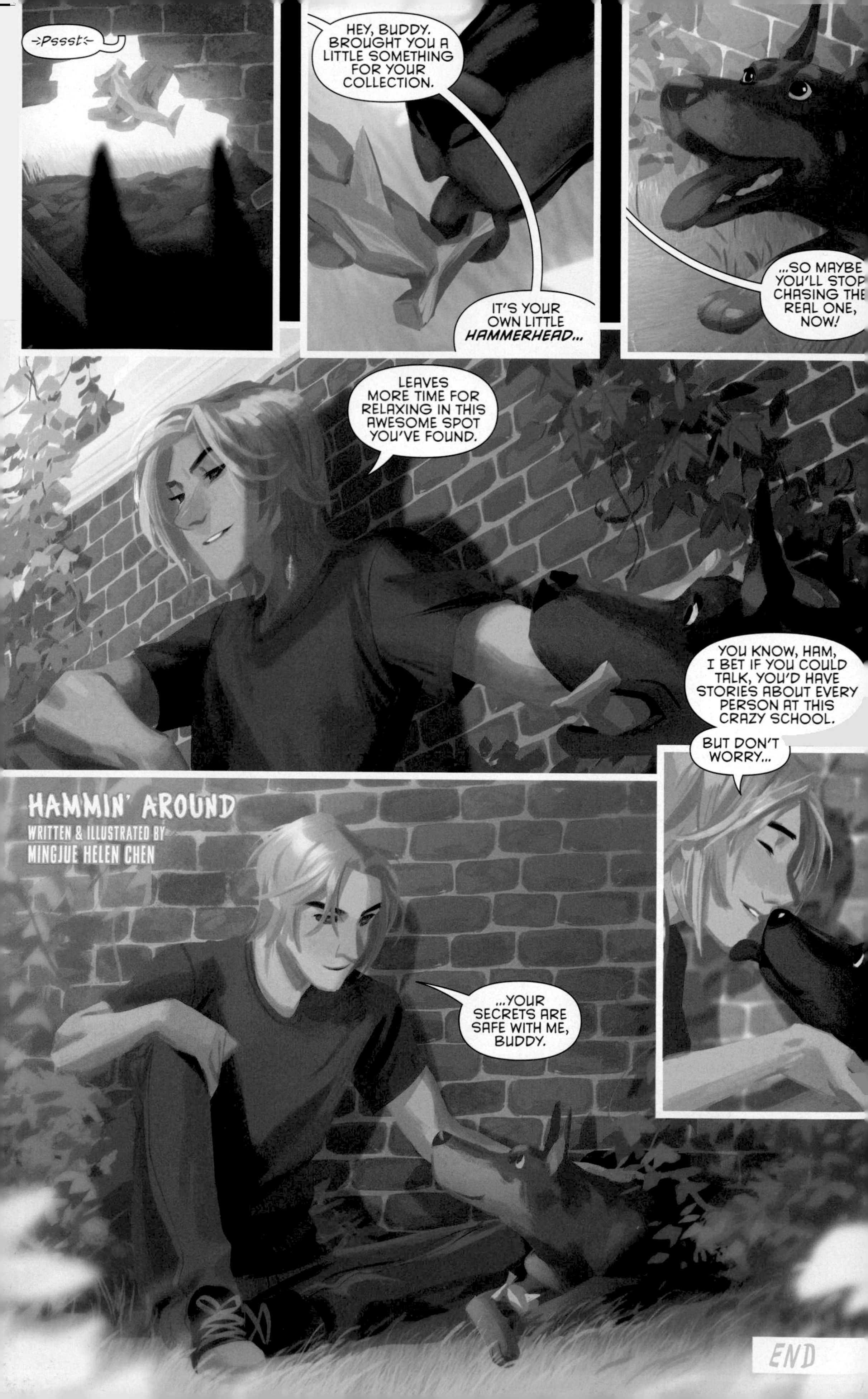

-Pssst-
HEY, BUDDY. BROUGHT YOU A LITTLE SOMETHING FOR YOUR COLLECTION.
IT'S YOUR OWN LITTLE *HAMMERHEAD...*
...SO MAYBE YOU'LL STOP CHASING THE REAL ONE, NOW!
LEAVES MORE TIME FOR RELAXING IN THIS AWESOME SPOT YOU'VE FOUND.
YOU KNOW, HAM, I BET IF YOU COULD TALK, YOU'D HAVE STORIES ABOUT EVERY PERSON AT THIS CRAZY SCHOOL.
BUT DON'T WORRY...
HAMMIN' AROUND
WRITTEN & ILLUSTRATED BY
MINGJUE HELEN CHEN
...YOUR SECRETS ARE SAFE WITH ME, BUDDY.
END

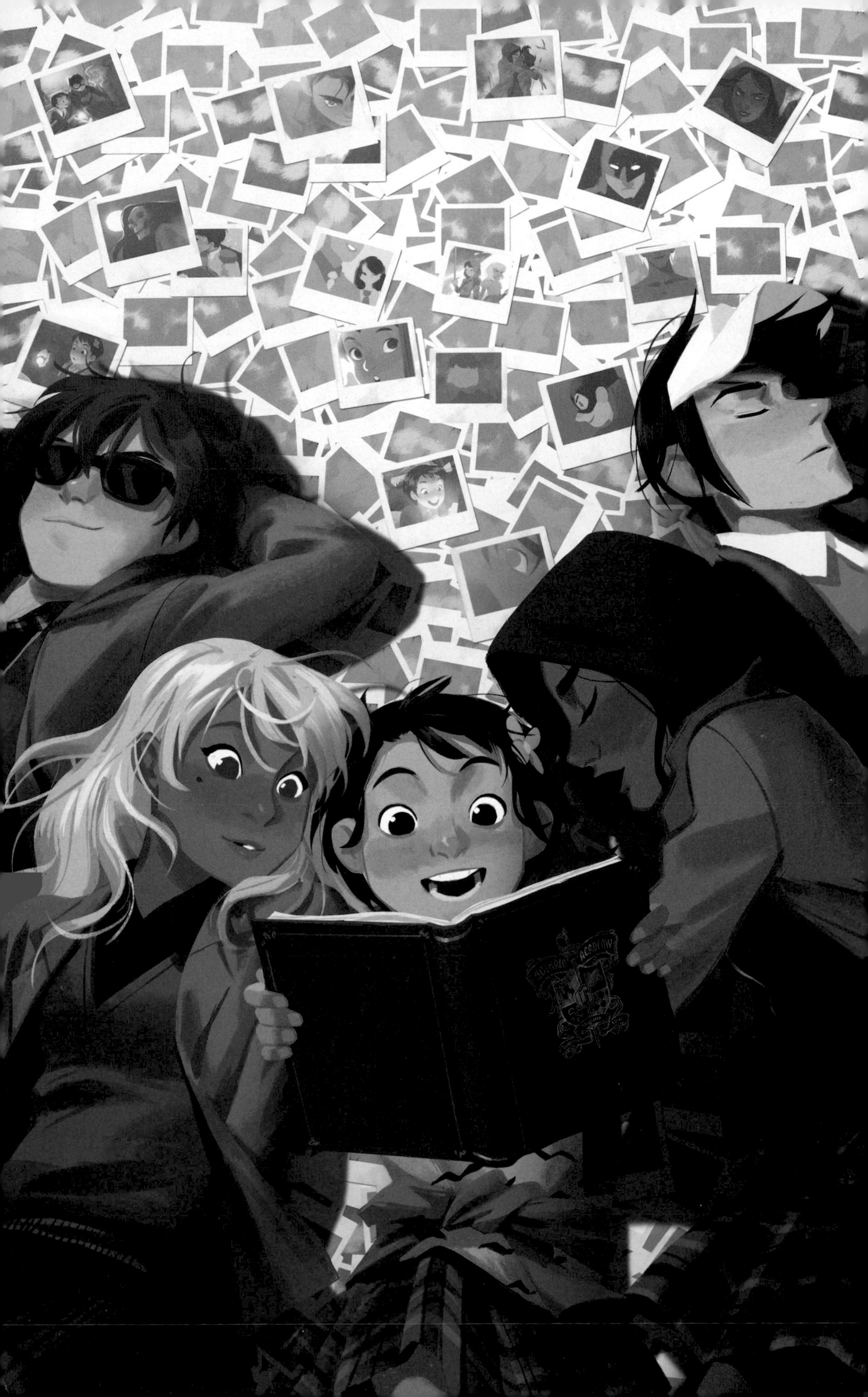

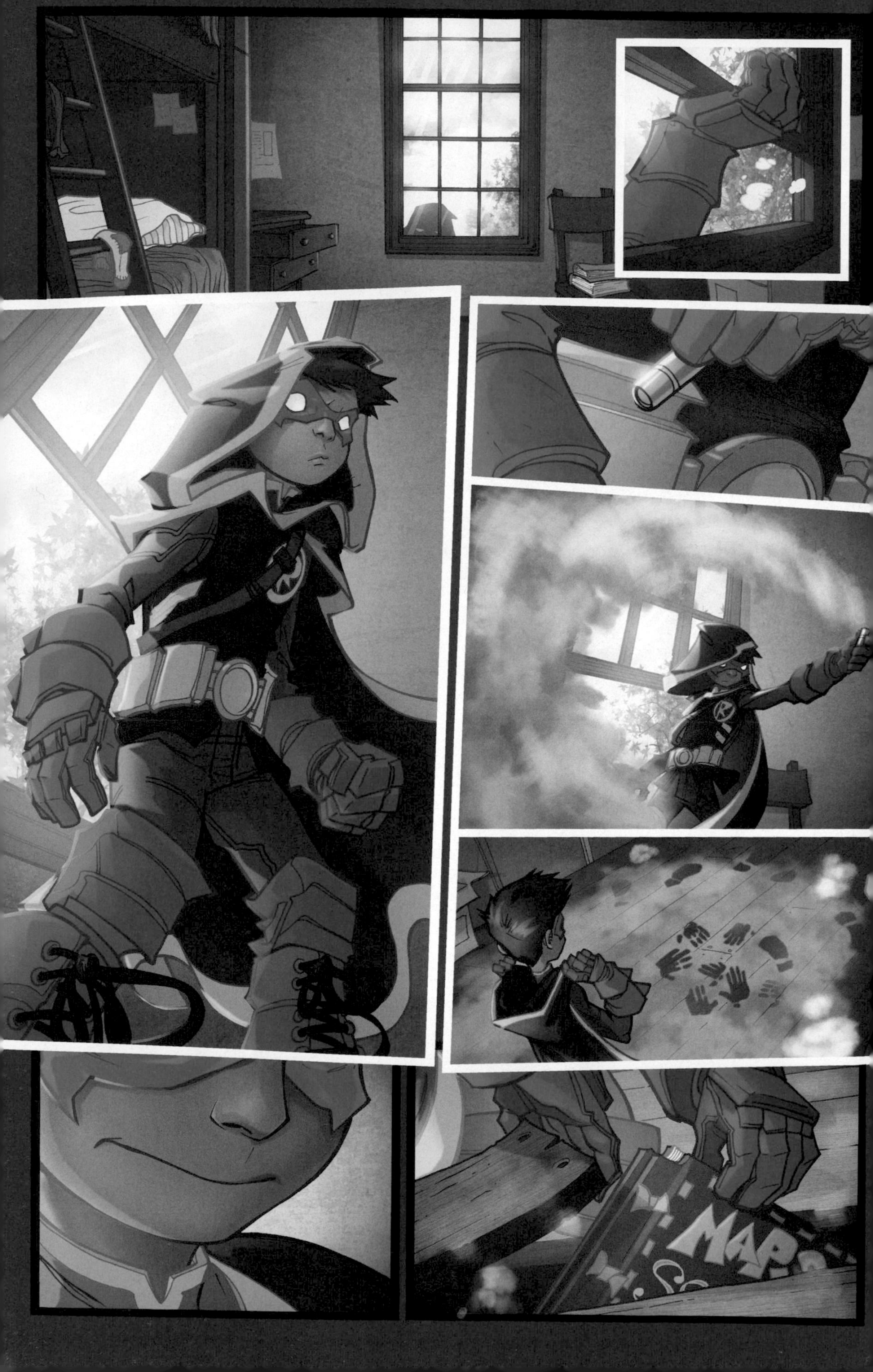

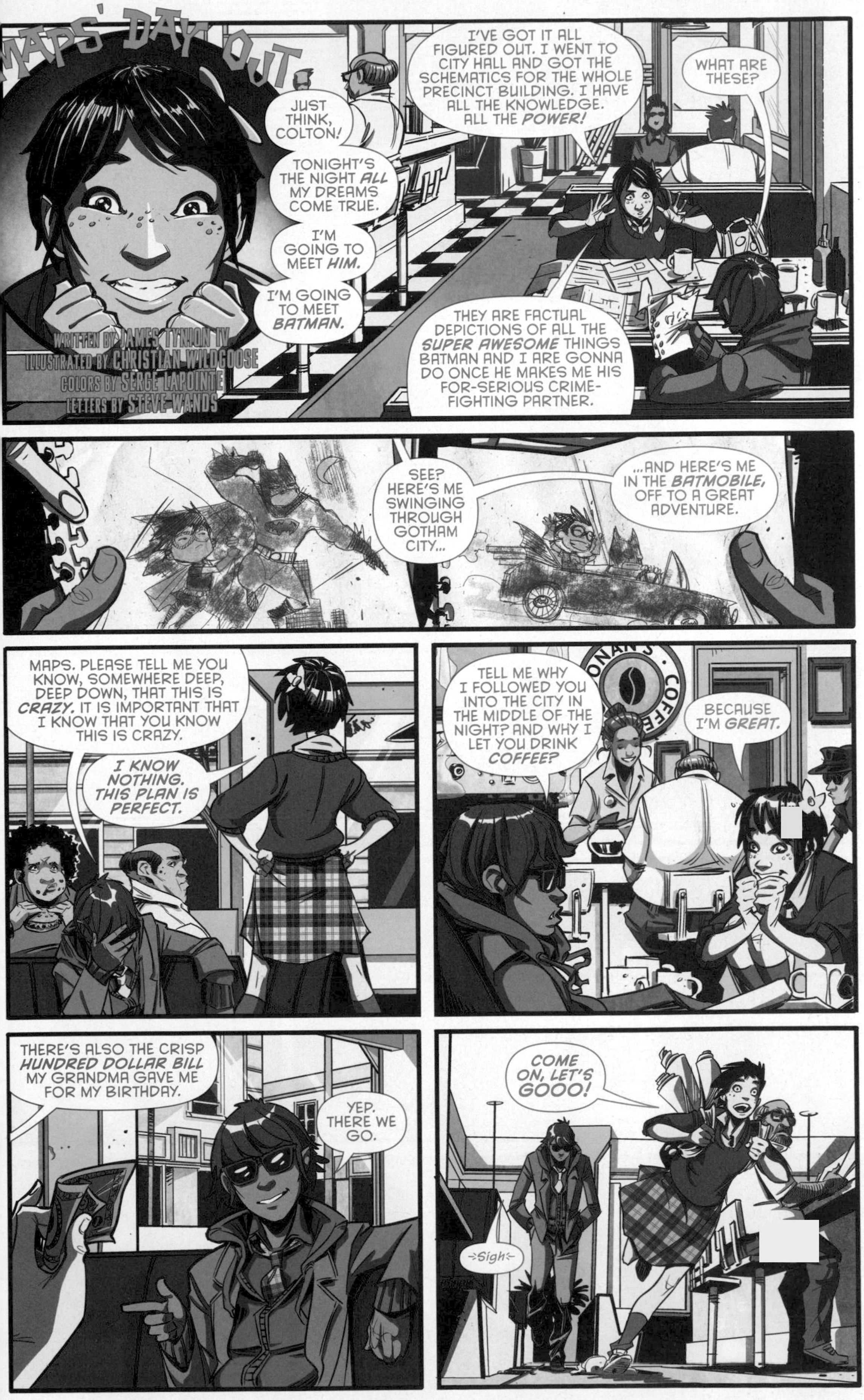
MAPS' DAY OUT
WRITTEN BY JAMES TYNION IV
ILLUSTRATED BY CHRISTIAN WILDGOOSE
COLORS BY SERGE LAPOINTE
LETTERS BY STEVE WANDS
JUST THINK, COLTON!
TONIGHT'S THE NIGHT *ALL* MY DREAMS COME TRUE.
I'M GOING TO MEET *HIM.*
I'M GOING TO MEET *BATMAN.*
I'VE GOT IT ALL FIGURED OUT. I WENT TO CITY HALL AND GOT THE SCHEMATICS FOR THE WHOLE PRECINCT BUILDING. I HAVE ALL THE KNOWLEDGE. ALL THE *POWER!*
WHAT ARE THESE?
THEY ARE FACTUAL DEPICTIONS OF ALL THE *SUPER AWESOME* THINGS BATMAN AND I ARE GONNA DO ONCE HE MAKES ME HIS FOR-SERIOUS CRIME-FIGHTING PARTNER.
SEE? HERE'S ME SWINGING THROUGH GOTHAM CITY...
...AND HERE'S ME IN THE *BATMOBILE,* OFF TO A GREAT ADVENTURE.
MAPS. PLEASE TELL ME YOU KNOW, SOMEWHERE DEEP, DEEP DOWN, THAT THIS IS *CRAZY.* IT IS IMPORTANT THAT I KNOW THAT YOU KNOW THIS IS CRAZY.
I KNOW NOTHING. THIS PLAN IS PERFECT.
TELL ME WHY I FOLLOWED YOU INTO THE CITY IN THE MIDDLE OF THE NIGHT? AND WHY I LET YOU DRINK *COFFEE?*
BECAUSE I'M *GREAT.*
THERE'S ALSO THE CRISP *HUNDRED DOLLAR BILL* MY GRANDMA GAVE ME FOR MY BIRTHDAY.
YEP. THERE WE GO.
COME ON, LET'S GOOO!
Sigh

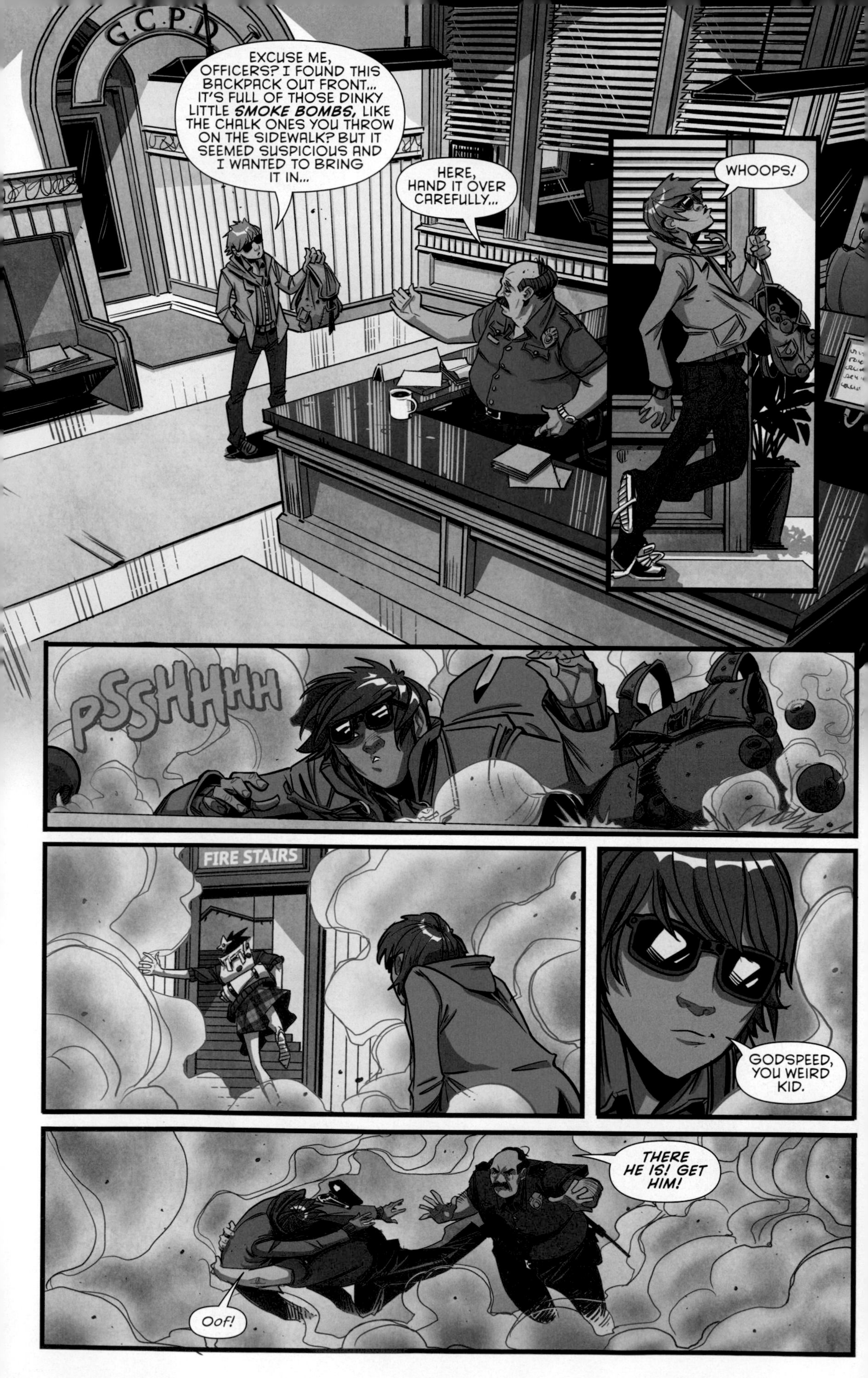
G.C.P.D.
EXCUSE ME, OFFICERS? I FOUND THIS BACKPACK OUT FRONT... IT'S FULL OF THOSE DINKY LITTLE SMOKE BOMBS, LIKE THE CHALK ONES YOU THROW ON THE SIDEWALK? BUT IT SEEMED SUSPICIOUS AND I WANTED TO BRING IT IN...
HERE, HAND IT OVER CAREFULLY...
WHOOPS!
PSSHHHH
FIRE STAIRS
GODSPEED, YOU WEIRD KID.
THERE HE IS! GET HIM!
Oof!

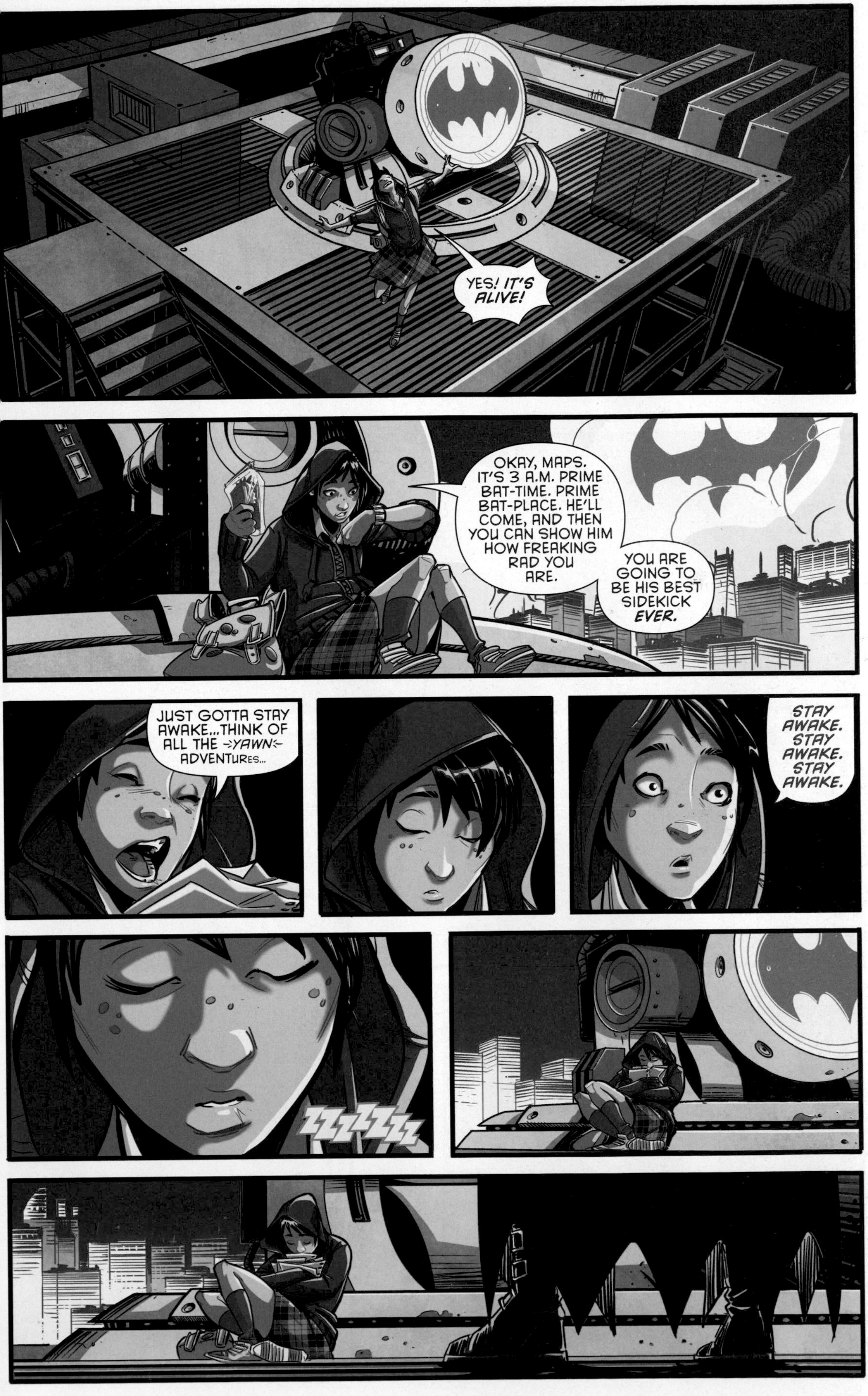
YES! IT'S ALIVE!
OKAY, MAPS. IT'S 3 A.M. PRIME BAT-TIME. PRIME BAT-PLACE. HE'LL COME, AND THEN YOU CAN SHOW HIM HOW FREAKING RAD YOU ARE.
YOU ARE GOING TO BE HIS BEST SIDEKICK EVER.
JUST GOTTA STAY AWAKE...THINK OF ALL THE =YAWN= ADVENTURes...
STAY AWAKE. STAY AWAKE. STAY AWAKE.
ZZZZZZZ

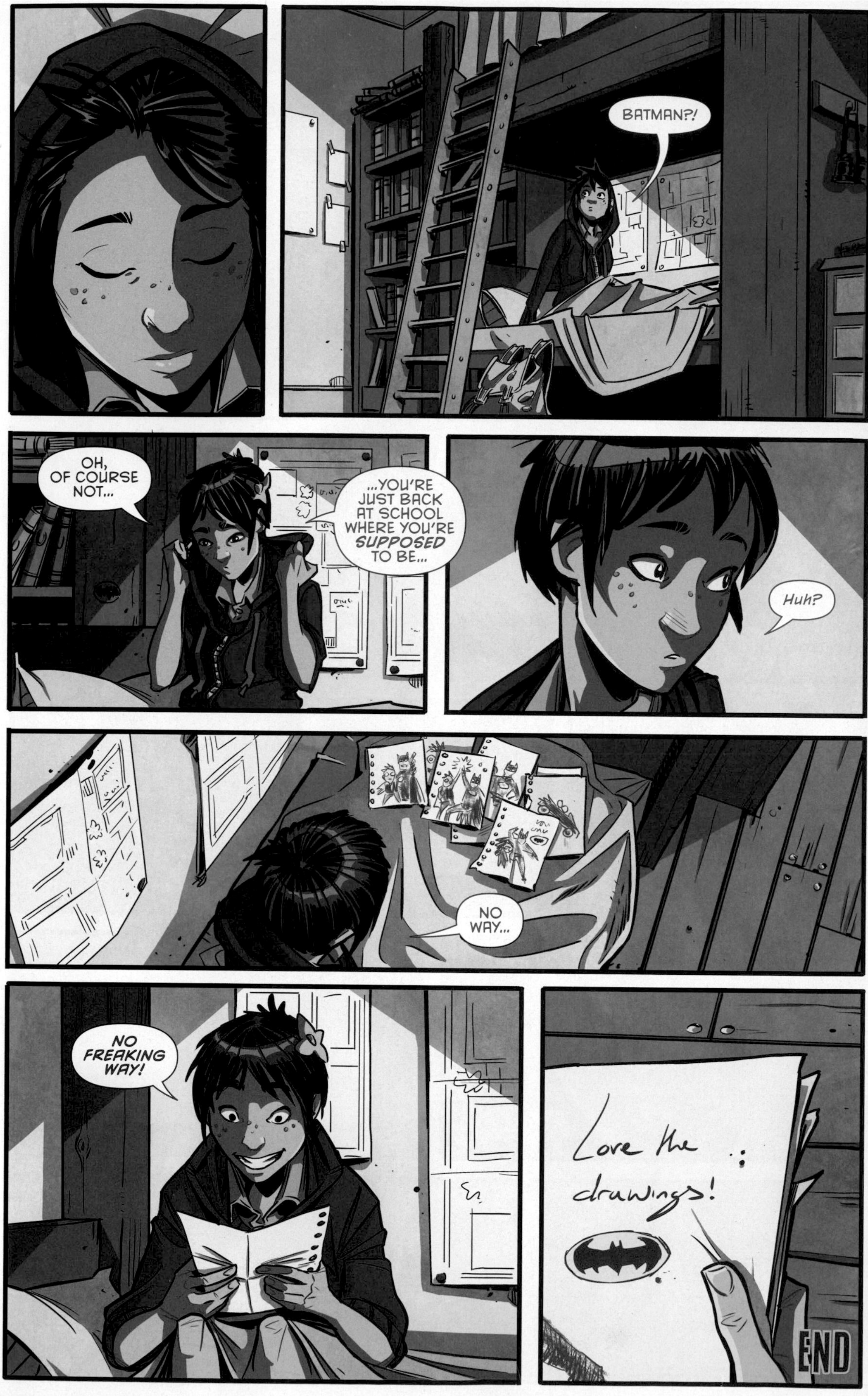
BATMAN?!
OH, OF COURSE NOT...
...YOU'RE JUST BACK AT SCHOOL WHERE YOU'RE SUPPOSED TO BE...
Huh?
NO WAY...
NO FREAKING WAY!
Love the drawings!
END

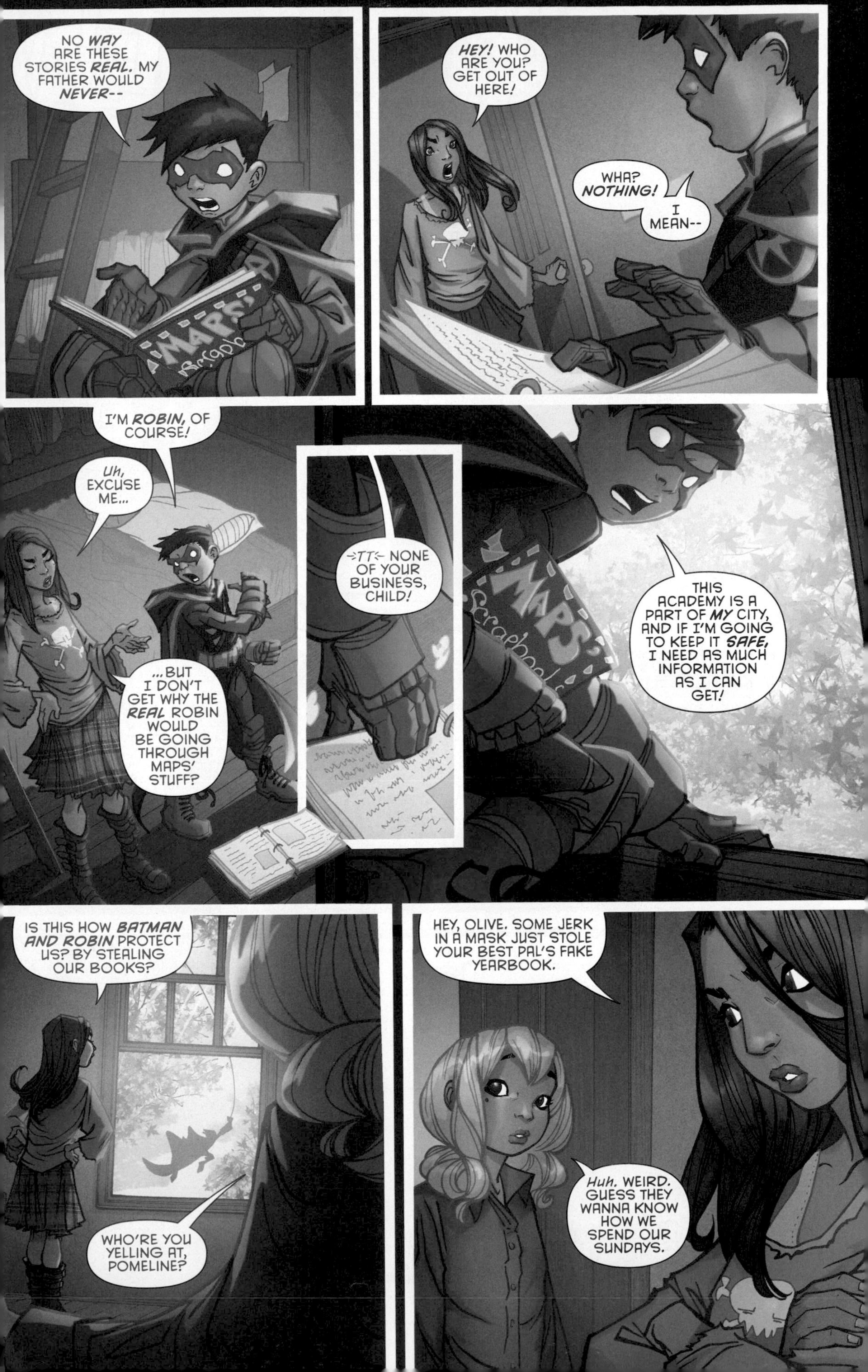
NO WAY ARE THESE STORIES REAL. MY FATHER WOULD NEVER--
MAPS' Scrapbook
HEY! WHO ARE YOU? GET OUT OF HERE!
WHA? NOTHING!
I MEAN--
I'M ROBIN, OF COURSE!
Uh, EXCUSE ME...
...BUT I DON'T GET WHY THE REAL ROBIN WOULD BE GOING THROUGH MAPS' STUFF?
-TT- NONE OF YOUR BUSINESS, CHILD!
THIS ACADEMY IS A PART OF MY CITY, AND IF I'M GOING TO KEEP IT SAFE, I NEED AS MUCH INFORMATION AS I CAN GET!
IS THIS HOW BATMAN AND ROBIN PROTECT US? BY STEALING OUR BOOKS?
WHO'RE YOU YELLING AT, POMELINE?
HEY, OLIVE. SOME JERK IN A MASK JUST STOLE YOUR BEST PAL'S FAKE YEARBOOK.
Huh. WEIRD. GUESS THEY WANNA KNOW HOW WE SPEND OUR SUNDAYS.

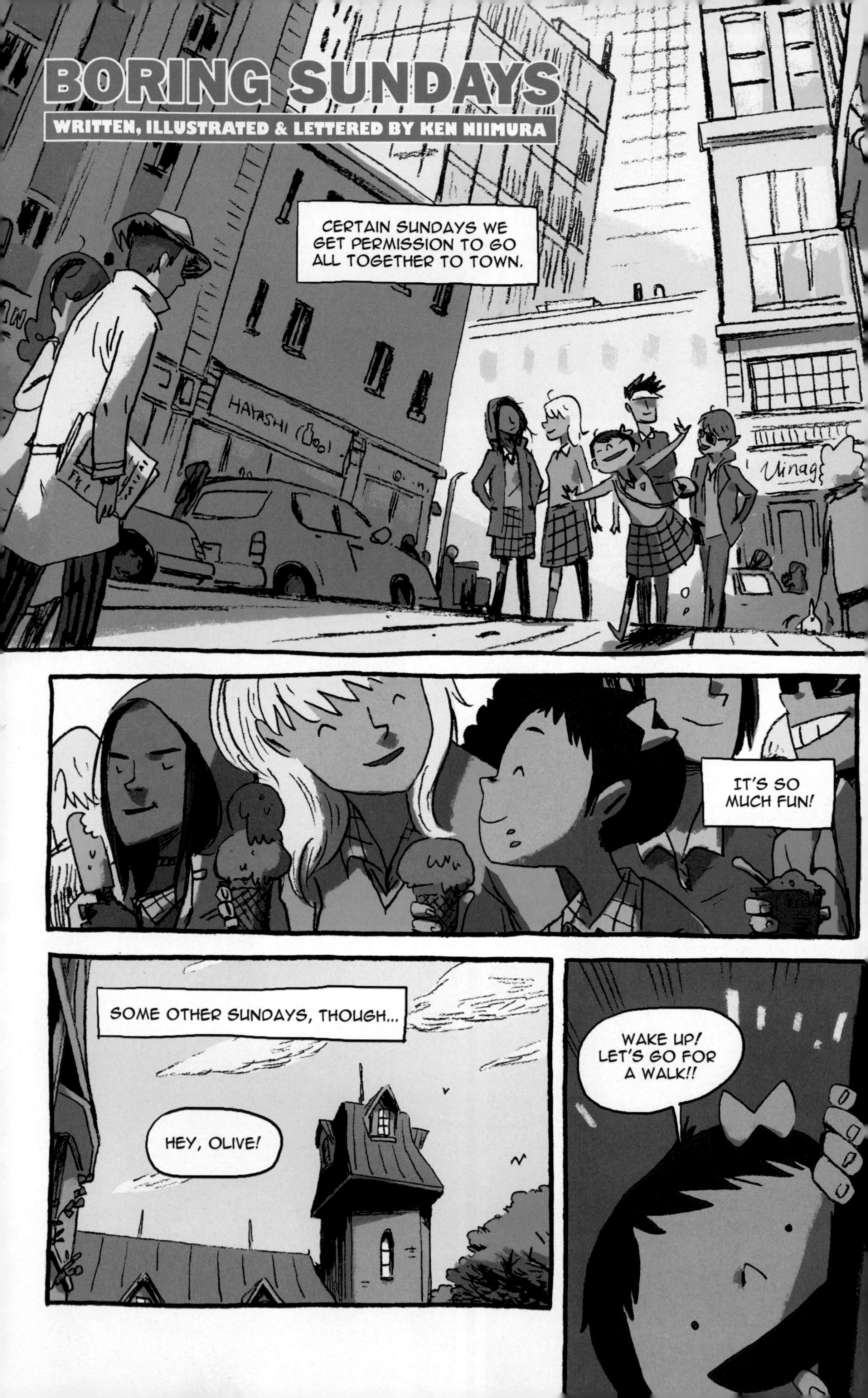
BORING SUNDAYS
WRITTEN, ILLUSTRATED & LETTERED BY KEN NIIMURA
CERTAIN SUNDAYS WE GET PERMISSION TO GO ALL TOGETHER TO TOWN.
HAYASHI
IT'S SO MUCH FUN!
SOME OTHER SUNDAYS, THOUGH...
HEY, OLIVE!
WAKE UP! LET'S GO FOR A WALK!!

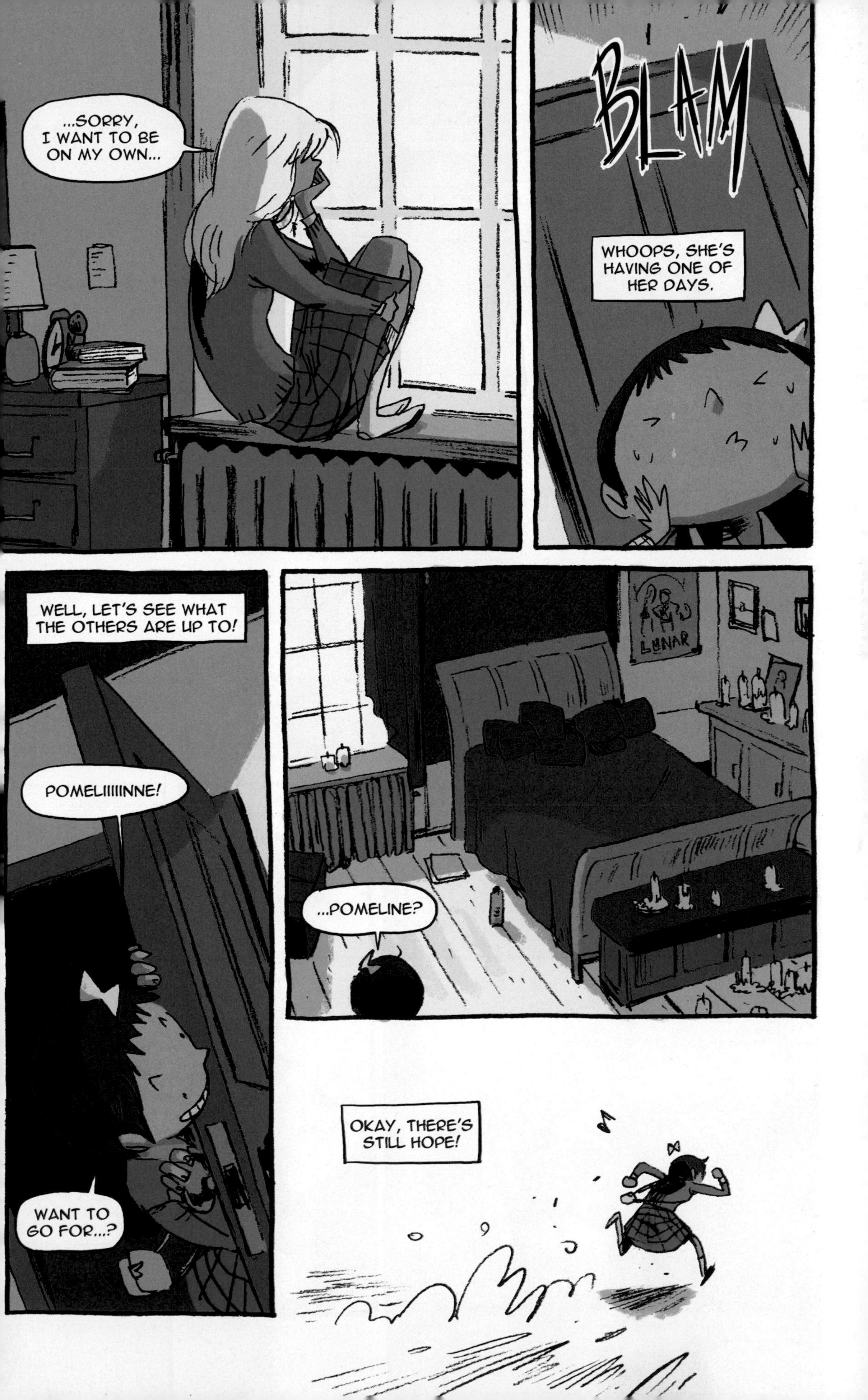
...SORRY, I WANT TO BE ON MY OWN...
BLAM
WHOOPS, SHE'S HAVING ONE OF HER DAYS.
WELL, LET'S SEE WHAT THE OTHERS ARE UP TO!
POMELIIIIIINNE!
WANT TO GO FOR...?
LUNAR
...POMELINE?
OKAY, THERE'S STILL HOPE!

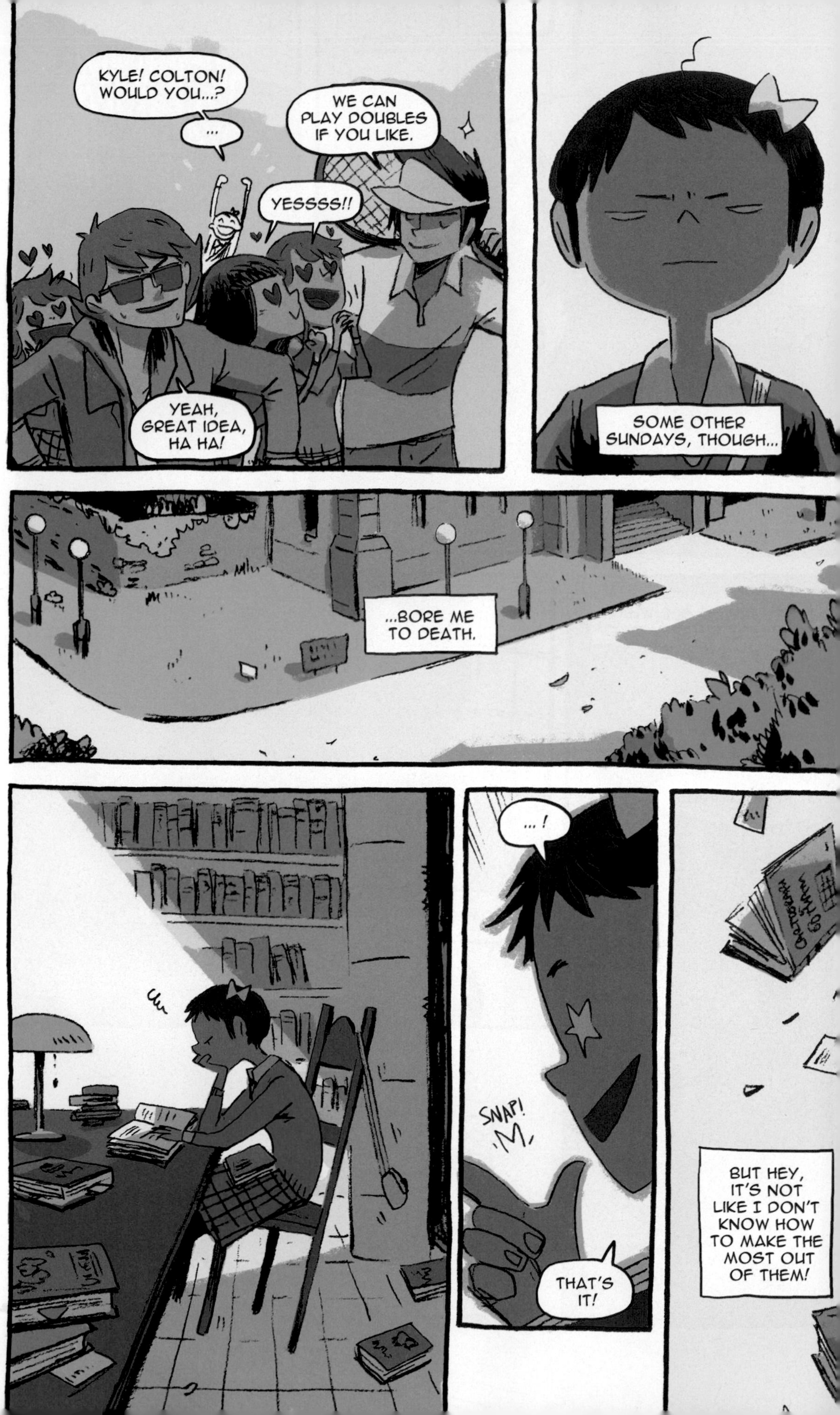
KYLE! COLTON! WOULD YOU...?
...
WE CAN PLAY DOUBLES IF YOU LIKE.
YESSSS!!
YEAH, GREAT IDEA, HA HA!
SOME OTHER SUNDAYS, THOUGH...
...BORE ME TO DEATH.
...!
SNAP!
THAT'S IT!
BUT HEY, IT'S NOT LIKE I DON'T KNOW HOW TO MAKE THE MOST OUT OF THEM!

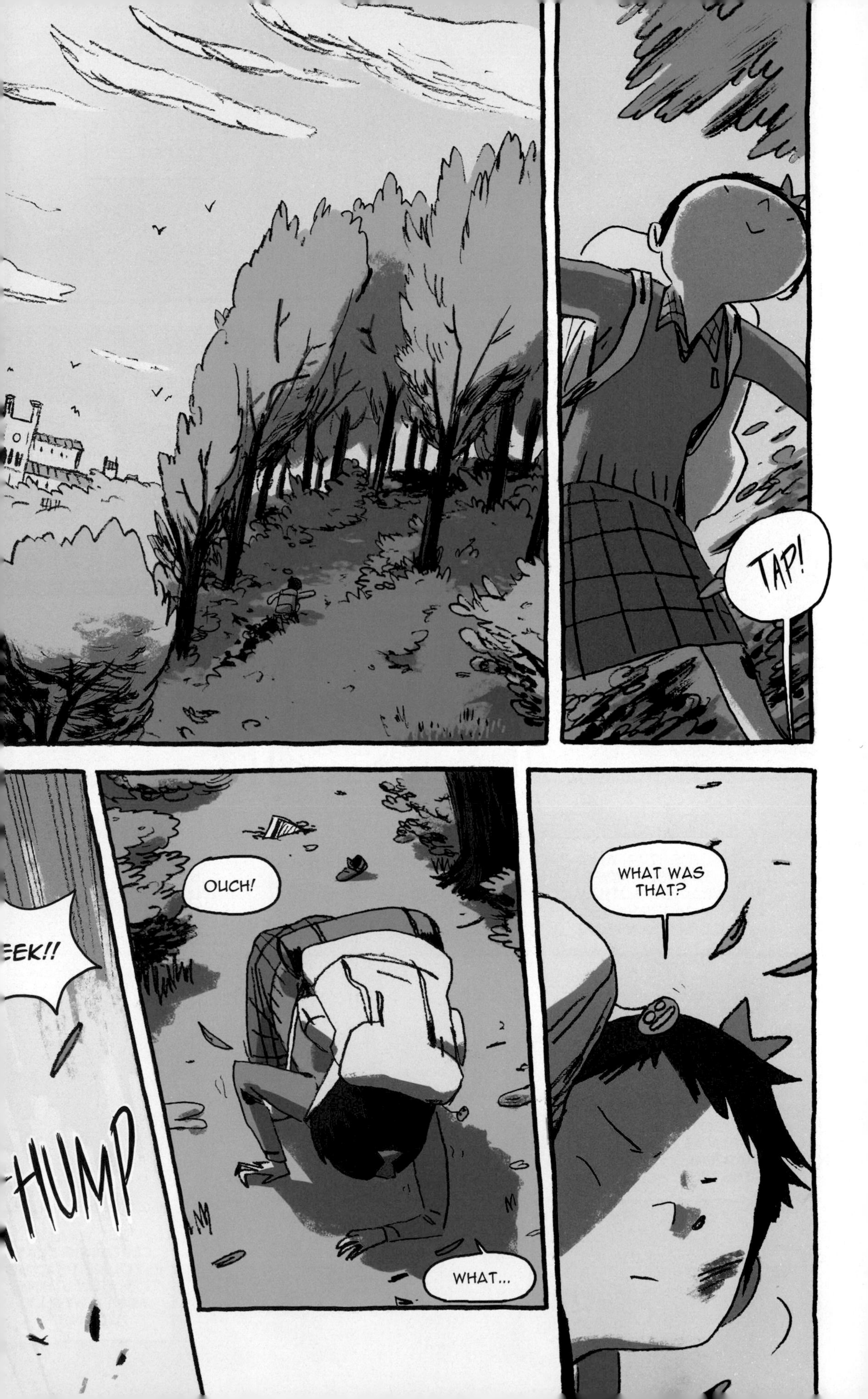
TAP!
EEK!!
THUMP
OUCH!
WHAT...
WHAT WAS THAT?

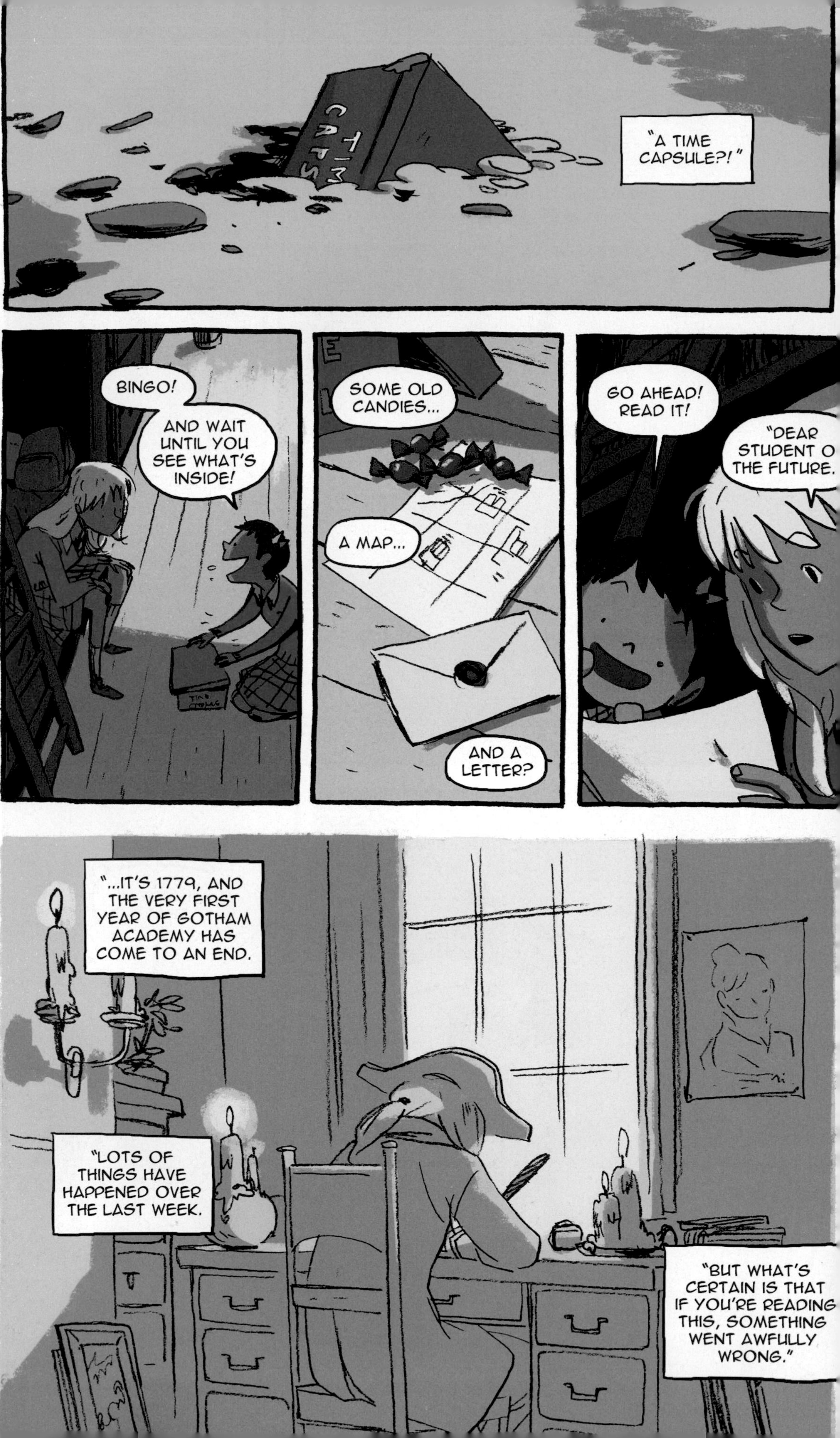
TIME CAPS
"A TIME CAPSULE?!"
BINGO!
AND WAIT UNTIL YOU SEE WHAT'S INSIDE!
SOME OLD CANDIES...
A MAP...
AND A LETTER?
GO AHEAD! READ IT!
"DEAR STUDENT O THE FUTURE.
"...IT'S 1779, AND THE VERY FIRST YEAR OF GOTHAM ACADEMY HAS COME TO AN END.
"LOTS OF THINGS HAVE HAPPENED OVER THE LAST WEEK.
"BUT WHAT'S CERTAIN IS THAT IF YOU'RE READING THIS, SOMETHING WENT AWFULLY WRONG."

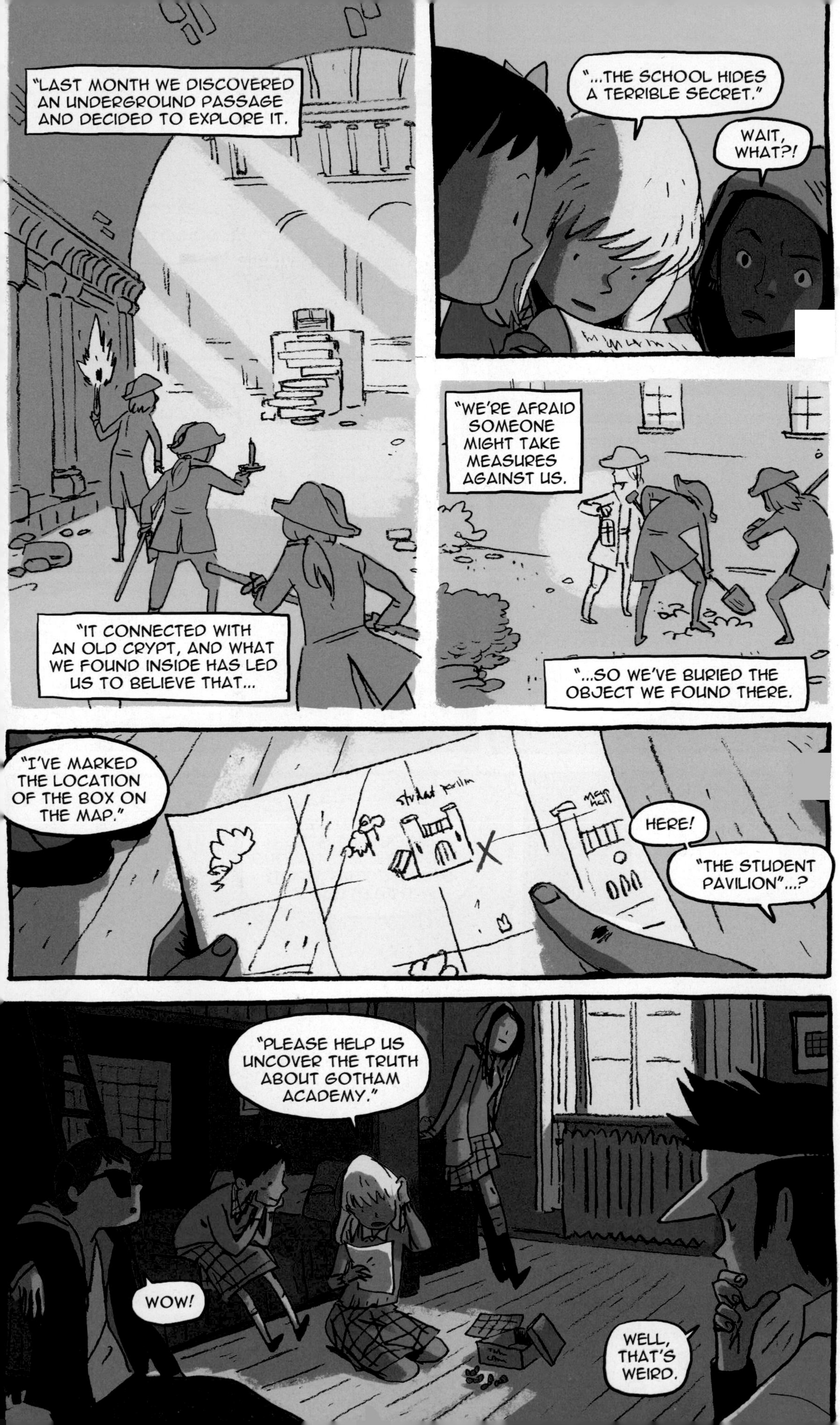
"LAST MONTH WE DISCOVERED AN UNDERGROUND PASSAGE AND DECIDED TO EXPLORE IT.
"IT CONNECTED WITH AN OLD CRYPT, AND WHAT WE FOUND INSIDE HAS LED US TO BELIEVE THAT...
"...THE SCHOOL HIDES A TERRIBLE SECRET."
WAIT, WHAT?!
"WE'RE AFRAID SOMEONE MIGHT TAKE MEASURES AGAINST US.
"...SO WE'VE BURIED THE OBJECT WE FOUND THERE.
"I'VE MARKED THE LOCATION OF THE BOX ON THE MAP."
HERE!
"THE STUDENT PAVILION"...?
"PLEASE HELP US UNCOVER THE TRUTH ABOUT GOTHAM ACADEMY."
WOW!
WELL, THAT'S WEIRD.

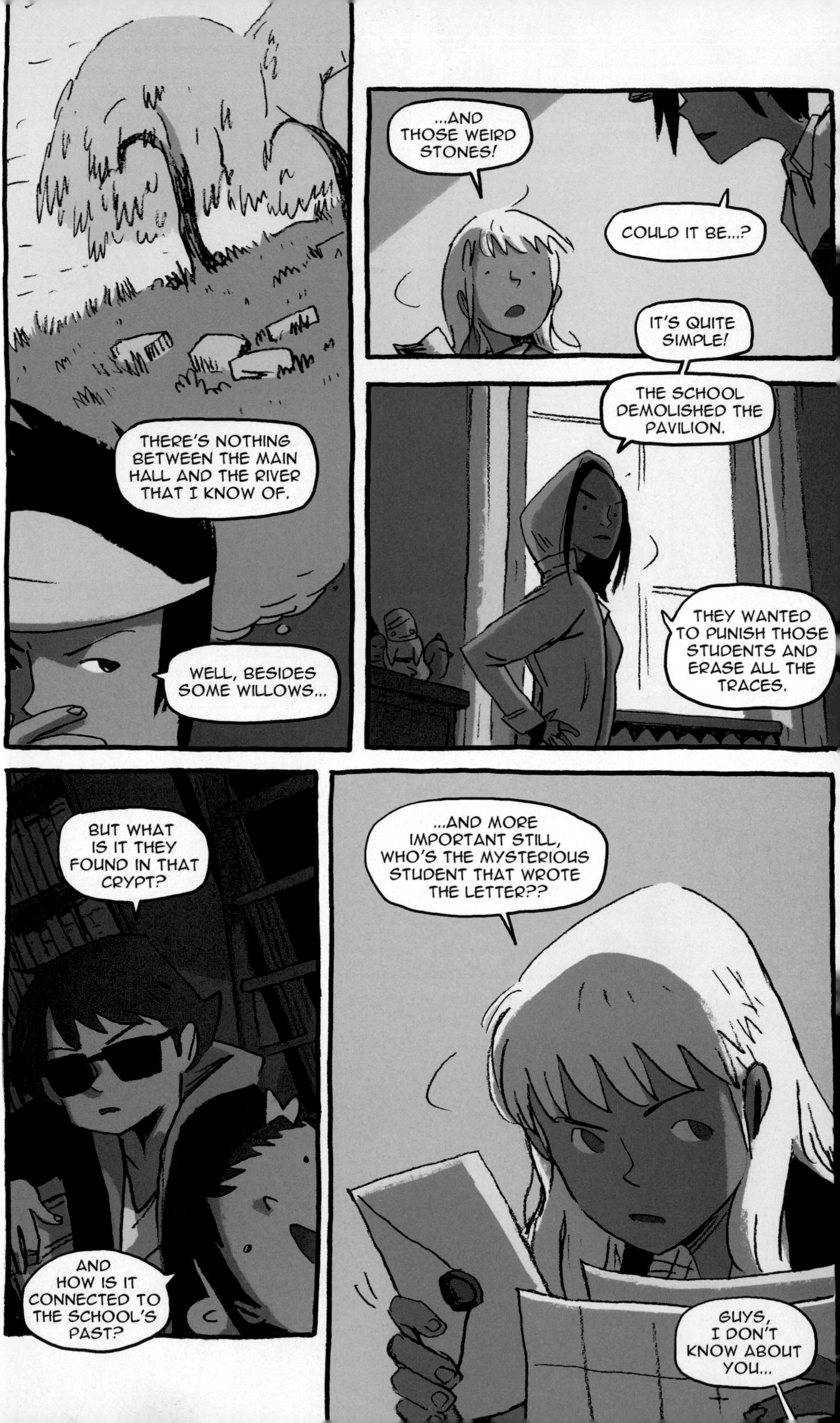

THERE'S NOTHING BETWEEN THE MAIN HALL AND THE RIVER THAT I KNOW OF.
WELL, BESIDES SOME WILLOWS...
...AND THOSE WEIRD STONES!
COULD IT BE...?
IT'S QUITE SIMPLE!
THE SCHOOL DEMOLISHED THE PAVILION.
THEY WANTED TO PUNISH THOSE STUDENTS AND ERASE ALL THE TRACES.
BUT WHAT IS IT THEY FOUND IN THAT CRYPT?
AND HOW IS IT CONNECTED TO THE SCHOOL'S PAST?
...AND MORE IMPORTANT STILL, WHO'S THE MYSTERIOUS STUDENT THAT WROTE THE LETTER??
GUYS, I DON'T KNOW ABOUT YOU...

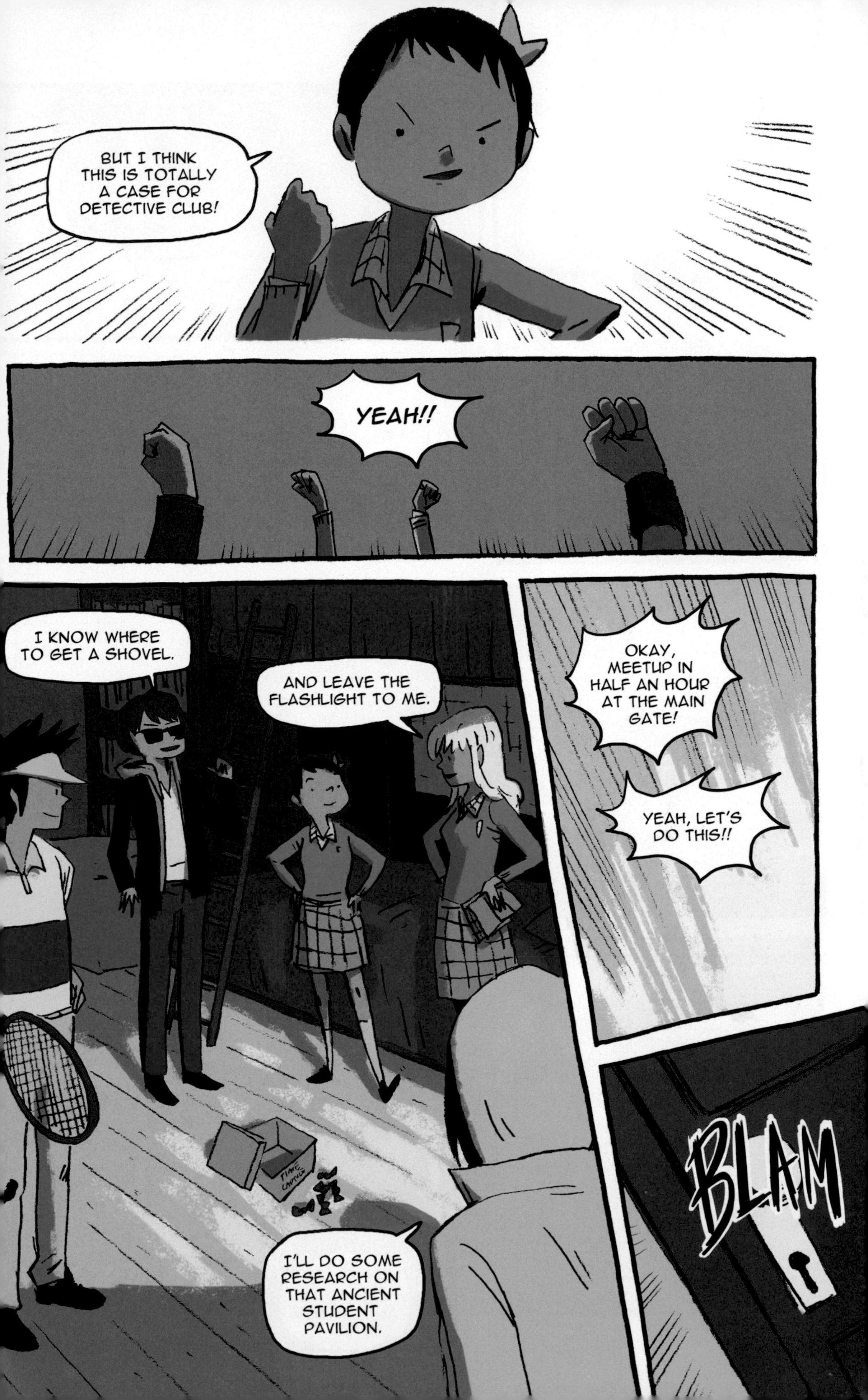
BUT I THINK THIS IS TOTALLY A CASE FOR DETECTIVE CLUB!
YEAH!!
I KNOW WHERE TO GET A SHOVEL.
AND LEAVE THE FLASHLIGHT TO ME.
I'LL DO SOME RESEARCH ON THAT ANCIENT STUDENT PAVILION.
OKAY, MEETUP IN HALF AN HOUR AT THE MAIN GATE!
YEAH, LET'S DO THIS!!
BLAM

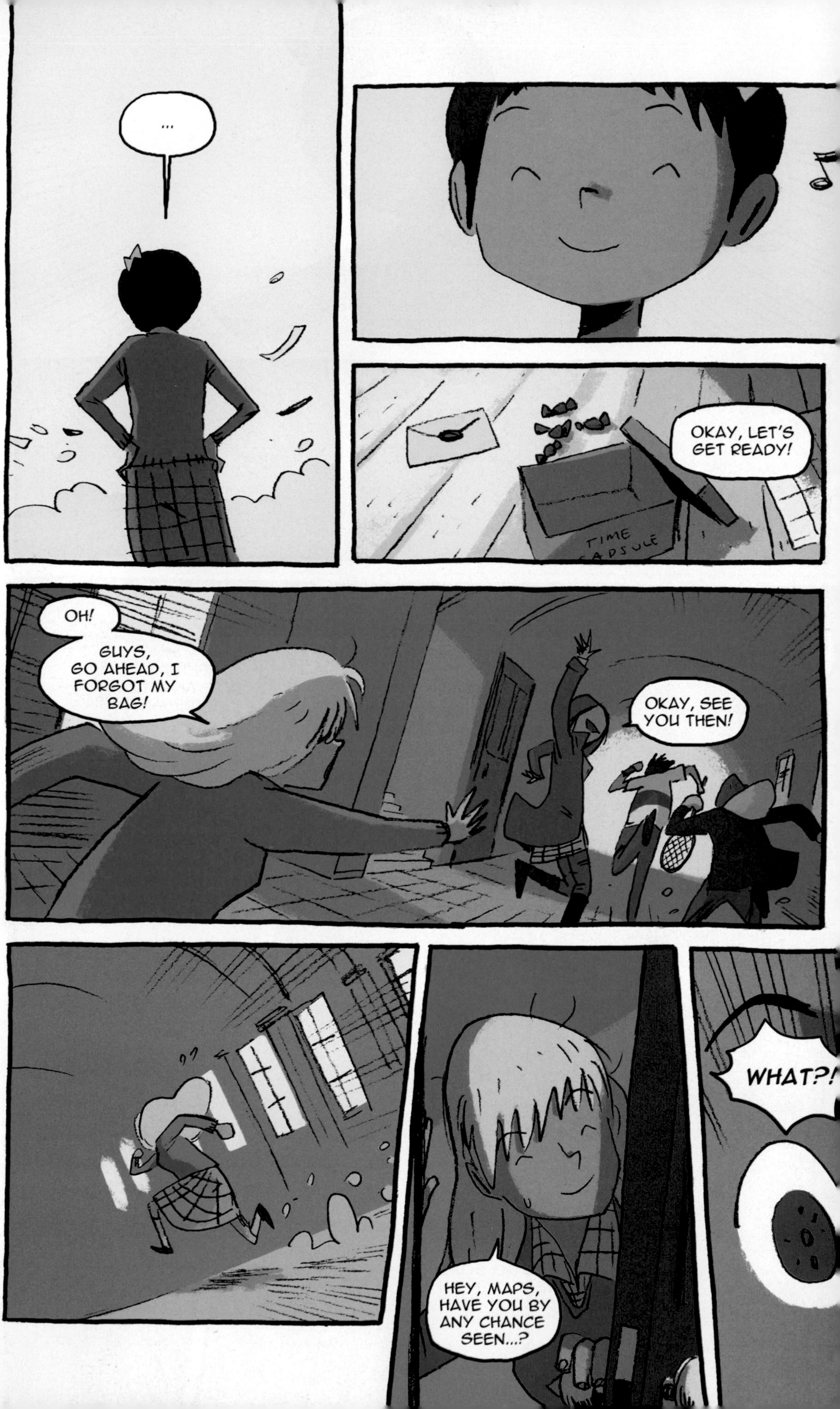
...
OKAY, LET'S GET READY!
TIME CAPSULE
OH!
GUYS, GO AHEAD, I FORGOT MY BAG!
OKAY, SEE YOU THEN!
HEY, MAPS, HAVE YOU BY ANY CHANCE SEEN...?
WHAT?!

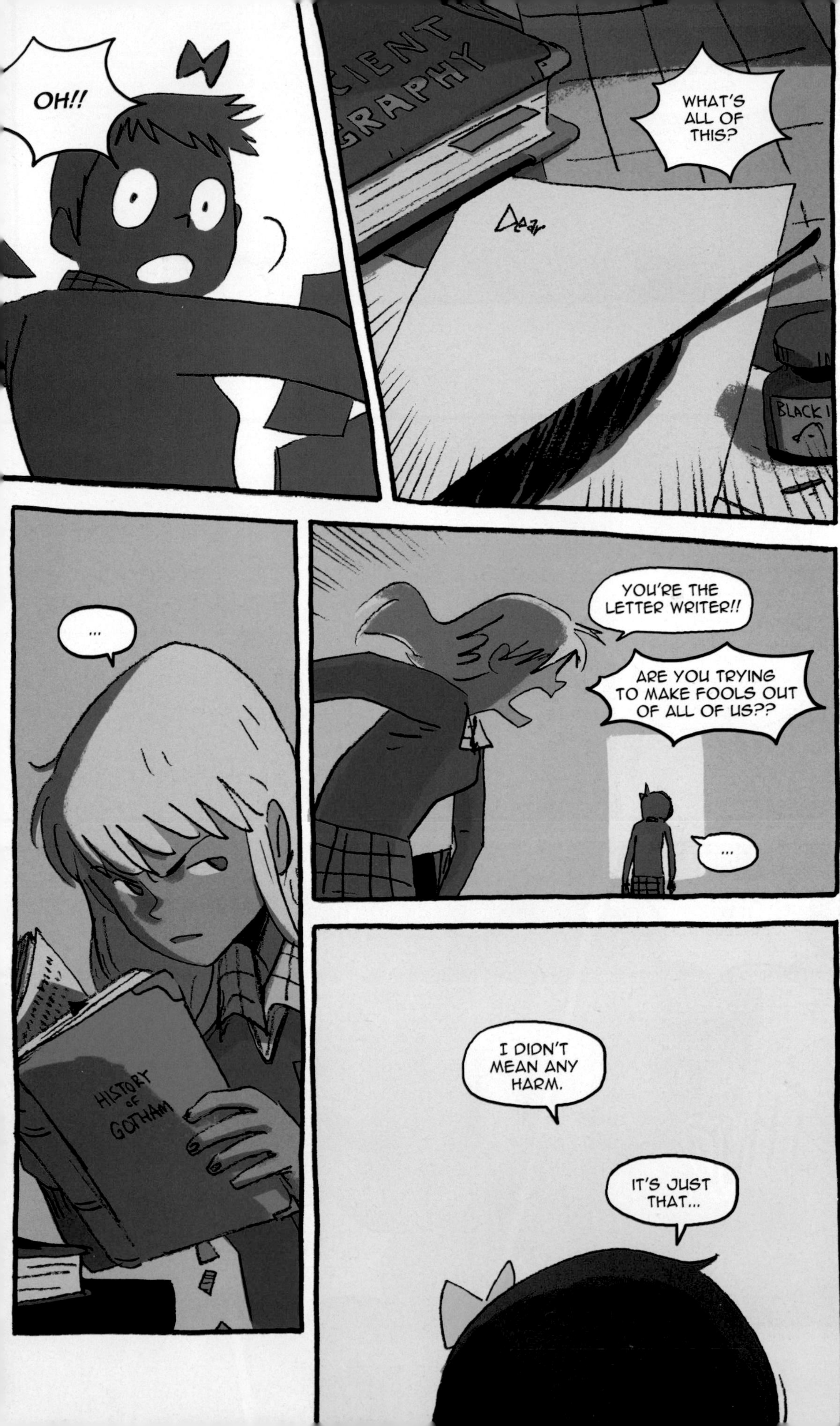
OH!!
CIENT
GRAPHY
WHAT'S ALL OF THIS?
Dear
BLACK I
...
HISTORY OF GOTHAM
YOU'RE THE LETTER WRITER!!
ARE YOU TRYING TO MAKE FOOLS OUT OF ALL OF US??
...
I DIDN'T MEAN ANY HARM.
IT'S JUST THAT...

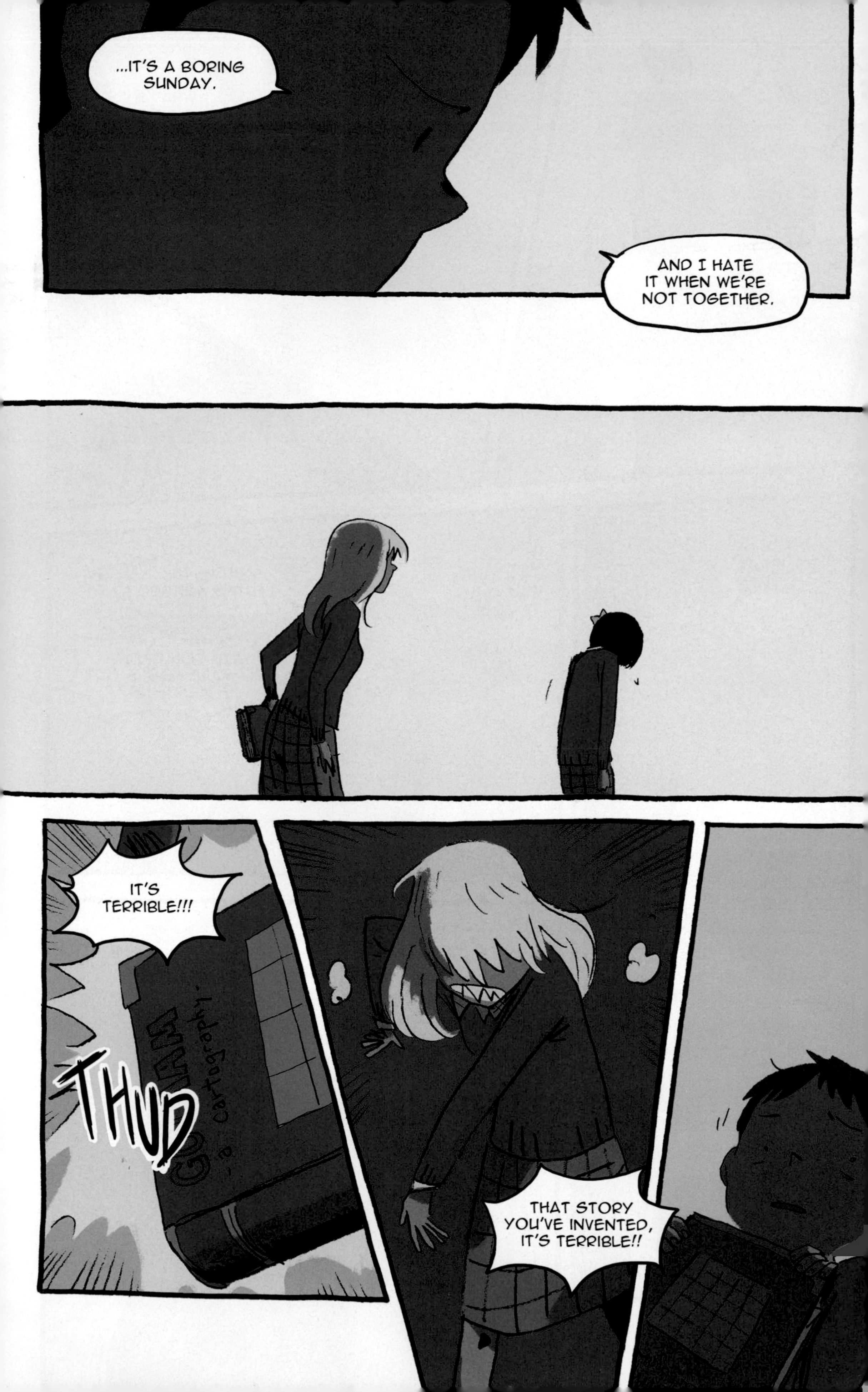
...IT'S A BORING SUNDAY.
AND I HATE IT WHEN WE'RE NOT TOGETHER.
IT'S TERRIBLE!!!
THUD
-a cartography
THAT STORY YOU'VE INVENTED, IT'S TERRIBLE!!

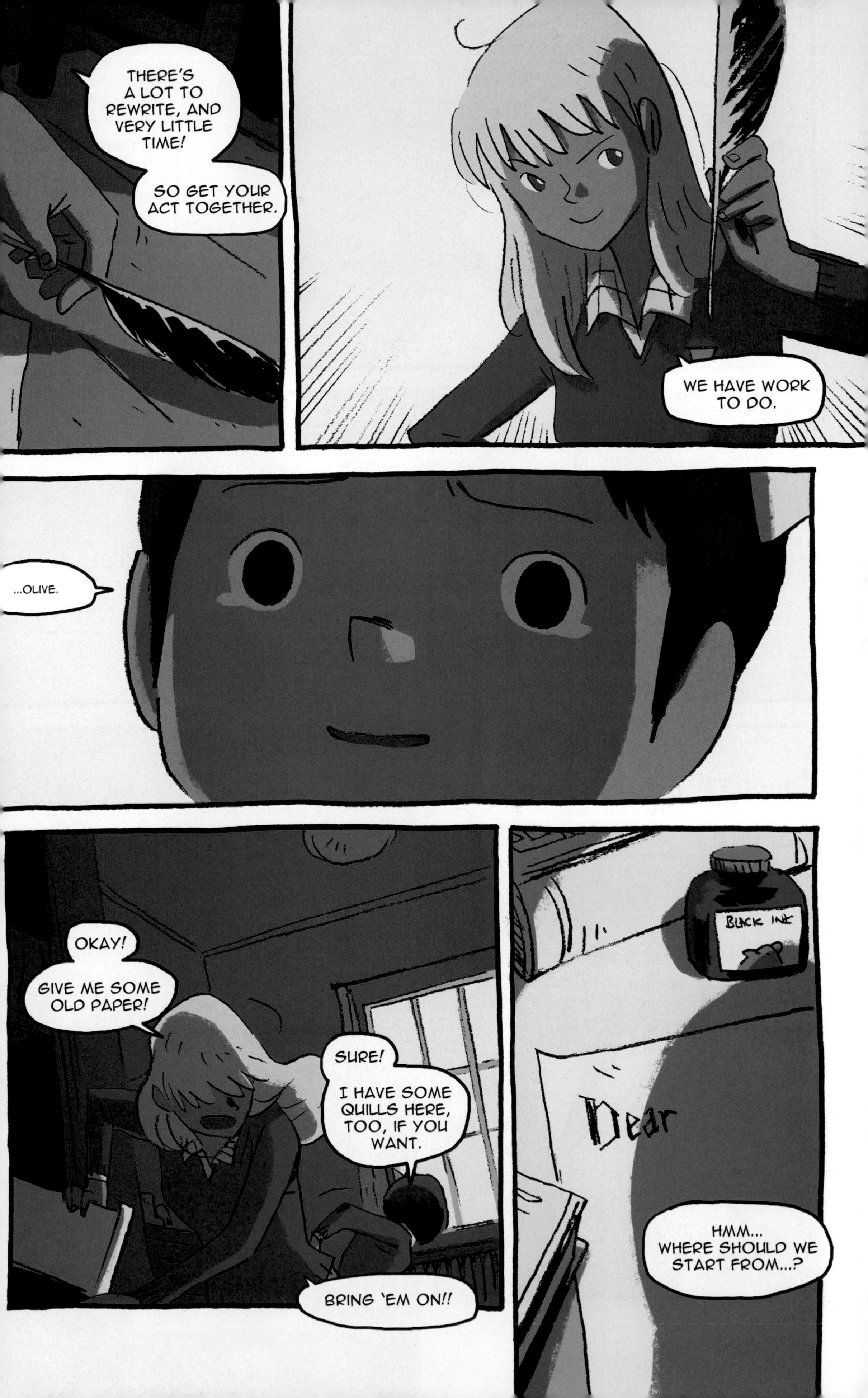
THERE'S A LOT TO REWRITE, AND VERY LITTLE TIME!
SO GET YOUR ACT TOGETHER.
WE HAVE WORK TO DO.
...OLIVE.
OKAY!
GIVE ME SOME OLD PAPER!
SURE!
I HAVE SOME QUILLS HERE, TOO, IF YOU WANT.
BRING 'EM ON!!
BLACK INK
Dear
HMM... WHERE SHOULD WE START FROM...?

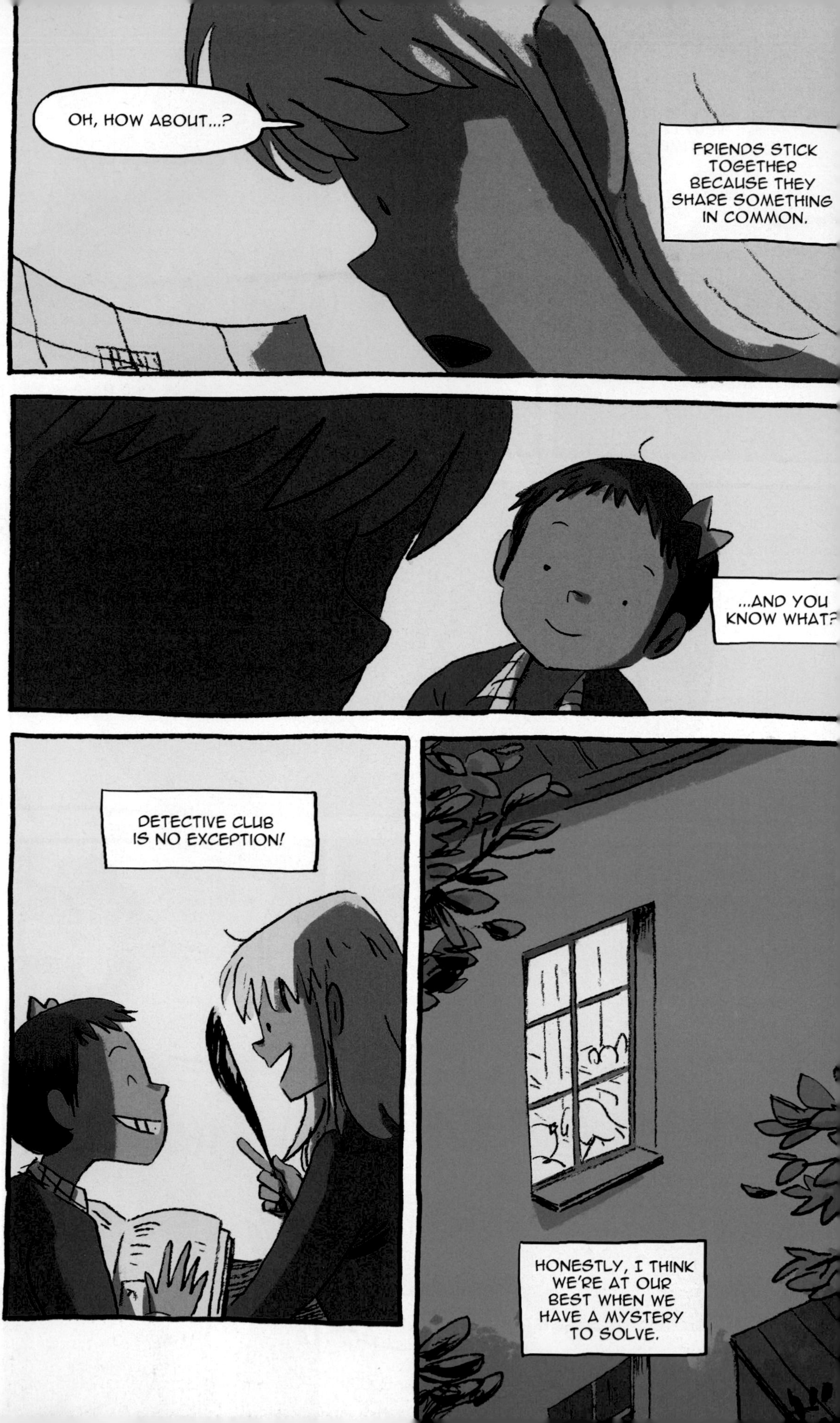

OH, HOW ABOUT...?
FRIENDS STICK TOGETHER BECAUSE THEY SHARE SOMETHING IN COMMON.
...AND YOU KNOW WHAT?
DETECTIVE CLUB IS NO EXCEPTION!
HONESTLY, I THINK WE'RE AT OUR BEST WHEN WE HAVE A MYSTERY TO SOLVE.

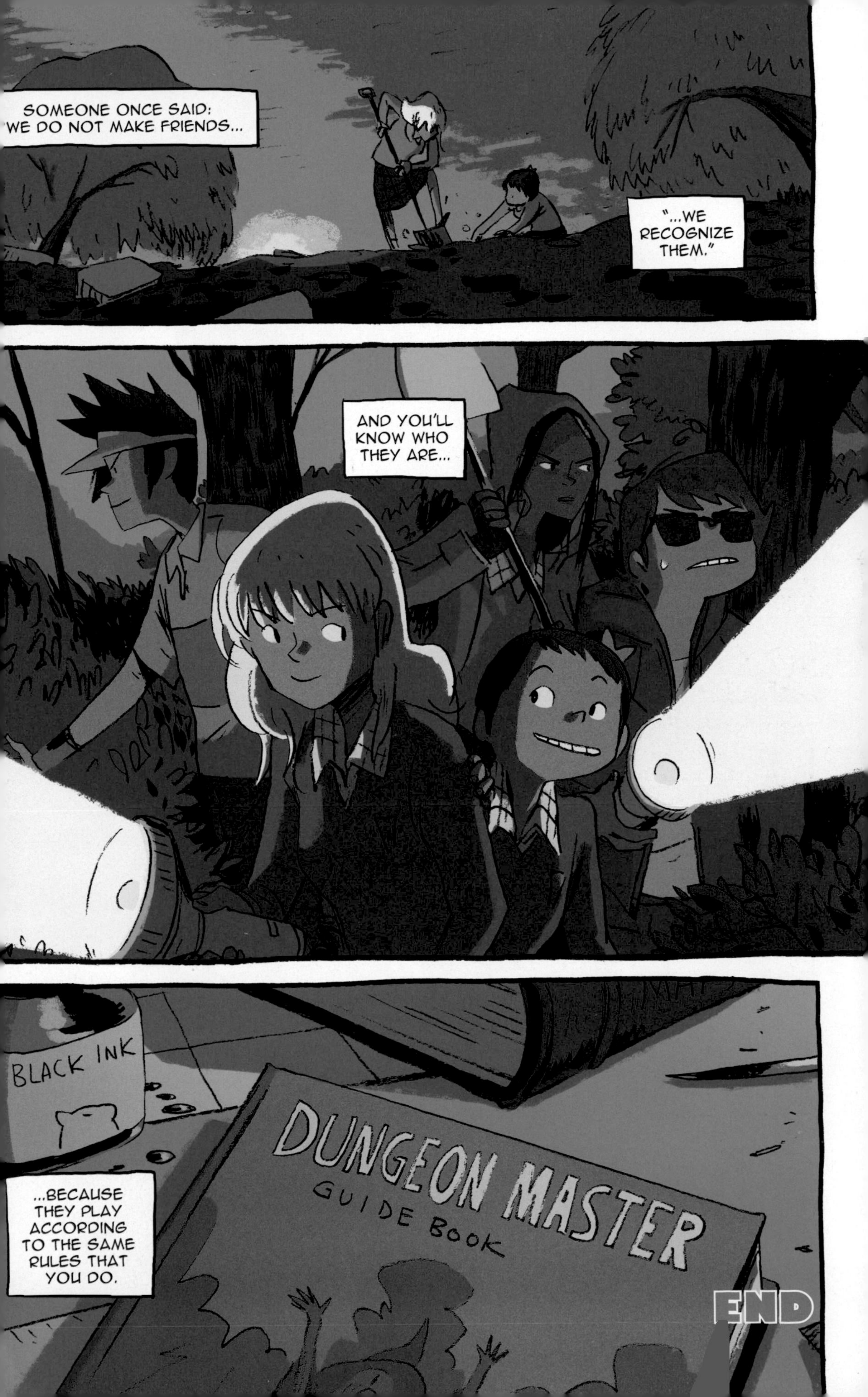
SOMEONE ONCE SAID: WE DO NOT MAKE FRIENDS...
"...WE RECOGNIZE THEM."
AND YOU'LL KNOW WHO THEY ARE...
BLACK INK
DUNGEON MASTER
GUIDE BOOK
...BECAUSE THEY PLAY ACCORDING TO THE SAME RULES THAT YOU DO.
END

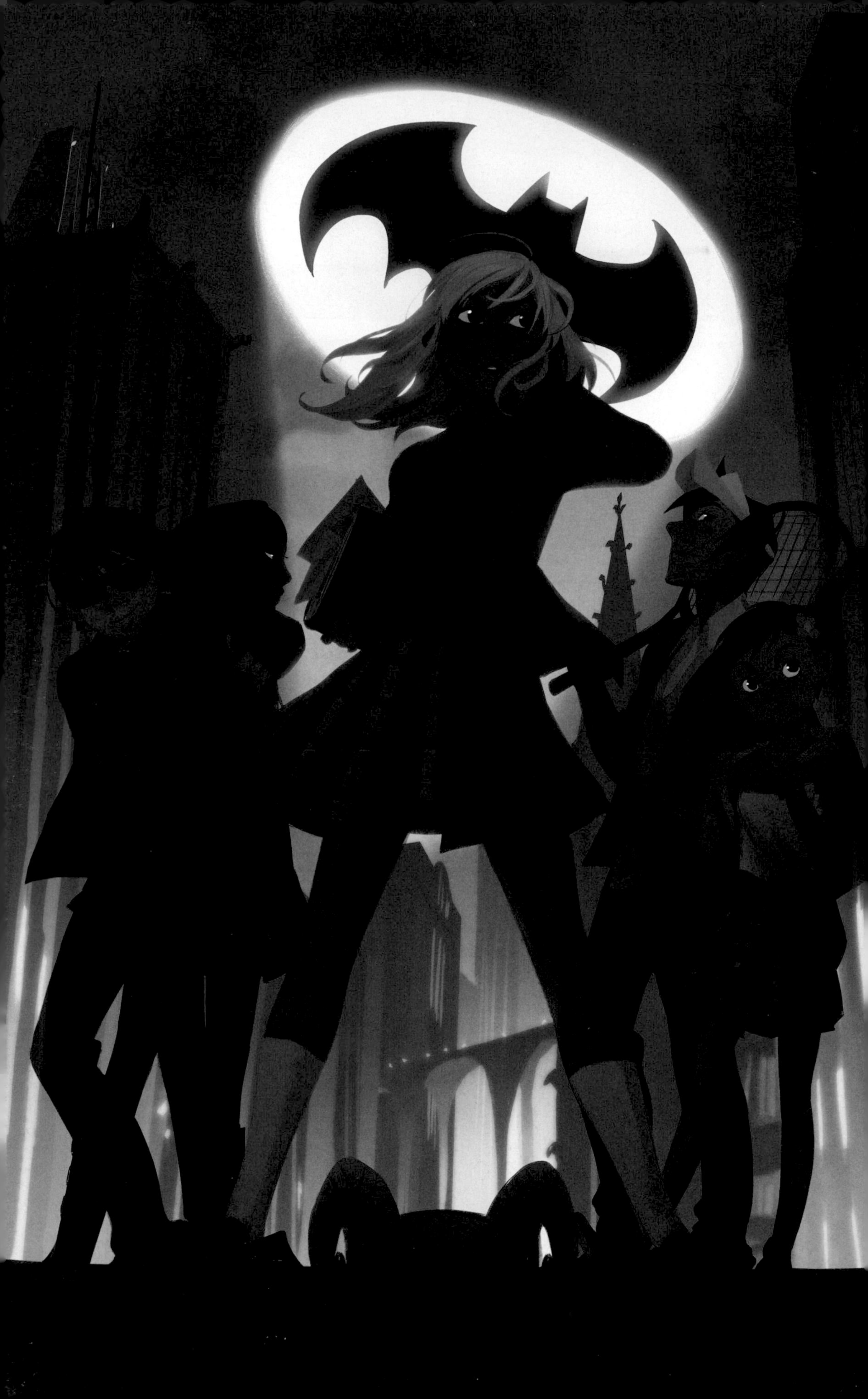

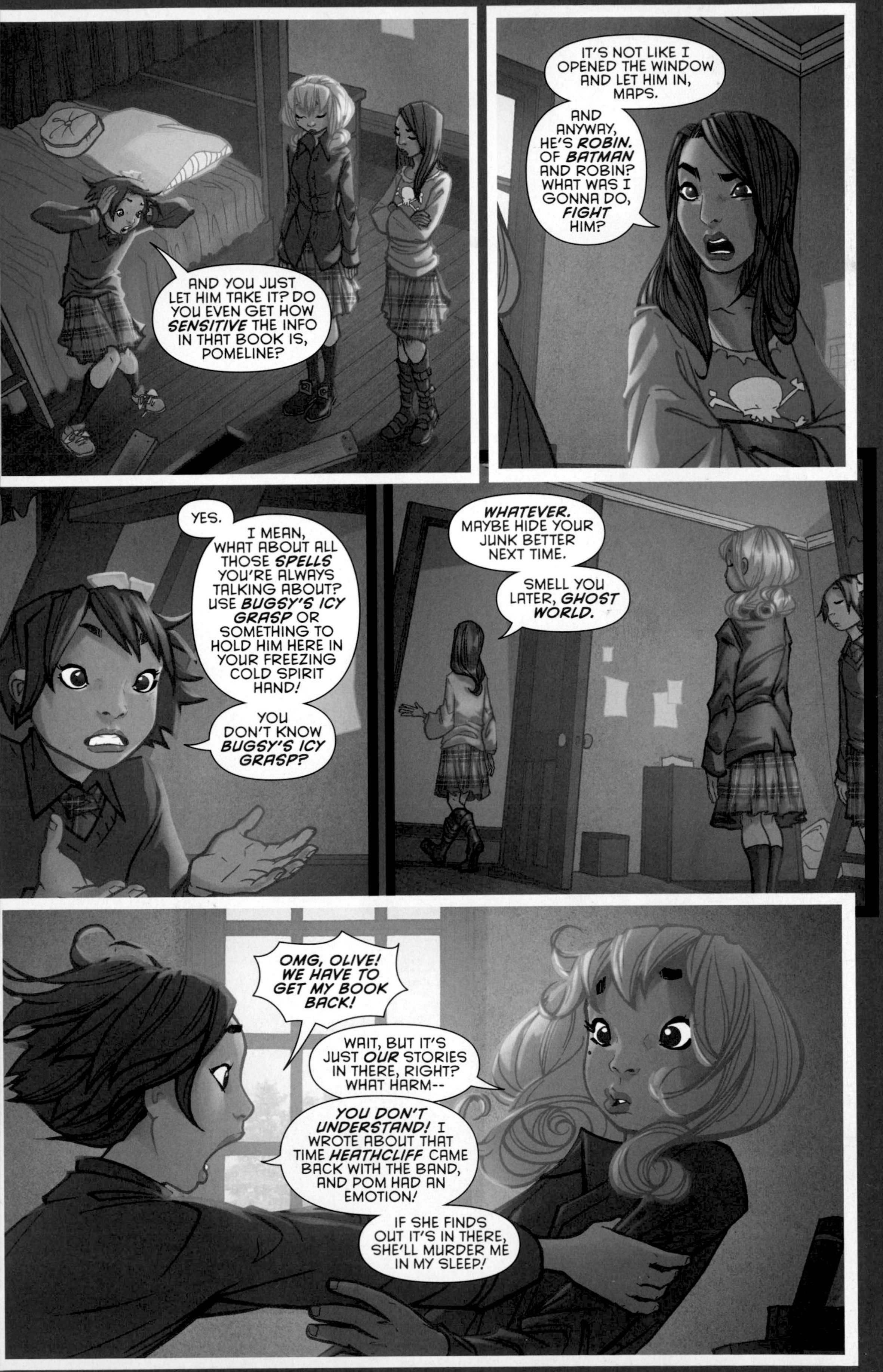
AND YOU JUST LET HIM TAKE IT? DO YOU EVEN GET HOW SENSITIVE THE INFO IN THAT BOOK IS, POMELINE?
IT'S NOT LIKE I OPENED THE WINDOW AND LET HIM IN, MAPS.
AND ANYWAY, HE'S ROBIN. OF BATMAN AND ROBIN? WHAT WAS I GONNA DO, FIGHT HIM?
YES.
I MEAN, WHAT ABOUT ALL THOSE SPELLS YOU'RE ALWAYS TALKING ABOUT? USE BUGSY'S ICY GRASP OR SOMETHING TO HOLD HIM HERE IN YOUR FREEZING COLD SPIRIT HAND!
YOU DON'T KNOW BUGSY'S ICY GRASP?
WHATEVER. MAYBE HIDE YOUR JUNK BETTER NEXT TIME.
SMELL YOU LATER, GHOST WORLD.
OMG, OLIVE! WE HAVE TO GET MY BOOK BACK!
WAIT, BUT IT'S JUST OUR STORIES IN THERE, RIGHT? WHAT HARM--
YOU DON'T UNDERSTAND! I WROTE ABOUT THAT TIME HEATHCLIFF CAME BACK WITH THE BAND, AND POM HAD AN EMOTION!
IF SHE FINDS OUT IT'S IN THERE, SHE'LL MURDER ME IN MY SLEEP!

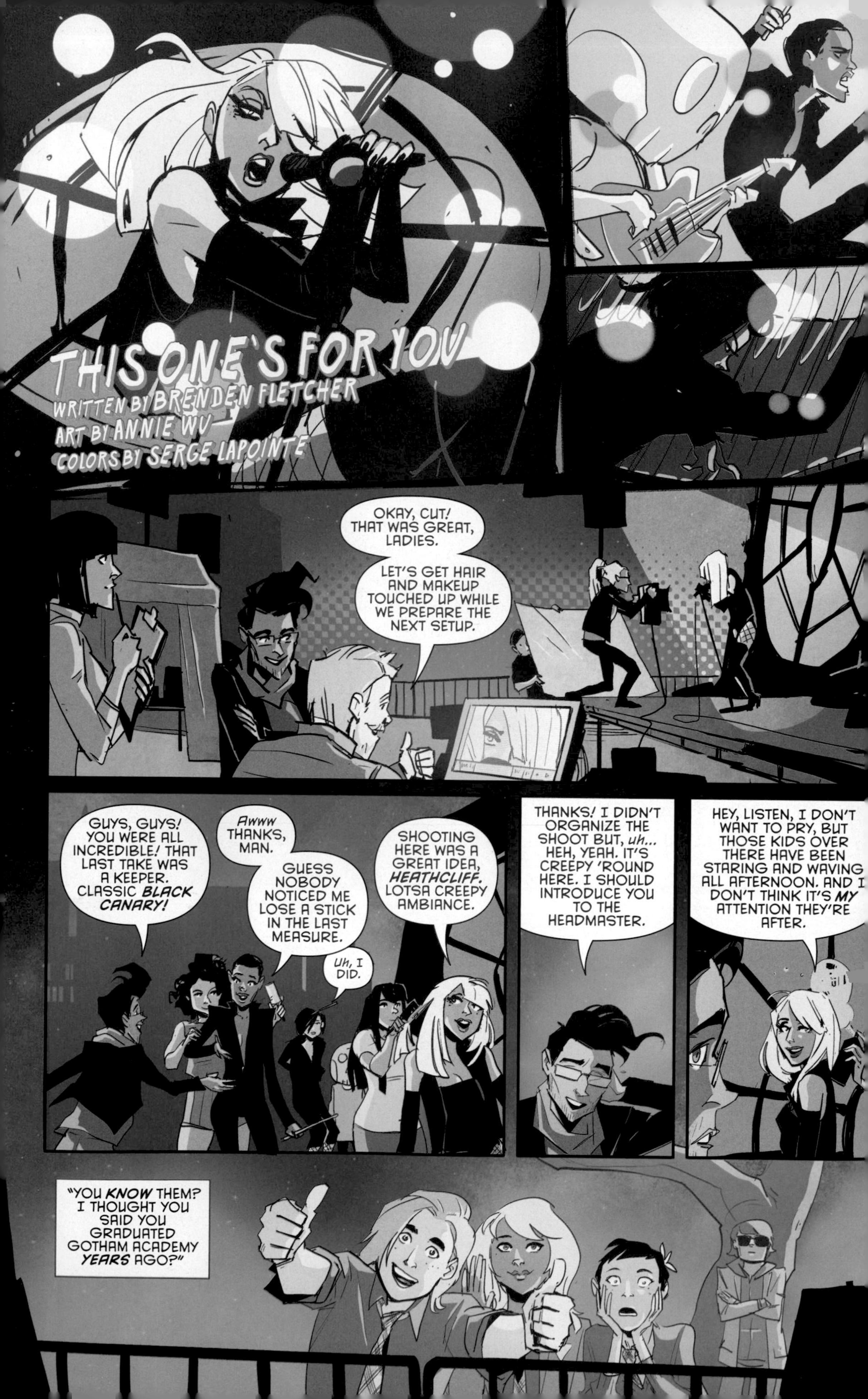
THIS ONE'S FOR YOU
WRITTEN BY BRENDEN FLETCHER
ART BY ANNIE WU
COLORS BY SERGE LAPOINTE
OKAY, CUT! THAT WAS GREAT, LADIES.
LET'S GET HAIR AND MAKEUP TOUCHED UP WHILE WE PREPARE THE NEXT SETUP.
GUYS, GUYS! YOU WERE ALL INCREDIBLE! THAT LAST TAKE WAS A KEEPER. CLASSIC BLACK CANARY!
Awww THANKS, MAN.
GUESS NOBODY NOTICED ME LOSE A STICK IN THE LAST MEASURE.
Uh, I DID.
SHOOTING HERE WAS A GREAT IDEA, HEATHCLIFF. LOTSA CREEPY AMBIANCE.
THANKS! I DIDN'T ORGANIZE THE SHOOT BUT, uh... HEH, YEAH. IT'S CREEPY 'ROUND HERE. I SHOULD INTRODUCE YOU TO THE HEADMASTER.
HEY, LISTEN, I DON'T WANT TO PRY, BUT THOSE KIDS OVER THERE HAVE BEEN STARING AND WAVING ALL AFTERNOON. AND I DON'T THINK IT'S MY ATTENTION THEY'RE AFTER.
"YOU KNOW THEM? I THOUGHT YOU SAID YOU GRADUATED GOTHAM ACADEMY YEARS AGO?"

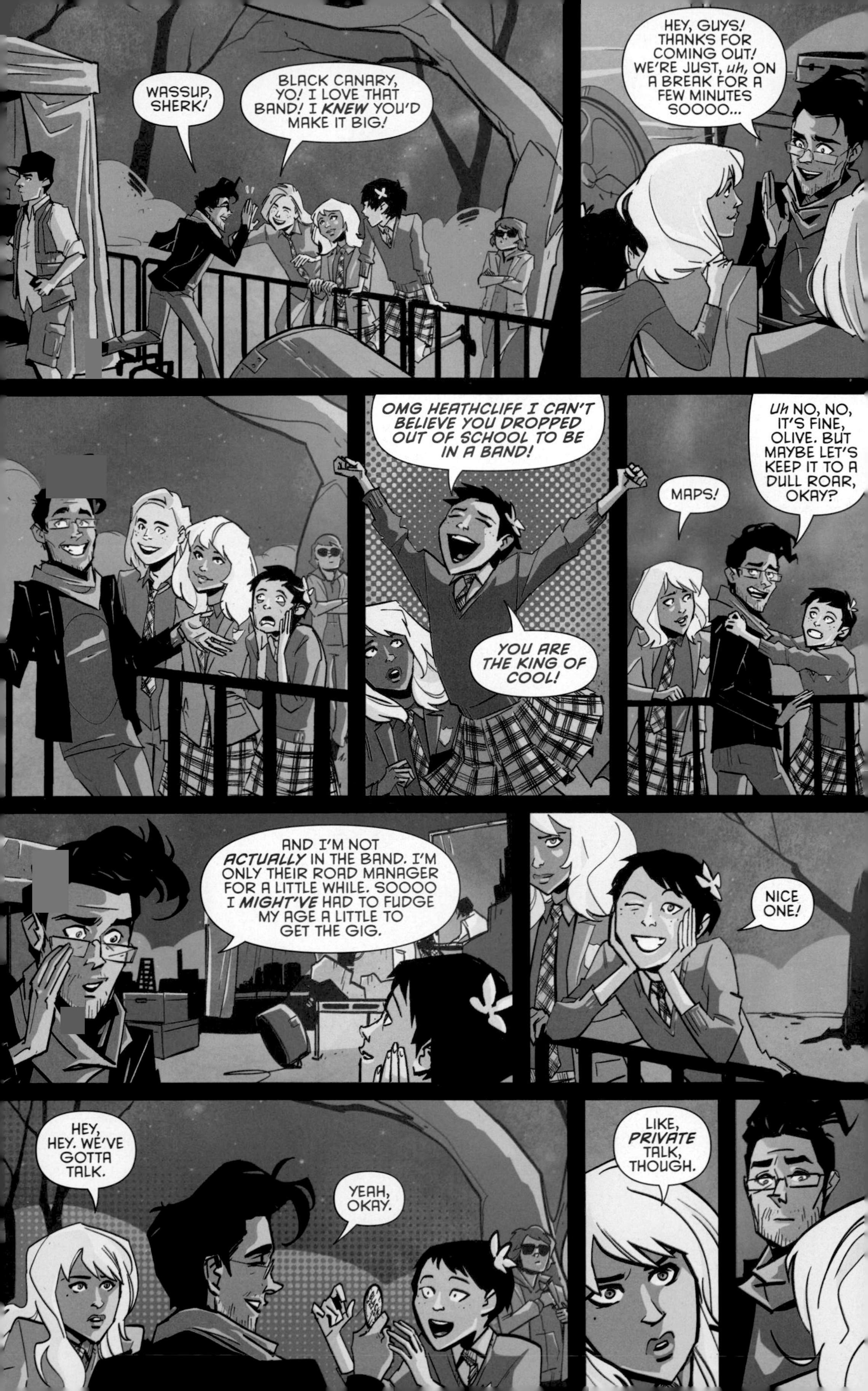
WASSUP, SHERK!
BLACK CANARY, YO! I LOVE THAT BAND! I *KNEW* YOU'D MAKE IT BIG!
HEY, GUYS! THANKS FOR COMING OUT! WE'RE JUST, *uh*, ON A BREAK FOR A FEW MINUTES SOOOO...
OMG HEATHCLIFF I CAN'T BELIEVE YOU DROPPED OUT OF SCHOOL TO BE IN A BAND!
YOU ARE THE KING OF COOL!
MAPS!
Uh NO, NO, IT'S FINE, OLIVE. BUT MAYBE LET'S KEEP IT TO A DULL ROAR, OKAY?
AND I'M NOT *ACTUALLY* IN THE BAND. I'M ONLY THEIR ROAD MANAGER FOR A LITTLE WHILE. SOOOO I *MIGHT'VE* HAD TO FUDGE MY AGE A LITTLE TO GET THE GIG.
NICE ONE!
HEY, HEY. WE'VE GOTTA TALK.
YEAH, OKAY.
LIKE, *PRIVATE* TALK, THOUGH.

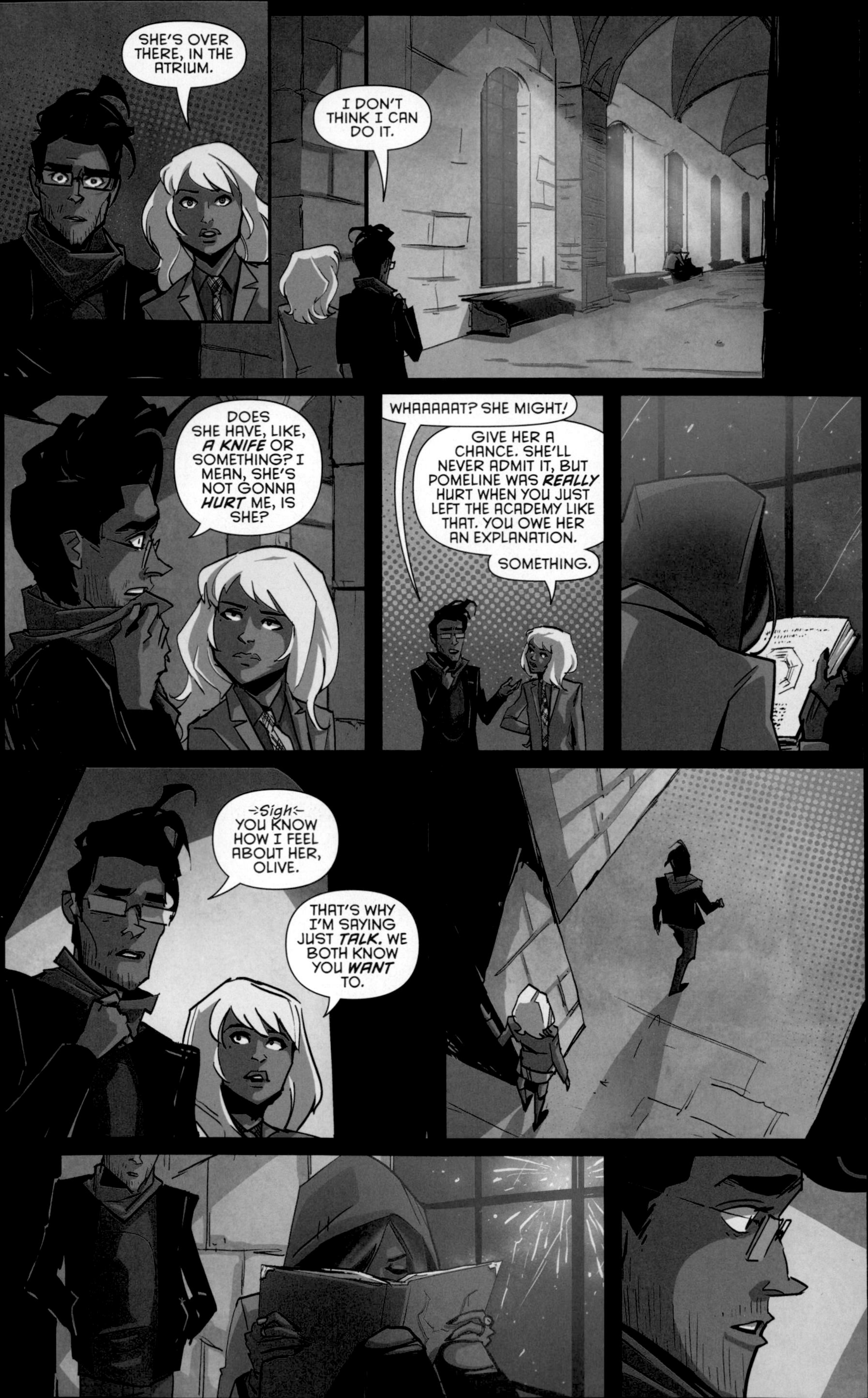
SHE'S OVER THERE, IN THE ATRIUM.
I DON'T THINK I CAN DO IT.
DOES SHE HAVE, LIKE, A KNIFE OR SOMETHING? I MEAN, SHE'S NOT GONNA HURT ME, IS SHE?
WHAAAAAT? SHE MIGHT!
GIVE HER A CHANCE. SHE'LL NEVER ADMIT IT, BUT POMELINE WAS REALLY HURT WHEN YOU JUST LEFT THE ACADEMY LIKE THAT. YOU OWE HER AN EXPLANATION.
SOMETHING.
Sigh
YOU KNOW HOW I FEEL ABOUT HER, OLIVE.
THAT'S WHY I'M SAYING JUST TALK. WE BOTH KNOW YOU WANT TO.

GUESS WHO'S BACK?

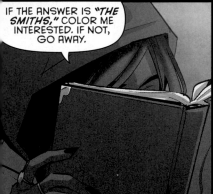

IF THE ANSWER IS *"THE SMITHS,"* COLOR ME INTERESTED. IF NOT, GO AWAY.

I'M... I'M SORRY, POM. SORRY I BOTHERED YOU. AND FOR ALL THE OTHER STUFF.

I WATCHED THAT CLIP WHERE BLACK CANARY GOT IN A FIGHT AND YOU HAD TO TAKE OVER A *PRESS CONFERENCE.*

THAT WAS PRETTY WILD.

YEAH. IT *WAS.* I NEARLY TOOK A MICROPHONE TO THE FACE.

WHAT'S THE BOOK?

OH.

HEY...

CULTS. SECRET SOCIETIES. NO BIG DEAL.

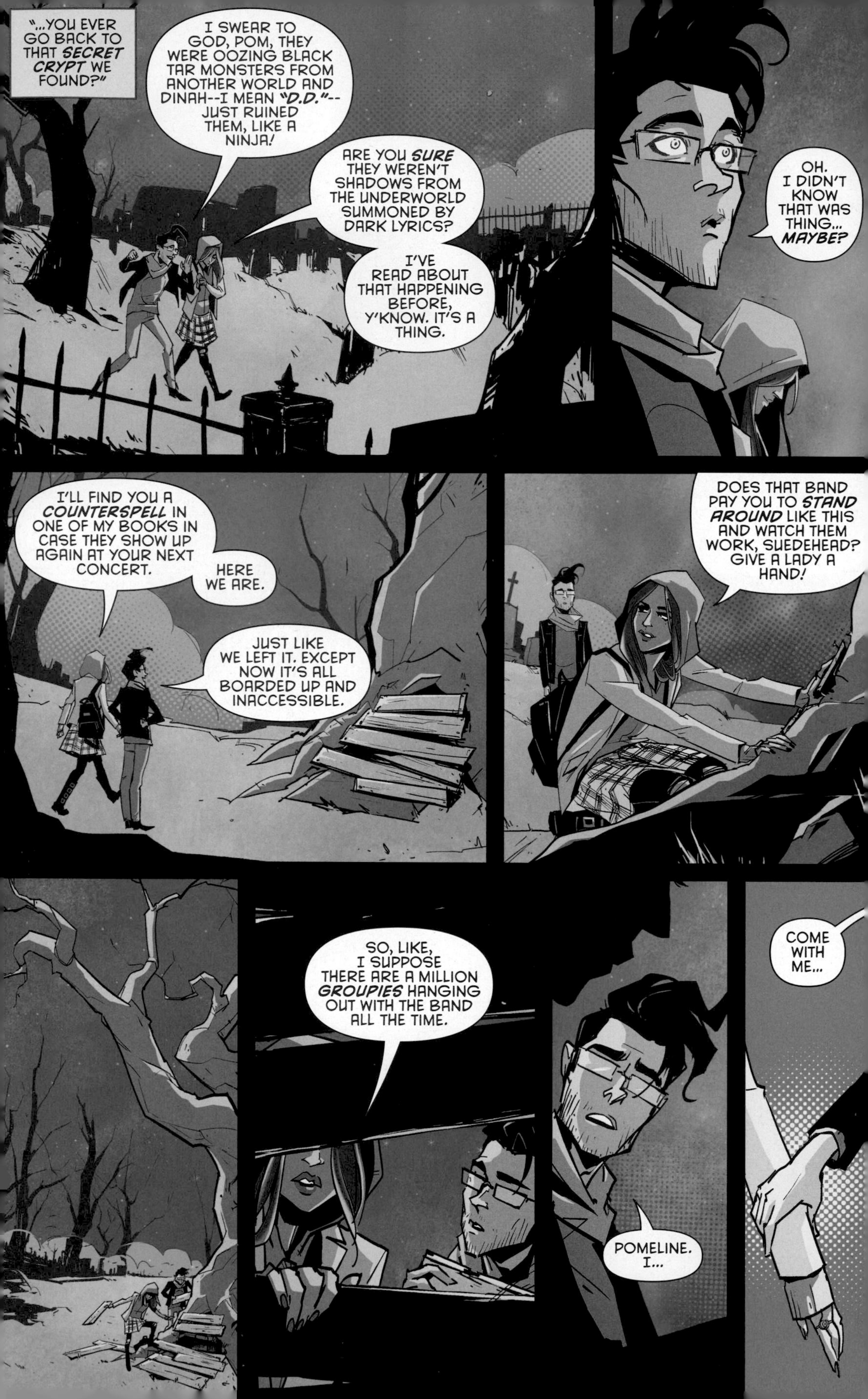
"...YOU EVER GO BACK TO THAT SECRET CRYPT WE FOUND?"
I SWEAR TO GOD, POM, THEY WERE OOZING BLACK TAR MONSTERS FROM ANOTHER WORLD AND DINAH--I MEAN "D.D."--JUST RUINED THEM, LIKE A NINJA!
ARE YOU SURE THEY WEREN'T SHADOWS FROM THE UNDERWORLD SUMMONED BY DARK LYRICS?
I'VE READ ABOUT THAT HAPPENING BEFORE, Y'KNOW. IT'S A THING.
OH. I DIDN'T KNOW THAT WAS THING... MAYBE?
I'LL FIND YOU A COUNTERSPELL IN ONE OF MY BOOKS IN CASE THEY SHOW UP AGAIN AT YOUR NEXT CONCERT.
HERE WE ARE.
JUST LIKE WE LEFT IT. EXCEPT NOW IT'S ALL BOARDED UP AND INACCESSIBLE.
DOES THAT BAND PAY YOU TO STAND AROUND LIKE THIS AND WATCH THEM WORK, SUEDEHEAD? GIVE A LADY A HAND!
SO, LIKE, I SUPPOSE THERE ARE A MILLION GROUPIES HANGING OUT WITH THE BAND ALL THE TIME.
POMELINE. I...
COME WITH ME...

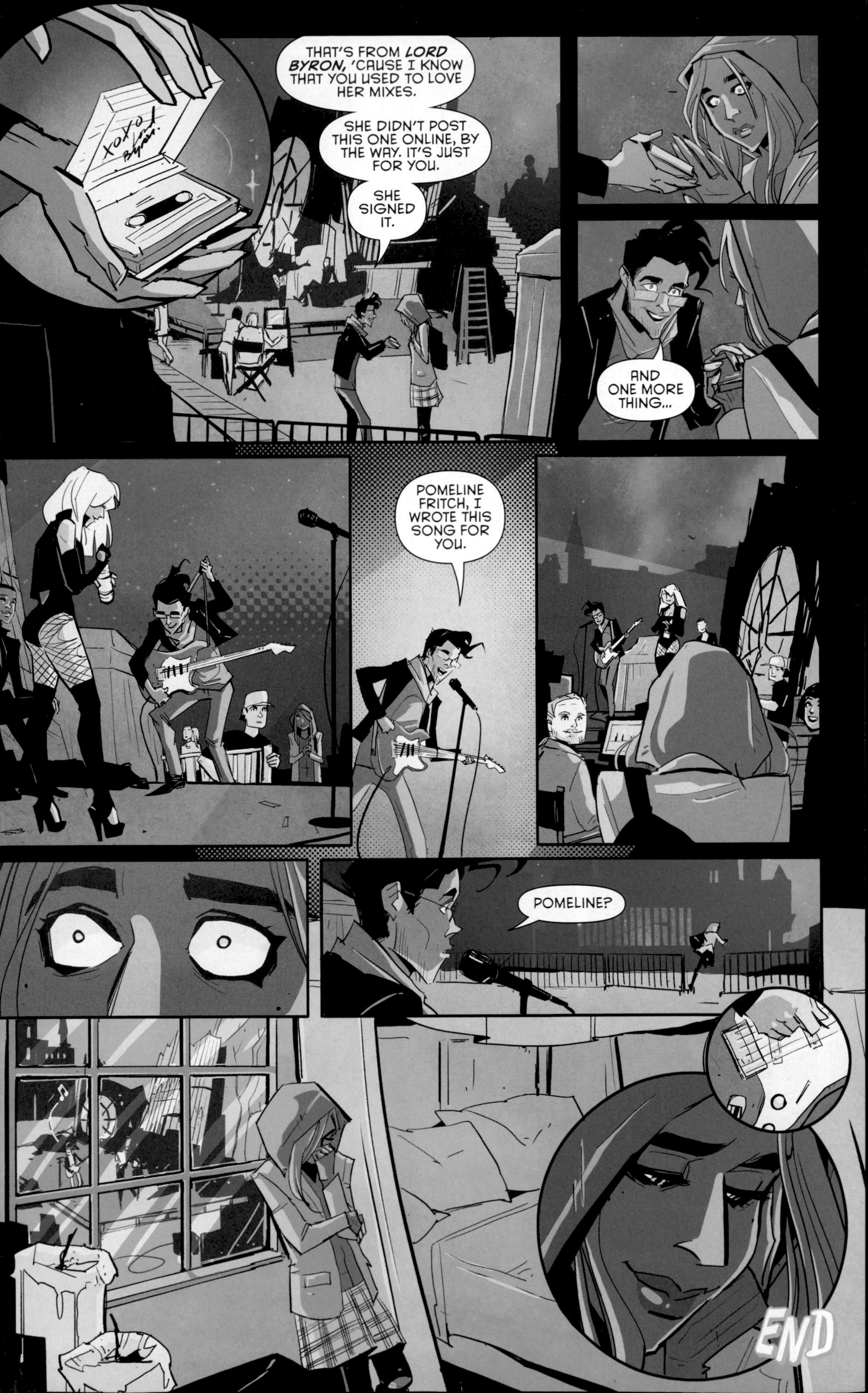
XOXO Lord Byron.
THAT'S FROM LORD BYRON, 'CAUSE I KNOW THAT YOU USED TO LOVE HER MIXES.
SHE DIDN'T POST THIS ONE ONLINE, BY THE WAY. IT'S JUST FOR YOU.
SHE SIGNED IT.
AND ONE MORE THING...
POMELINE FRITCH, I WROTE THIS SONG FOR YOU.
POMELINE?
END

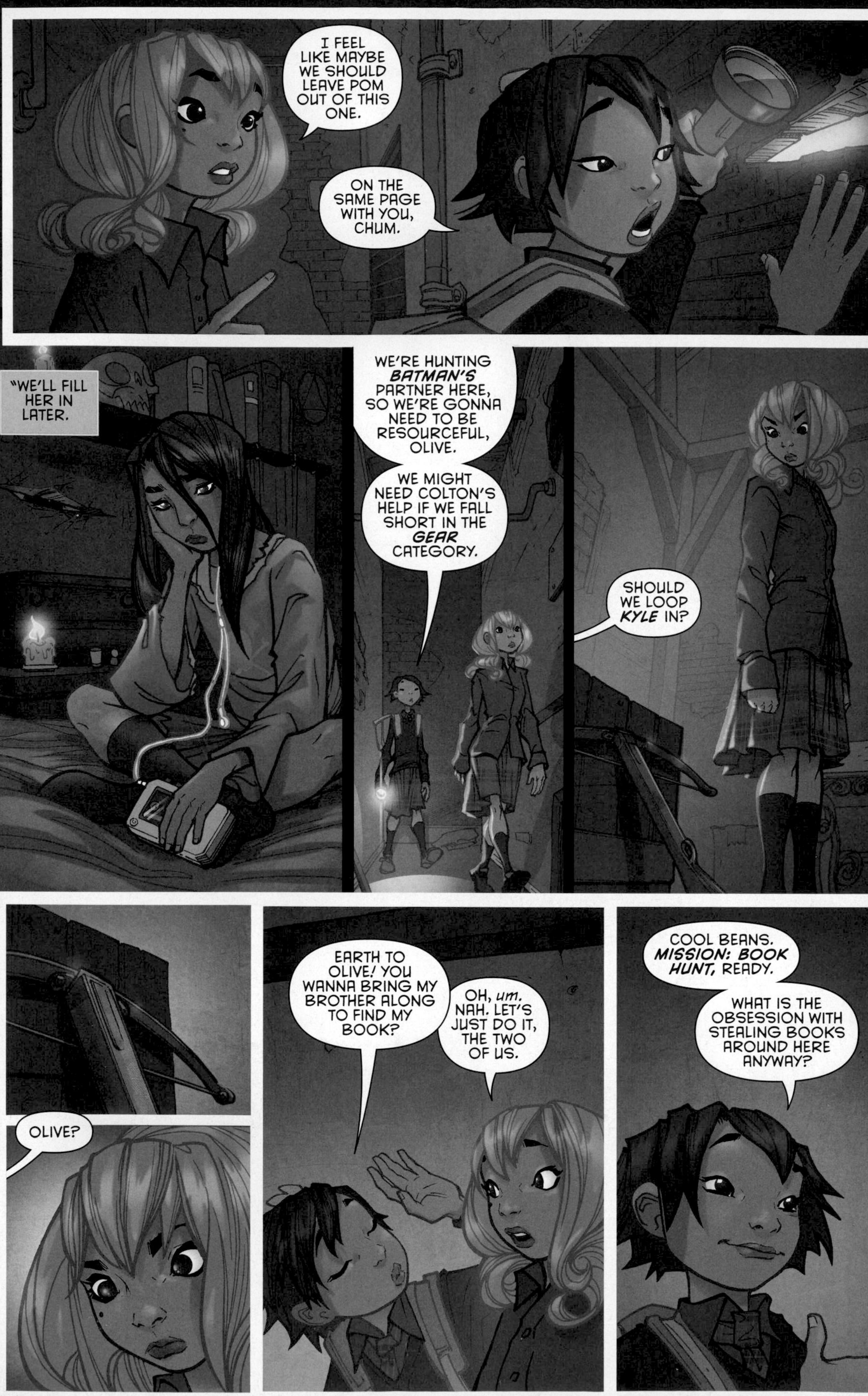
I FEEL LIKE MAYBE WE SHOULD LEAVE POM OUT OF THIS ONE.
ON THE SAME PAGE WITH YOU, CHUM.
"WE'LL FILL HER IN LATER.
WE'RE HUNTING BATMAN'S PARTNER HERE, SO WE'RE GONNA NEED TO BE RESOURCEFUL, OLIVE.
WE MIGHT NEED COLTON'S HELP IF WE FALL SHORT IN THE GEAR CATEGORY.
SHOULD WE LOOP KYLE IN?
OLIVE?
EARTH TO OLIVE! YOU WANNA BRING MY BROTHER ALONG TO FIND MY BOOK?
OH, um. NAH. LET'S JUST DO IT, THE TWO OF US.
COOL BEANS. MISSION: BOOK HUNT, READY.
WHAT IS THE OBSESSION WITH STEALING BOOKS AROUND HERE ANYWAY?

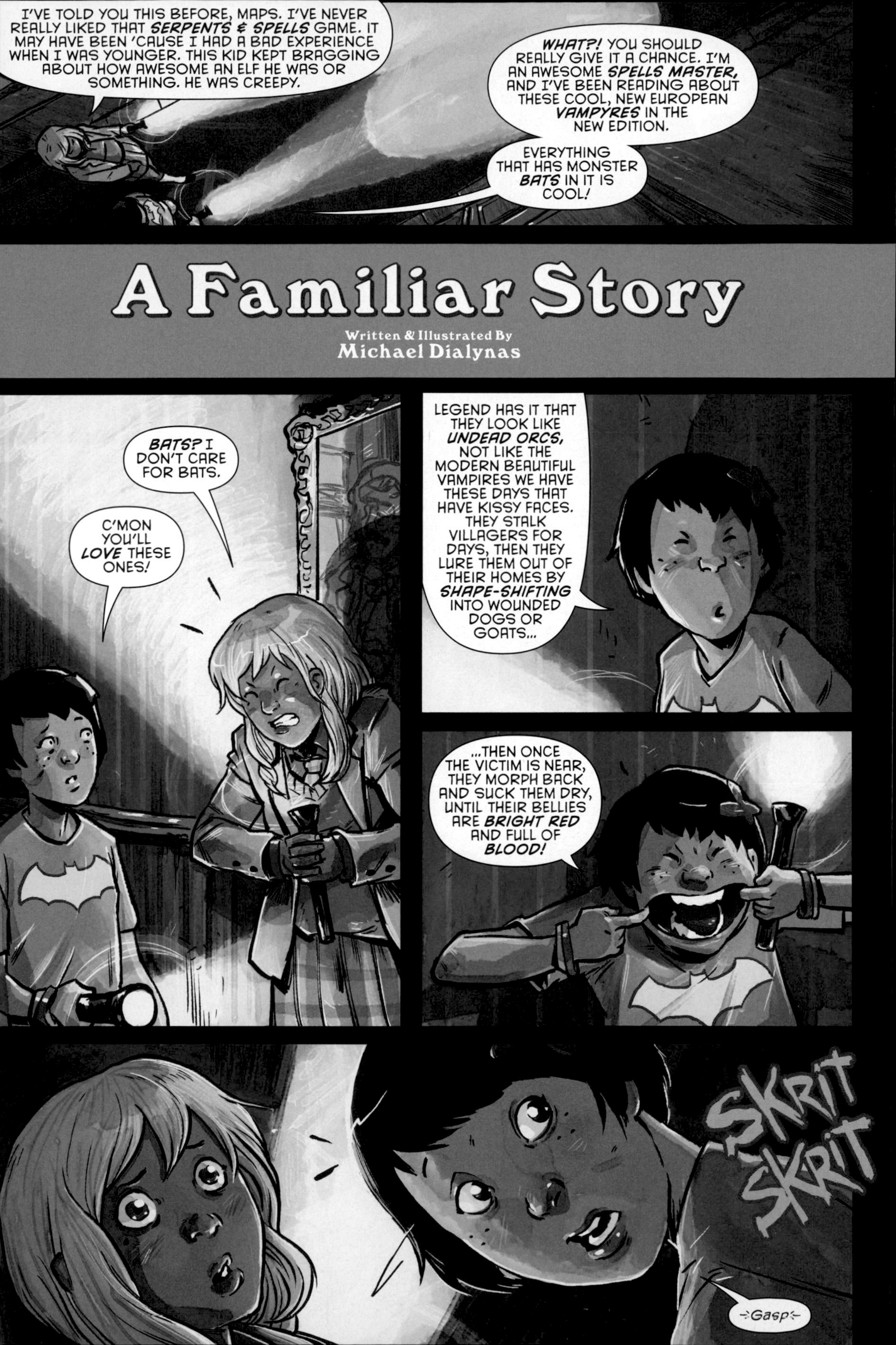
I'VE TOLD YOU THIS BEFORE, MAPS. I'VE NEVER REALLY LIKED THAT SERPENTS & SPELLS GAME. IT MAY HAVE BEEN 'CAUSE I HAD A BAD EXPERIENCE WHEN I WAS YOUNGER. THIS KID KEPT BRAGGING ABOUT HOW AWESOME AN ELF HE WAS OR SOMETHING. HE WAS CREEPY.
WHAT?! YOU SHOULD REALLY GIVE IT A CHANCE. I'M AN AWESOME SPELLS MASTER, AND I'VE BEEN READING ABOUT THESE COOL, NEW EUROPEAN VAMPYRES IN THE NEW EDITION.
EVERYTHING THAT HAS MONSTER BATS IN IT IS COOL!
A Familiar Story
Written & Illustrated By
Michael Dialynas
BATS? I DON'T CARE FOR BATS.
C'MON YOU'LL LOVE THESE ONES!
LEGEND HAS IT THAT THEY LOOK LIKE UNDEAD ORCS, NOT LIKE THE MODERN BEAUTIFUL VAMPIRES WE HAVE THESE DAYS THAT HAVE KISSY FACES. THEY STALK VILLAGERS FOR DAYS, THEN THEY LURE THEM OUT OF THEIR HOMES BY SHAPE-SHIFTING INTO WOUNDED DOGS OR GOATS...
...THEN ONCE THE VICTIM IS NEAR, THEY MORPH BACK AND SUCK THEM DRY, UNTIL THEIR BELLIES ARE BRIGHT RED AND FULL OF BLOOD!
SKRIT SKRIT
Gasp

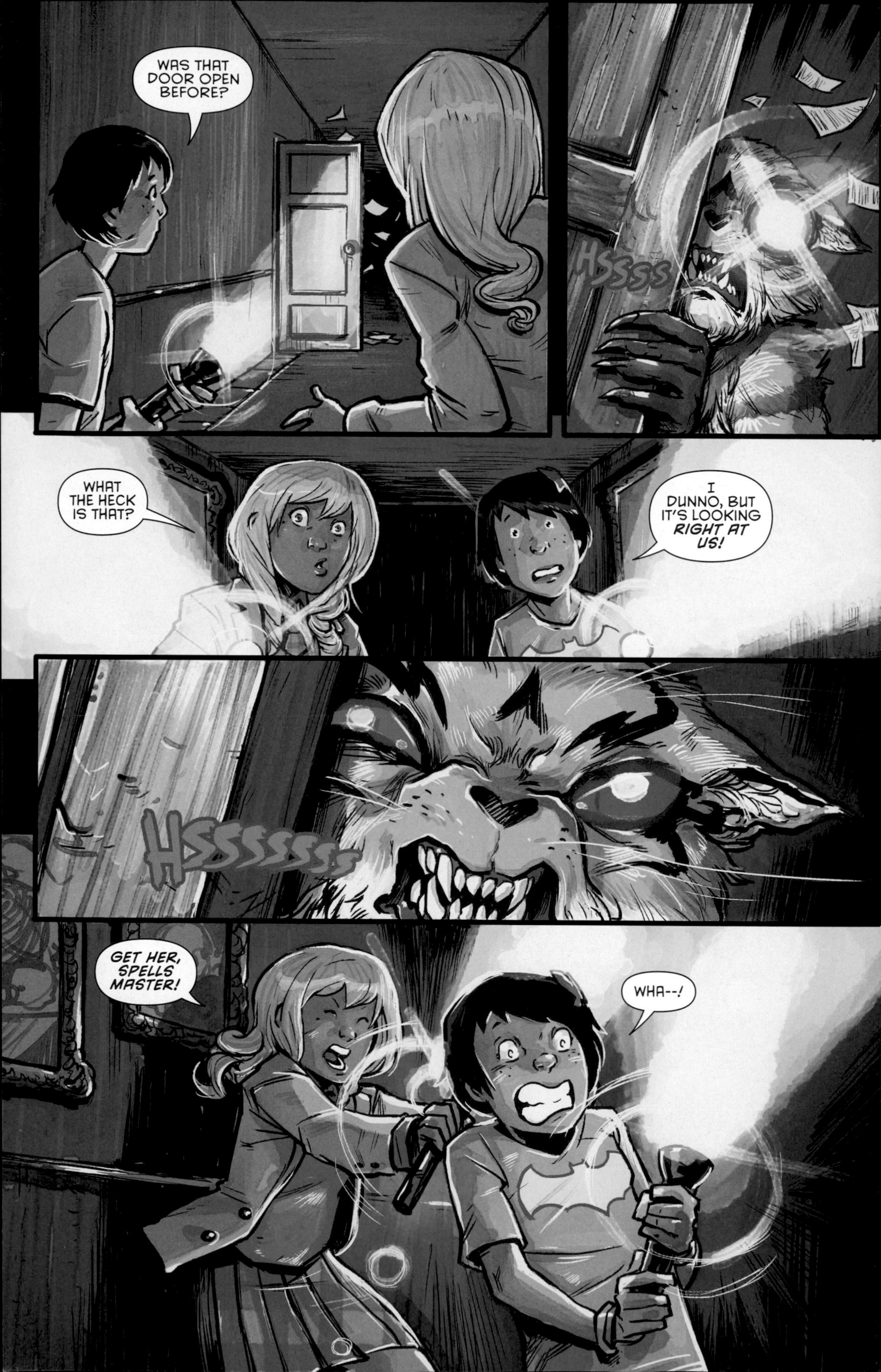
WAS THAT DOOR OPEN BEFORE?
HSSSS
WHAT THE HECK IS THAT?
I DUNNO, BUT IT'S LOOKING *RIGHT AT US!*
HSSSSSSS
GET HER, SPELLS MASTER!
WHA--!

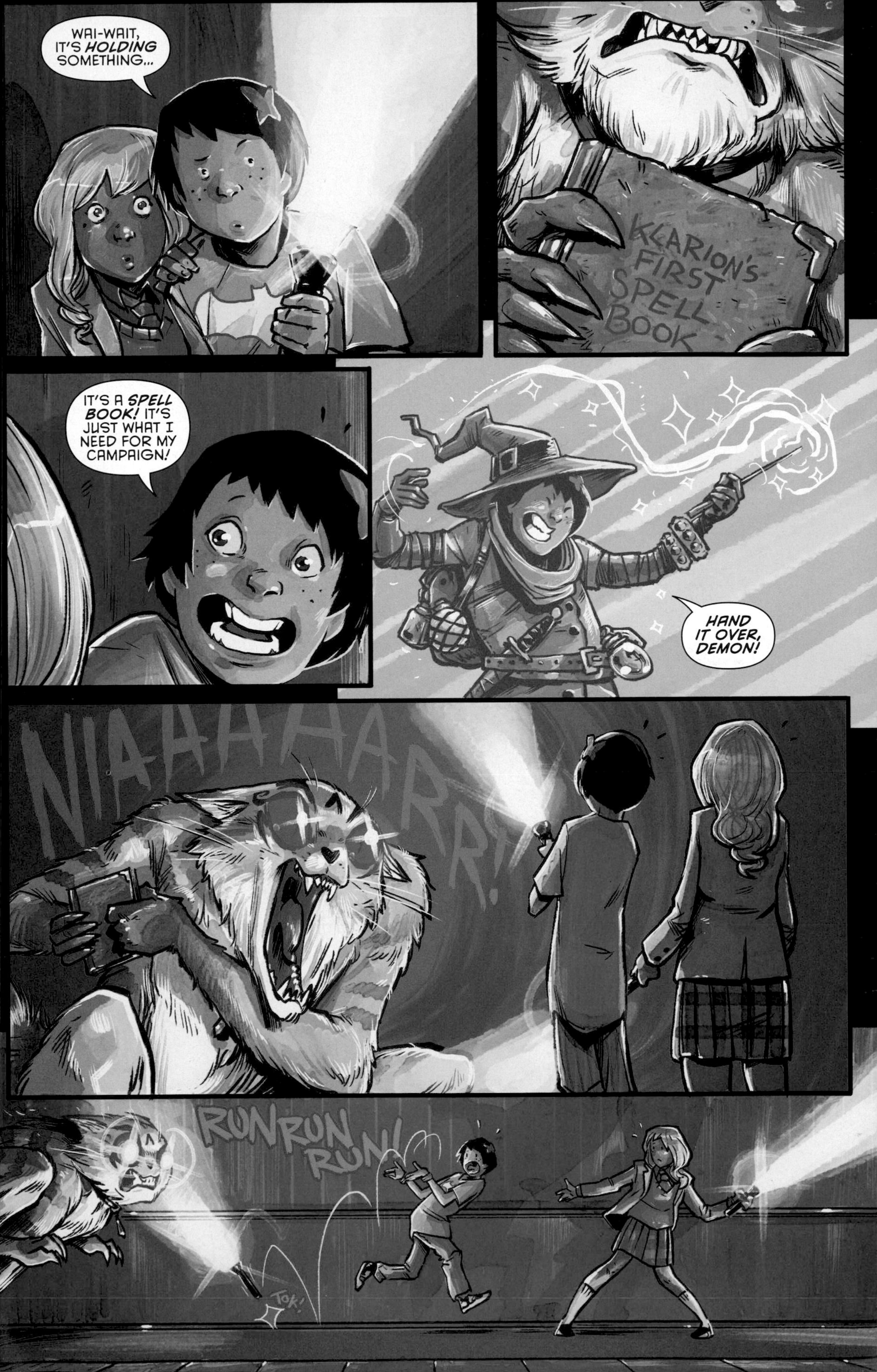
WAI-WAIT, IT'S HOLDING SOMETHING...
KLARION'S FIRST SPELL BOOK
IT'S A SPELL BOOK! IT'S JUST WHAT I NEED FOR MY CAMPAIGN!
HAND IT OVER, DEMON!
NIAAAHAARR!
RUNRUN RUN!
TOK!

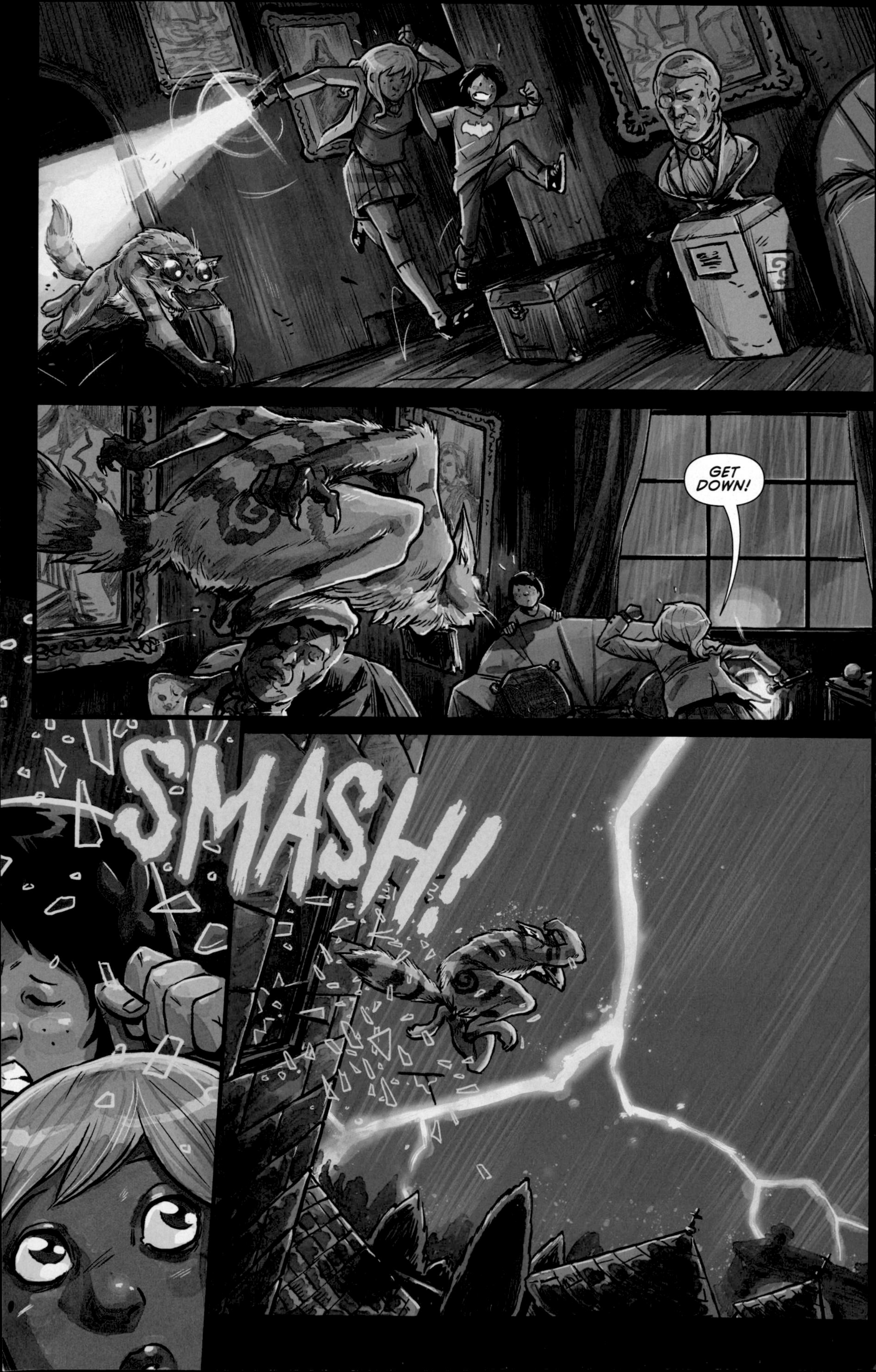
GET DOWN!
SMASH!

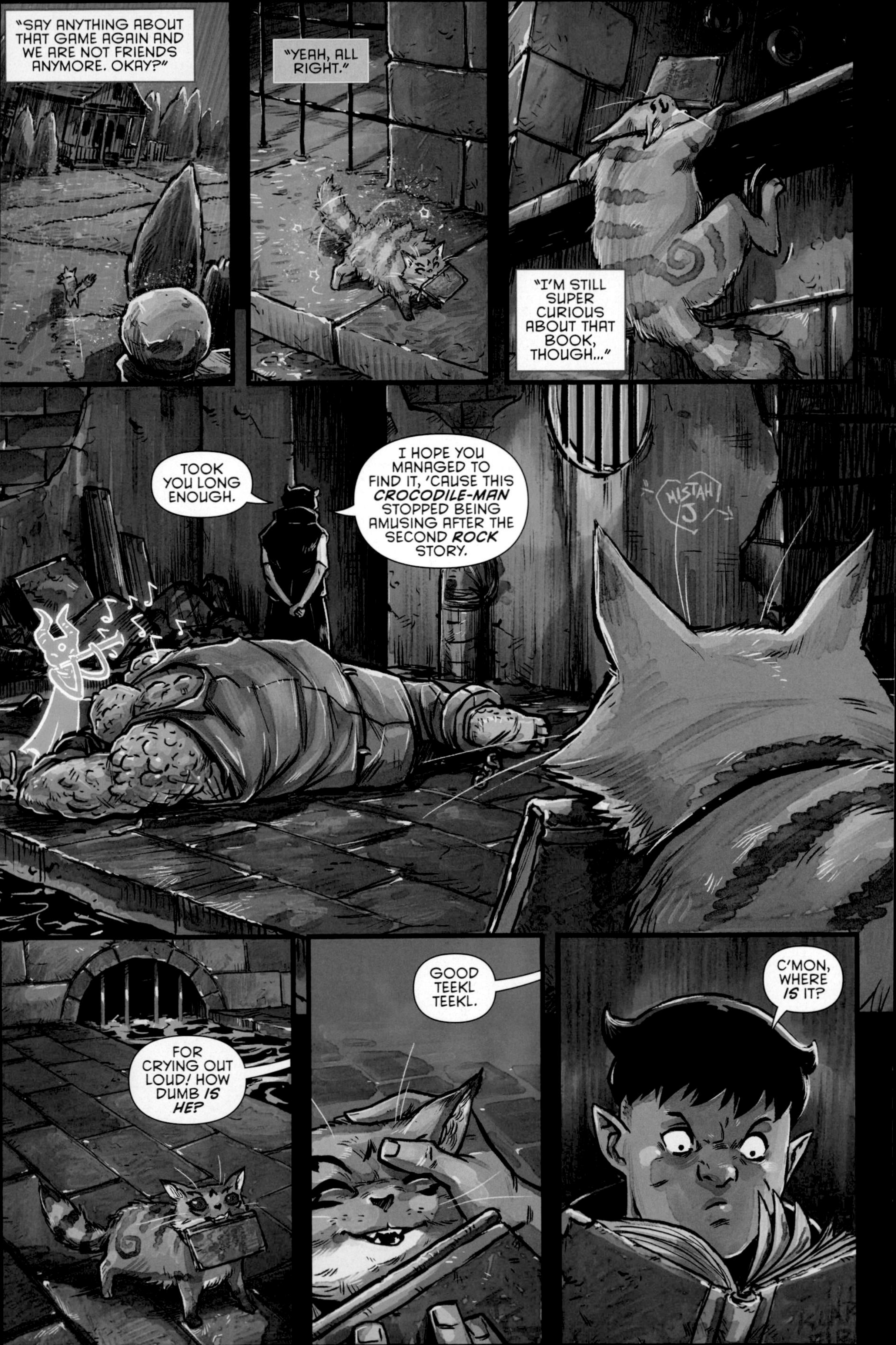
"SAY ANYTHING ABOUT THAT GAME AGAIN AND WE ARE NOT FRIENDS ANYMORE. OKAY?"
"YEAH, ALL RIGHT."
"I'M STILL SUPER CURIOUS ABOUT THAT BOOK, THOUGH..."
TOOK YOU LONG ENOUGH.
I HOPE YOU MANAGED TO FIND IT, 'CAUSE THIS CROCODILE-MAN STOPPED BEING AMUSING AFTER THE SECOND ROCK STORY.
MISTAH J
FOR CRYING OUT LOUD! HOW DUMB IS HE?
GOOD TEEKL TEEKL.
C'MON, WHERE IS IT?

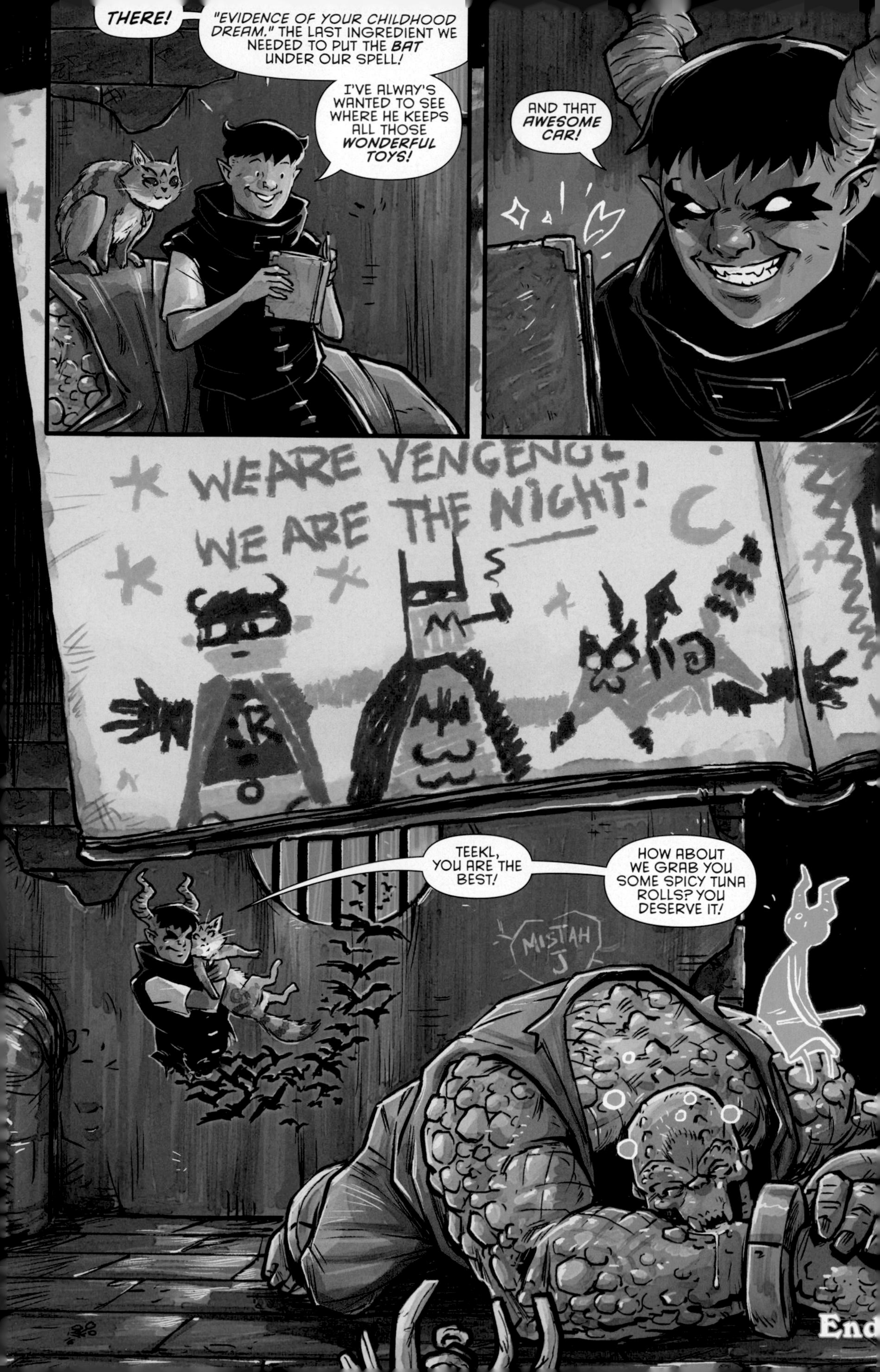
THERE!
"EVIDENCE OF YOUR CHILDHOOD DREAM." THE LAST INGREDIENT WE NEEDED TO PUT THE BAT UNDER OUR SPELL!
I'VE ALWAY'S WANTED TO SEE WHERE HE KEEPS ALL THOSE WONDERFUL TOYS!
AND THAT AWESOME CAR!
WEARE VENGEN
WE ARE THE NIGHT!
TEEKL, YOU ARE THE BEST!
HOW ABOUT WE GRAB YOU SOME SPICY TUNA ROLLS? YOU DESERVE IT!
MISTAH J
End

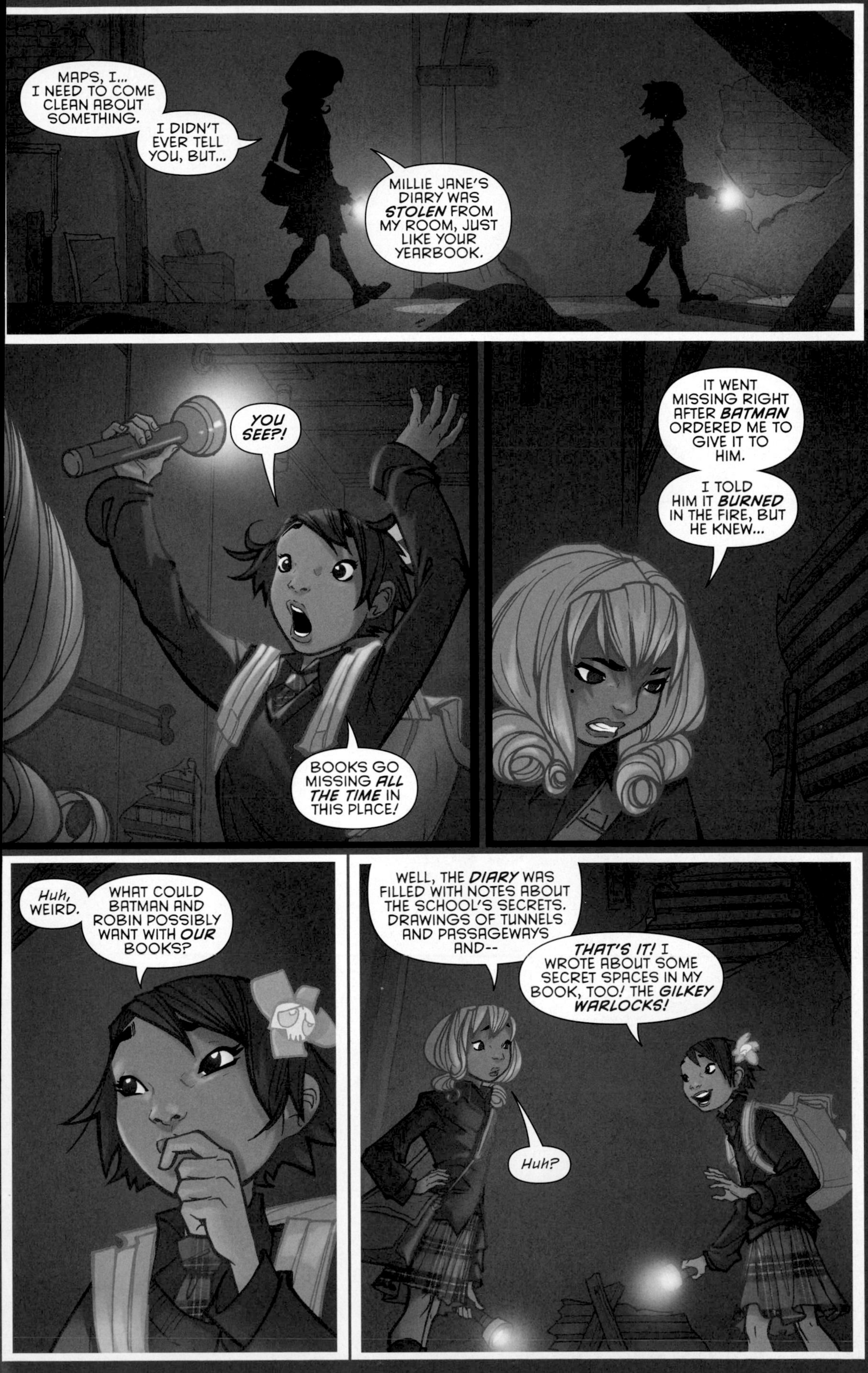
MAPS, I... I NEED TO COME CLEAN ABOUT SOMETHING.
I DIDN'T EVER TELL YOU, BUT...
MILLIE JANE'S DIARY WAS *STOLEN* FROM MY ROOM, JUST LIKE YOUR YEARBOOK.
YOU SEE?!
BOOKS GO MISSING *ALL THE TIME* IN THIS PLACE!
IT WENT MISSING RIGHT AFTER *BATMAN* ORDERED ME TO GIVE IT TO HIM.
I TOLD HIM IT *BURNED* IN THE FIRE, BUT HE KNEW...
Huh, WEIRD.
WHAT COULD BATMAN AND ROBIN POSSIBLY WANT WITH *OUR* BOOKS?
WELL, THE *DIARY* WAS FILLED WITH NOTES ABOUT THE SCHOOL'S SECRETS. DRAWINGS OF TUNNELS AND PASSAGEWAYS AND--
THAT'S IT! I WROTE ABOUT SOME SECRET SPACES IN MY BOOK, TOO! THE *GILKEY WARLOCKS!*
Huh?

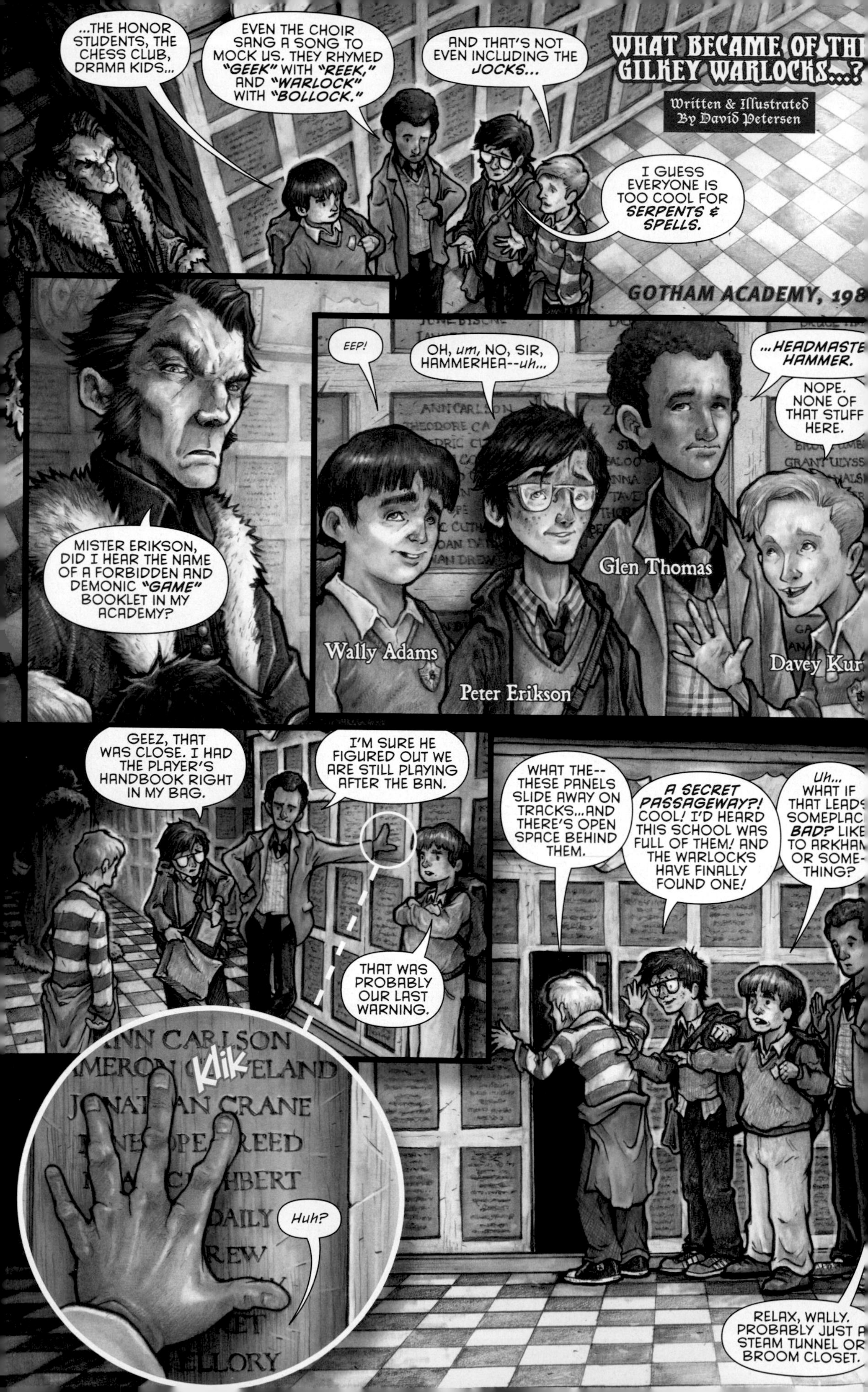

WHAT BECAME OF TH
GILKEY WARLOCKS...?
Written & Illustrated
By David Petersen
...THE HONOR STUDENTS, THE CHESS CLUB, DRAMA KIDS...
EVEN THE CHOIR SANG A SONG TO MOCK US. THEY RHYMED "GEEK" WITH "REEK," AND "WARLOCK" WITH "BOLLOCK."
AND THAT'S NOT EVEN INCLUDING THE JOCKS...
I GUESS EVERYONE IS TOO COOL FOR SERPENTS & SPELLS.
GOTHAM ACADEMY, 198
MISTER ERIKSON, DID I HEAR THE NAME OF A FORBIDDEN AND DEMONIC "GAME" BOOKLET IN MY ACADEMY?
EEP!
OH, um, NO, SIR, HAMMERHEA--uh...
...HEADMASTE HAMMER.
NOPE. NONE OF THAT STUFF HERE.
Wally Adams
Peter Erikson
Glen Thomas
Davey Kur
GEEZ, THAT WAS CLOSE. I HAD THE PLAYER'S HANDBOOK RIGHT IN MY BAG.
I'M SURE HE FIGURED OUT WE ARE STILL PLAYING AFTER THE BAN.
THAT WAS PROBABLY OUR LAST WARNING.
KLIK
Huh?
WHAT THE-- THESE PANELS SLIDE AWAY ON TRACKS...AND THERE'S OPEN SPACE BEHIND THEM.
A SECRET PASSAGEWAY?! COOL! I'D HEARD THIS SCHOOL WAS FULL OF THEM! AND THE WARLOCKS HAVE FINALLY FOUND ONE!
Uh... WHAT IF THAT LEADS SOMEPLAC BAD? LIKE TO ARKHAM OR SOME-THING?
RELAX, WALLY. PROBABLY JUST A STEAM TUNNEL OR BROOM CLOSET.

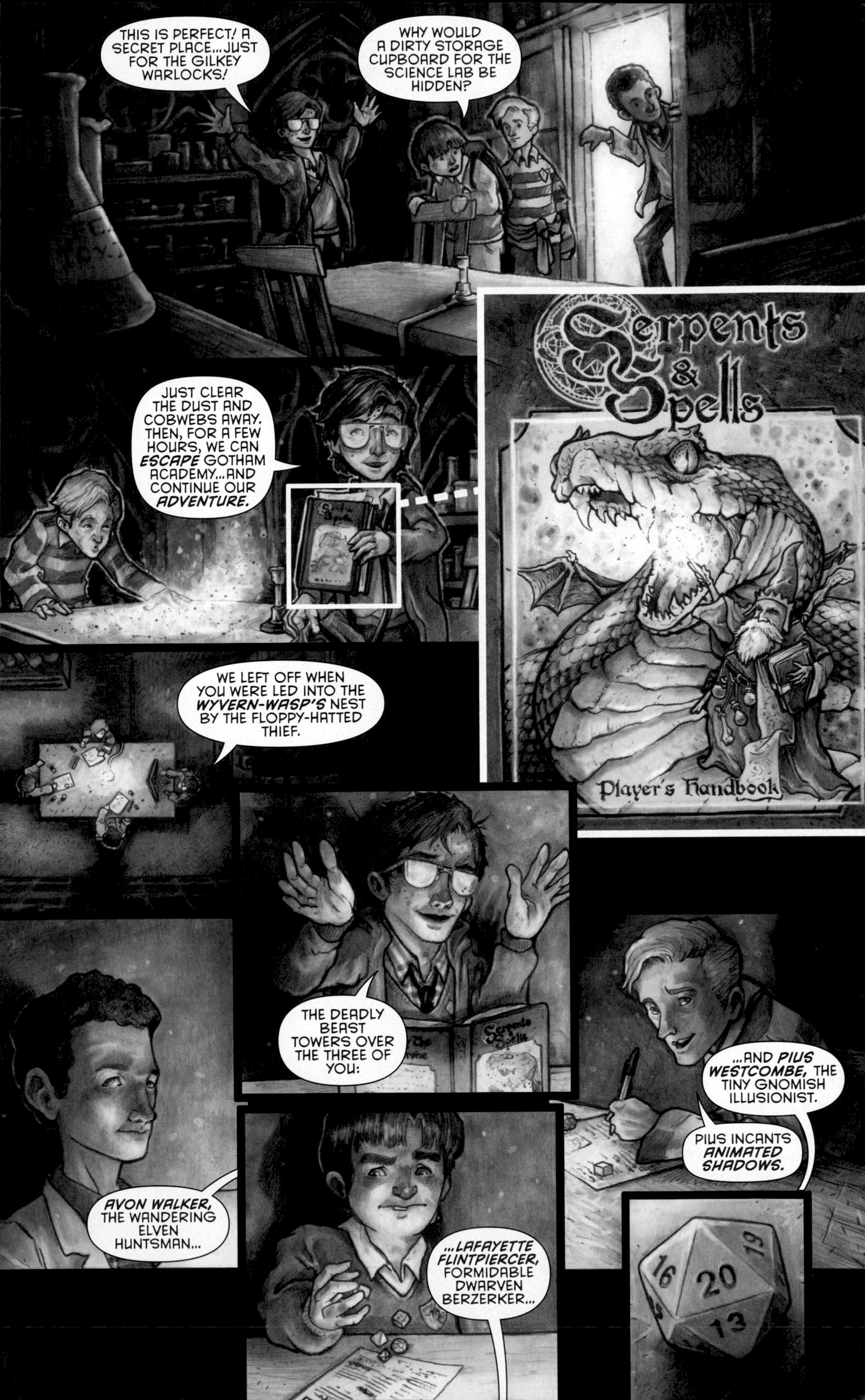
THIS IS PERFECT! A SECRET PLACE...JUST FOR THE GILKEY WARLOCKS!
WHY WOULD A DIRTY STORAGE CUPBOARD FOR THE SCIENCE LAB BE HIDDEN?
JUST CLEAR THE DUST AND COBWEBS AWAY. THEN, FOR A FEW HOURS, WE CAN *ESCAPE* GOTHAM ACADEMY...AND CONTINUE OUR *ADVENTURE.*
Serpents & Spells
Player's Handbook
WE LEFT OFF WHEN YOU WERE LED INTO THE *WYVERN-WASP'S* NEST BY THE FLOPPY-HATTED THIEF.
THE DEADLY BEAST TOWERS OVER THE THREE OF YOU:
AVON WALKER, THE WANDERING ELVEN HUNTSMAN...
...*LAFAYETTE FLINTPIERCER,* FORMIDABLE DWARVEN BERZERKER...
...AND *PIUS WESTCOMBE,* THE TINY GNOMISH ILLUSIONIST.
PIUS INCANTS *ANIMATED SHADOWS.*
16
20
19
13

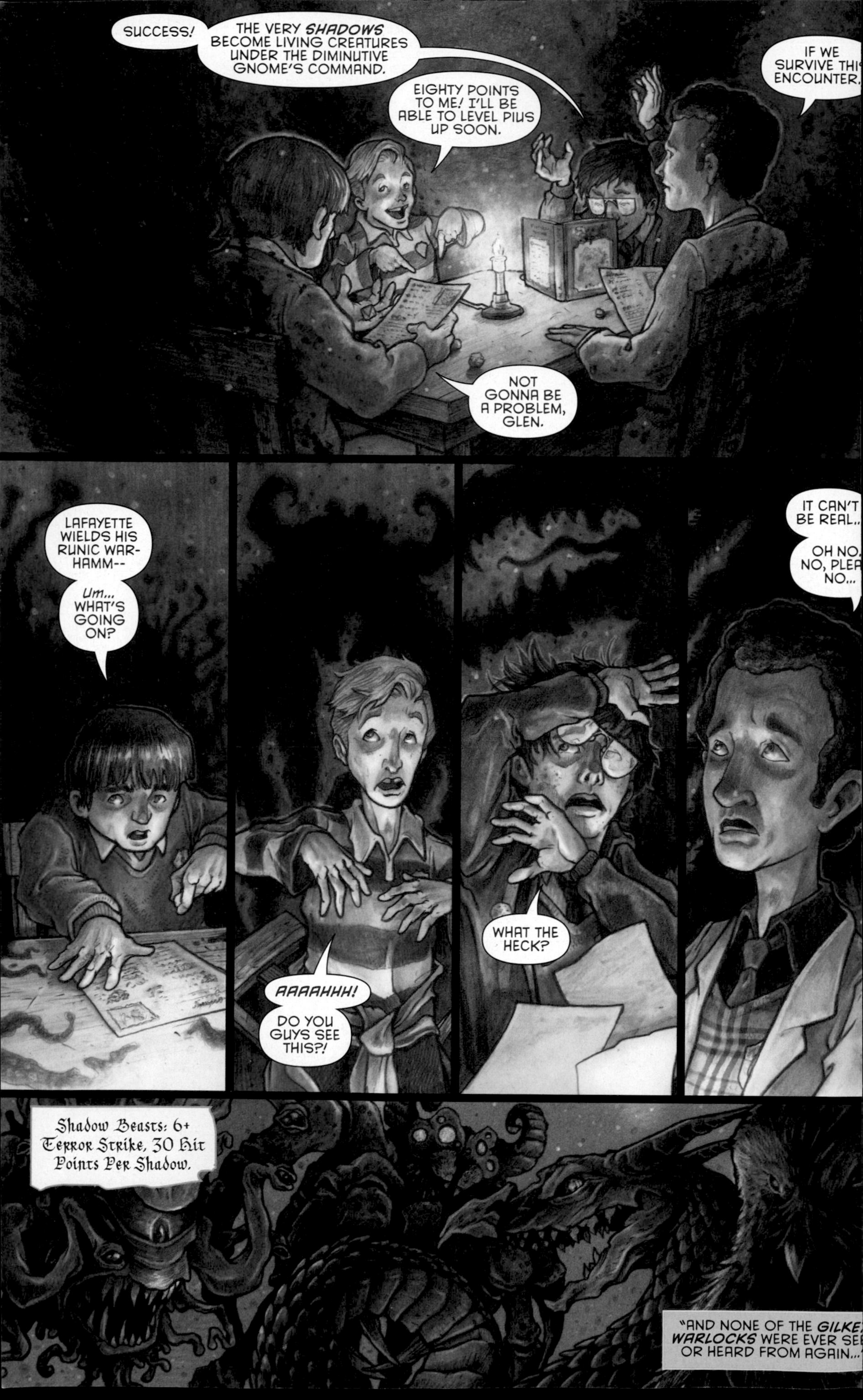
SUCCESS!
THE VERY SHADOWS BECOME LIVING CREATURES UNDER THE DIMINUTIVE GNOME'S COMMAND.
EIGHTY POINTS TO ME! I'LL BE ABLE TO LEVEL PIUS UP SOON.
IF WE SURVIVE THI ENCOUNTER,
NOT GONNA BE A PROBLEM, GLEN.
LAFAYETTE WIELDS HIS RUNIC WAR-HAMM--
Um... WHAT'S GOING ON?
AAAAHHH!
DO YOU GUYS SEE THIS?!
WHAT THE HECK?
IT CAN'T BE REAL..
OH NO. NO, PLEA NO...
Shadow Beasts: 6+ Terror Strike, 30 Hit Points Per Shadow.
"AND NONE OF THE GILKE WARLOCKS WERE EVER SE OR HEARD FROM AGAIN...

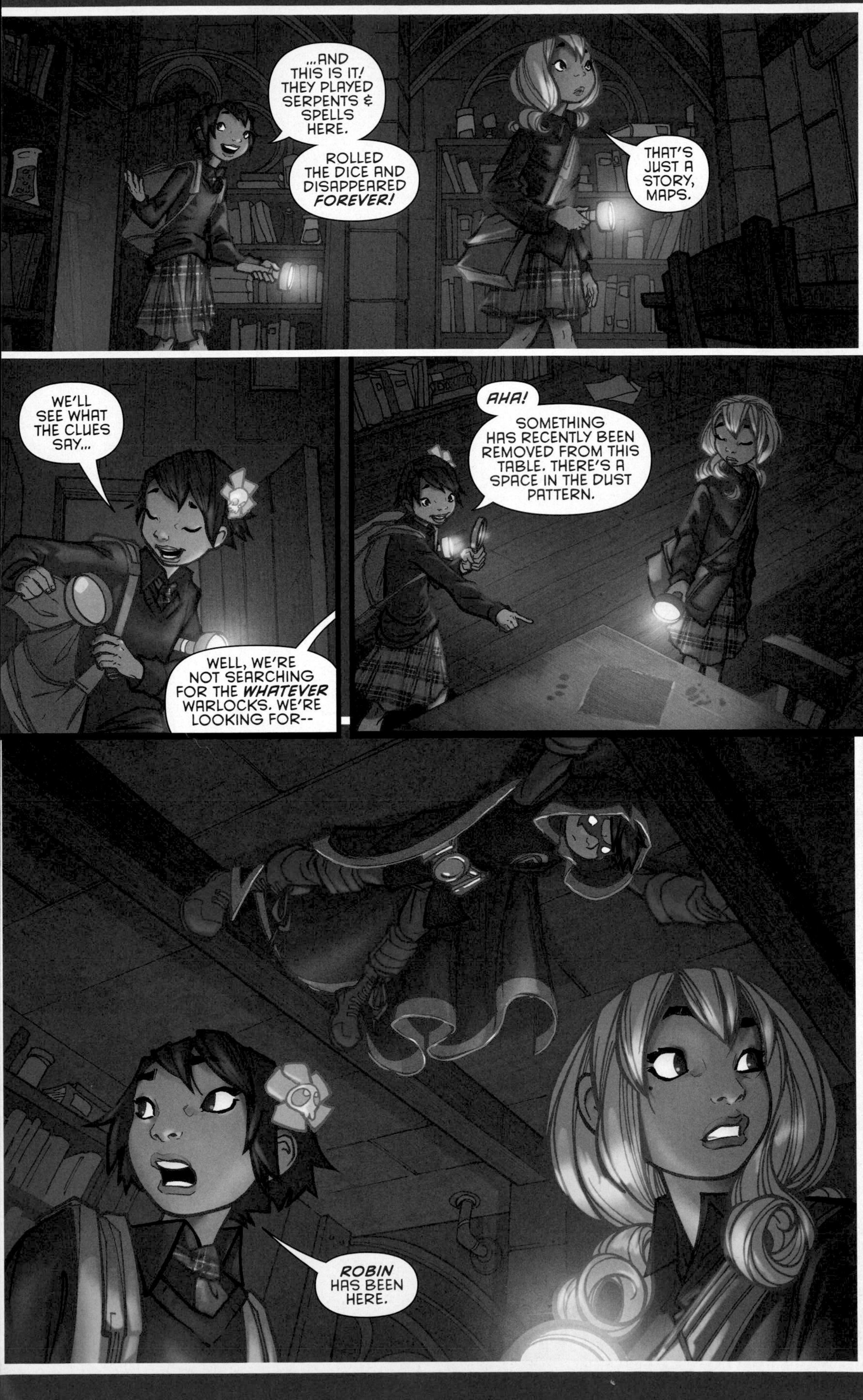
...AND THIS IS IT! THEY PLAYED SERPENTS & SPELLS HERE.
ROLLED THE DICE AND DISAPPEARED *FOREVER!*
THAT'S JUST A STORY, MAPS.
WE'LL SEE WHAT THE CLUES SAY...
WELL, WE'RE NOT SEARCHING FOR THE *WHATEVER* WARLOCKS. WE'RE LOOKING FOR--
AHA!
SOMETHING HAS RECENTLY BEEN REMOVED FROM THIS TABLE. THERE'S A SPACE IN THE DUST PATTERN.
ROBIN HAS BEEN HERE.

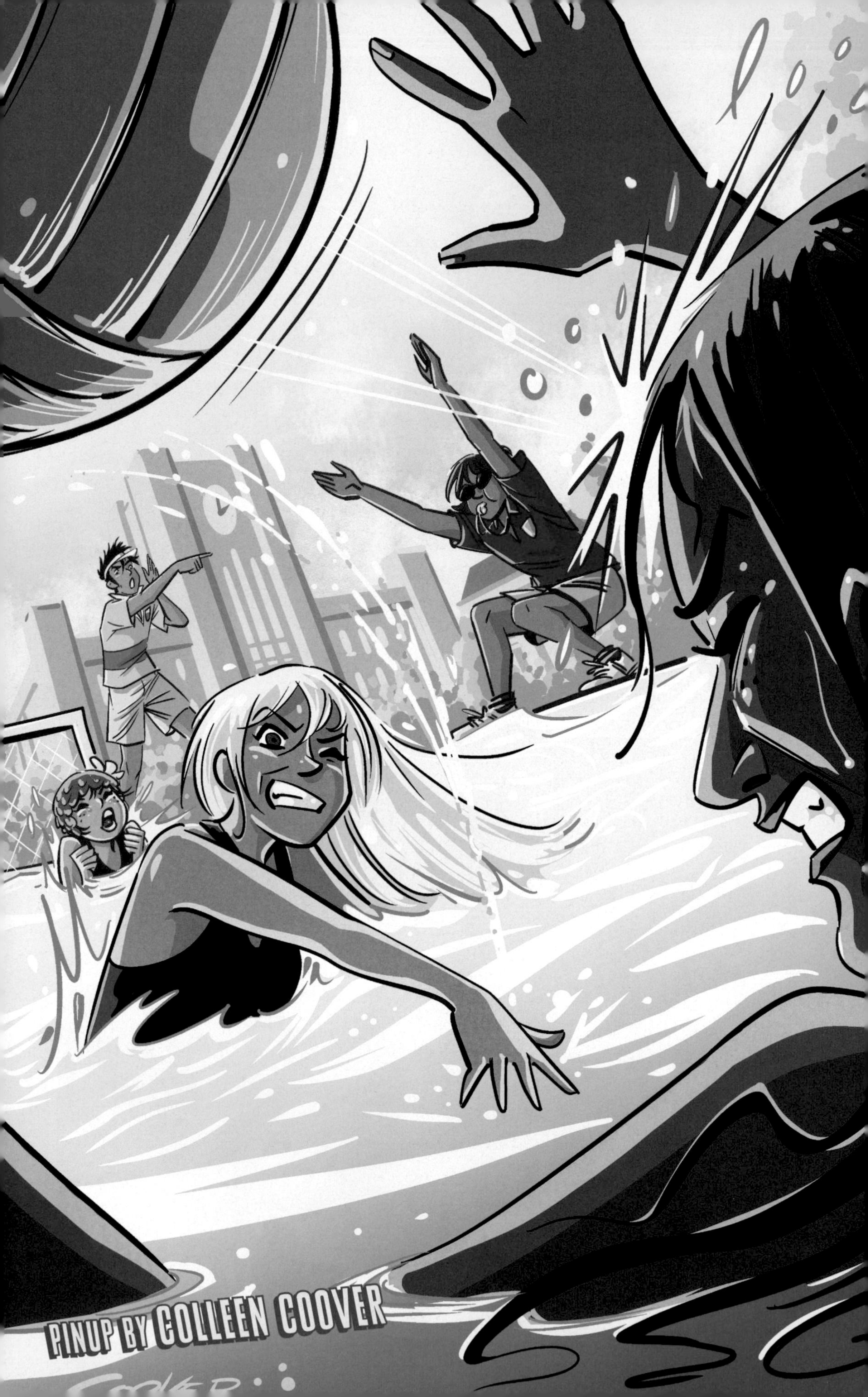
PINUP BY COLLEEN COOVER

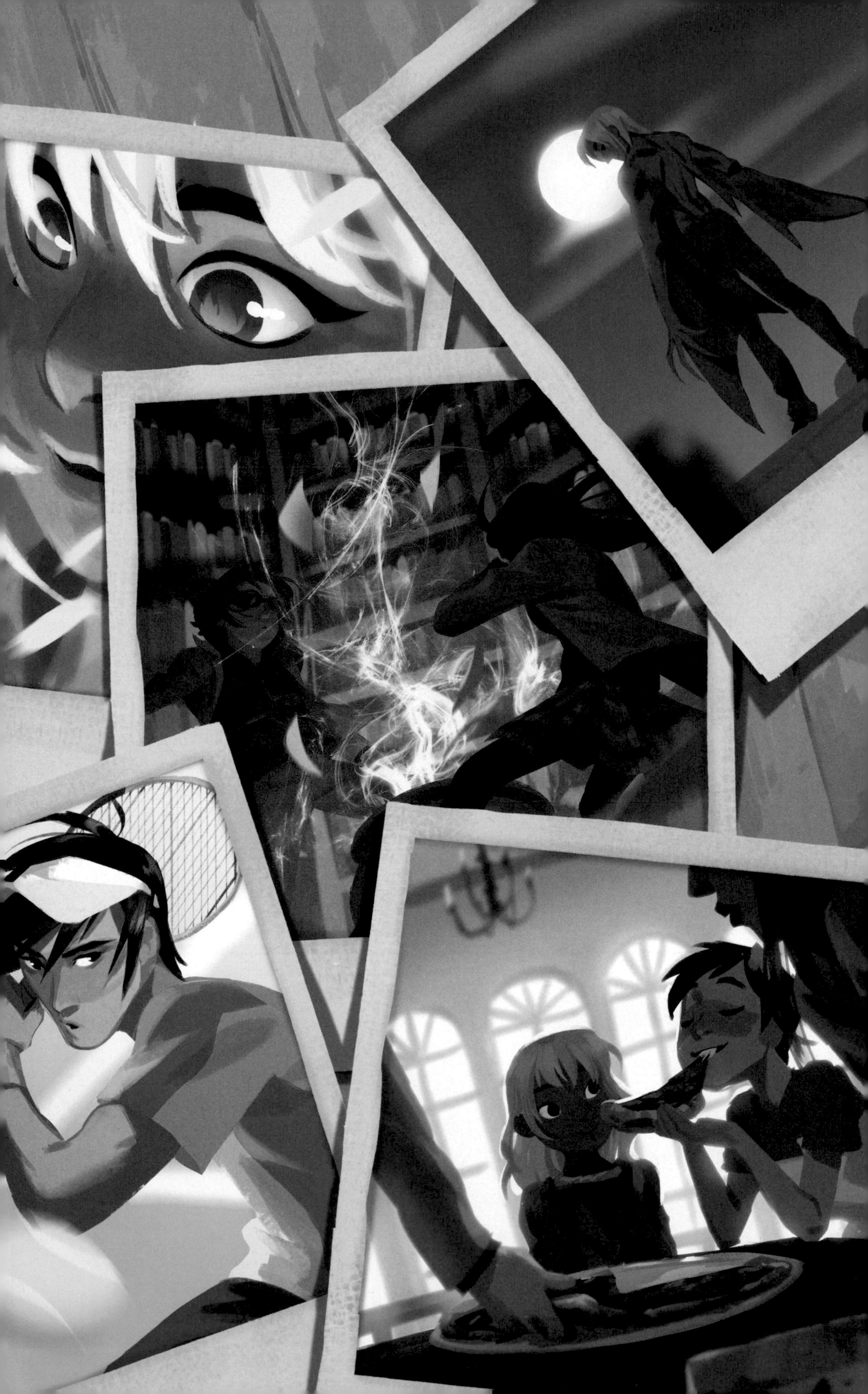

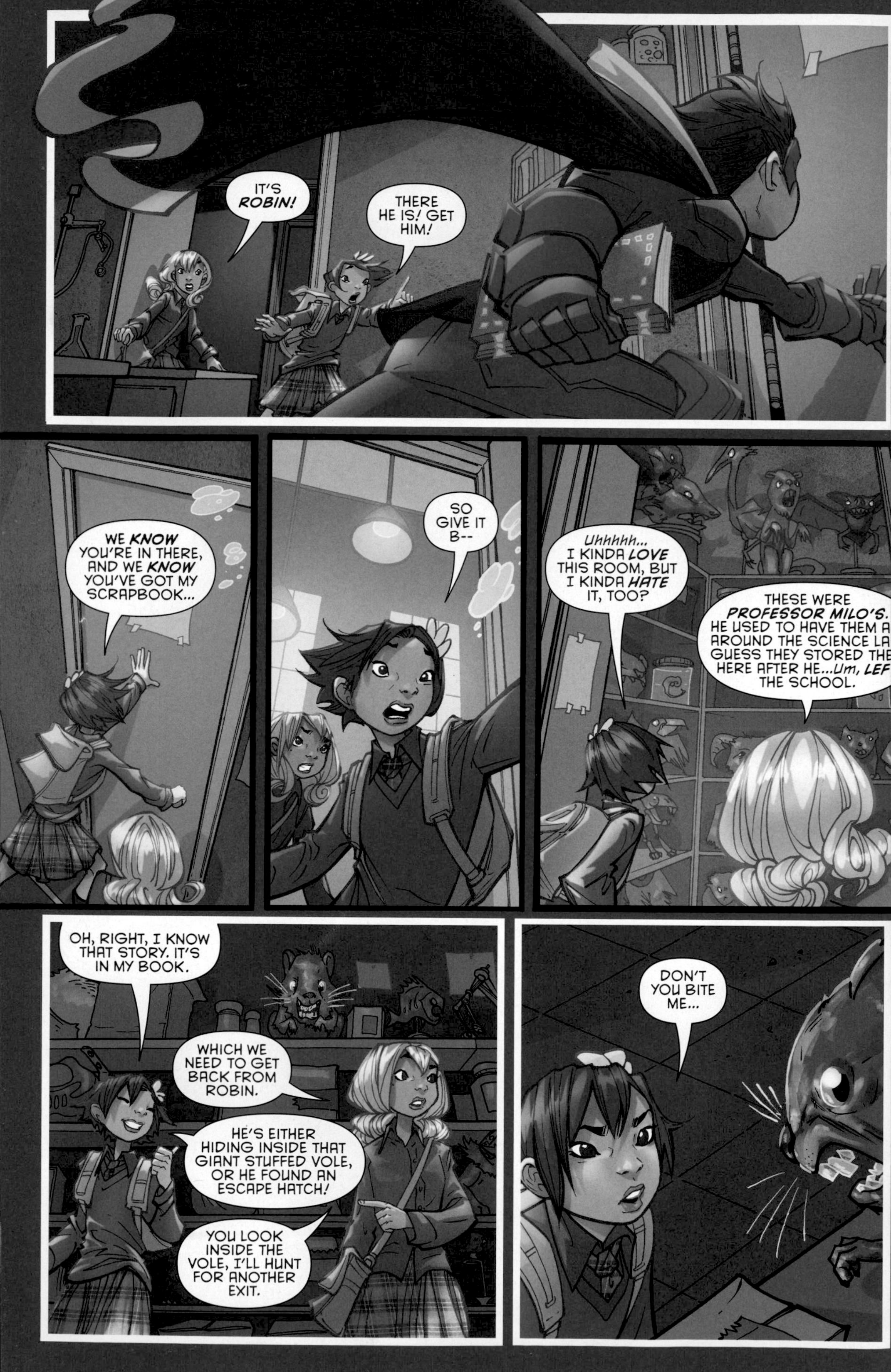

IT'S ROBIN!
THERE HE IS! GET HIM!
WE KNOW YOU'RE IN THERE, AND WE KNOW YOU'VE GOT MY SCRAPBOOK...
SO GIVE IT B--
Uhhhhh... I KINDA LOVE THIS ROOM, BUT I KINDA HATE IT, TOO?
THESE WERE PROFESSOR MILO'S. HE USED TO HAVE THEM A AROUND THE SCIENCE LA GUESS THEY STORED THE HERE AFTER HE...Um, LEF THE SCHOOL.
OH, RIGHT, I KNOW THAT STORY. IT'S IN MY BOOK.
WHICH WE NEED TO GET BACK FROM ROBIN.
HE'S EITHER HIDING INSIDE THAT GIANT STUFFED VOLE, OR HE FOUND AN ESCAPE HATCH!
YOU LOOK INSIDE THE VOLE, I'LL HUNT FOR ANOTHER EXIT.
DON'T YOU BITE ME...

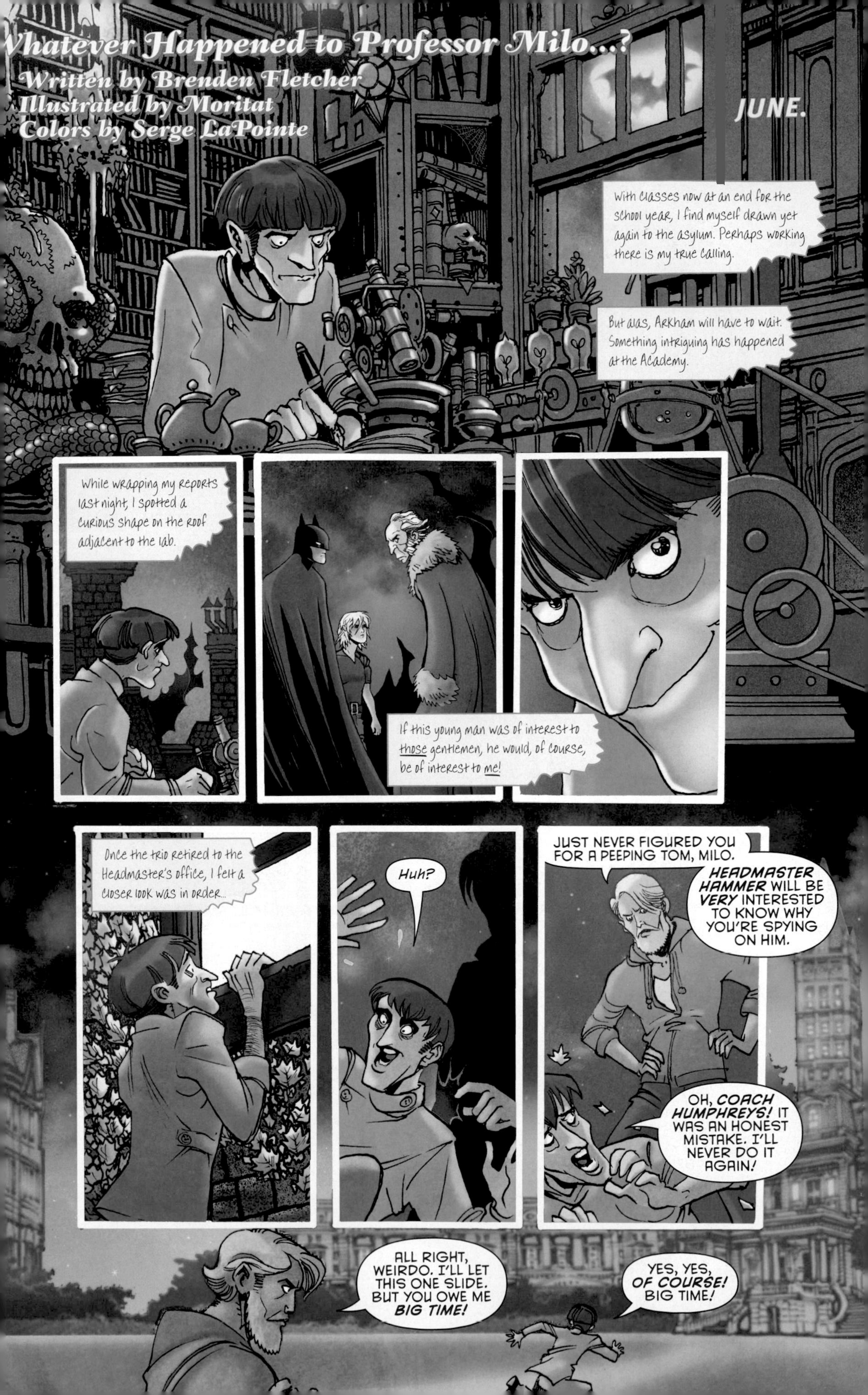
Whatever Happened to Professor Milo...?
Written by Brenden Fletcher
Illustrated by Moritat
Colors by Serge LaPointe
JUNE.
With classes now at an end for the school year, I find myself drawn yet again to the asylum. Perhaps working there is my true calling.
But alas, Arkham will have to wait. Something intriguing has happened at the Academy.
While wrapping my reports last night, I spotted a curious shape on the roof adjacent to the lab.
If this young man was of interest to those gentlemen, he would, of course, be of interest to me!
Once the trio retired to the Headmaster's office, I felt a closer look was in order...
Huh?
JUST NEVER FIGURED YOU FOR A PEEPING TOM, MILO.
HEADMASTER HAMMER WILL BE VERY INTERESTED TO KNOW WHY YOU'RE SPYING ON HIM.
OH, COACH HUMPHREYS! IT WAS AN HONEST MISTAKE. I'LL NEVER DO IT AGAIN!
ALL RIGHT, WEIRDO. I'LL LET THIS ONE SLIDE. BUT YOU OWE ME BIG TIME!
YES, YES, OF COURSE! BIG TIME!

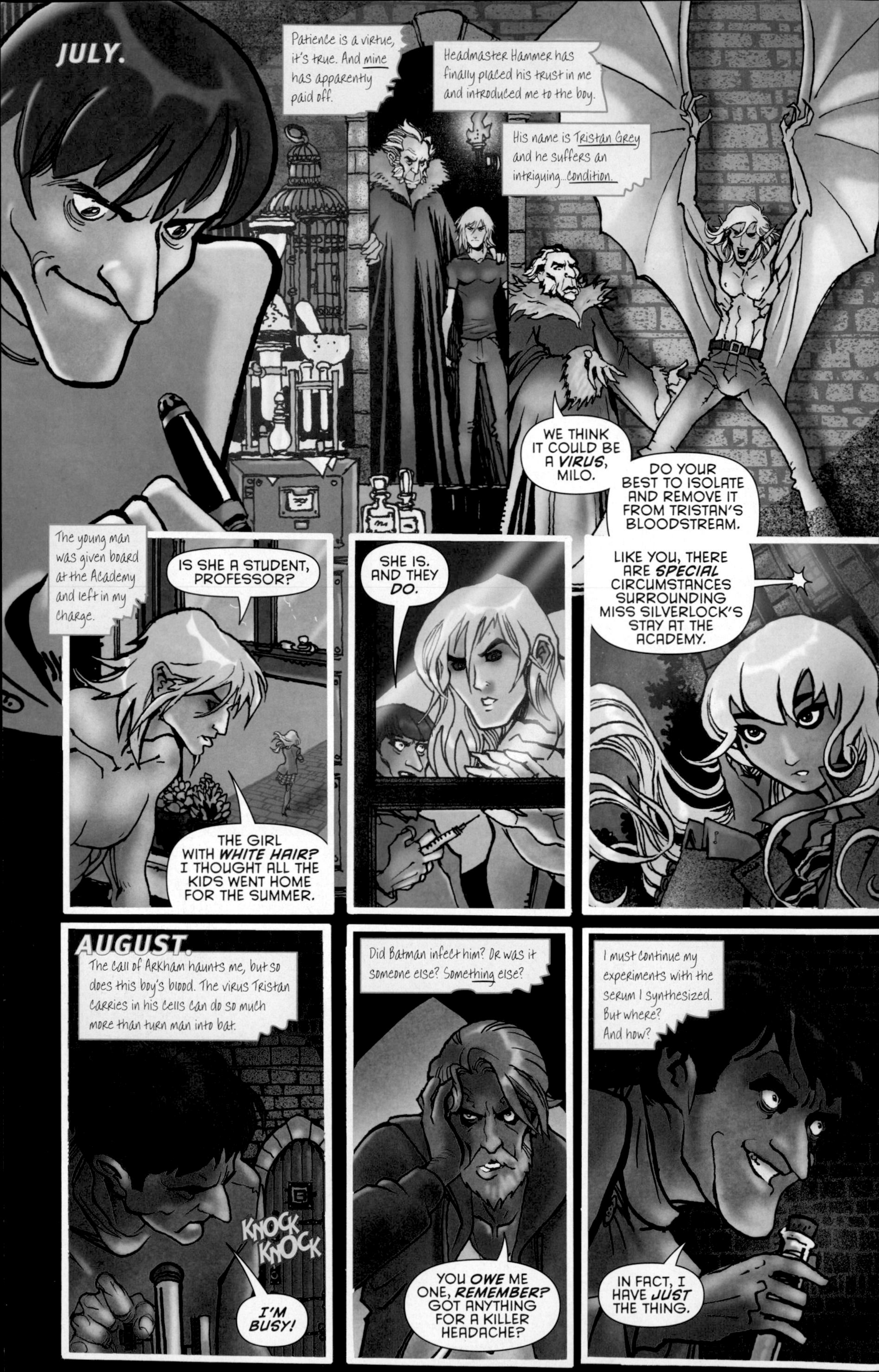
JULY.
Patience is a virtue, it's true. And mine has apparently paid off.
Headmaster Hammer has finally placed his trust in me and introduced me to the boy.
His name is Tristan Grey and he suffers an intriguing...condition.
WE THINK IT COULD BE A VIRUS, MILO.
DO YOUR BEST TO ISOLATE AND REMOVE IT FROM TRISTAN'S BLOODSTREAM.
The young man was given board at the Academy and left in my charge.
IS SHE A STUDENT, PROFESSOR?
THE GIRL WITH WHITE HAIR? I THOUGHT ALL THE KIDS WENT HOME FOR THE SUMMER.
SHE IS. AND THEY DO.
LIKE YOU, THERE ARE SPECIAL CIRCUMSTANCES SURROUNDING MISS SILVERLOCK'S STAY AT THE ACADEMY.
AUGUST.
The call of Arkham haunts me, but so does this boy's blood. The virus Tristan carries in his cells can do so much more than turn man into bat.
KNOCK KNOCK
I'M BUSY!
Did Batman infect him? Or was it someone else? Something else?
YOU OWE ME ONE, REMEMBER? GOT ANYTHING FOR A KILLER HEADACHE?
I must continue my experiments with the serum I synthesized. But where? And how?
IN FACT, I HAVE JUST THE THING.

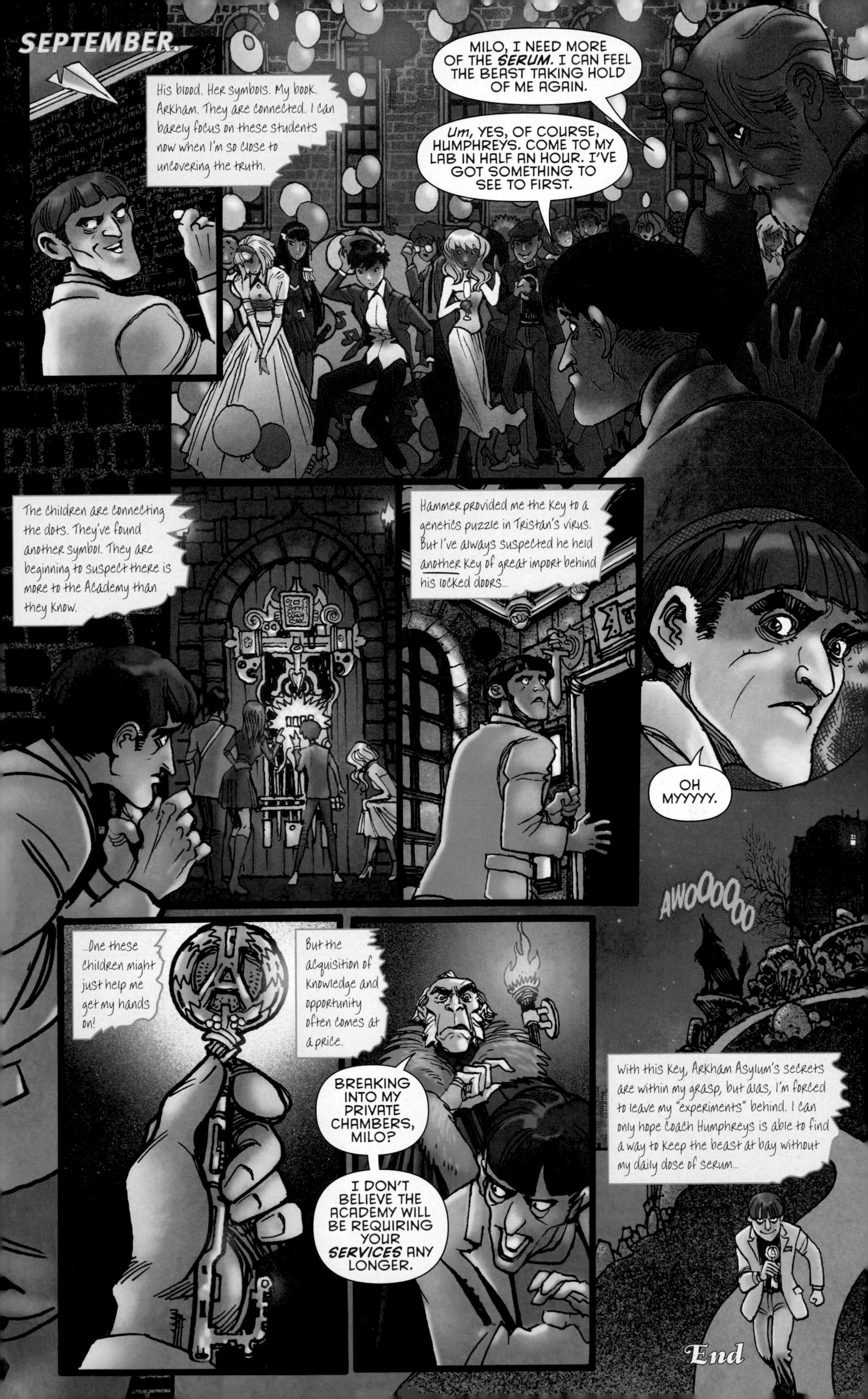
SEPTEMBER.
His blood. Her symbols. My book. Arkham. They are connected. I can barely focus on these students now when I'm so close to uncovering the truth.
MILO, I NEED MORE OF THE SERUM. I CAN FEEL THE BEAST TAKING HOLD OF ME AGAIN.
Um, YES, OF COURSE, HUMPHREYS. COME TO MY LAB IN HALF AN HOUR. I'VE GOT SOMETHING TO SEE TO FIRST.
The children are connecting the dots. They've found another symbol. They are beginning to suspect there is more to the Academy than they know.
Hammer provided me the key to a genetics puzzle in Tristan's virus. But I've always suspected he held another key of great import behind his locked doors...
OH MYYYYY.
AWOOOOOO
...One these children might just help me get my hands on!
But the acquisition of knowledge and opportunity often comes at a price.
BREAKING INTO MY PRIVATE CHAMBERS, MILO?
I DON'T BELIEVE THE ACADEMY WILL BE REQUIRING YOUR SERVICES ANY LONGER.
With this key, Arkham Asylum's secrets are within my grasp, but alas, I'm forced to leave my "experiments" behind. I can only hope Coach Humphreys is able to find a way to keep the beast at bay without my daily dose of serum...
End

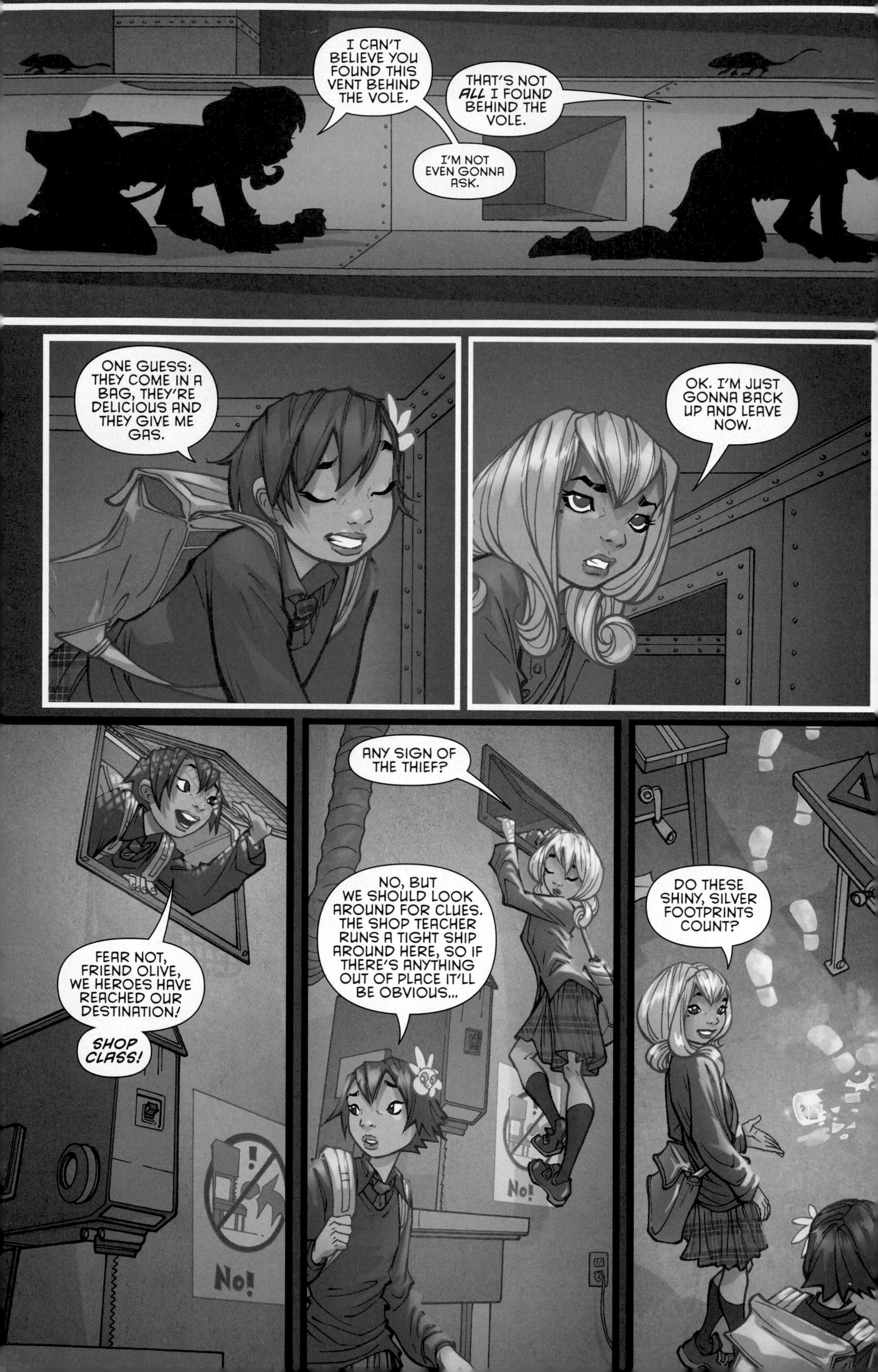
I CAN'T BELIEVE YOU FOUND THIS VENT BEHIND THE VOLE.
THAT'S NOT ALL I FOUND BEHIND THE VOLE.
I'M NOT EVEN GONNA ASK.
ONE GUESS: THEY COME IN A BAG, THEY'RE DELICIOUS AND THEY GIVE ME GAS.
OK. I'M JUST GONNA BACK UP AND LEAVE NOW.
FEAR NOT, FRIEND OLIVE, WE HEROES HAVE REACHED OUR DESTINATION!
SHOP CLASS!
No!
ANY SIGN OF THE THIEF?
NO, BUT WE SHOULD LOOK AROUND FOR CLUES. THE SHOP TEACHER RUNS A TIGHT SHIP AROUND HERE, SO IF THERE'S ANYTHING OUT OF PLACE IT'LL BE OBVIOUS...
No!
DO THESE SHINY, SILVER FOOTPRINTS COUNT?

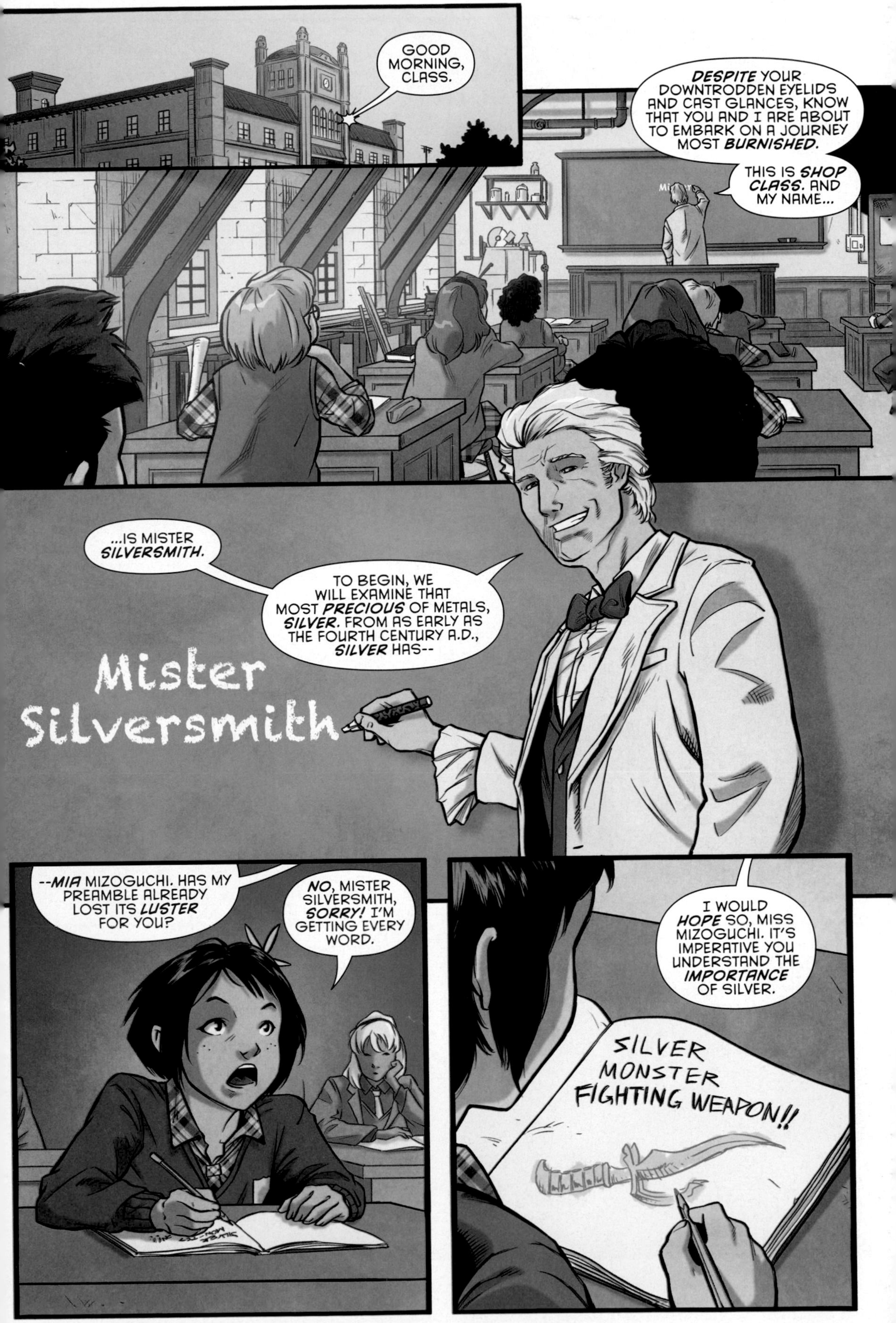
GOOD MORNING, CLASS.
DESPITE YOUR DOWNTRODDEN EYELIDS AND CAST GLANCES, KNOW THAT YOU AND I ARE ABOUT TO EMBARK ON A JOURNEY MOST BURNISHED.
THIS IS SHOP CLASS. AND MY NAME...
...IS MISTER SILVERSMITH.
TO BEGIN, WE WILL EXAMINE THAT MOST PRECIOUS OF METALS, SILVER. FROM AS EARLY AS THE FOURTH CENTURY A.D., SILVER HAS--
Mister Silversmith
--MIA MIZOGUCHI. HAS MY PREAMBLE ALREADY LOST ITS LUSTER FOR YOU?
NO, MISTER SILVERSMITH, SORRY! I'M GETTING EVERY WORD.
I WOULD HOPE SO, MISS MIZOGUCHI. IT'S IMPERATIVE YOU UNDERSTAND THE IMPORTANCE OF SILVER.
SILVER MONSTER FIGHTING WEAPON!!

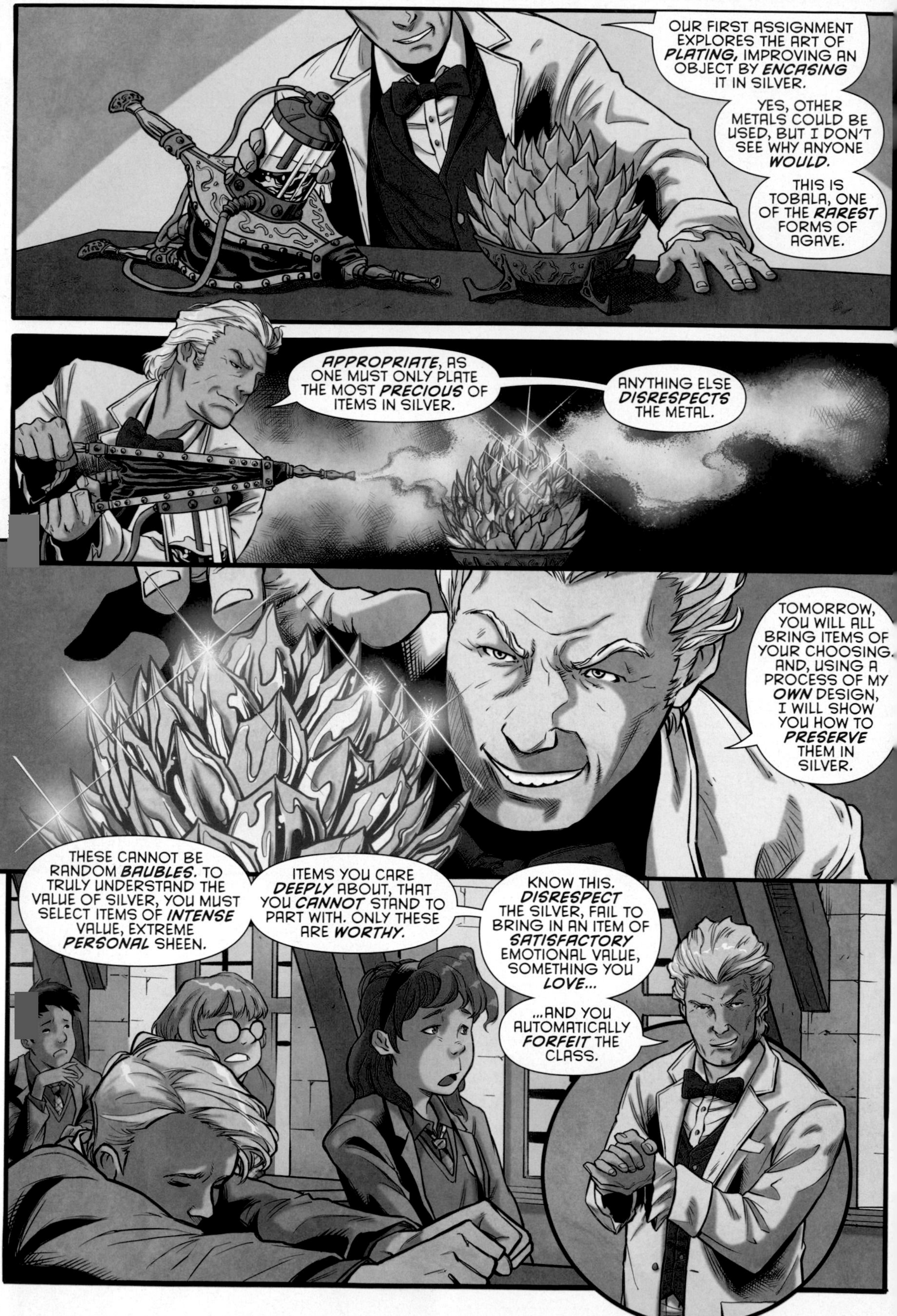
OUR FIRST ASSIGNMENT EXPLORES THE ART OF PLATING, IMPROVING AN OBJECT BY ENCASING IT IN SILVER.
YES, OTHER METALS COULD BE USED, BUT I DON'T SEE WHY ANYONE WOULD.
THIS IS TOBALA, ONE OF THE RAREST FORMS OF AGAVE.
APPROPRIATE, AS ONE MUST ONLY PLATE THE MOST PRECIOUS OF ITEMS IN SILVER.
ANYTHING ELSE DISRESPECTS THE METAL.
TOMORROW, YOU WILL ALL BRING ITEMS OF YOUR CHOOSING. AND, USING A PROCESS OF MY OWN DESIGN, I WILL SHOW YOU HOW TO PRESERVE THEM IN SILVER.
THESE CANNOT BE RANDOM BAUBLES. TO TRULY UNDERSTAND THE VALUE OF SILVER, YOU MUST SELECT ITEMS OF INTENSE VALUE, EXTREME PERSONAL SHEEN.
ITEMS YOU CARE DEEPLY ABOUT, THAT YOU CANNOT STAND TO PART WITH. ONLY THESE ARE WORTHY.
KNOW THIS. DISRESPECT THE SILVER, FAIL TO BRING IN AN ITEM OF SATISFACTORY EMOTIONAL VALUE, SOMETHING YOU LOVE...
...AND YOU AUTOMATICALLY FORFEIT THE CLASS.

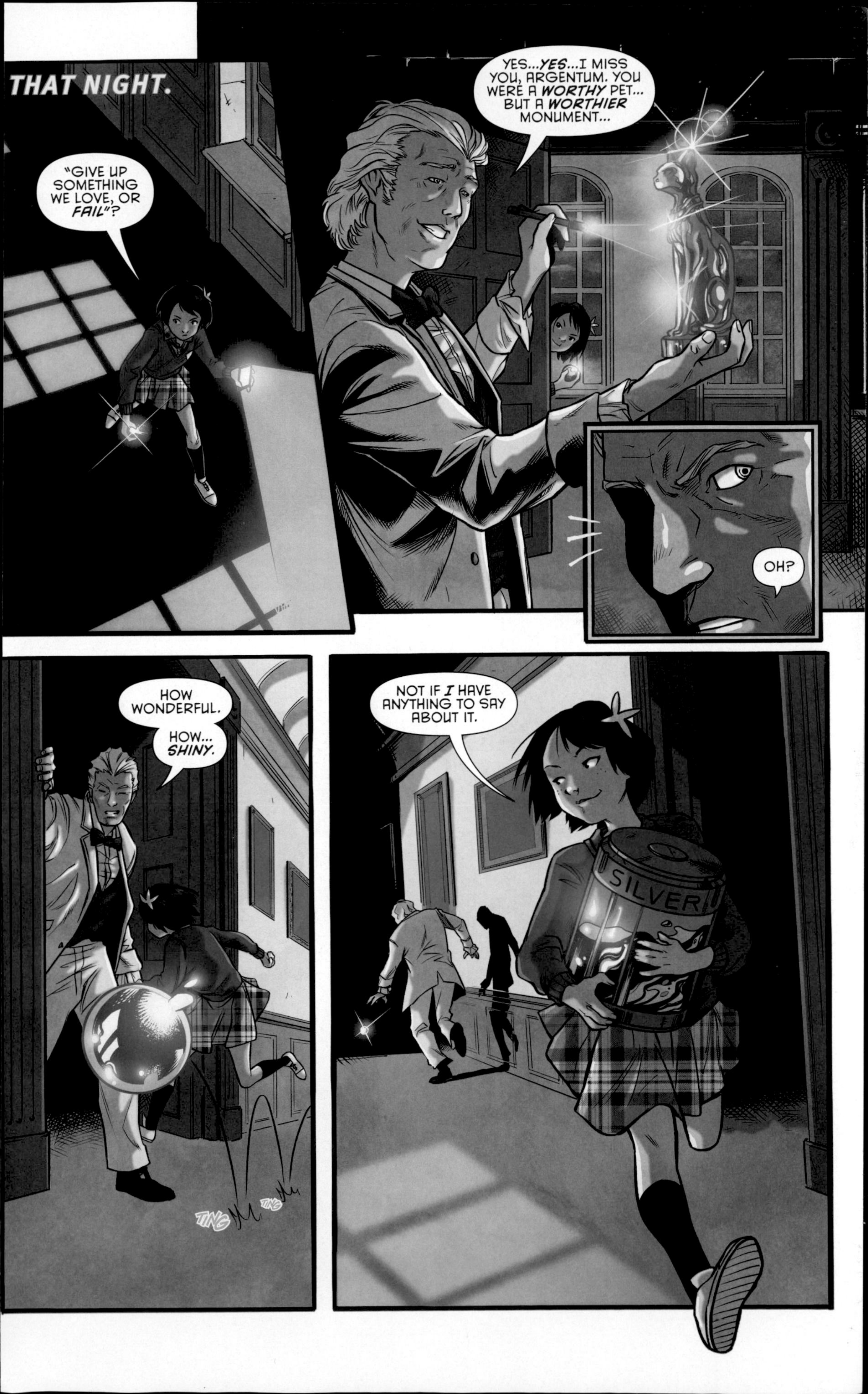
THAT NIGHT.
"GIVE UP SOMETHING WE LOVE, OR FAIL"?
YES...YES...I MISS YOU, ARGENTUM. YOU WERE A WORTHY PET... BUT A WORTHIER MONUMENT...
OH?
HOW WONDERFUL.
HOW... SHINY.
TING
TING
NOT IF I HAVE ANYTHING TO SAY ABOUT IT.
SILVER

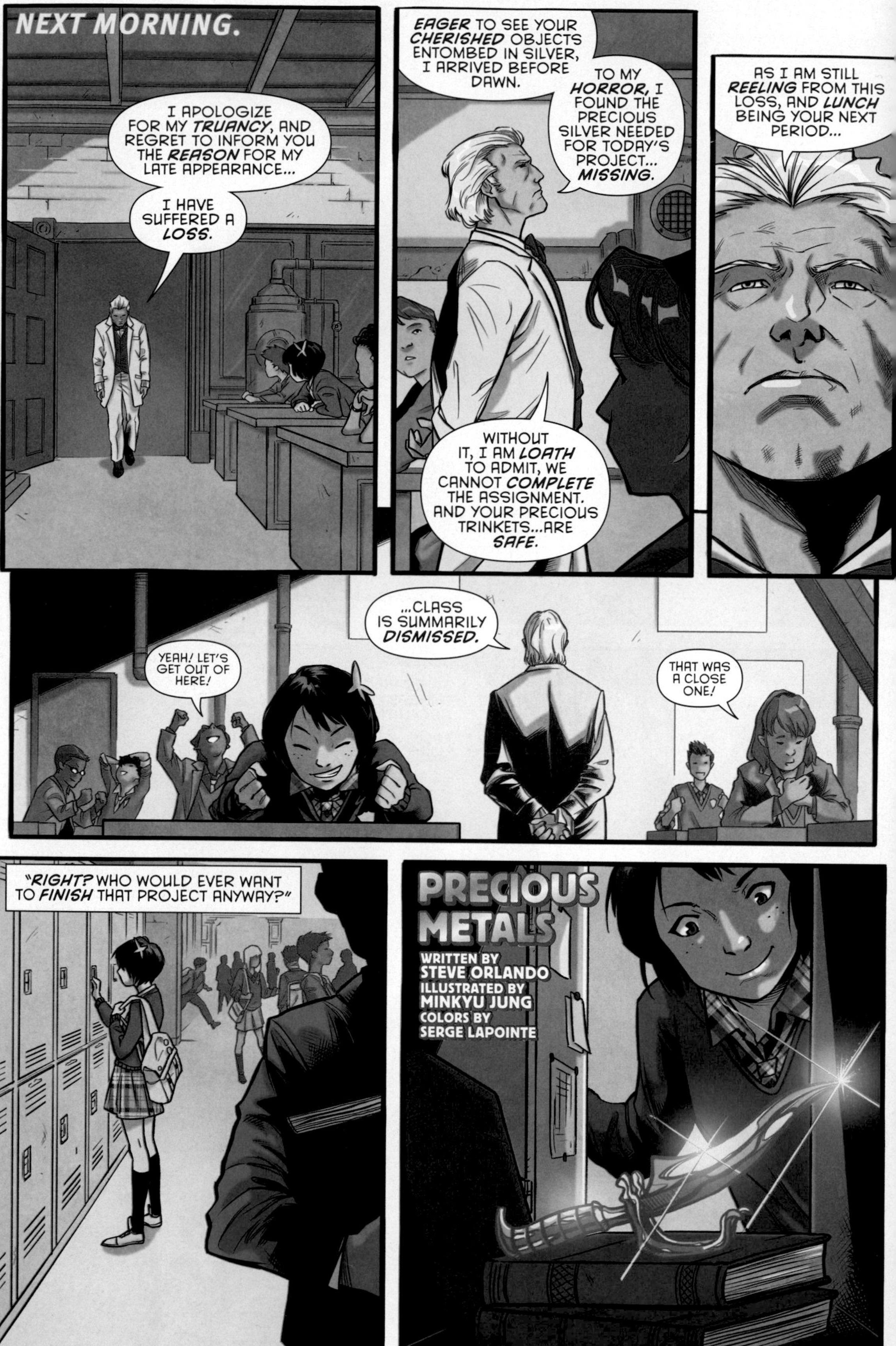
NEXT MORNING.
I APOLOGIZE FOR MY TRUANCY, AND REGRET TO INFORM YOU THE REASON FOR MY LATE APPEARANCE...
I HAVE SUFFERED A LOSS.
EAGER TO SEE YOUR CHERISHED OBJECTS ENTOMBED IN SILVER, I ARRIVED BEFORE DAWN.
TO MY HORROR, I FOUND THE PRECIOUS SILVER NEEDED FOR TODAY'S PROJECT... MISSING.
WITHOUT IT, I AM LOATH TO ADMIT, WE CANNOT COMPLETE THE ASSIGNMENT. AND YOUR PRECIOUS TRINKETS...ARE SAFE.
AS I AM STILL REELING FROM THIS LOSS, AND LUNCH BEING YOUR NEXT PERIOD...
...CLASS IS SUMMARILY DISMISSED.
YEAH! LET'S GET OUT OF HERE!
THAT WAS A CLOSE ONE!
"RIGHT? WHO WOULD EVER WANT TO FINISH THAT PROJECT ANYWAY?"
PRECIOUS METALS
WRITTEN BY STEVE ORLANDO
ILLUSTRATED BY MINKYU JUNG
COLORS BY SERGE LAPOINTE

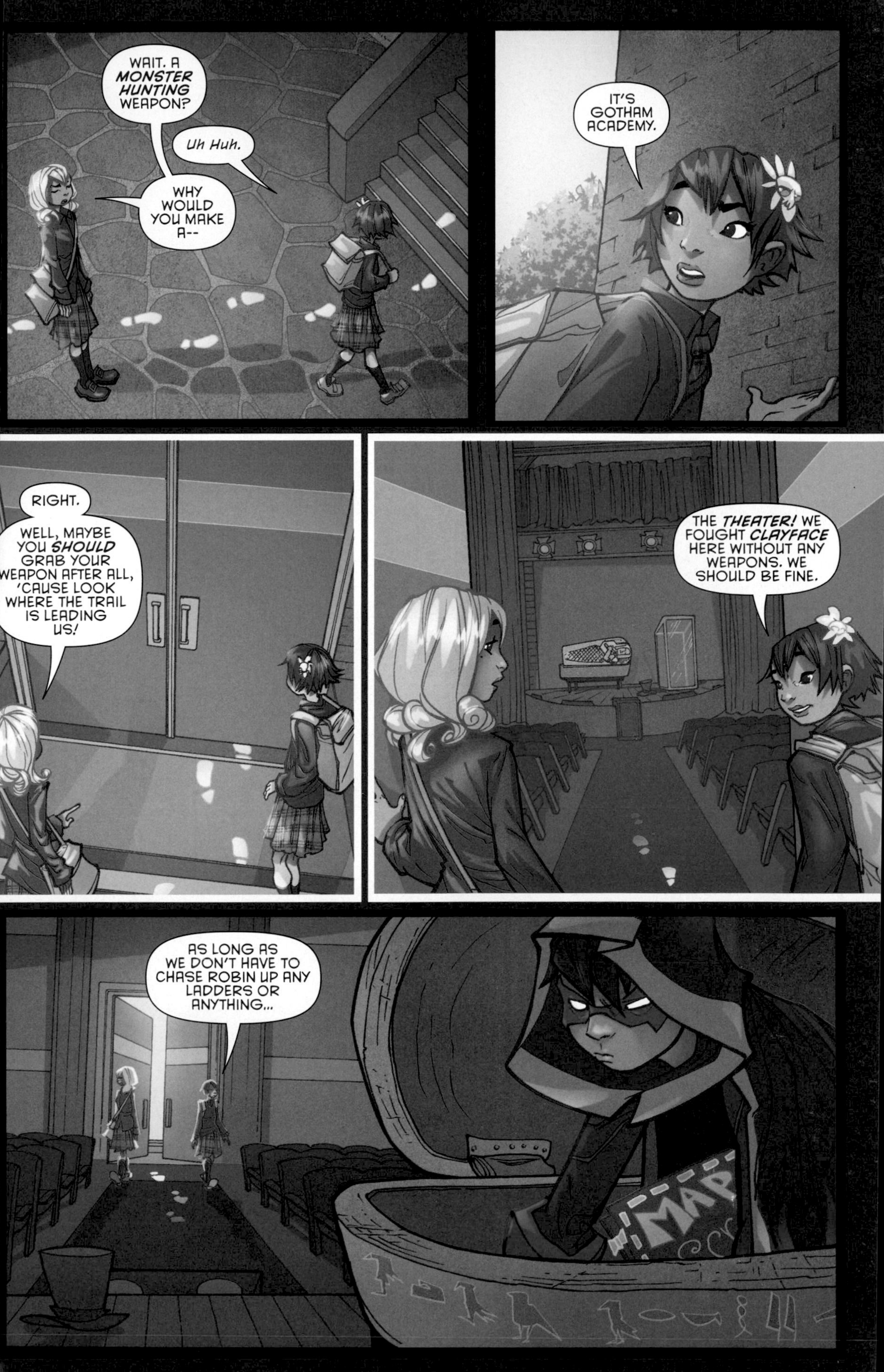

WAIT. A *MONSTER HUNTING* WEAPON?
Uh Huh.
WHY WOULD YOU MAKE A--
IT'S GOTHAM ACADEMY.
RIGHT.
WELL, MAYBE YOU *SHOULD* GRAB YOUR WEAPON AFTER ALL, 'CAUSE LOOK WHERE THE TRAIL IS LEADING US!
THE *THEATER!* WE FOUGHT *CLAYFACE* HERE WITHOUT ANY WEAPONS. WE SHOULD BE FINE.
AS LONG AS WE DON'T HAVE TO CHASE ROBIN UP ANY LADDERS OR ANYTHING...
MAP

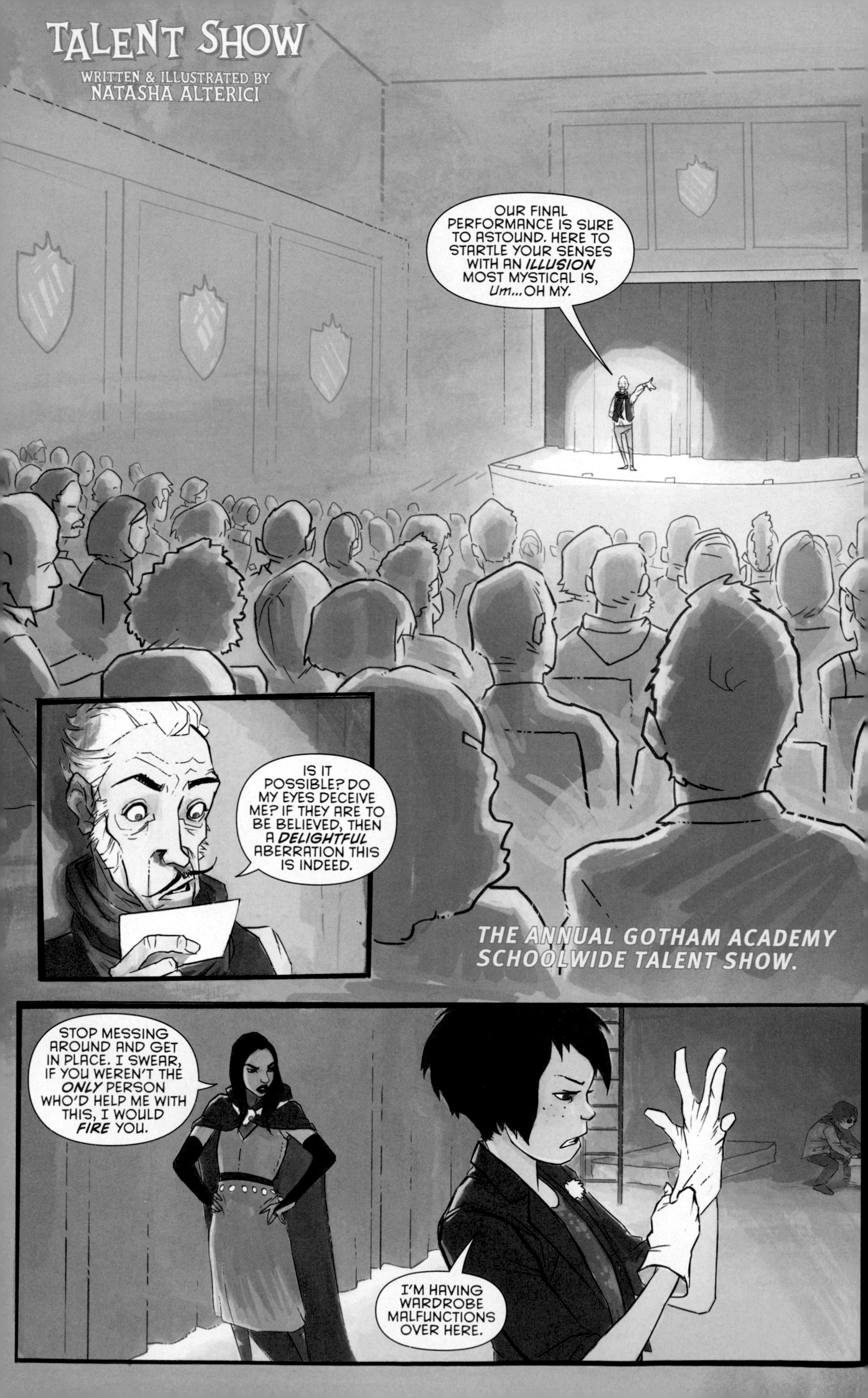
TALENT SHOW
WRITTEN & ILLUSTRATED BY
NATASHA ALTERICI
OUR FINAL PERFORMANCE IS SURE TO ASTOUND. HERE TO STARTLE YOUR SENSES WITH AN ILLUSION MOST MYSTICAL IS, Um...OH MY.
IS IT POSSIBLE? DO MY EYES DECEIVE ME? IF THEY ARE TO BE BELIEVED, THEN A DELIGHTFUL ABERRATION THIS IS INDEED.
THE ANNUAL GOTHAM ACADEMY SCHOOLWIDE TALENT SHOW.
STOP MESSING AROUND AND GET IN PLACE. I SWEAR, IF YOU WEREN'T THE ONLY PERSON WHO'D HELP ME WITH THIS, I WOULD FIRE YOU.
I'M HAVING WARDROBE MALFUNCTIONS OVER HERE.

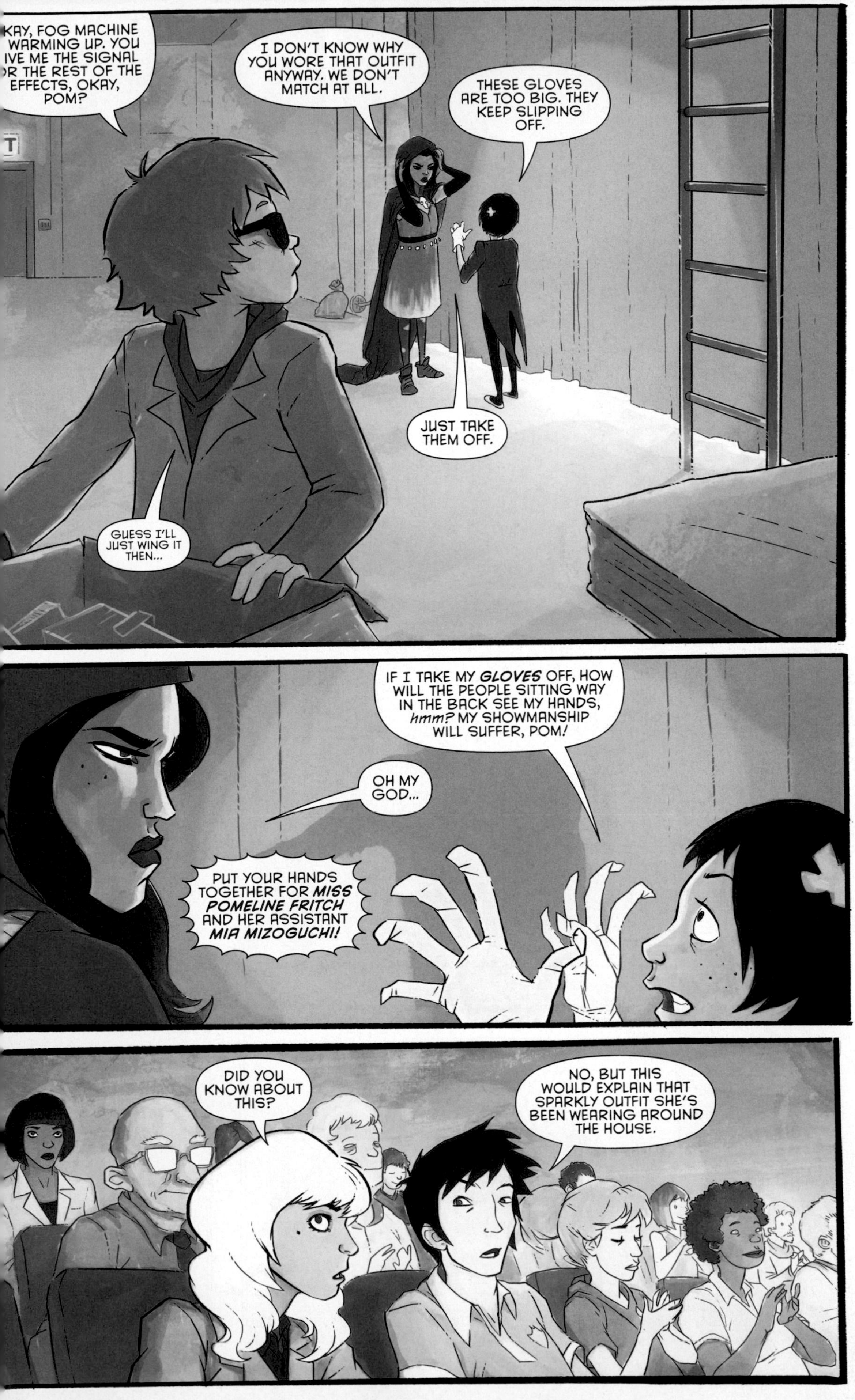
KAY, FOG MACHINE WARMING UP. YOU IVE ME THE SIGNAL OR THE REST OF THE EFFECTS, OKAY, POM?
I DON'T KNOW WHY YOU WORE THAT OUTFIT ANYWAY. WE DON'T MATCH AT ALL.
THESE GLOVES ARE TOO BIG. THEY KEEP SLIPPING OFF.
JUST TAKE THEM OFF.
GUESS I'LL JUST WING IT THEN...
IF I TAKE MY *GLOVES* OFF, HOW WILL THE PEOPLE SITTING WAY IN THE BACK SEE MY HANDS, *hmm?* MY SHOWMANSHIP WILL SUFFER, POM!
OH MY GOD...
PUT YOUR HANDS TOGETHER FOR *MISS POMELINE FRITCH* AND HER ASSISTANT *MIA MIZOGUCHI!*
DID YOU KNOW ABOUT THIS?
NO, BUT THIS WOULD EXPLAIN THAT SPARKLY OUTFIT SHE'S BEEN WEARING AROUND THE HOUSE.

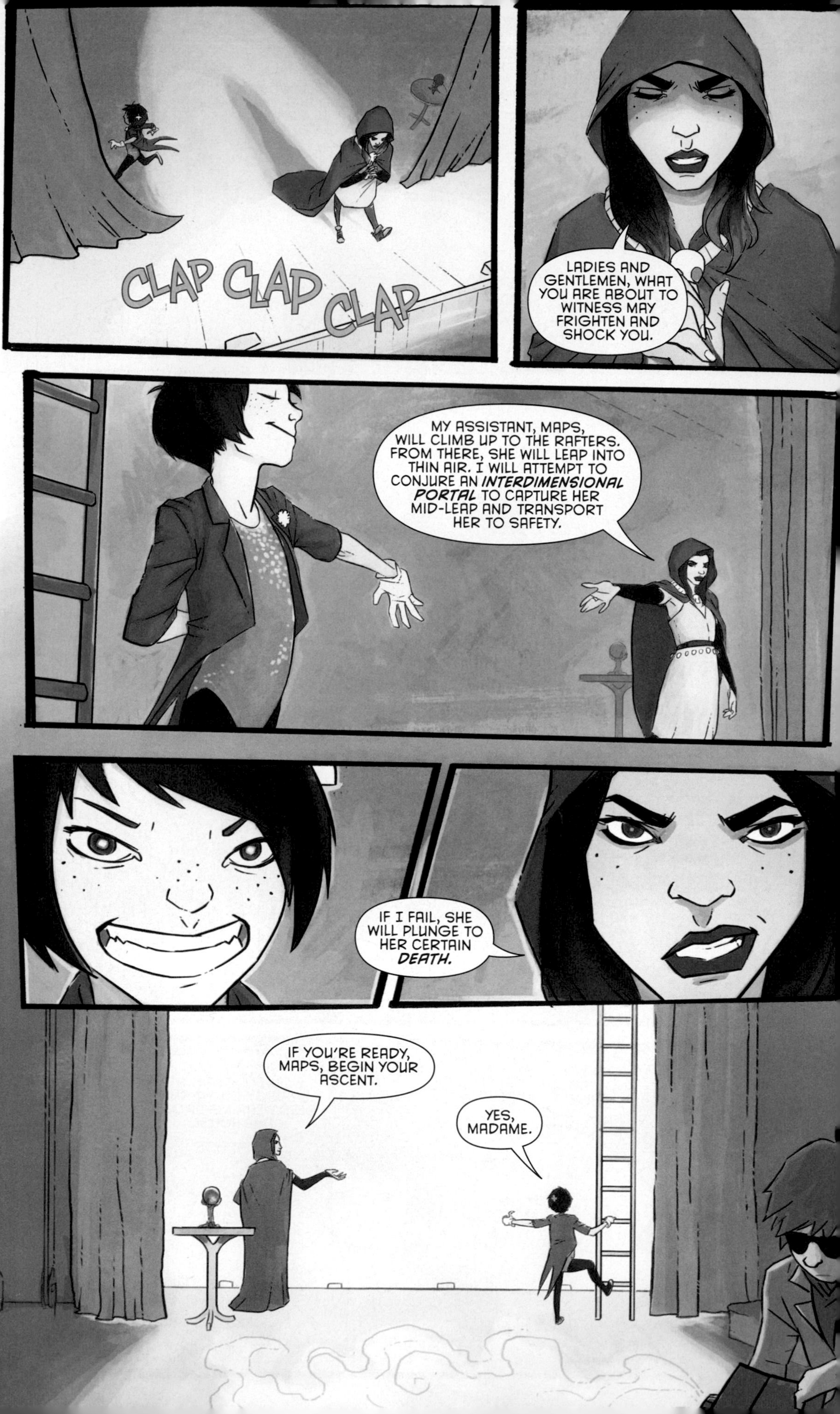
CLAP CLAP CLAP
LADIES AND GENTLEMEN, WHAT YOU ARE ABOUT TO WITNESS MAY FRIGHTEN AND SHOCK YOU.
MY ASSISTANT, MAPS, WILL CLIMB UP TO THE RAFTERS. FROM THERE, SHE WILL LEAP INTO THIN AIR. I WILL ATTEMPT TO CONJURE AN *INTERDIMENSIONAL PORTAL* TO CAPTURE HER MID-LEAP AND TRANSPORT HER TO SAFETY.
IF I FAIL, SHE WILL PLUNGE TO HER CERTAIN *DEATH.*
IF YOU'RE READY, MAPS, BEGIN YOUR ASCENT.
YES, MADAME.

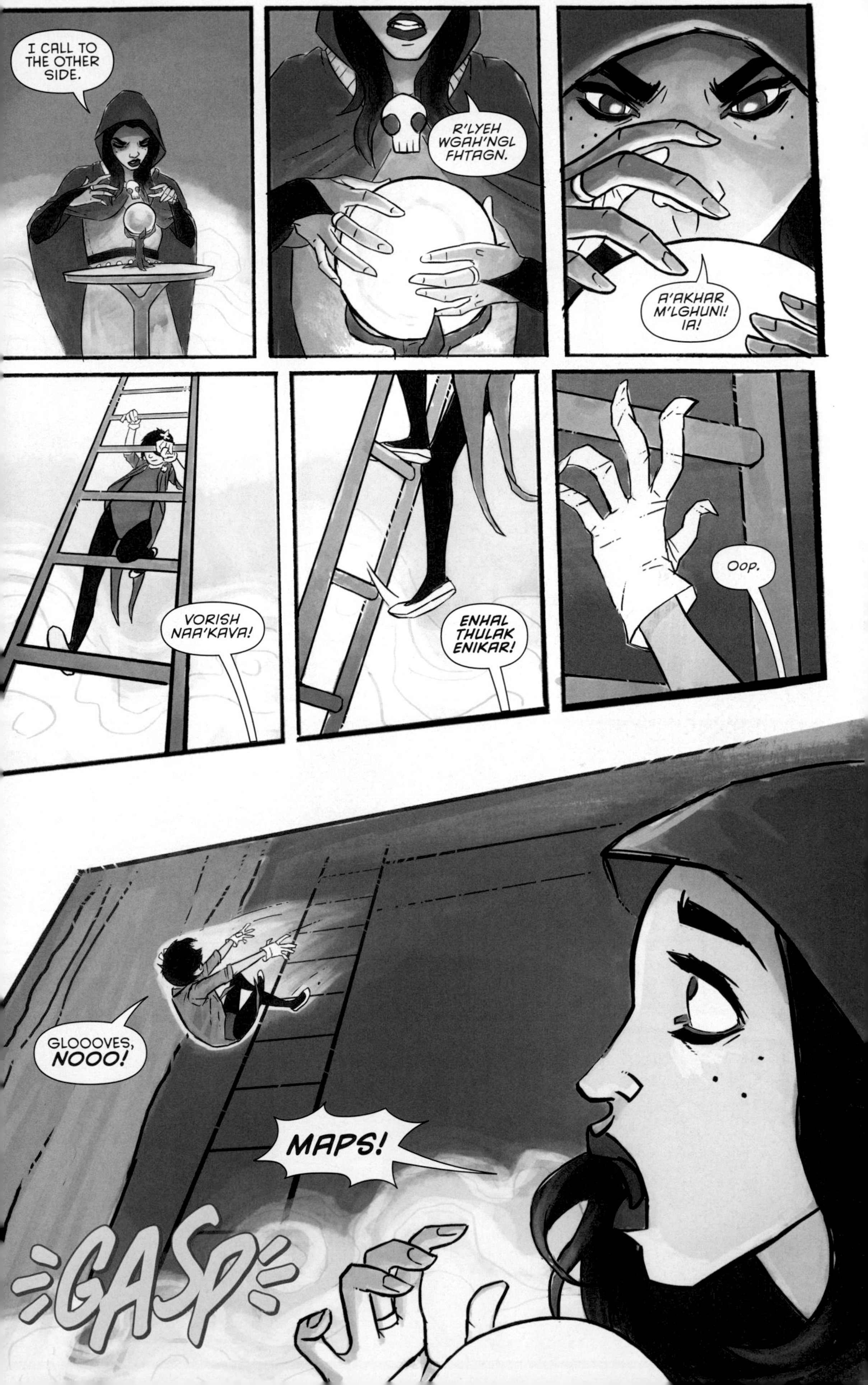
I CALL TO THE OTHER SIDE.
R'LYEH WGAH'NGL FHTAGN.
A'AKHAR M'LGHUNI! IA!
VORISH NAA'KAVA!
ENHAL THULAK ENIKAR!
Oop.
GLOOOVES, NOOO!
MAPS!
GASP

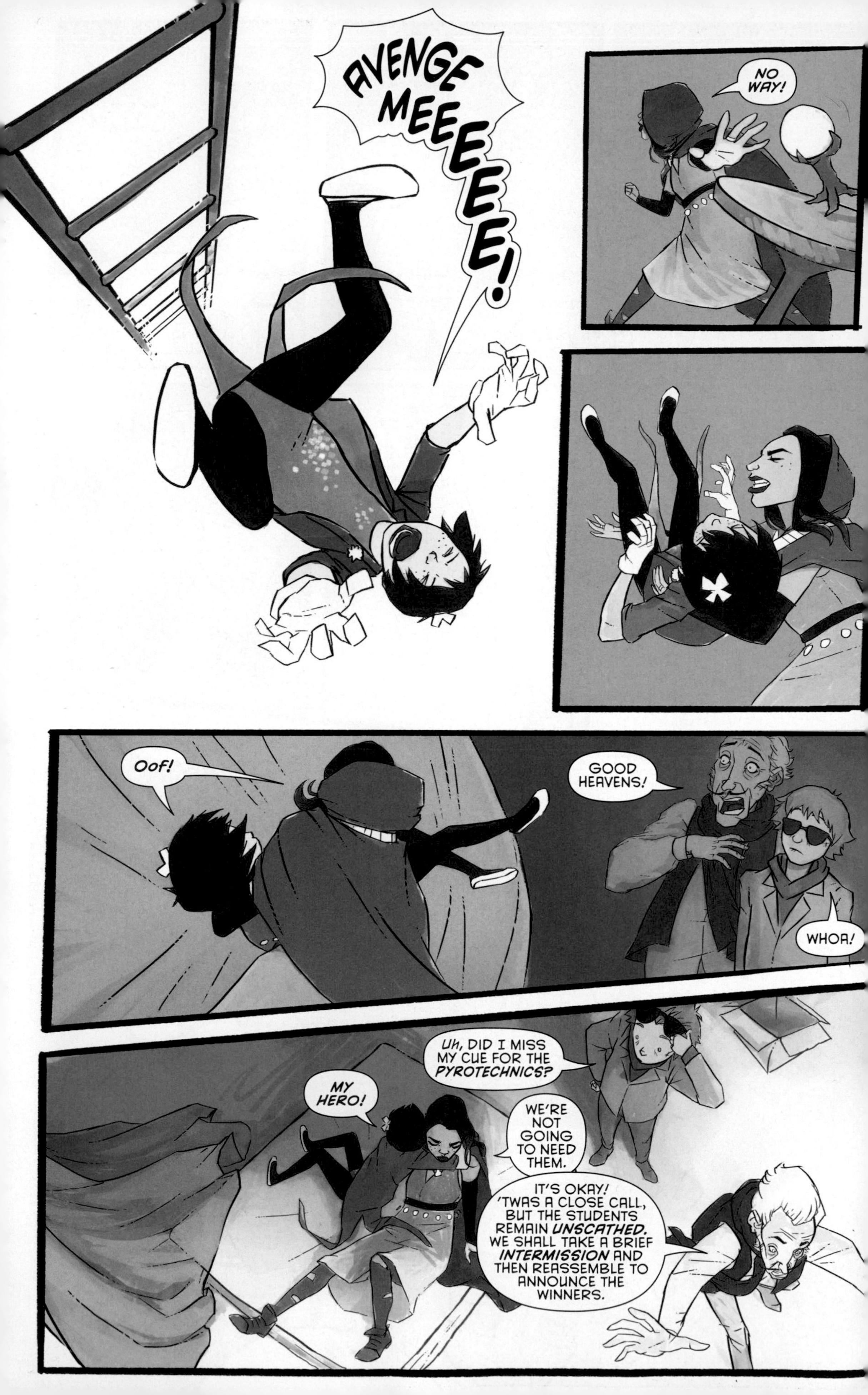
AVENGE MEEEEEE!
NO WAY!
Oof!
GOOD HEAVENS!
WHOA!
Uh, DID I MISS MY CUE FOR THE PYROTECHNICS?
MY HERO!
WE'RE NOT GOING TO NEED THEM.
IT'S OKAY! 'TWAS A CLOSE CALL, BUT THE STUDENTS REMAIN UNSCATHED. WE SHALL TAKE A BRIEF INTERMISSION AND THEN REASSEMBLE TO ANNOUNCE THE WINNERS.

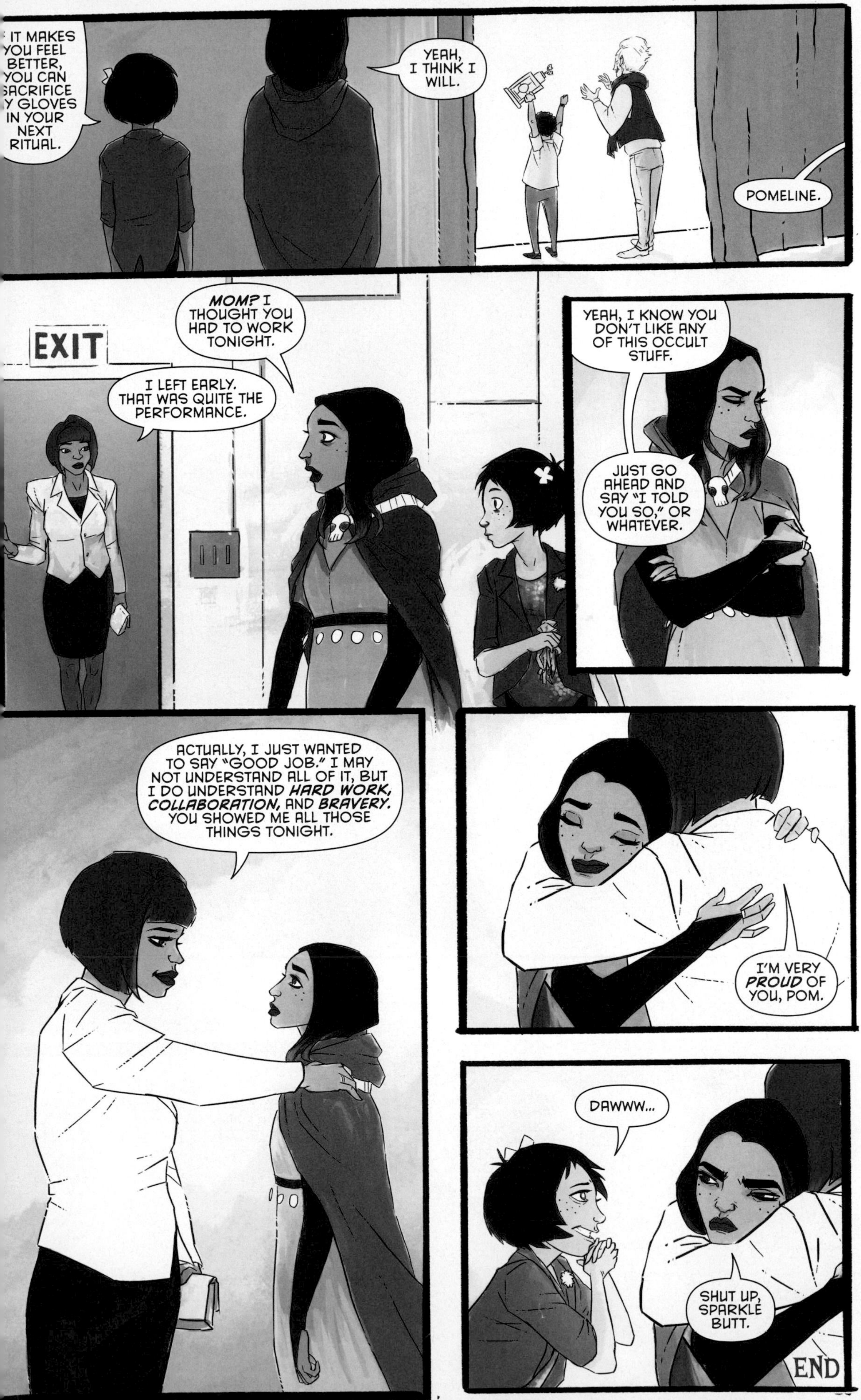

IT MAKES YOU FEEL BETTER, YOU CAN SACRIFICE Y GLOVES IN YOUR NEXT RITUAL.
YEAH, I THINK I WILL.
POMELINE.
EXIT
MOM? I THOUGHT YOU HAD TO WORK TONIGHT.
I LEFT EARLY. THAT WAS QUITE THE PERFORMANCE.
YEAH, I KNOW YOU DON'T LIKE ANY OF THIS OCCULT STUFF.
JUST GO AHEAD AND SAY "I TOLD YOU SO," OR WHATEVER.
ACTUALLY, I JUST WANTED TO SAY "GOOD JOB." I MAY NOT UNDERSTAND ALL OF IT, BUT I DO UNDERSTAND HARD WORK, COLLABORATION, AND BRAVERY. YOU SHOWED ME ALL THOSE THINGS TONIGHT.
I'M VERY PROUD OF YOU, POM.
DAWWW...
SHUT UP, SPARKLE BUTT.
END

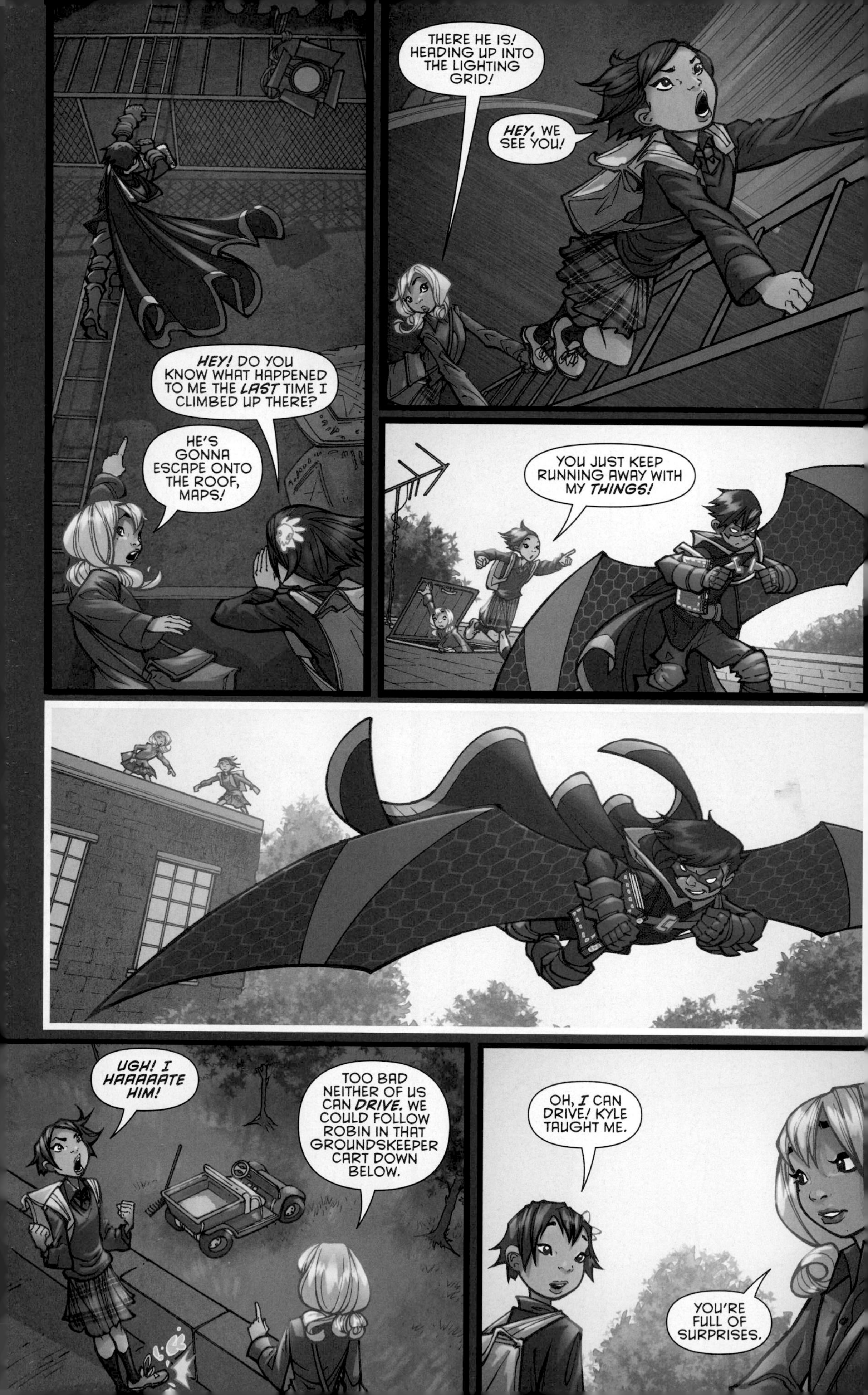
THERE HE IS! HEADING UP INTO THE LIGHTING GRID!
HEY, WE SEE YOU!
HEY! DO YOU KNOW WHAT HAPPENED TO ME THE LAST TIME I CLIMBED UP THERE?
HE'S GONNA ESCAPE ONTO THE ROOF, MAPS!
YOU JUST KEEP RUNNING AWAY WITH MY THINGS!
UGH! I HAAAAATE HIM!
TOO BAD NEITHER OF US CAN DRIVE. WE COULD FOLLOW ROBIN IN THAT GROUNDSKEEPER CART DOWN BELOW.
OH, I CAN DRIVE! KYLE TAUGHT ME.
YOU'RE FULL OF SURPRISES.

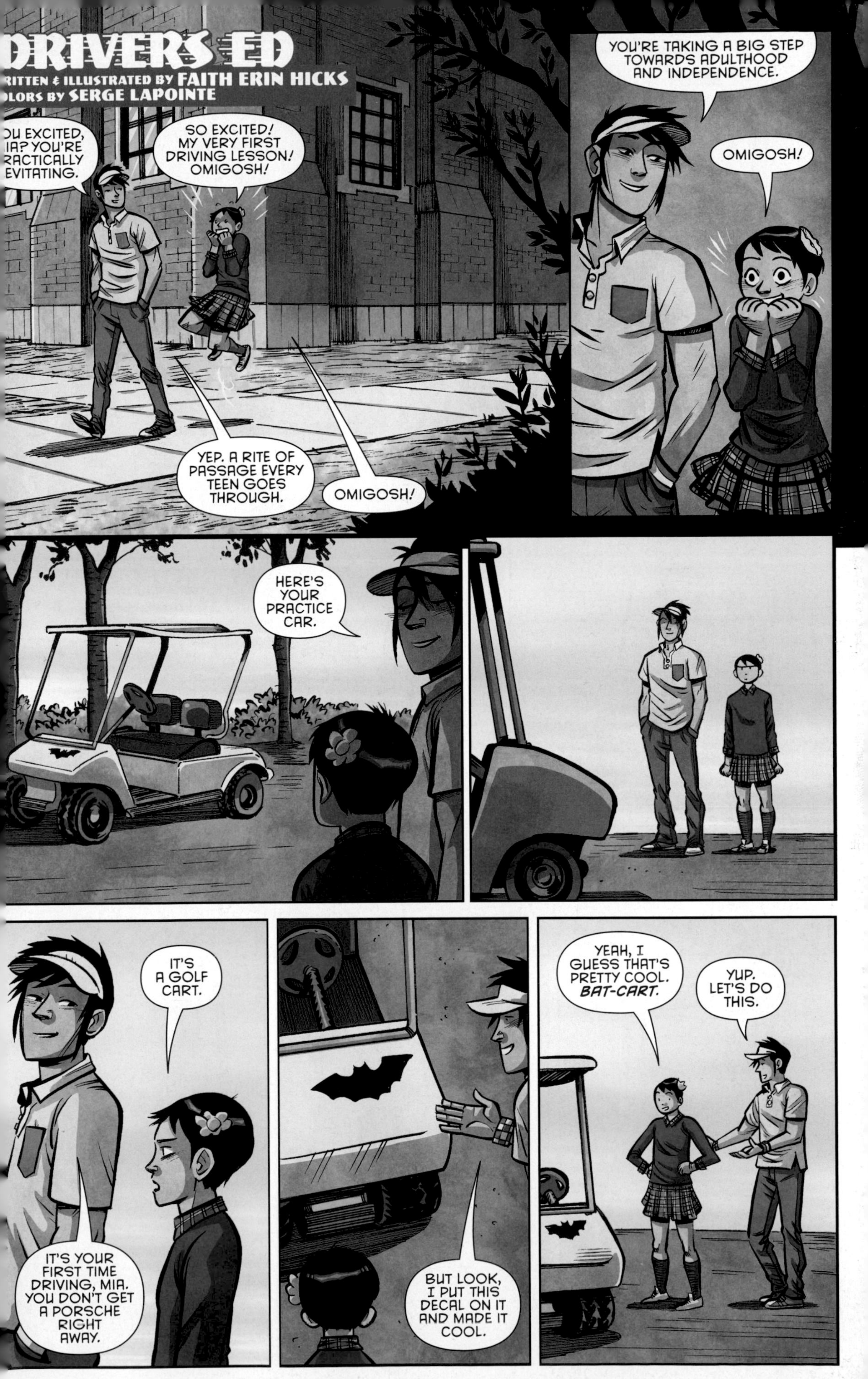
DRIVERS ED
RITTEN & ILLUSTRATED BY FAITH ERIN HICKS
OLORS BY SERGE LAPOINTE
OU EXCITED, IA? YOU'RE RACTICALLY EVITATING.
SO EXCITED! MY VERY FIRST DRIVING LESSON! OMIGOSH!
YEP. A RITE OF PASSAGE EVERY TEEN GOES THROUGH.
OMIGOSH!
YOU'RE TAKING A BIG STEP TOWARDS ADULTHOOD AND INDEPENDENCE.
OMIGOSH!
HERE'S YOUR PRACTICE CAR.
IT'S A GOLF CART.
IT'S YOUR FIRST TIME DRIVING, MIA. YOU DON'T GET A PORSCHE RIGHT AWAY.
BUT LOOK, I PUT THIS DECAL ON IT AND MADE IT COOL.
YEAH, I GUESS THAT'S PRETTY COOL. BAT-CART.
YUP. LET'S DO THIS.

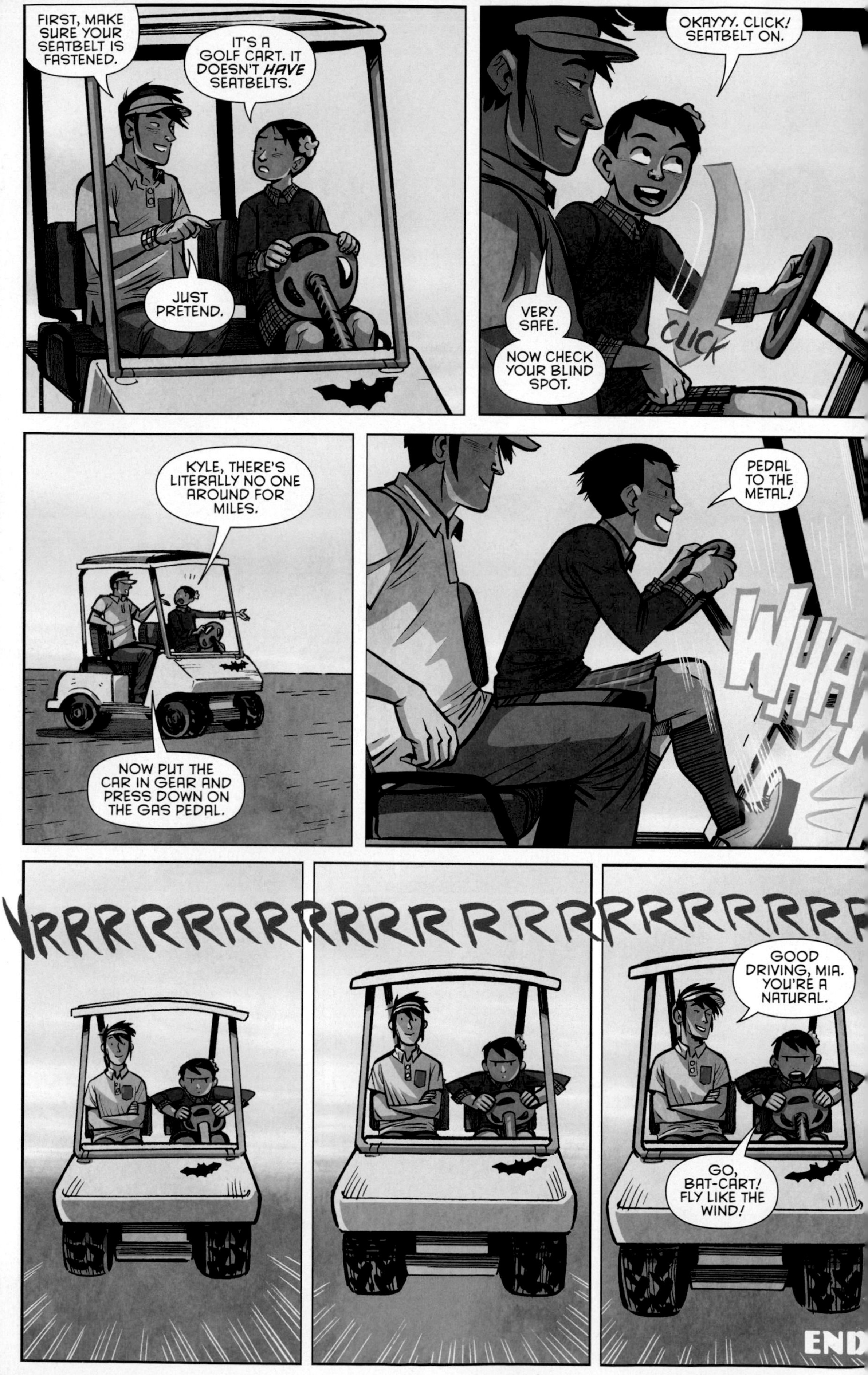
FIRST, MAKE SURE YOUR SEATBELT IS FASTENED.
IT'S A GOLF CART. IT DOESN'T *HAVE* SEATBELTS.
JUST PRETEND.
OKAYYY. CLICK! SEATBELT ON.
CLICK
VERY SAFE.
NOW CHECK YOUR BLIND SPOT.
KYLE, THERE'S LITERALLY NO ONE AROUND FOR MILES.
NOW PUT THE CAR IN GEAR AND PRESS DOWN ON THE GAS PEDAL.
PEDAL TO THE METAL!
VRRRRRRRRRRRRRRRRRRRRR
GOOD DRIVING, MIA. YOU'RE A NATURAL.
GO, BAT-CART! FLY LIKE THE WIND!
END

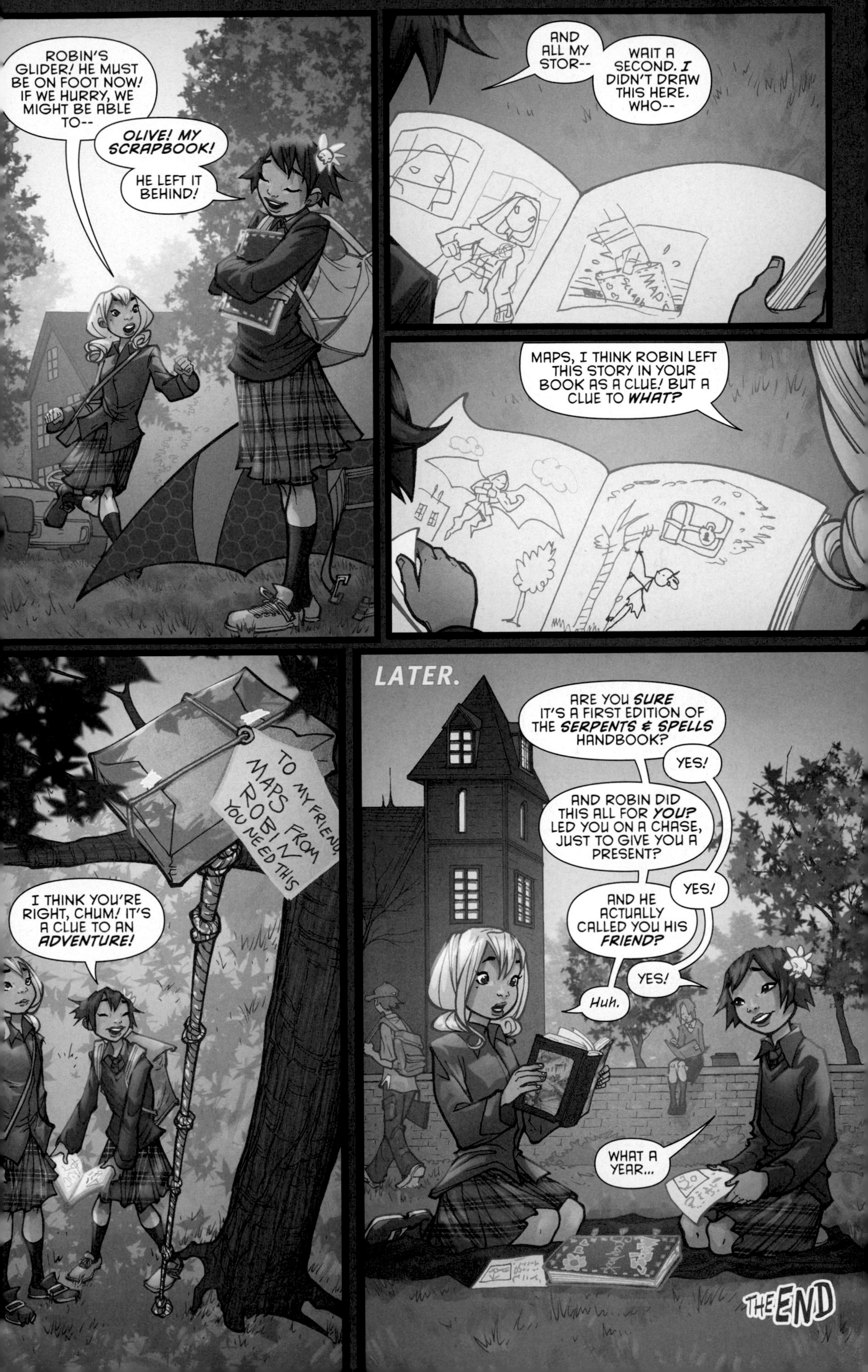
ROBIN'S GLIDER! HE MUST BE ON FOOT NOW! IF WE HURRY, WE MIGHT BE ABLE TO--
OLIVE! MY SCRAPBOOK!
HE LEFT IT BEHIND!
AND ALL MY STOR--
WAIT A SECOND. I DIDN'T DRAW THIS HERE. WHO--
MAPS, I THINK ROBIN LEFT THIS STORY IN YOUR BOOK AS A CLUE! BUT A CLUE TO WHAT?
TO MY FRIEND, MAPS FROM ROBIN YOU NEED THIS
I THINK YOU'RE RIGHT, CHUM! IT'S A CLUE TO AN ADVENTURE!
LATER.
ARE YOU SURE IT'S A FIRST EDITION OF THE SERPENTS & SPELLS HANDBOOK?
YES!
AND ROBIN DID THIS ALL FOR YOU? LED YOU ON A CHASE, JUST TO GIVE YOU A PRESENT?
YES!
AND HE ACTUALLY CALLED YOU HIS FRIEND?
YES!
Huh.
WHAT A YEAR...
THE END

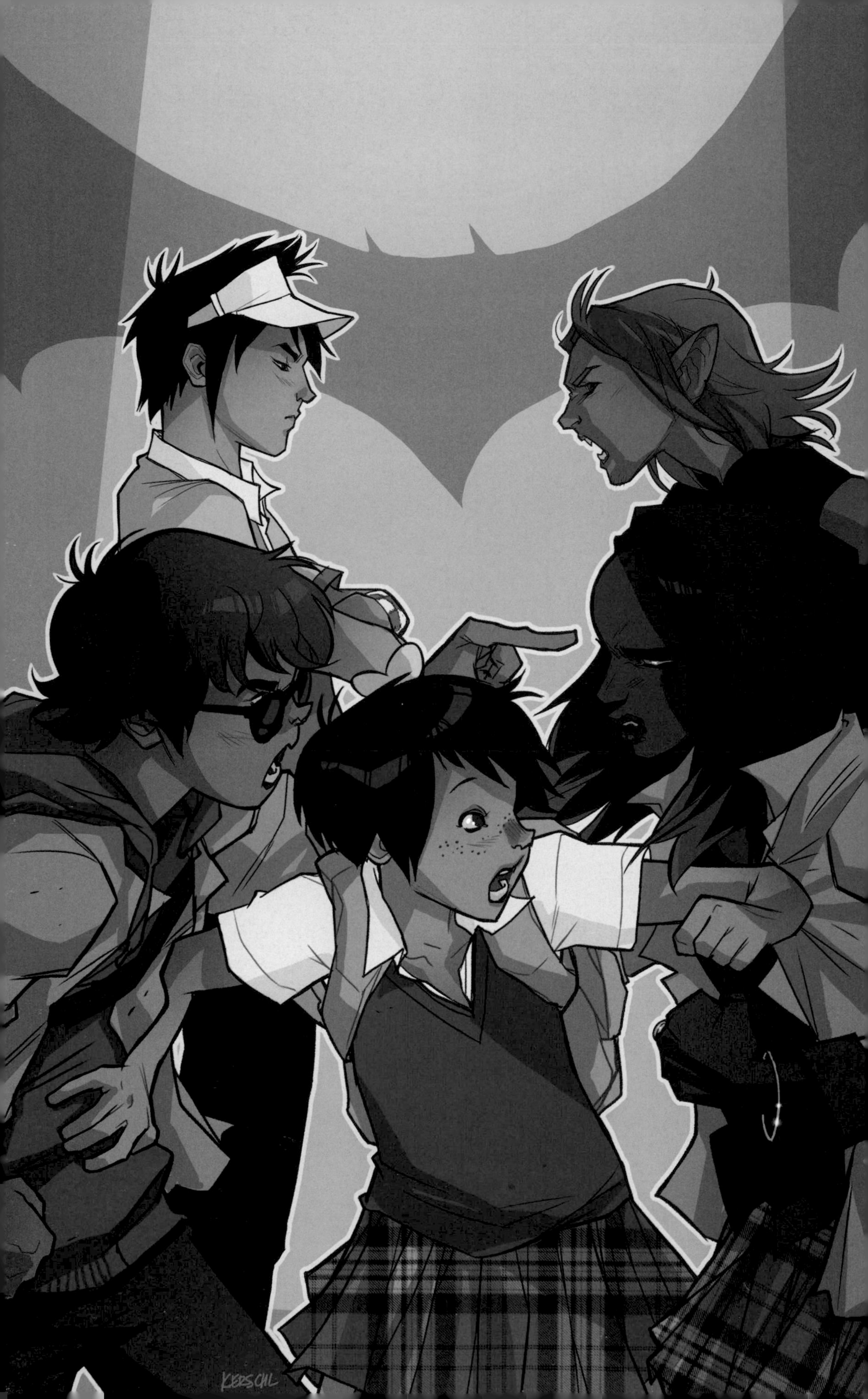
KERSCHL

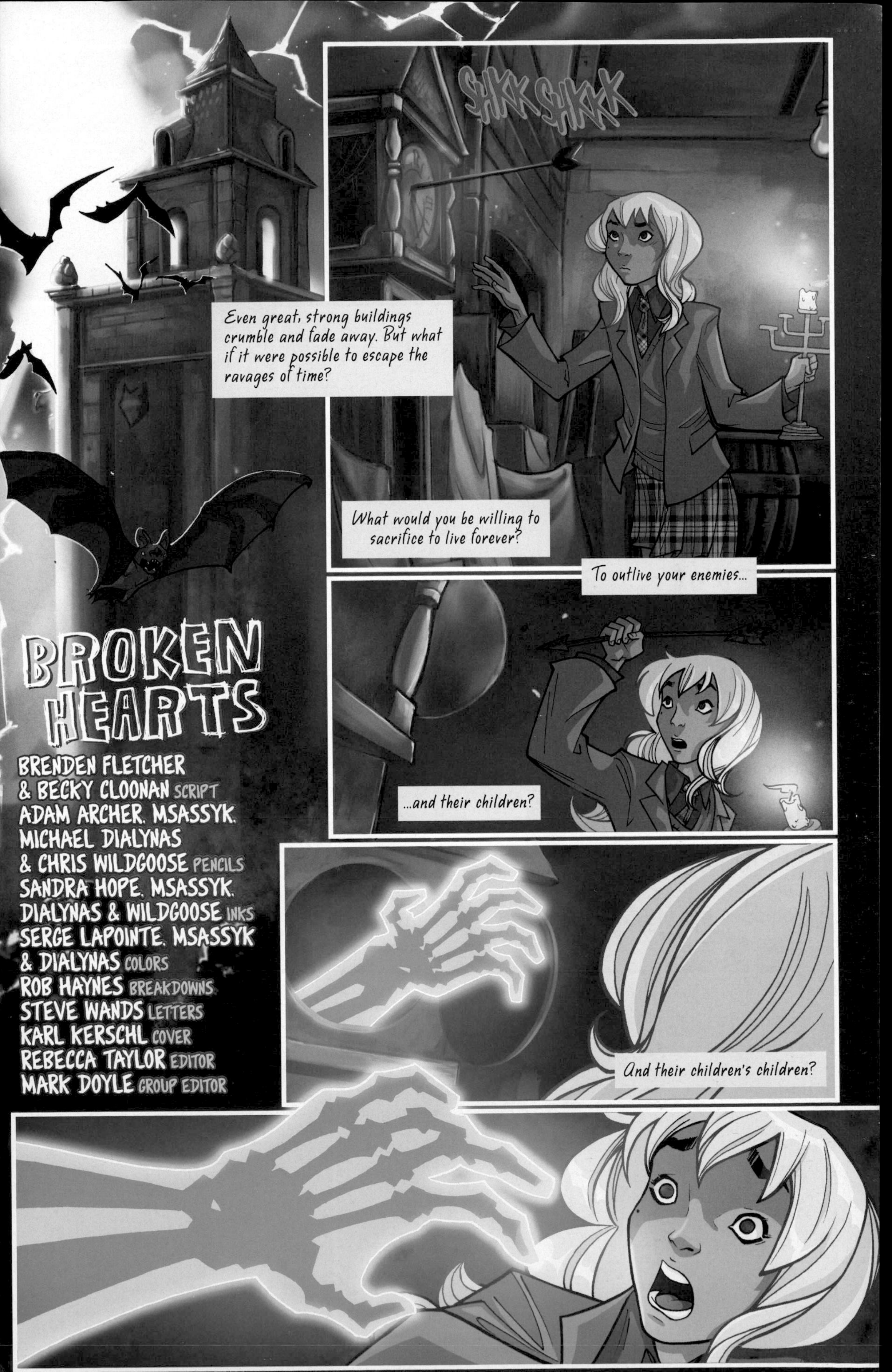
SHKK SHKKK
Even great, strong buildings crumble and fade away. But what if it were possible to escape the ravages of time?
What would you be willing to sacrifice to live forever?
To outlive your enemies...
...and their children?
BROKEN HEARTS
BRENDEN FLETCHER & BECKY CLOONAN SCRIPT
ADAM ARCHER, MSASSYK, MICHAEL DIALYNAS & CHRIS WILDGOOSE PENCILS
SANDRA HOPE, MSASSYK, DIALYNAS & WILDGOOSE INKS
SERGE LAPOINTE, MSASSYK & DIALYNAS COLORS
ROB HAYNES BREAKDOWNS
STEVE WANDS LETTERS
KARL KERSCHL COVER
REBECCA TAYLOR EDITOR
MARK DOYLE GROUP EDITOR
And their children's children?

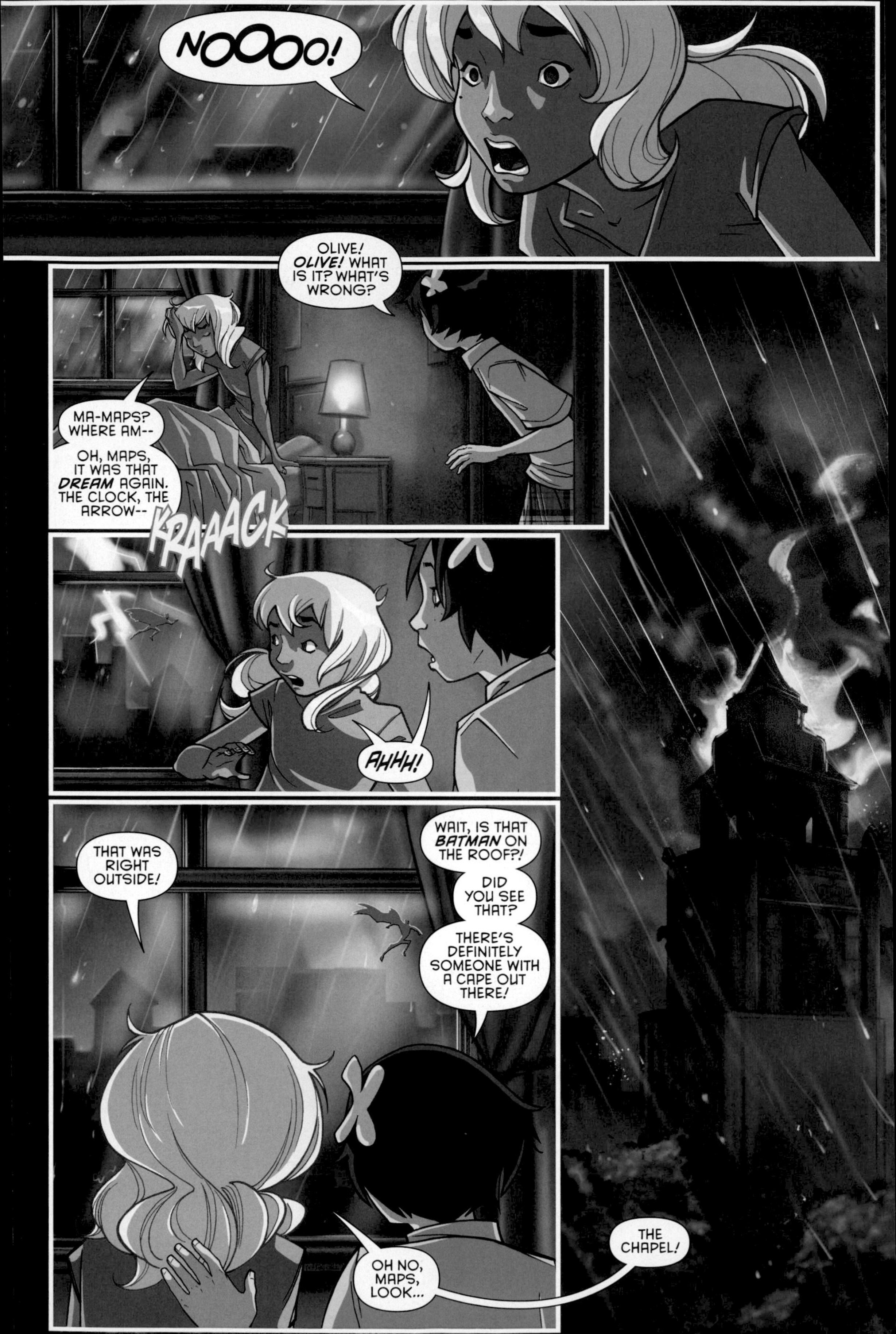
NOOOO!
OLIVE! OLIVE! WHAT IS IT? WHAT'S WRONG?
MA-MAPS? WHERE AM--
OH, MAPS, IT WAS THAT DREAM AGAIN. THE CLOCK, THE ARROW--
KRAAACK
AHHH!
THAT WAS RIGHT OUTSIDE!
WAIT, IS THAT BATMAN ON THE ROOF?!
DID YOU SEE THAT?
THERE'S DEFINITELY SOMEONE WITH A CAPE OUT THERE!
OH NO, MAPS, LOOK...
THE CHAPEL!

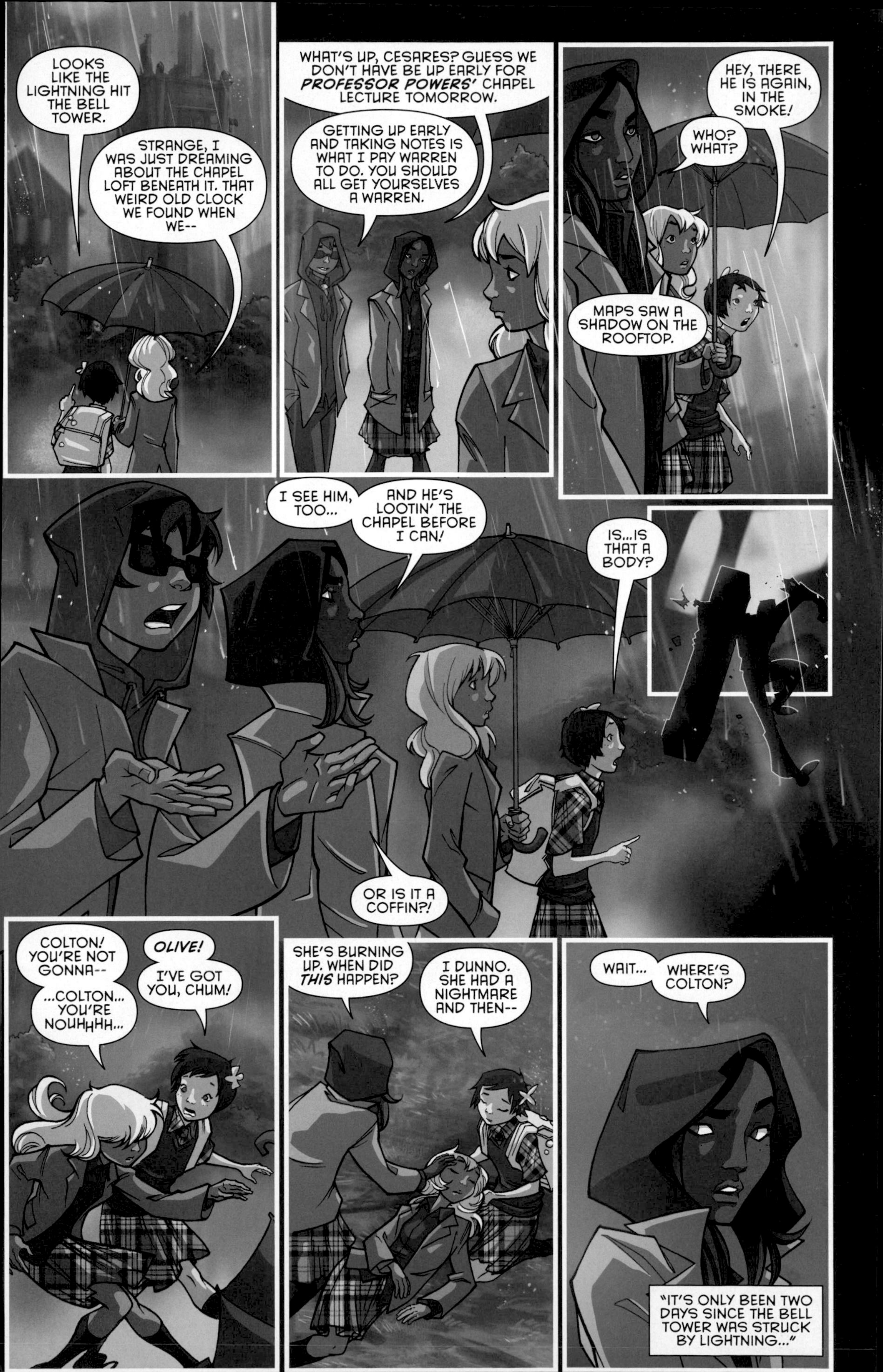
LOOKS LIKE THE LIGHTNING HIT THE BELL TOWER.
STRANGE, I WAS JUST DREAMING ABOUT THE CHAPEL LOFT BENEATH IT. THAT WEIRD OLD CLOCK WE FOUND WHEN WE--
WHAT'S UP, CESARES? GUESS WE DON'T HAVE BE UP EARLY FOR PROFESSOR POWERS' CHAPEL LECTURE TOMORROW.
GETTING UP EARLY AND TAKING NOTES IS WHAT I PAY WARREN TO DO. YOU SHOULD ALL GET YOURSELVES A WARREN.
HEY, THERE HE IS AGAIN, IN THE SMOKE!
WHO? WHAT?
MAPS SAW A SHADOW ON THE ROOFTOP.
I SEE HIM, TOO...
AND HE'S LOOTIN' THE CHAPEL BEFORE I CAN!
IS...IS THAT A BODY?
OR IS IT A COFFIN?!
COLTON! YOU'RE NOT GONNA--
...COLTON... YOU'RE NOUHHHH...
OLIVE!
I'VE GOT YOU, CHUM!
SHE'S BURNING UP. WHEN DID THIS HAPPEN?
I DUNNO. SHE HAD A NIGHTMARE AND THEN--
WAIT...
WHERE'S COLTON?
"IT'S ONLY BEEN TWO DAYS SINCE THE BELL TOWER WAS STRUCK BY LIGHTNING..."

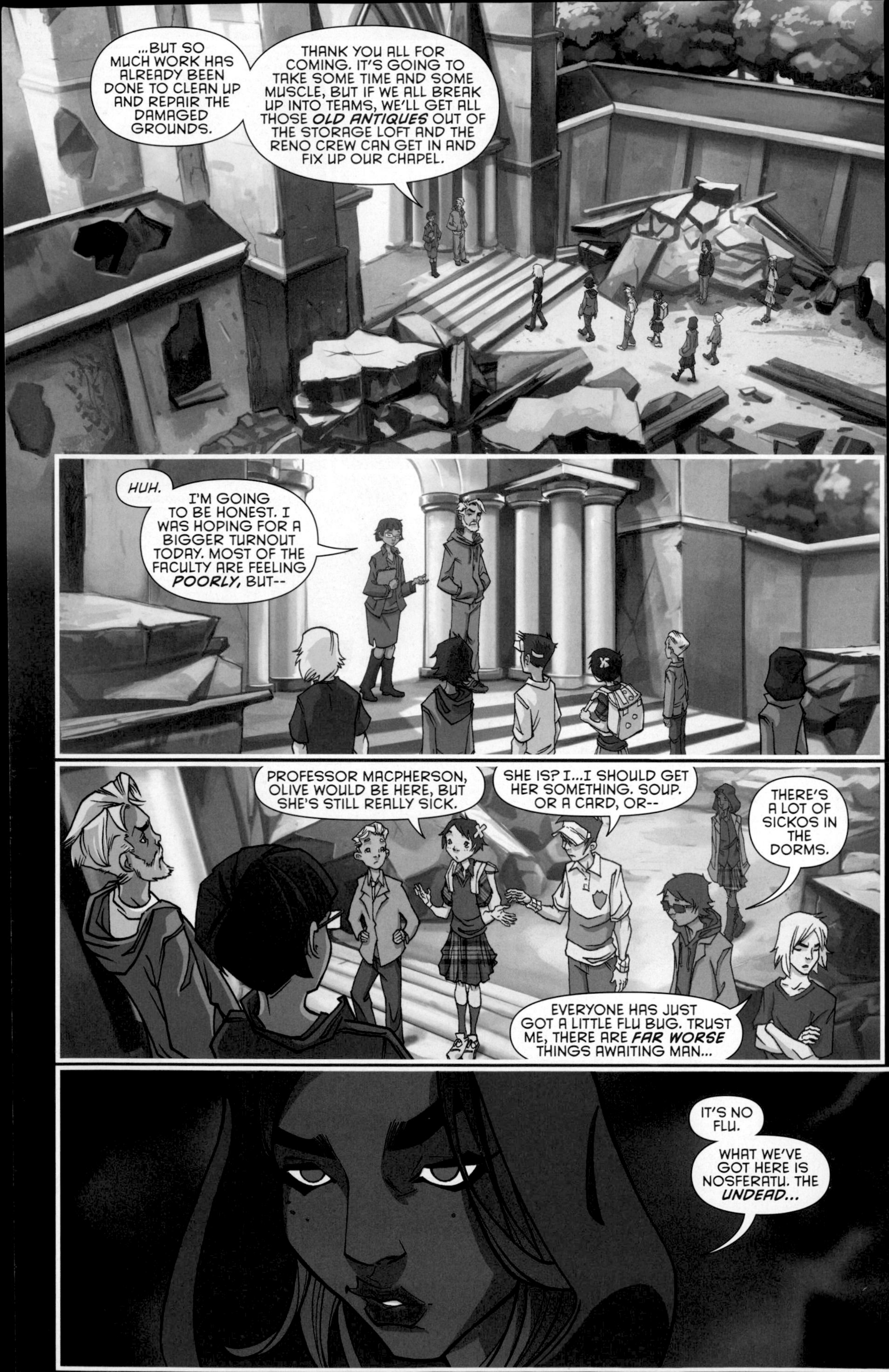
...BUT SO MUCH WORK HAS ALREADY BEEN DONE TO CLEAN UP AND REPAIR THE DAMAGED GROUNDS.
THANK YOU ALL FOR COMING. IT'S GOING TO TAKE SOME TIME AND SOME MUSCLE, BUT IF WE ALL BREAK UP INTO TEAMS, WE'LL GET ALL THOSE *OLD ANTIQUES* OUT OF THE STORAGE LOFT AND THE RENO CREW CAN GET IN AND FIX UP OUR CHAPEL.
HUH.
I'M GOING TO BE HONEST. I WAS HOPING FOR A BIGGER TURNOUT TODAY. MOST OF THE FACULTY ARE FEELING ***POORLY,*** BUT--
PROFESSOR MACPHERSON, OLIVE WOULD BE HERE, BUT SHE'S STILL REALLY SICK.
SHE IS? I...I SHOULD GET HER SOMETHING. SOUP. OR A CARD, OR--
THERE'S A LOT OF SICKOS IN THE DORMS.
EVERYONE HAS JUST GOT A LITTLE FLU BUG. TRUST ME, THERE ARE ***FAR WORSE*** THINGS AWAITING MAN...
IT'S NO FLU.
WHAT WE'VE GOT HERE IS NOSFERATU. THE ***UNDEAD...***

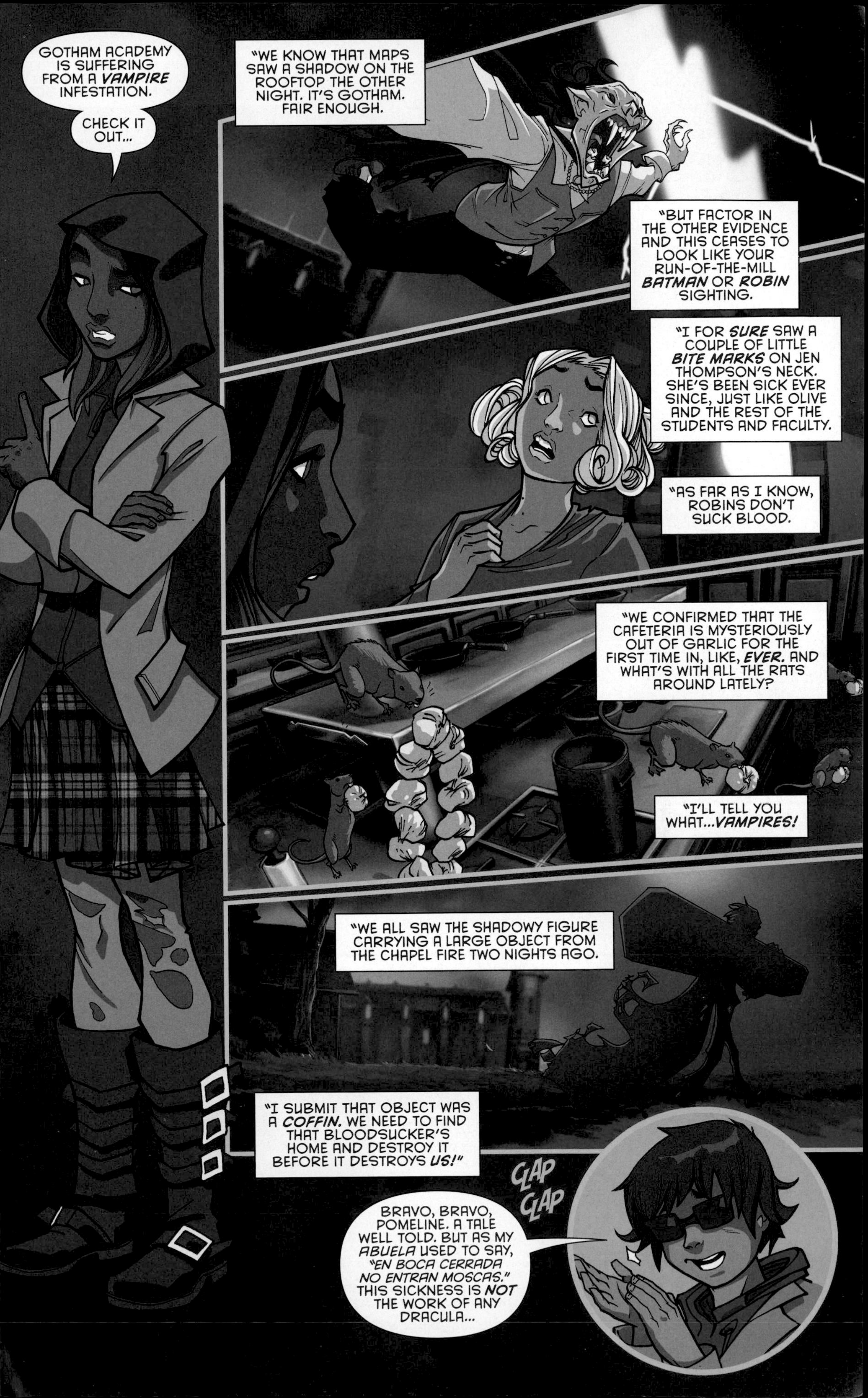
GOTHAM ACADEMY IS SUFFERING FROM A VAMPIRE INFESTATION.
CHECK IT OUT...
"WE KNOW THAT MAPS SAW A SHADOW ON THE ROOFTOP THE OTHER NIGHT. IT'S GOTHAM. FAIR ENOUGH.
"BUT FACTOR IN THE OTHER EVIDENCE AND THIS CEASES TO LOOK LIKE YOUR RUN-OF-THE-MILL BATMAN OR ROBIN SIGHTING.
"I FOR SURE SAW A COUPLE OF LITTLE BITE MARKS ON JEN THOMPSON'S NECK. SHE'S BEEN SICK EVER SINCE, JUST LIKE OLIVE AND THE REST OF THE STUDENTS AND FACULTY.
"AS FAR AS I KNOW, ROBINS DON'T SUCK BLOOD.
"WE CONFIRMED THAT THE CAFETERIA IS MYSTERIOUSLY OUT OF GARLIC FOR THE FIRST TIME IN, LIKE, EVER. AND WHAT'S WITH ALL THE RATS AROUND LATELY?
"I'LL TELL YOU WHAT...VAMPIRES!
"WE ALL SAW THE SHADOWY FIGURE CARRYING A LARGE OBJECT FROM THE CHAPEL FIRE TWO NIGHTS AGO.
"I SUBMIT THAT OBJECT WAS A COFFIN. WE NEED TO FIND THAT BLOODSUCKER'S HOME AND DESTROY IT BEFORE IT DESTROYS US!"
CLAP CLAP
BRAVO, BRAVO, POMELINE. A TALE WELL TOLD. BUT AS MY ABUELA USED TO SAY, "EN BOCA CERRADA NO ENTRAN MOSCAS." THIS SICKNESS IS NOT THE WORK OF ANY DRACULA...

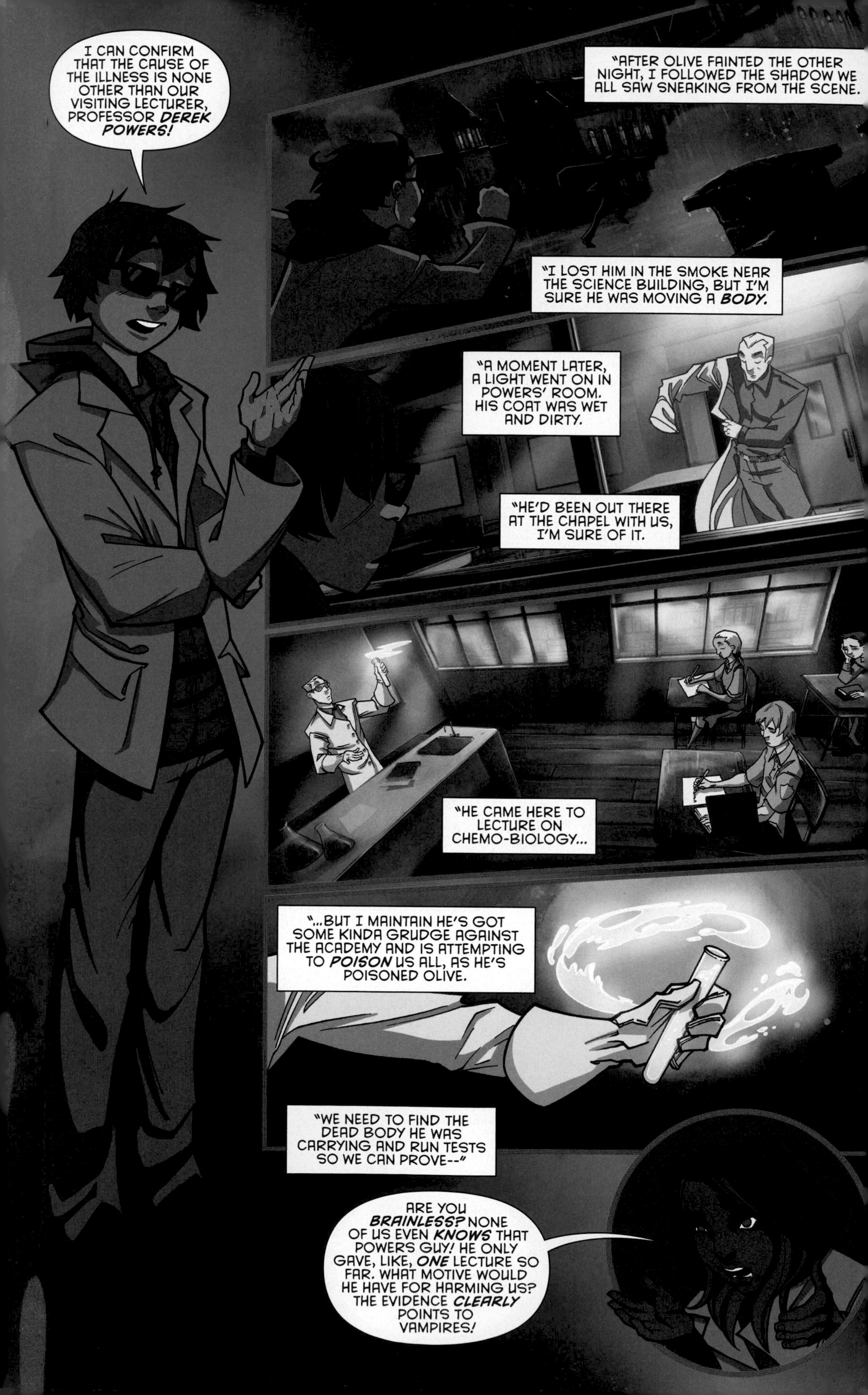
I CAN CONFIRM THAT THE CAUSE OF THE ILLNESS IS NONE OTHER THAN OUR VISITING LECTURER, PROFESSOR DEREK POWERS!
"AFTER OLIVE FAINTED THE OTHER NIGHT, I FOLLOWED THE SHADOW WE ALL SAW SNEAKING FROM THE SCENE.
"I LOST HIM IN THE SMOKE NEAR THE SCIENCE BUILDING, BUT I'M SURE HE WAS MOVING A BODY.
"A MOMENT LATER, A LIGHT WENT ON IN POWERS' ROOM. HIS COAT WAS WET AND DIRTY.
"HE'D BEEN OUT THERE AT THE CHAPEL WITH US, I'M SURE OF IT.
"HE CAME HERE TO LECTURE ON CHEMO-BIOLOGY...
"...BUT I MAINTAIN HE'S GOT SOME KINDA GRUDGE AGAINST THE ACADEMY AND IS ATTEMPTING TO POISON US ALL, AS HE'S POISONED OLIVE.
"WE NEED TO FIND THE DEAD BODY HE WAS CARRYING AND RUN TESTS SO WE CAN PROVE--"
ARE YOU BRAINLESS? NONE OF US EVEN KNOWS THAT POWERS GUY! HE ONLY GAVE, LIKE, ONE LECTURE SO FAR. WHAT MOTIVE WOULD HE HAVE FOR HARMING US? THE EVIDENCE CLEARLY POINTS TO VAMPIRES!

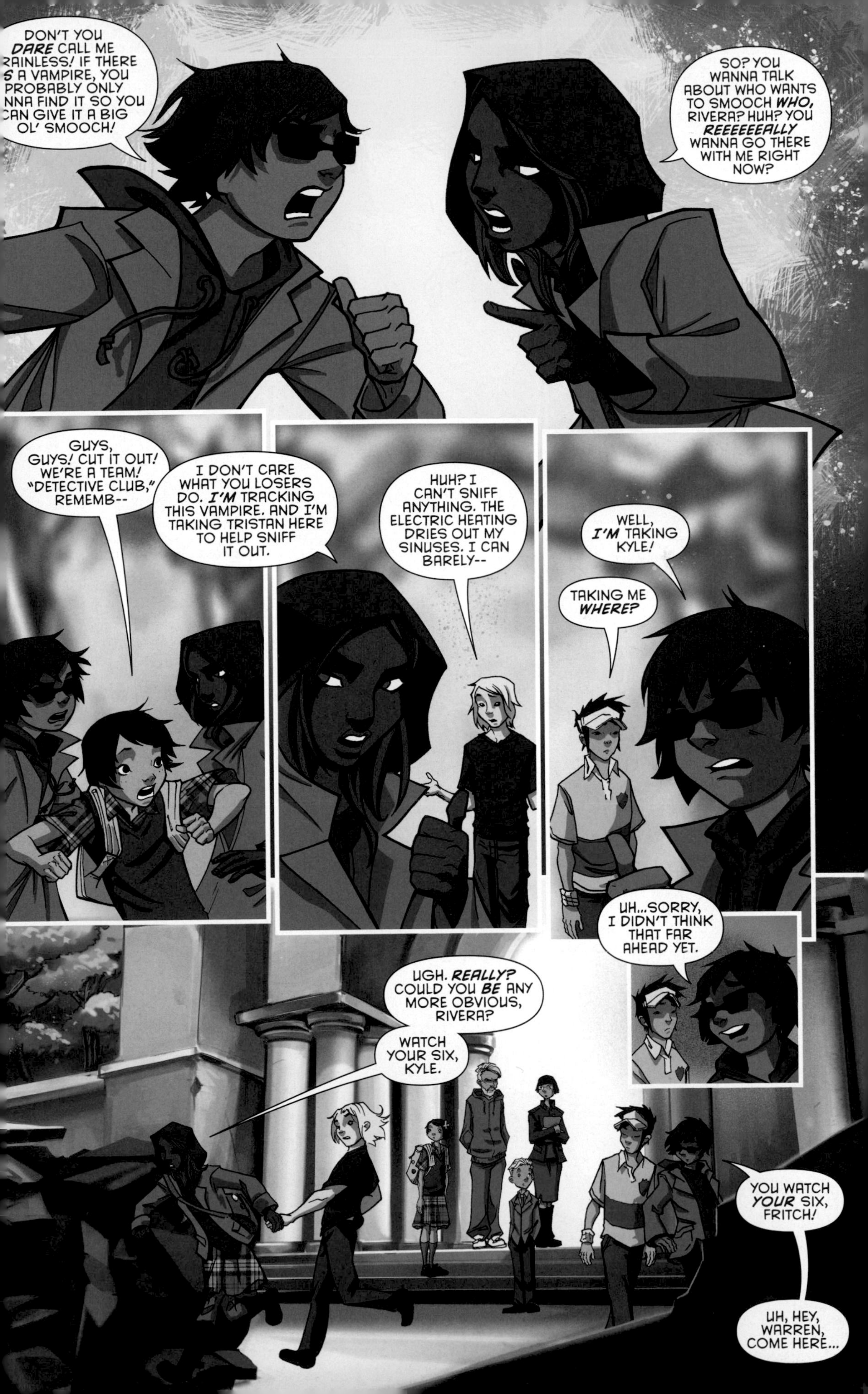

DON'T YOU DARE CALL ME BRAINLESS! IF THERE IS A VAMPIRE, YOU PROBABLY ONLY WANNA FIND IT SO YOU CAN GIVE IT A BIG OL' SMOOCH!
SO? YOU WANNA TALK ABOUT WHO WANTS TO SMOOCH WHO, RIVERA? HUH? YOU REEEEEEALLY WANNA GO THERE WITH ME RIGHT NOW?
GUYS, GUYS! CUT IT OUT! WE'RE A TEAM! "DETECTIVE CLUB," REMEMB--
I DON'T CARE WHAT YOU LOSERS DO. I'M TRACKING THIS VAMPIRE. AND I'M TAKING TRISTAN HERE TO HELP SNIFF IT OUT.
HUH? I CAN'T SNIFF ANYTHING. THE ELECTRIC HEATING DRIES OUT MY SINUSES. I CAN BARELY--
WELL, I'M TAKING KYLE!
TAKING ME WHERE?
UH...SORRY, I DIDN'T THINK THAT FAR AHEAD YET.
UGH. REALLY? COULD YOU BE ANY MORE OBVIOUS, RIVERA?
WATCH YOUR SIX, KYLE.
YOU WATCH YOUR SIX, FRITCH!
UH, HEY, WARREN, COME HERE...

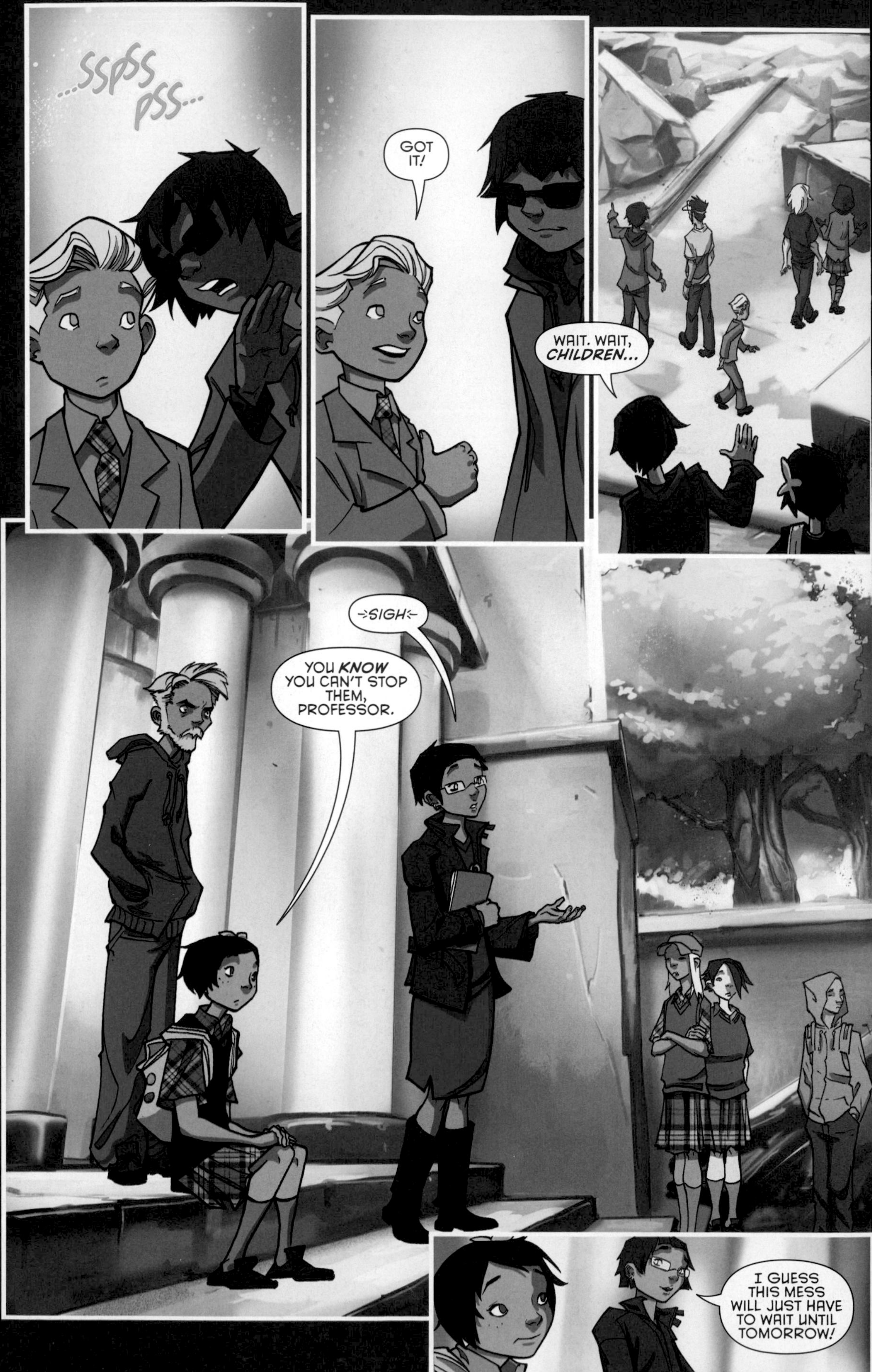
...SSPSS PSS...
GOT IT!
WAIT. WAIT, CHILDREN...
-SIGH-
YOU KNOW YOU CAN'T STOP THEM, PROFESSOR.
I GUESS THIS MESS WILL JUST HAVE TO WAIT UNTIL TOMORROW!

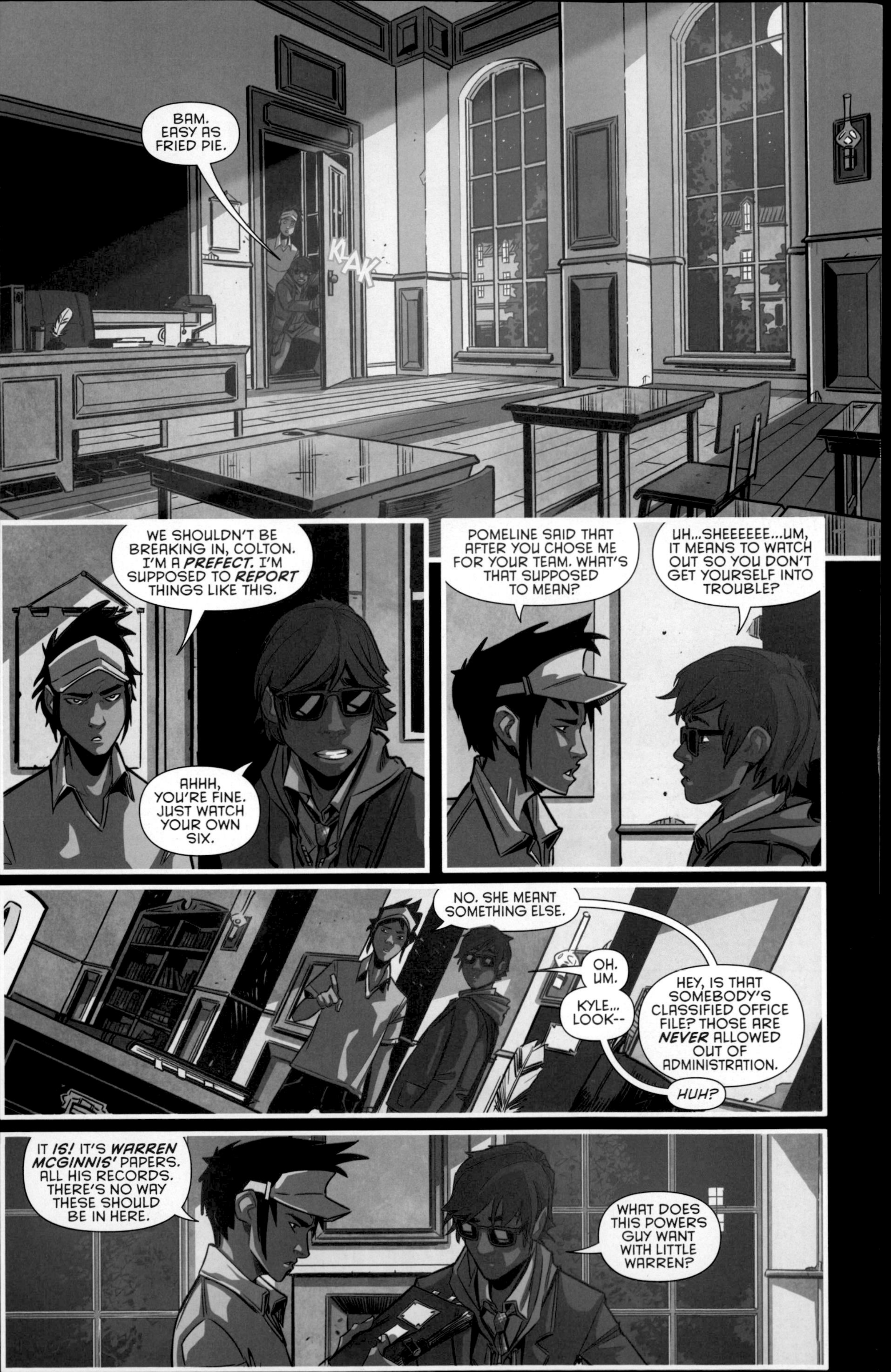
BAM. EASY AS FRIED PIE.
KLAK
WE SHOULDN'T BE BREAKING IN, COLTON. I'M A *PREFECT.* I'M SUPPOSED TO *REPORT* THINGS LIKE THIS.
AHHH, YOU'RE FINE. JUST WATCH YOUR OWN SIX.
POMELINE SAID THAT AFTER YOU CHOSE ME FOR YOUR TEAM. WHAT'S THAT SUPPOSED TO MEAN?
UH...SHEEEEEE...UM, IT MEANS TO WATCH OUT SO YOU DON'T GET YOURSELF INTO TROUBLE?
NO. SHE MEANT SOMETHING ELSE.
OH. UM.
KYLE... LOOK--
HEY, IS THAT SOMEBODY'S CLASSIFIED OFFICE FILE? THOSE ARE *NEVER* ALLOWED OUT OF ADMINISTRATION.
HUH?
IT *IS!* IT'S *WARREN MCGINNIS'* PAPERS. ALL HIS RECORDS. THERE'S NO WAY THESE SHOULD BE IN HERE.
WHAT DOES THIS POWERS GUY WANT WITH LITTLE WARREN?

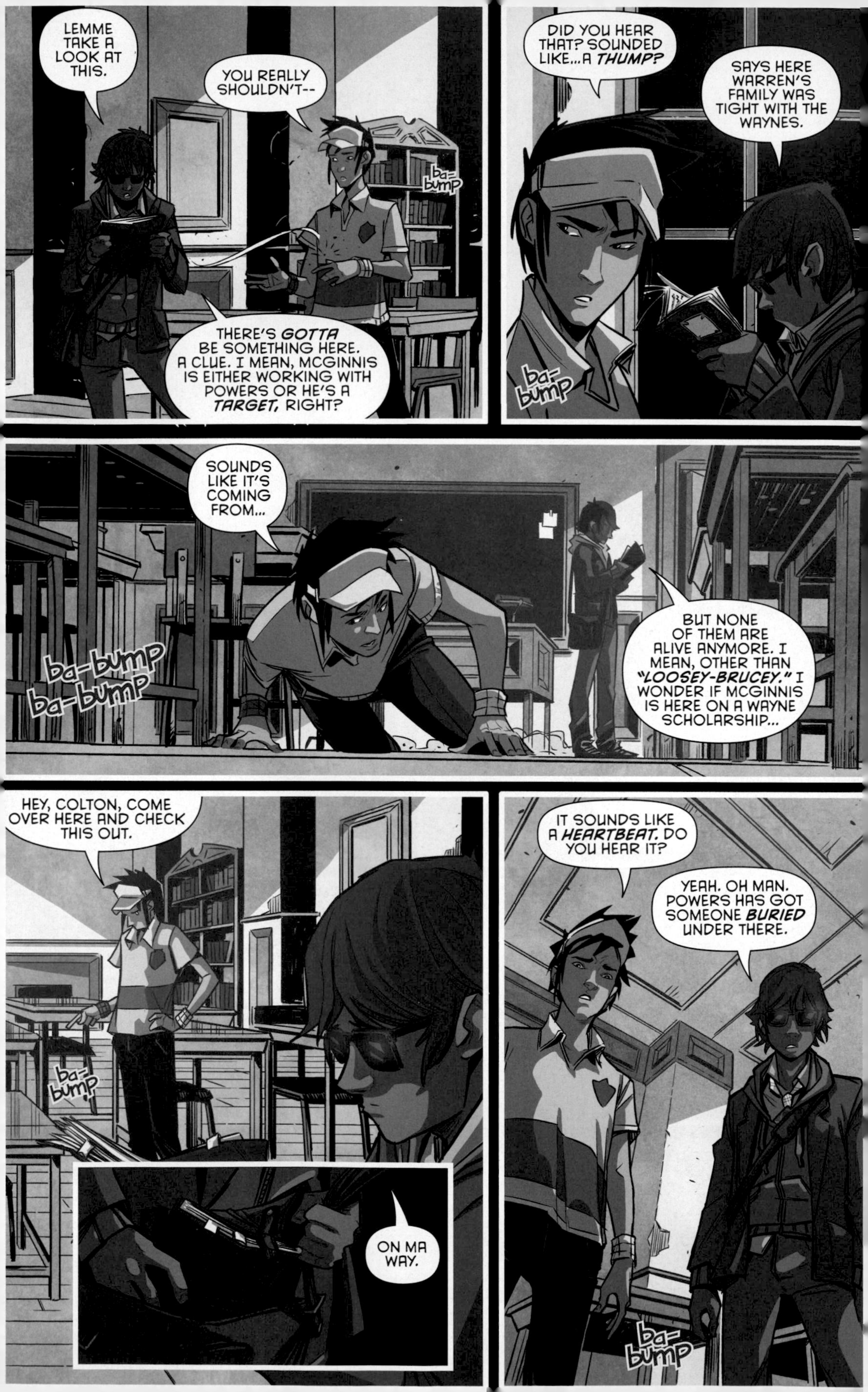
LEMME TAKE A LOOK AT THIS.
YOU REALLY SHOULDN'T--
ba-bump
THERE'S GOTTA BE SOMETHING HERE. A CLUE. I MEAN, MCGINNIS IS EITHER WORKING WITH POWERS OR HE'S A TARGET, RIGHT?
DID YOU HEAR THAT? SOUNDED LIKE...A THUMP?
SAYS HERE WARREN'S FAMILY WAS TIGHT WITH THE WAYNES.
ba-bump
SOUNDS LIKE IT'S COMING FROM...
ba-bump ba-bump
BUT NONE OF THEM ARE ALIVE ANYMORE. I MEAN, OTHER THAN "LOOSEY-BRUCEY." I WONDER IF MCGINNIS IS HERE ON A WAYNE SCHOLARSHIP...
HEY, COLTON, COME OVER HERE AND CHECK THIS OUT.
ba-bump
ON MA WAY.
IT SOUNDS LIKE A HEARTBEAT. DO YOU HEAR IT?
YEAH. OH MAN. POWERS HAS GOT SOMEONE BURIED UNDER THERE.
ba-bump

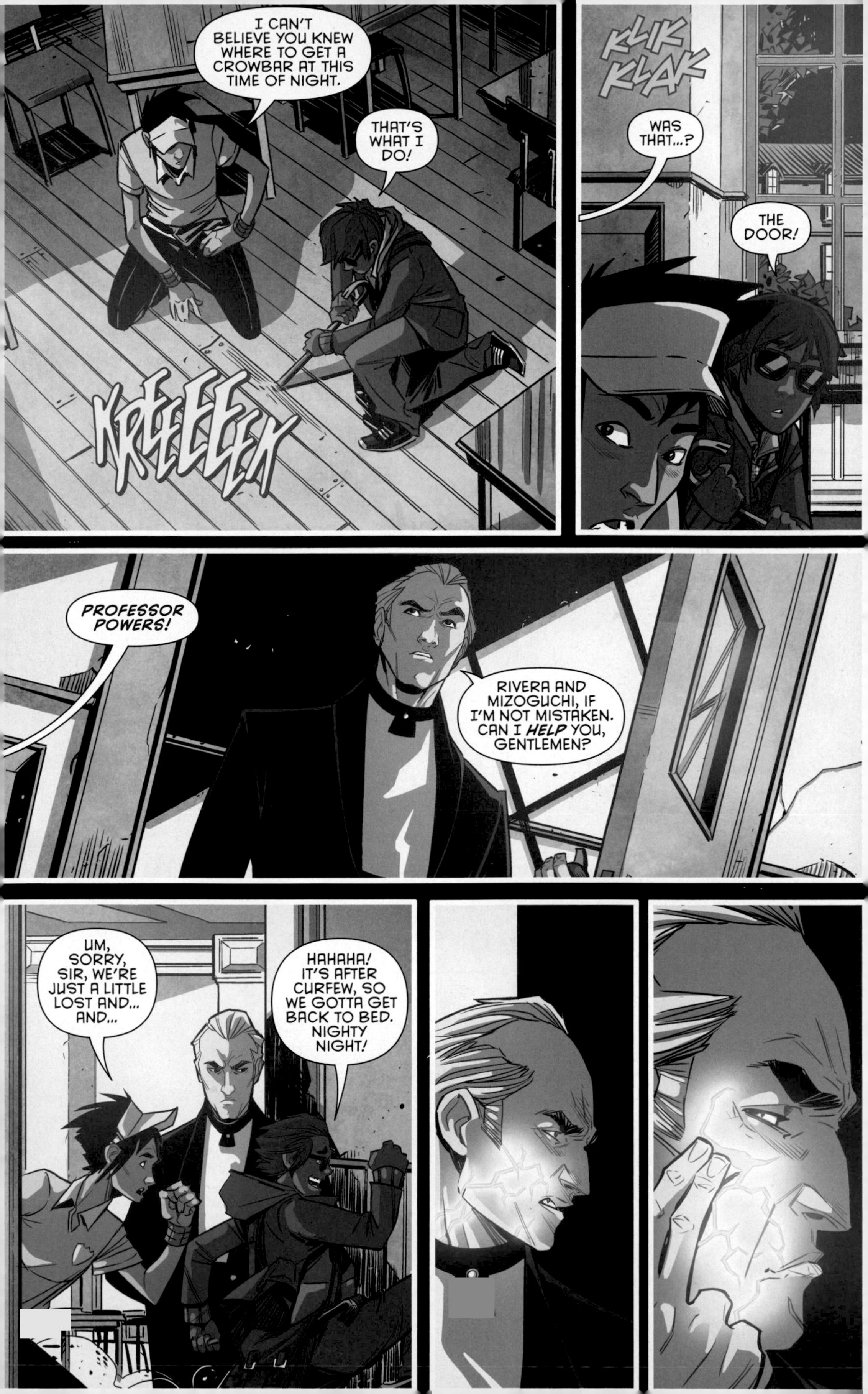
I CAN'T BELIEVE YOU KNEW WHERE TO GET A CROWBAR AT THIS TIME OF NIGHT.
THAT'S WHAT I DO!
KREEEEEK
KLIK KLAK
WAS THAT...?
THE DOOR!
PROFESSOR POWERS!
RIVERA AND MIZOGUCHI, IF I'M NOT MISTAKEN. CAN I HELP YOU, GENTLEMEN?
UM, SORRY, SIR, WE'RE JUST A LITTLE LOST AND... AND...
HAHAHA! IT'S AFTER CURFEW, SO WE GOTTA GET BACK TO BED. NIGHTY NIGHT!

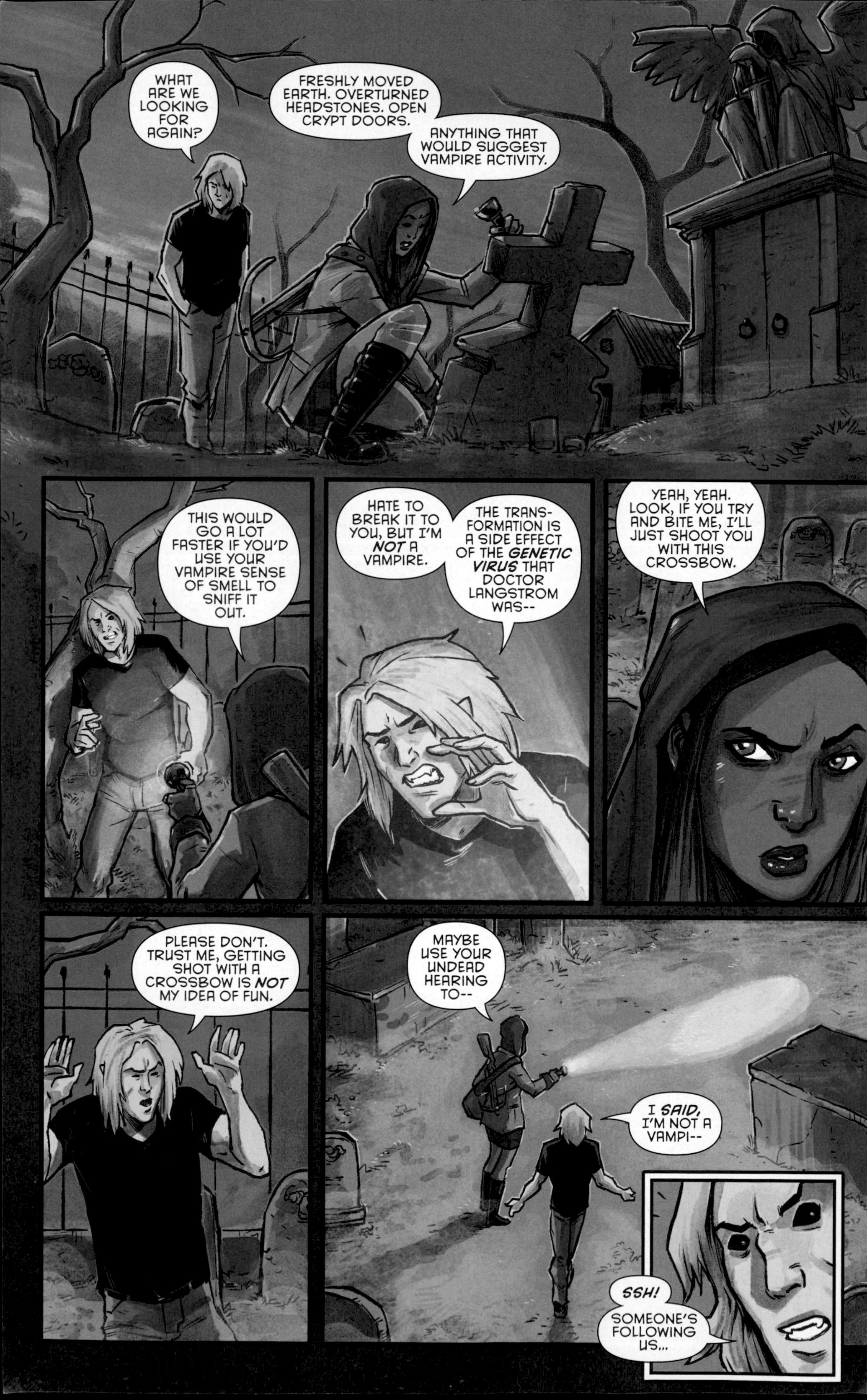
WHAT ARE WE LOOKING FOR AGAIN?
FRESHLY MOVED EARTH. OVERTURNED HEADSTONES. OPEN CRYPT DOORS.
ANYTHING THAT WOULD SUGGEST VAMPIRE ACTIVITY.
THIS WOULD GO A LOT FASTER IF YOU'D USE YOUR VAMPIRE SENSE OF SMELL TO SNIFF IT OUT.
HATE TO BREAK IT TO YOU, BUT I'M NOT A VAMPIRE.
THE TRANS-FORMATION IS A SIDE EFFECT OF THE GENETIC VIRUS THAT DOCTOR LANGSTROM WAS--
YEAH, YEAH. LOOK, IF YOU TRY AND BITE ME, I'LL JUST SHOOT YOU WITH THIS CROSSBOW.
PLEASE DON'T. TRUST ME, GETTING SHOT WITH A CROSSBOW IS NOT MY IDEA OF FUN.
MAYBE USE YOUR UNDEAD HEARING TO--
I SAID, I'M NOT A VAMPI--
SSH!
SOMEONE'S FOLLOWING US...

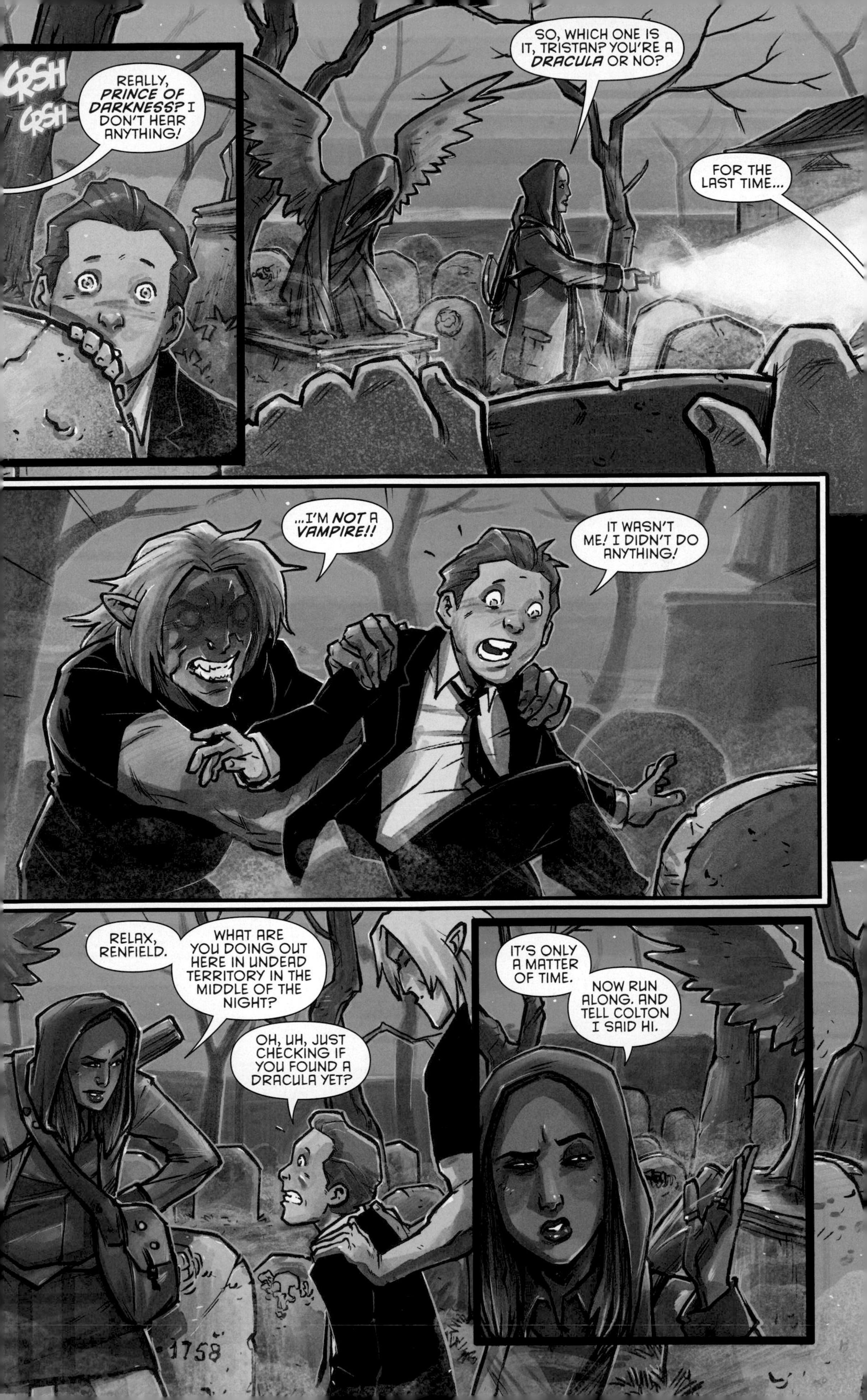
CRSH
CRSH
REALLY, PRINCE OF DARKNESS? I DON'T HEAR ANYTHING!
SO, WHICH ONE IS IT, TRISTAN? YOU'RE A DRACULA OR NO?
FOR THE LAST TIME...
...I'M NOT A VAMPIRE!!
IT WASN'T ME! I DIDN'T DO ANYTHING!
RELAX, RENFIELD.
WHAT ARE YOU DOING OUT HERE IN UNDEAD TERRITORY IN THE MIDDLE OF THE NIGHT?
OH, UH, JUST CHECKING IF YOU FOUND A DRACULA YET?
IT'S ONLY A MATTER OF TIME.
NOW RUN ALONG. AND TELL COLTON I SAID HI.
1758

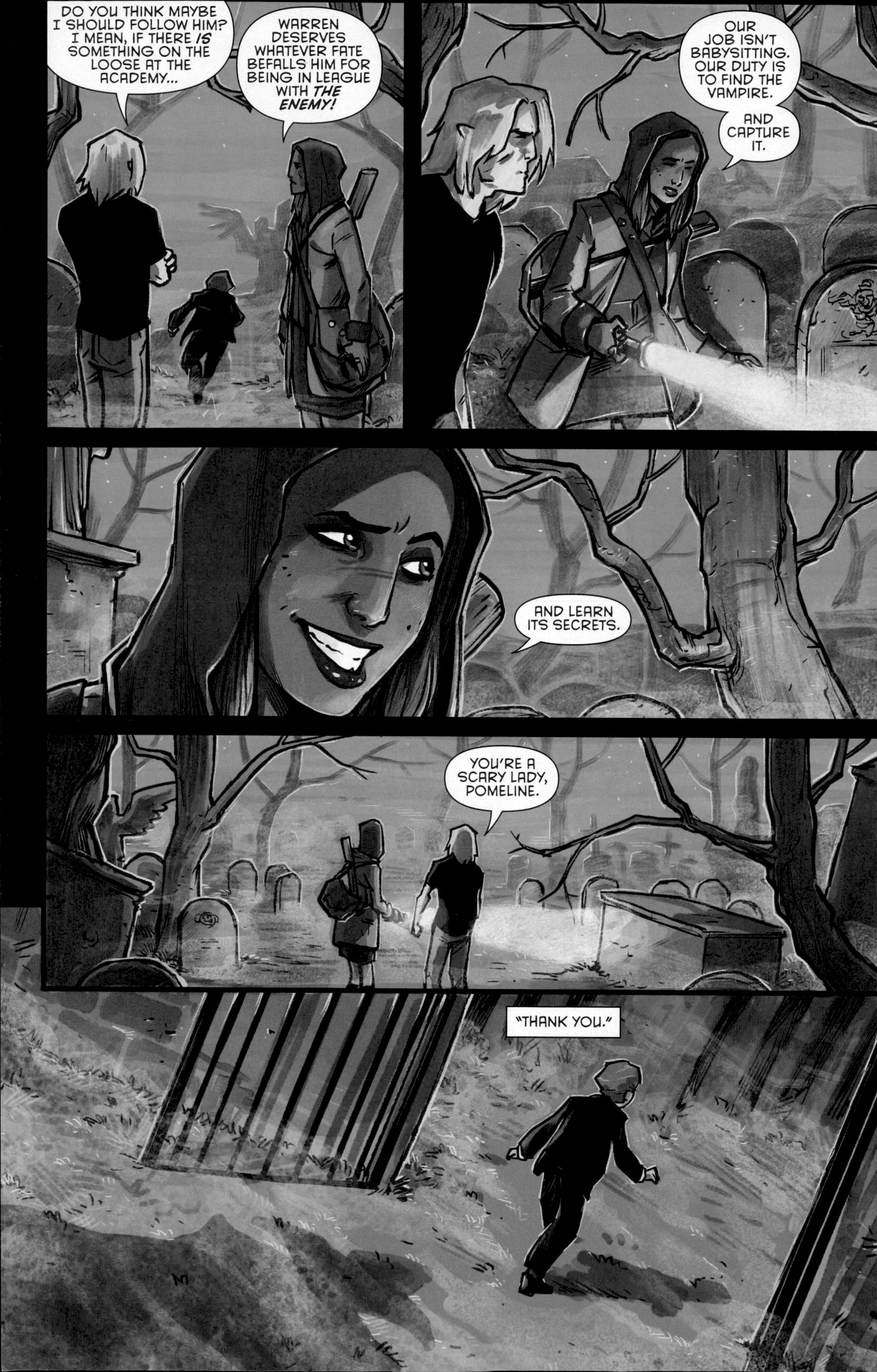
DO YOU THINK MAYBE I SHOULD FOLLOW HIM? I MEAN, IF THERE *IS* SOMETHING ON THE LOOSE AT THE ACADEMY...
WARREN DESERVES WHATEVER FATE BEFALLS HIM FOR BEING IN LEAGUE WITH *THE ENEMY!*
OUR JOB ISN'T BABYSITTING. OUR DUTY IS TO FIND THE VAMPIRE.
AND CAPTURE IT.
AND LEARN ITS SECRETS.
YOU'RE A SCARY LADY, POMELINE.
"THANK YOU."

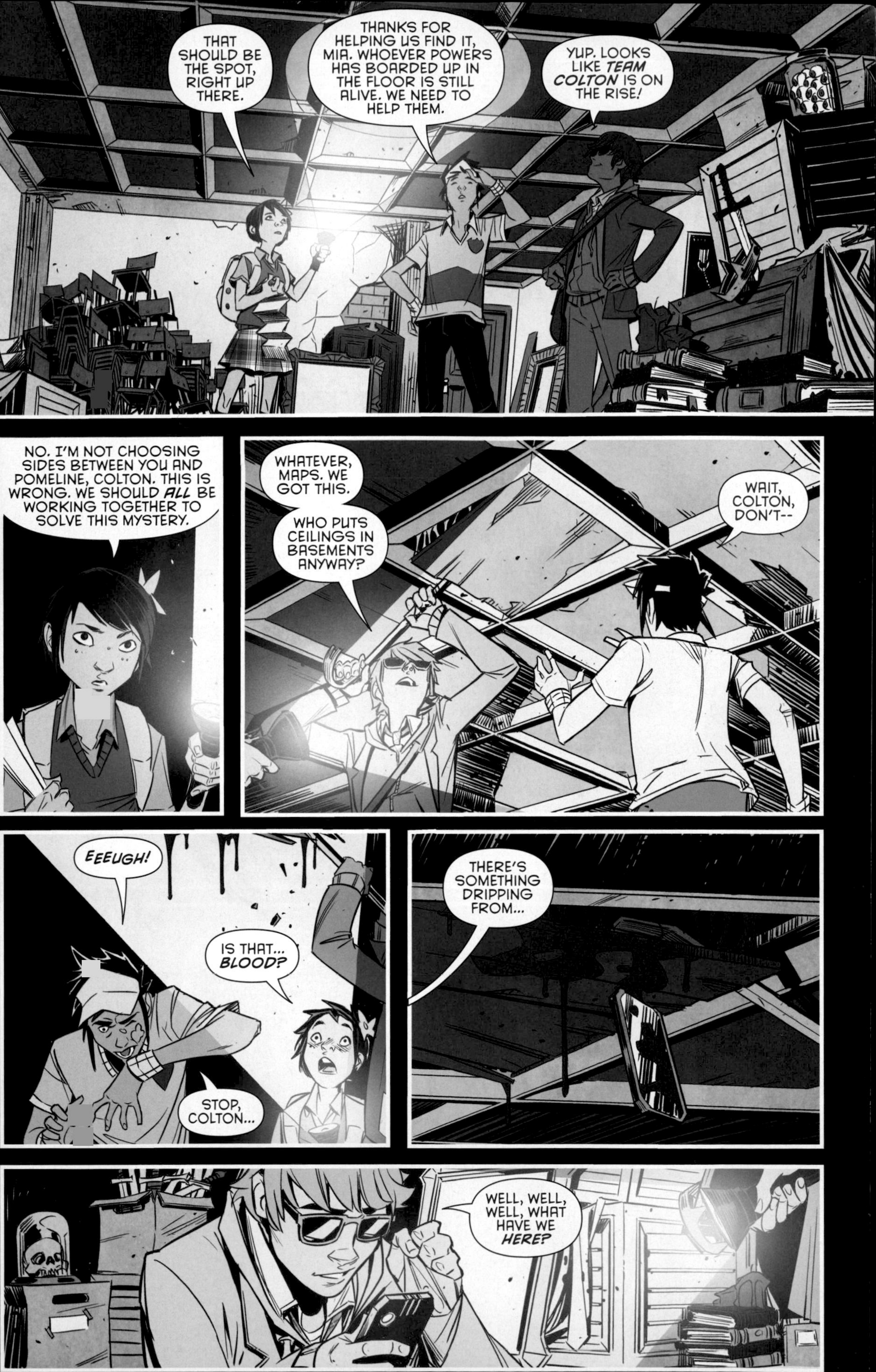

THAT SHOULD BE THE SPOT, RIGHT UP THERE.
THANKS FOR HELPING US FIND IT, MIA. WHOEVER POWERS HAS BOARDED UP IN THE FLOOR IS STILL ALIVE. WE NEED TO HELP THEM.
YUP. LOOKS LIKE TEAM COLTON IS ON THE RISE!
NO. I'M NOT CHOOSING SIDES BETWEEN YOU AND POMELINE, COLTON. THIS IS WRONG. WE SHOULD ALL BE WORKING TOGETHER TO SOLVE THIS MYSTERY.
WHATEVER, MAPS. WE GOT THIS.
WHO PUTS CEILINGS IN BASEMENTS ANYWAY?
WAIT, COLTON, DON'T--
EEEUGH!
IS THAT... BLOOD?
STOP, COLTON...
THERE'S SOMETHING DRIPPING FROM...
WELL, WELL, WELL, WHAT HAVE WE HERE?

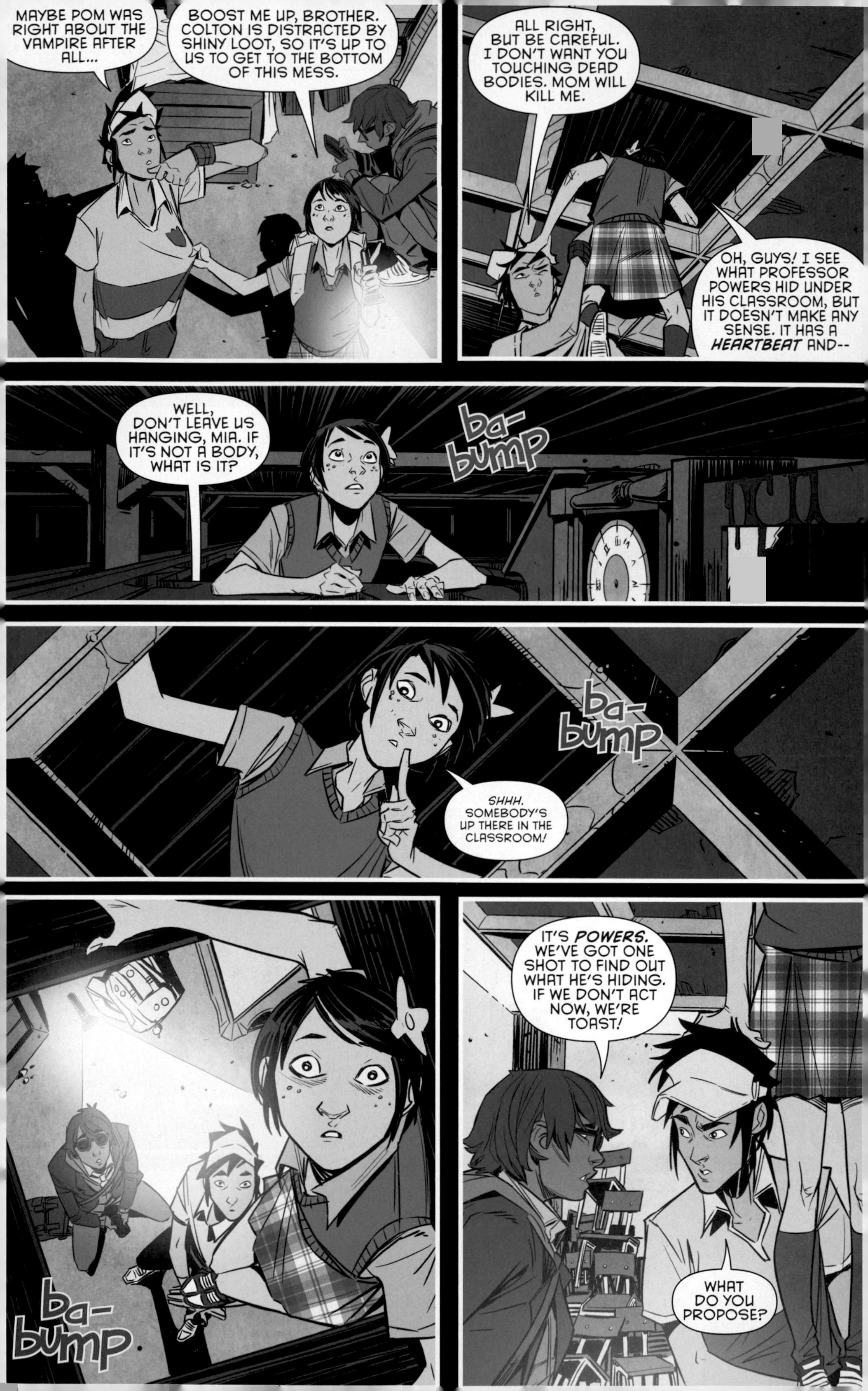
MAYBE POM WAS RIGHT ABOUT THE VAMPIRE AFTER ALL...
BOOST ME UP, BROTHER. COLTON IS DISTRACTED BY SHINY LOOT, SO IT'S UP TO US TO GET TO THE BOTTOM OF THIS MESS.
ALL RIGHT, BUT BE CAREFUL. I DON'T WANT YOU TOUCHING DEAD BODIES. MOM WILL KILL ME.
OH, GUYS! I SEE WHAT PROFESSOR POWERS HID UNDER HIS CLASSROOM, BUT IT DOESN'T MAKE ANY SENSE. IT HAS A *HEARTBEAT* AND--
WELL, DON'T LEAVE US HANGING, MIA. IF IT'S NOT A BODY, WHAT IS IT?
ba-bump
ba-bump
SHHH. SOMEBODY'S UP THERE IN THE CLASSROOM!
ba-bump
IT'S *POWERS.* WE'VE GOT ONE SHOT TO FIND OUT WHAT HE'S HIDING. IF WE DON'T ACT NOW, WE'RE TOAST!
WHAT DO YOU PROPOSE?

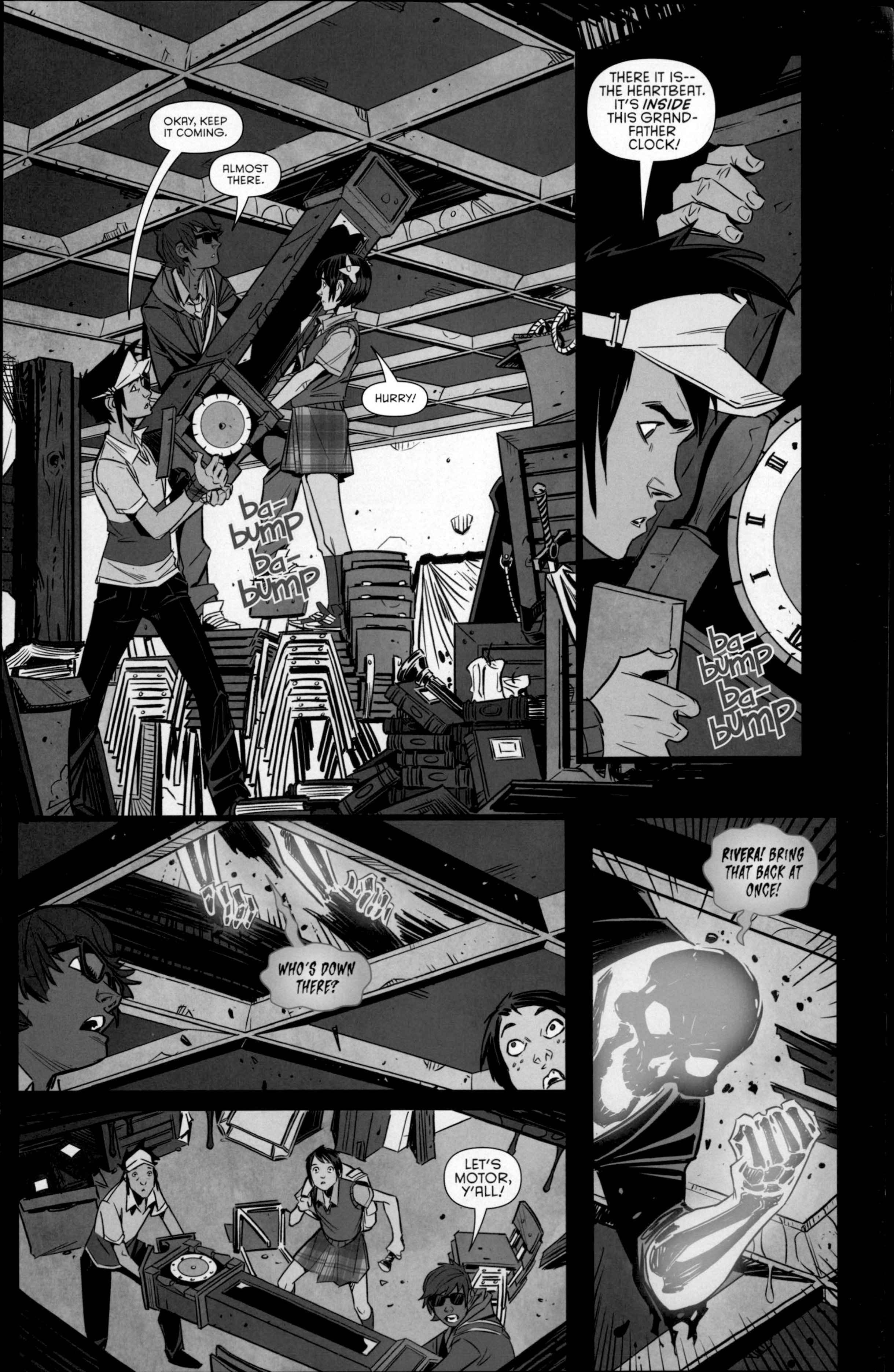

OKAY, KEEP IT COMING.
ALMOST THERE.
HURRY!
ba-bump ba-bump
THERE IT IS-- THE HEARTBEAT. IT'S *INSIDE* THIS GRAND-FATHER CLOCK!
ba-bump ba-bump
WHO'S DOWN THERE?
RIVERA! BRING THAT BACK AT ONCE!
LET'S MOTOR, Y'ALL!

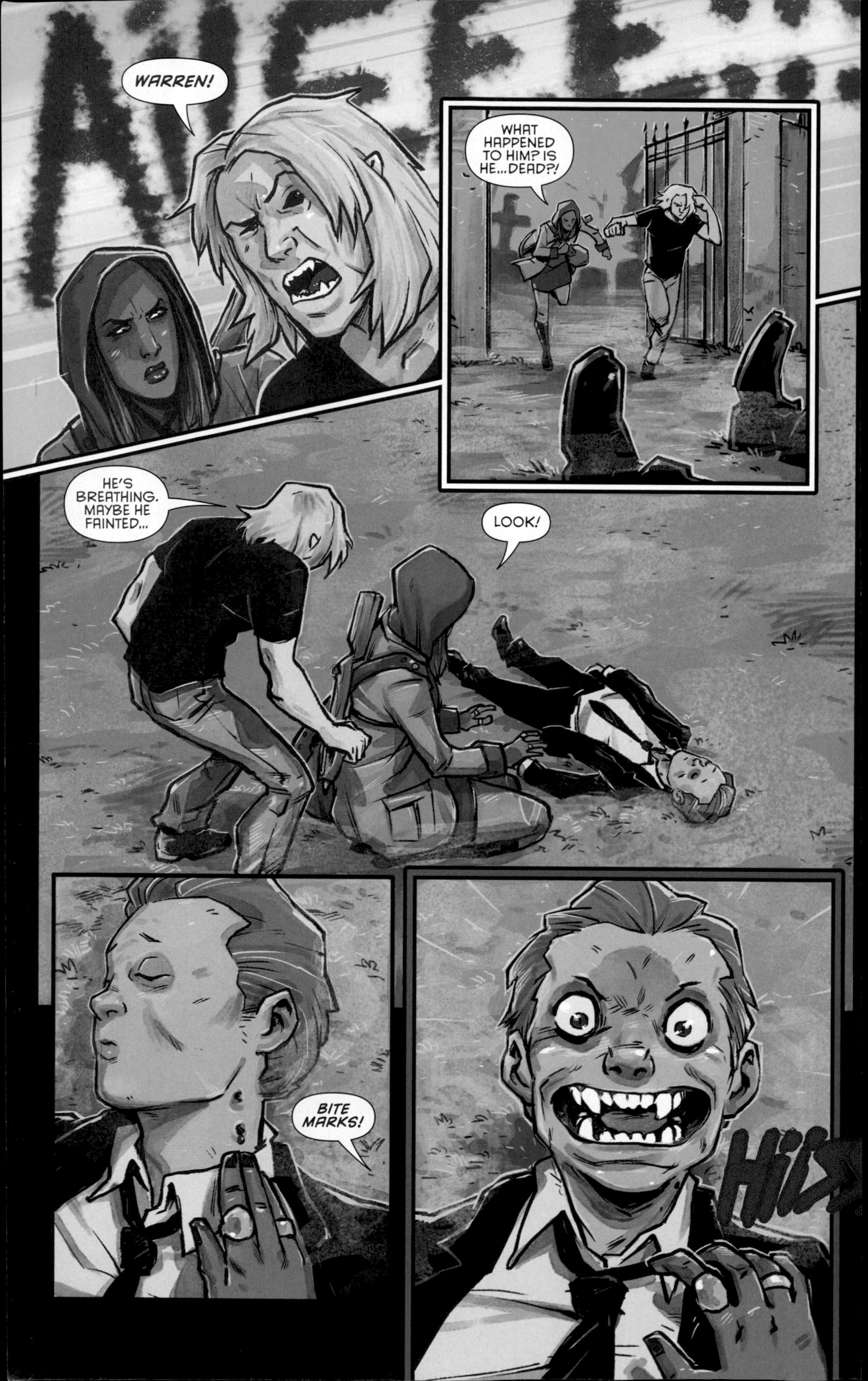
WARREN!
WHAT HAPPENED TO HIM? IS HE...DEAD?!
HE'S BREATHING. MAYBE HE FAINTED...
LOOK!
BITE MARKS!

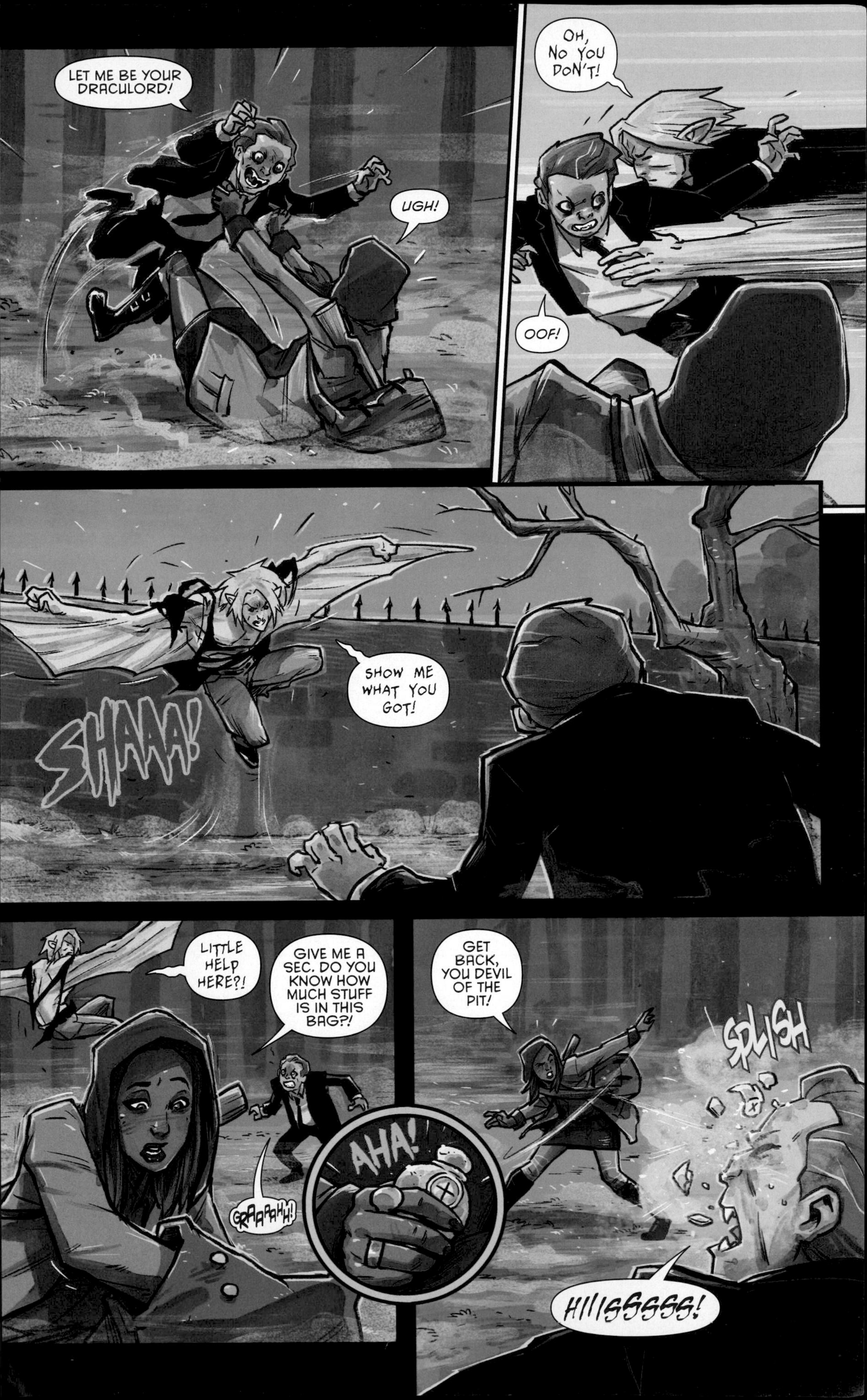
LET ME BE YOUR DRACULORD!
UGH!
OH, NO YOU DON'T!
OOF!
SHOW ME WHAT YOU GOT!
SHAAA!
LITTLE HELP HERE?!
GIVE ME A SEC. DO YOU KNOW HOW MUCH STUFF IS IN THIS BAG?!
GRAAAAHH!
AHA!
GET BACK, YOU DEVIL OF THE PIT!
SPLISH
HIIISSSSS!

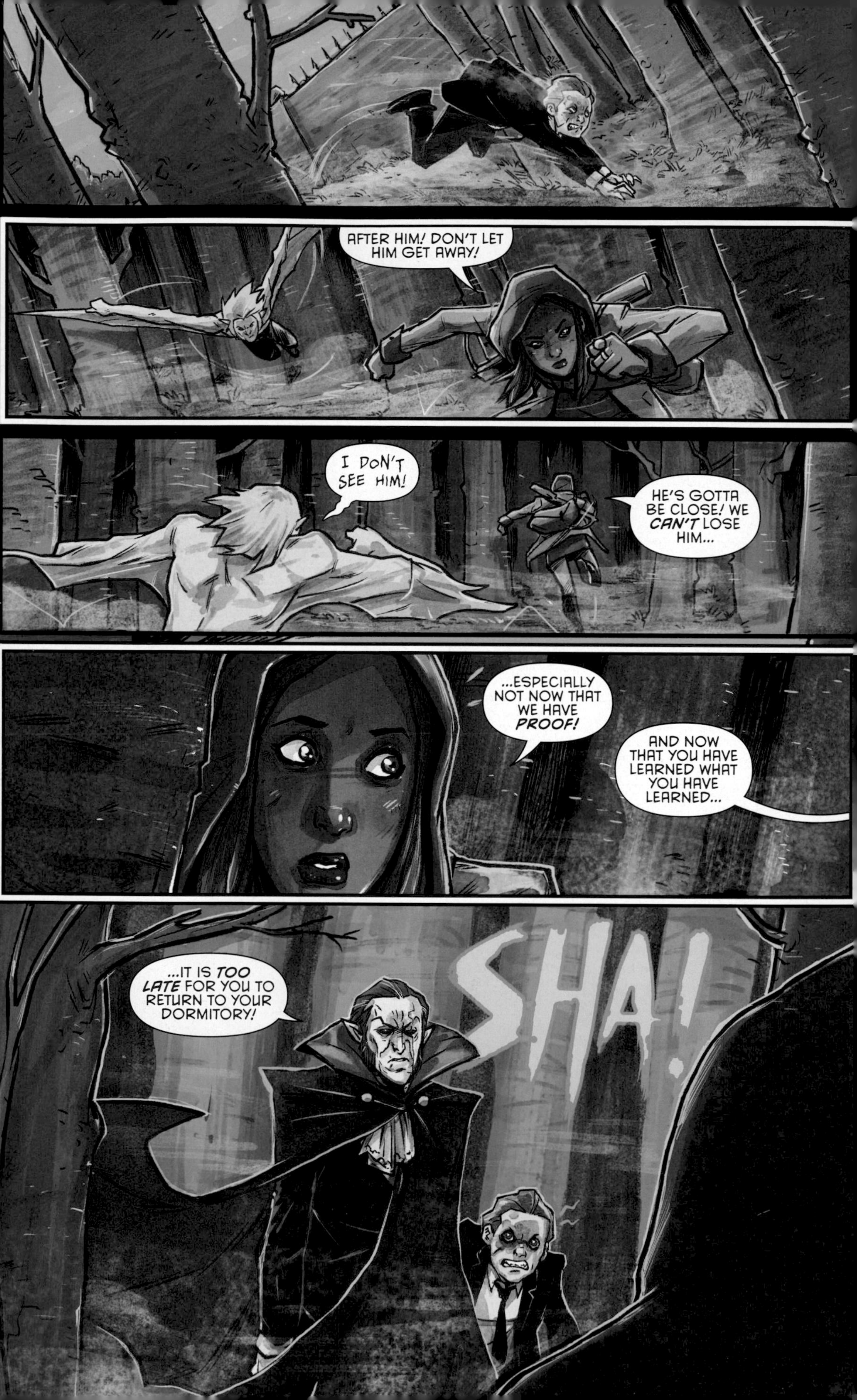
AFTER HIM! DON'T LET HIM GET AWAY!
I DON'T SEE HIM!
HE'S GOTTA BE CLOSE! WE CAN'T LOSE HIM...
...ESPECIALLY NOT NOW THAT WE HAVE PROOF!
AND NOW THAT YOU HAVE LEARNED WHAT YOU HAVE LEARNED...
...IT IS TOO LATE FOR YOU TO RETURN TO YOUR DORMITORY!
SHA!

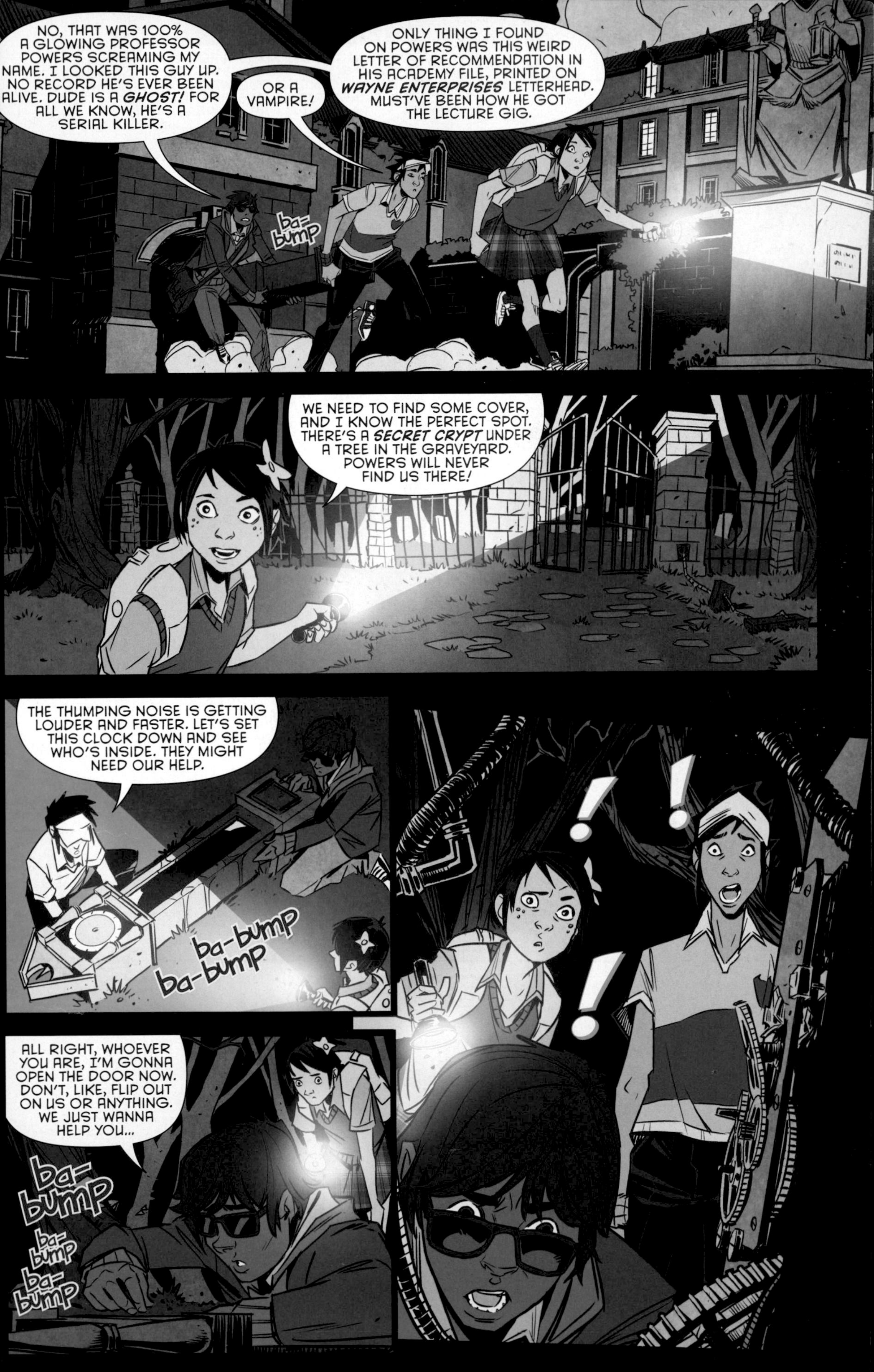
NO, THAT WAS 100% A GLOWING PROFESSOR POWERS SCREAMING MY NAME. I LOOKED THIS GUY UP. NO RECORD HE'S EVER BEEN ALIVE. DUDE IS A *GHOST!* FOR ALL WE KNOW, HE'S A SERIAL KILLER.
OR A VAMPIRE!
ONLY THING I FOUND ON POWERS WAS THIS WEIRD LETTER OF RECOMMENDATION IN HIS ACADEMY FILE, PRINTED ON *WAYNE ENTERPRISES* LETTERHEAD. MUST'VE BEEN HOW HE GOT THE LECTURE GIG.
ba-bump
WE NEED TO FIND SOME COVER, AND I KNOW THE PERFECT SPOT. THERE'S A *SECRET CRYPT* UNDER A TREE IN THE GRAVEYARD. POWERS WILL NEVER FIND US THERE!
THE THUMPING NOISE IS GETTING LOUDER AND FASTER. LET'S SET THIS CLOCK DOWN AND SEE WHO'S INSIDE. THEY MIGHT NEED OUR HELP.
ba-bump ba-bump
ALL RIGHT, WHOEVER YOU ARE, I'M GONNA OPEN THE DOOR NOW. DON'T, LIKE, FLIP OUT ON US OR ANYTHING. WE JUST WANNA HELP YOU...
ba-bump
ba-bump
ba-bump
!
!
!

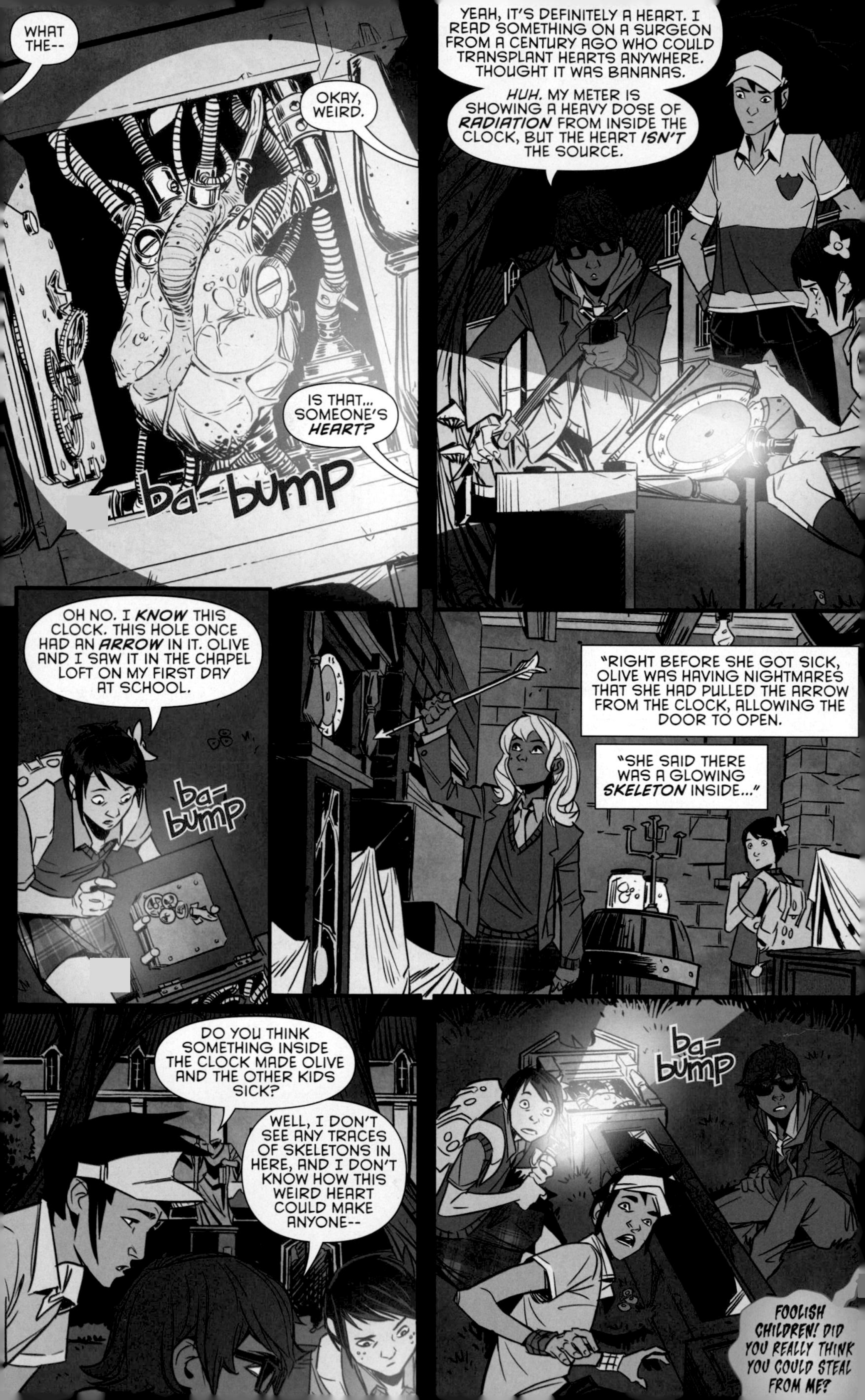
WHAT THE--
OKAY, WEIRD.
IS THAT... SOMEONE'S HEART?
ba-bump
YEAH, IT'S DEFINITELY A HEART. I READ SOMETHING ON A SURGEON FROM A CENTURY AGO WHO COULD TRANSPLANT HEARTS ANYWHERE. THOUGHT IT WAS BANANAS.
HUH. MY METER IS SHOWING A HEAVY DOSE OF RADIATION FROM INSIDE THE CLOCK, BUT THE HEART ISN'T THE SOURCE.
OH NO. I KNOW THIS CLOCK. THIS HOLE ONCE HAD AN ARROW IN IT. OLIVE AND I SAW IT IN THE CHAPEL LOFT ON MY FIRST DAY AT SCHOOL.
ba-bump
"RIGHT BEFORE SHE GOT SICK, OLIVE WAS HAVING NIGHTMARES THAT SHE HAD PULLED THE ARROW FROM THE CLOCK, ALLOWING THE DOOR TO OPEN.
"SHE SAID THERE WAS A GLOWING SKELETON INSIDE..."
DO YOU THINK SOMETHING INSIDE THE CLOCK MADE OLIVE AND THE OTHER KIDS SICK?
WELL, I DON'T SEE ANY TRACES OF SKELETONS IN HERE, AND I DON'T KNOW HOW THIS WEIRD HEART COULD MAKE ANYONE--
ba-bump
FOOLISH CHILDREN! DID YOU REALLY THINK YOU COULD STEAL FROM ME?

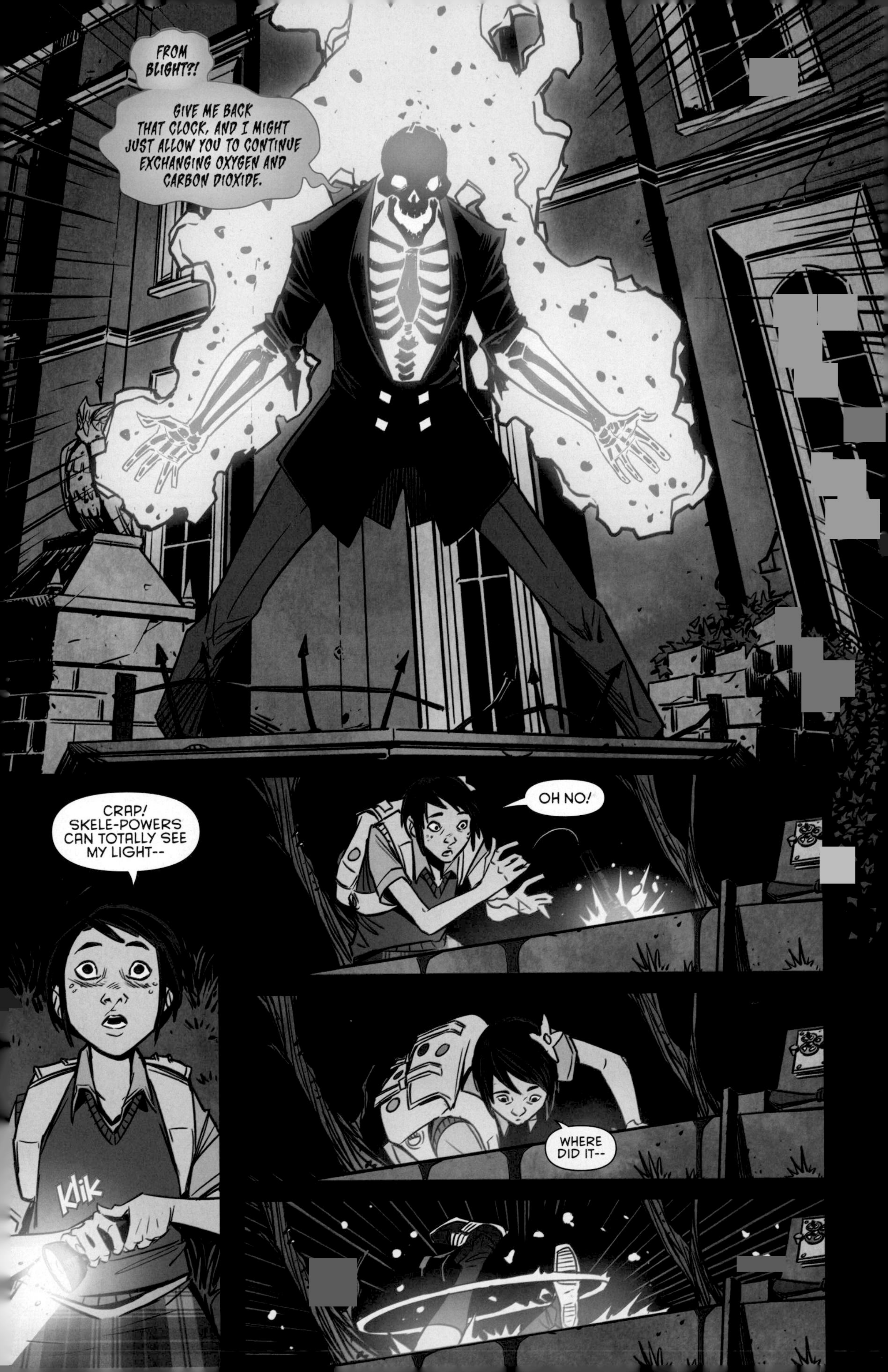
FROM BLIGHT?!
GIVE ME BACK THAT CLOCK, AND I MIGHT JUST ALLOW YOU TO CONTINUE EXCHANGING OXYGEN AND CARBON DIOXIDE.
CRAP! SKELE-POWERS CAN TOTALLY SEE MY LIGHT--
klik
OH NO!
WHERE DID IT--

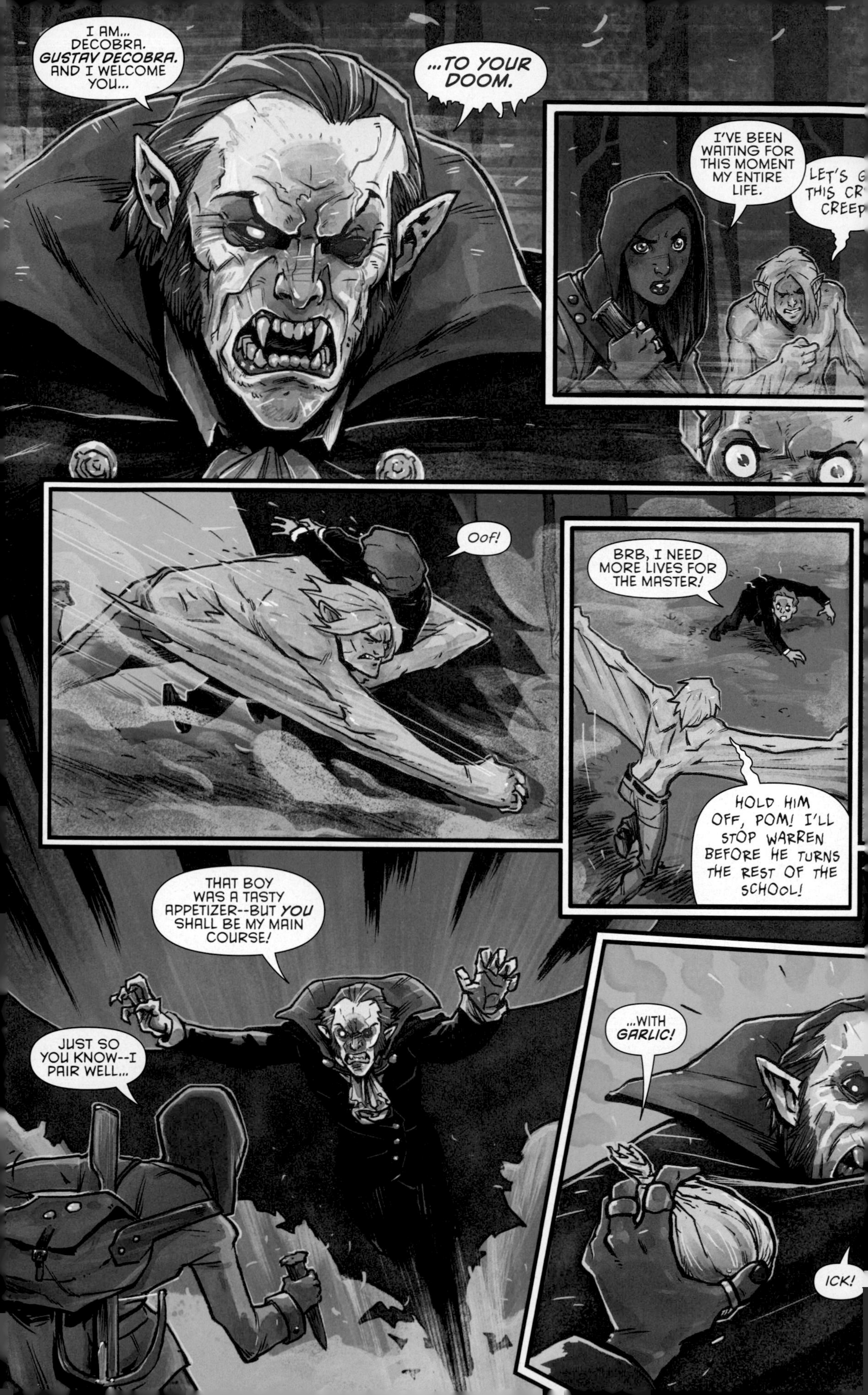
I AM... DECOBRA. *GUSTAV DECOBRA.* AND I WELCOME YOU...
...TO YOUR DOOM.
I'VE BEEN WAITING FOR THIS MOMENT MY ENTIRE LIFE.
Oof!
BRB, I NEED MORE LIVES FOR THE MASTER!
HOLD HIM OFF, POM! I'LL STOP WARREN BEFORE HE TURNS THE REST OF THE SCHOOL!
THAT BOY WAS A TASTY APPETIZER--BUT *YOU* SHALL BE MY MAIN COURSE!
JUST SO YOU KNOW--I PAIR WELL...
...WITH *GARLIC!*
ICK!

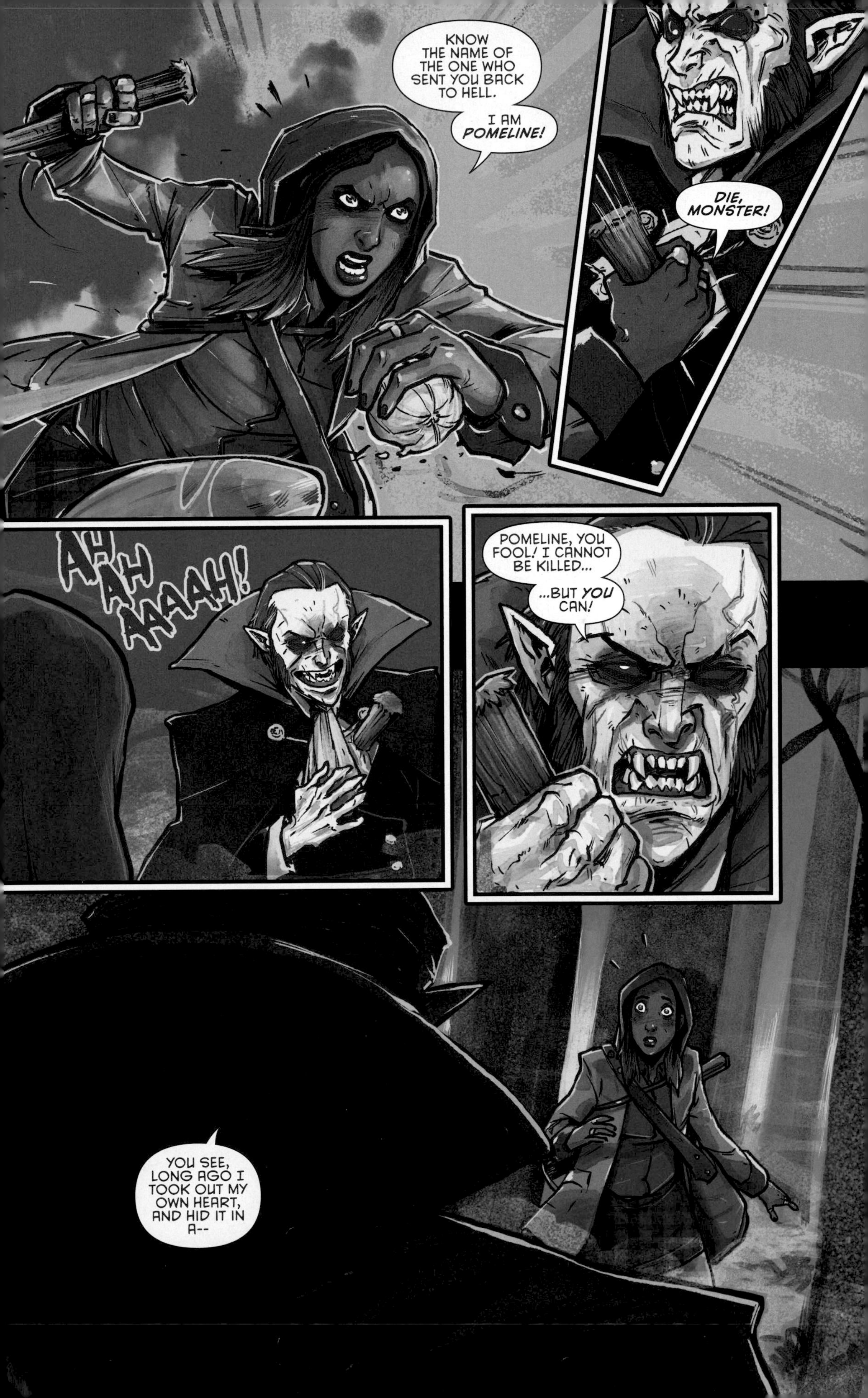
KNOW THE NAME OF THE ONE WHO SENT YOU BACK TO HELL.
I AM *POMELINE!*
DIE, MONSTER!
AH AH AAAAH!
POMELINE, YOU FOOL! I CANNOT BE KILLED...
...BUT *YOU* CAN!
YOU SEE, LONG AGO I TOOK OUT MY OWN HEART, AND HID IT IN A--

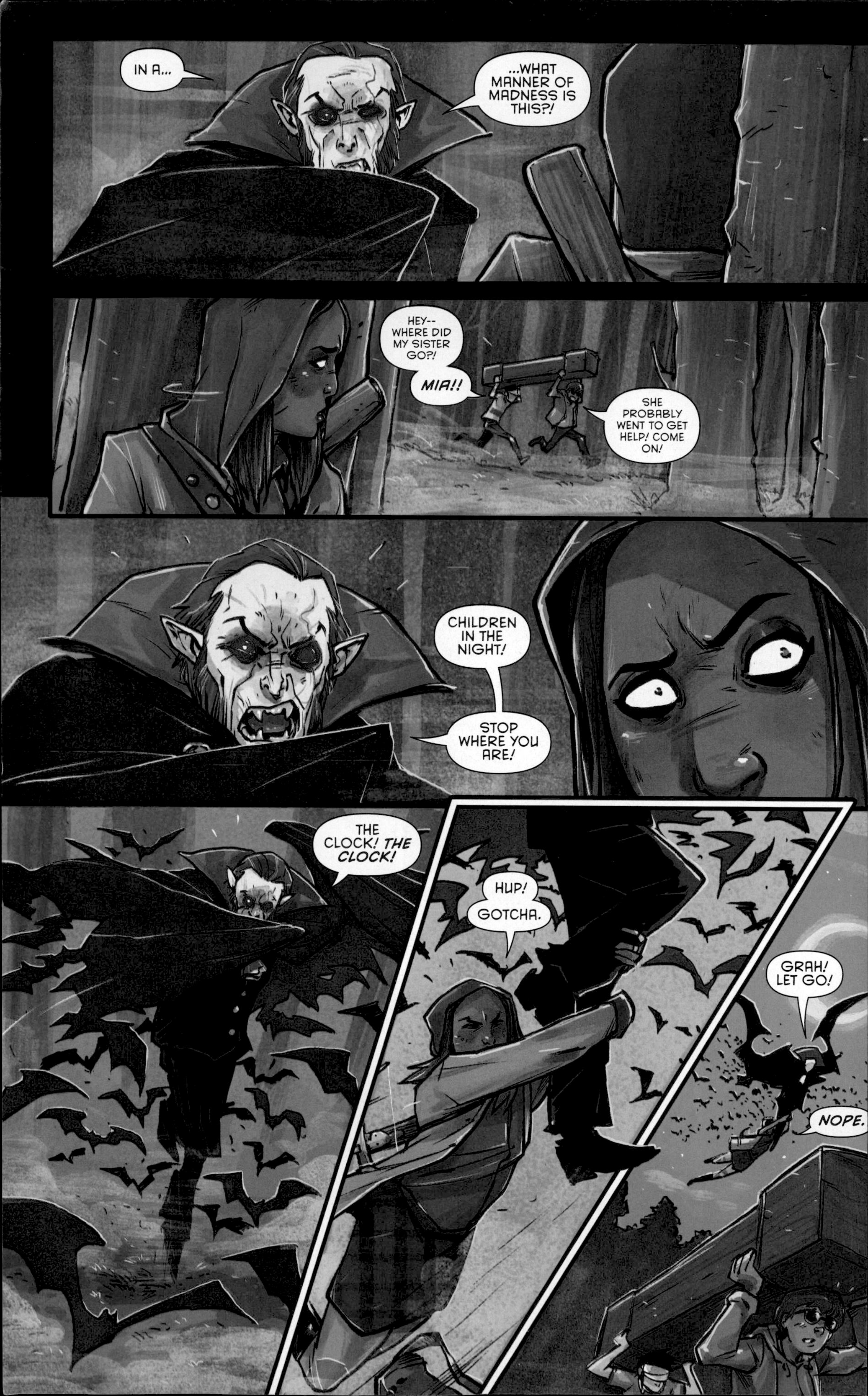
IN A...
...WHAT MANNER OF MADNESS IS THIS?!
HEY-- WHERE DID MY SISTER GO?!
MIA!!
SHE PROBABLY WENT TO GET HELP! COME ON!
CHILDREN IN THE NIGHT!
STOP WHERE YOU ARE!
THE CLOCK! THE CLOCK!
HUP!
GOTCHA.
GRAH! LET GO!
NOPE.

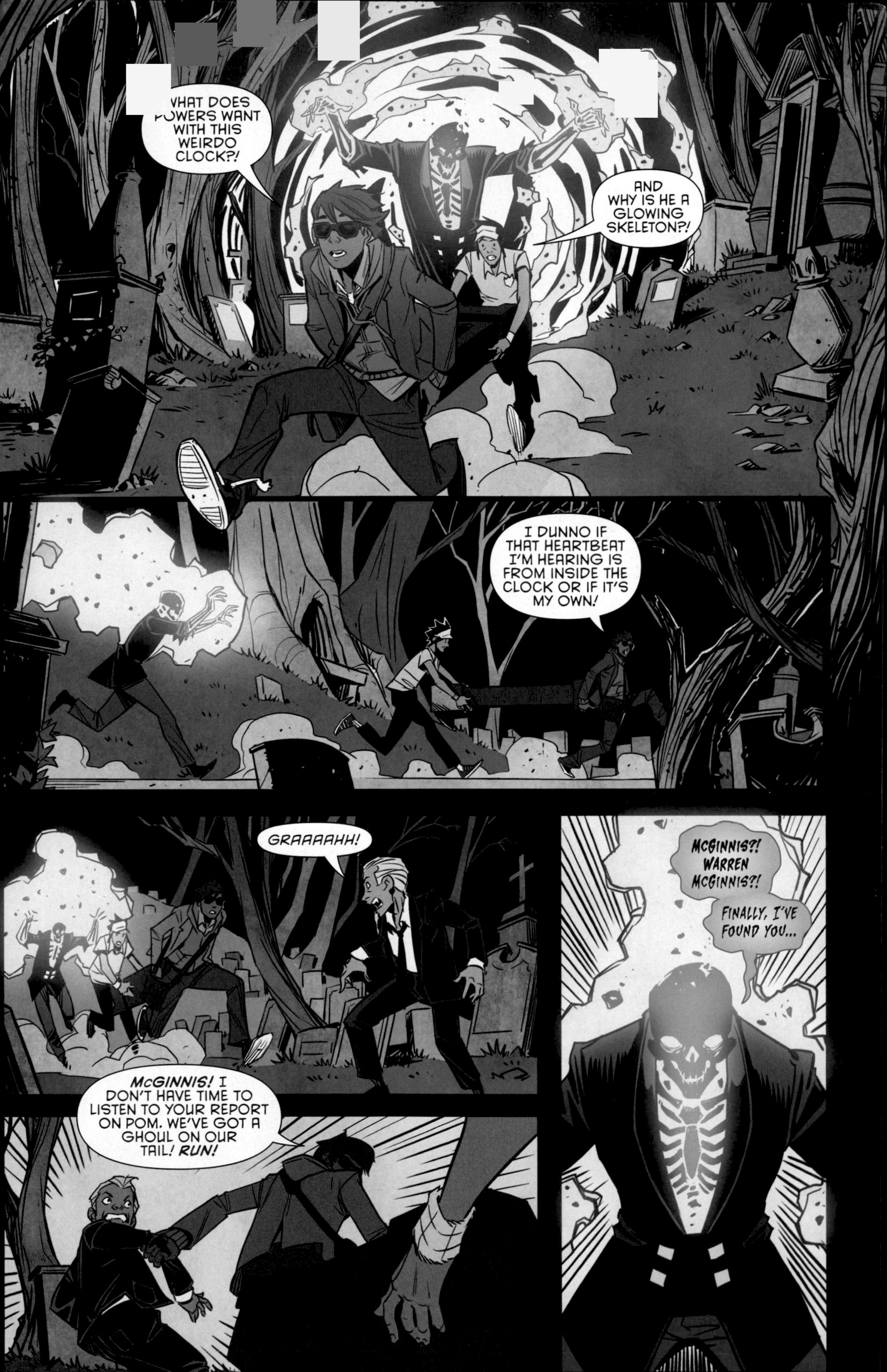
WHAT DOES POWERS WANT WITH THIS WEIRDO CLOCK?!
AND WHY IS HE A GLOWING SKELETON?!
I DUNNO IF THAT HEARTBEAT I'M HEARING IS FROM INSIDE THE CLOCK OR IF IT'S MY OWN!
GRAAAAAH!
McGINNIS! I DON'T HAVE TIME TO LISTEN TO YOUR REPORT ON POM. WE'VE GOT A GHOUL ON OUR TAIL! RUN!
McGINNIS?! WARREN McGINNIS?!
FINALLY, I'VE FOUND YOU...

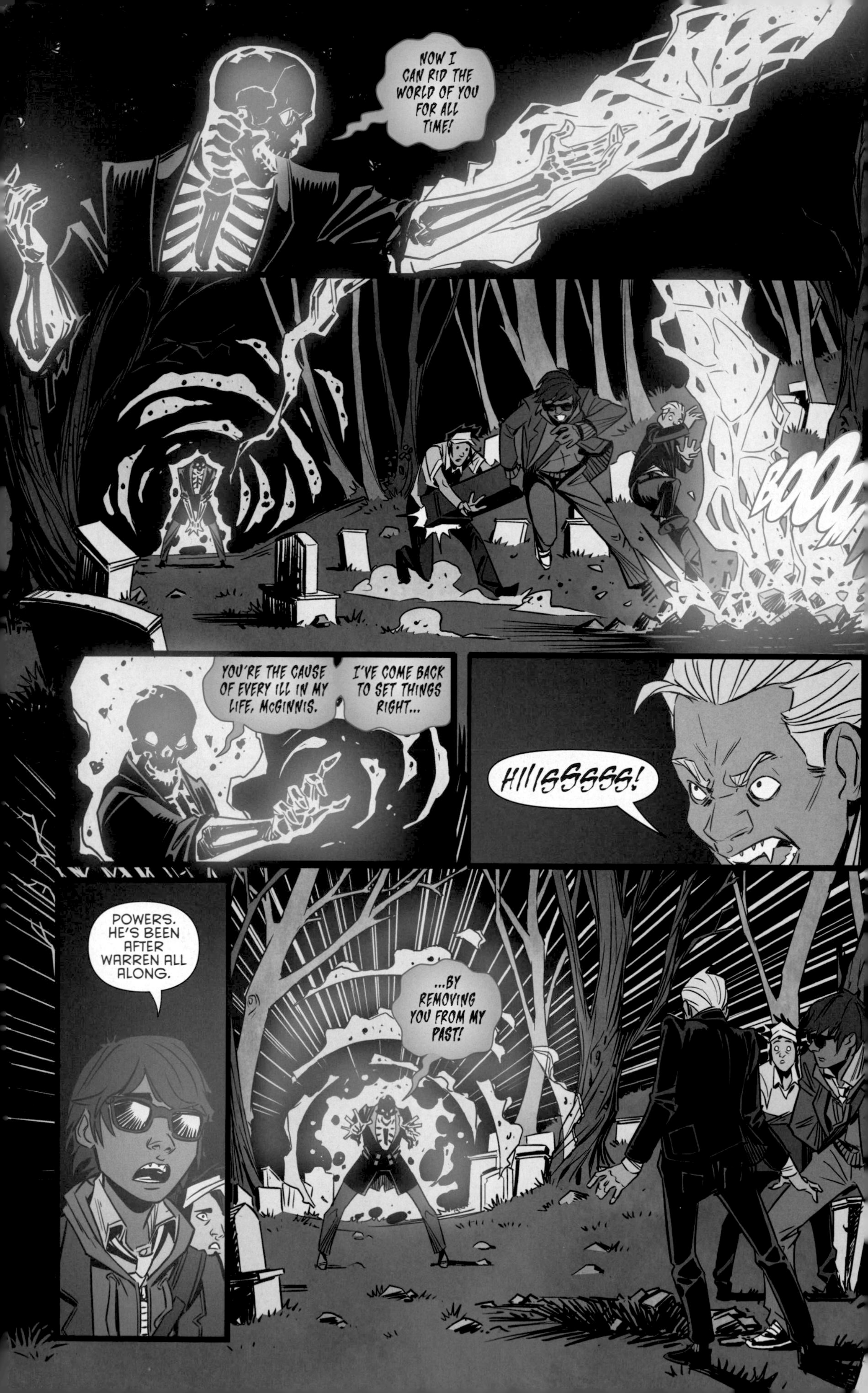
NOW I CAN RID THE WORLD OF YOU FOR ALL TIME!
BOOO
YOU'RE THE CAUSE OF EVERY ILL IN MY LIFE, McGINNIS.
I'VE COME BACK TO SET THINGS RIGHT...
HIIISSSSS!
POWERS. HE'S BEEN AFTER WARREN ALL ALONG.
...BY REMOVING YOU FROM MY PAST!

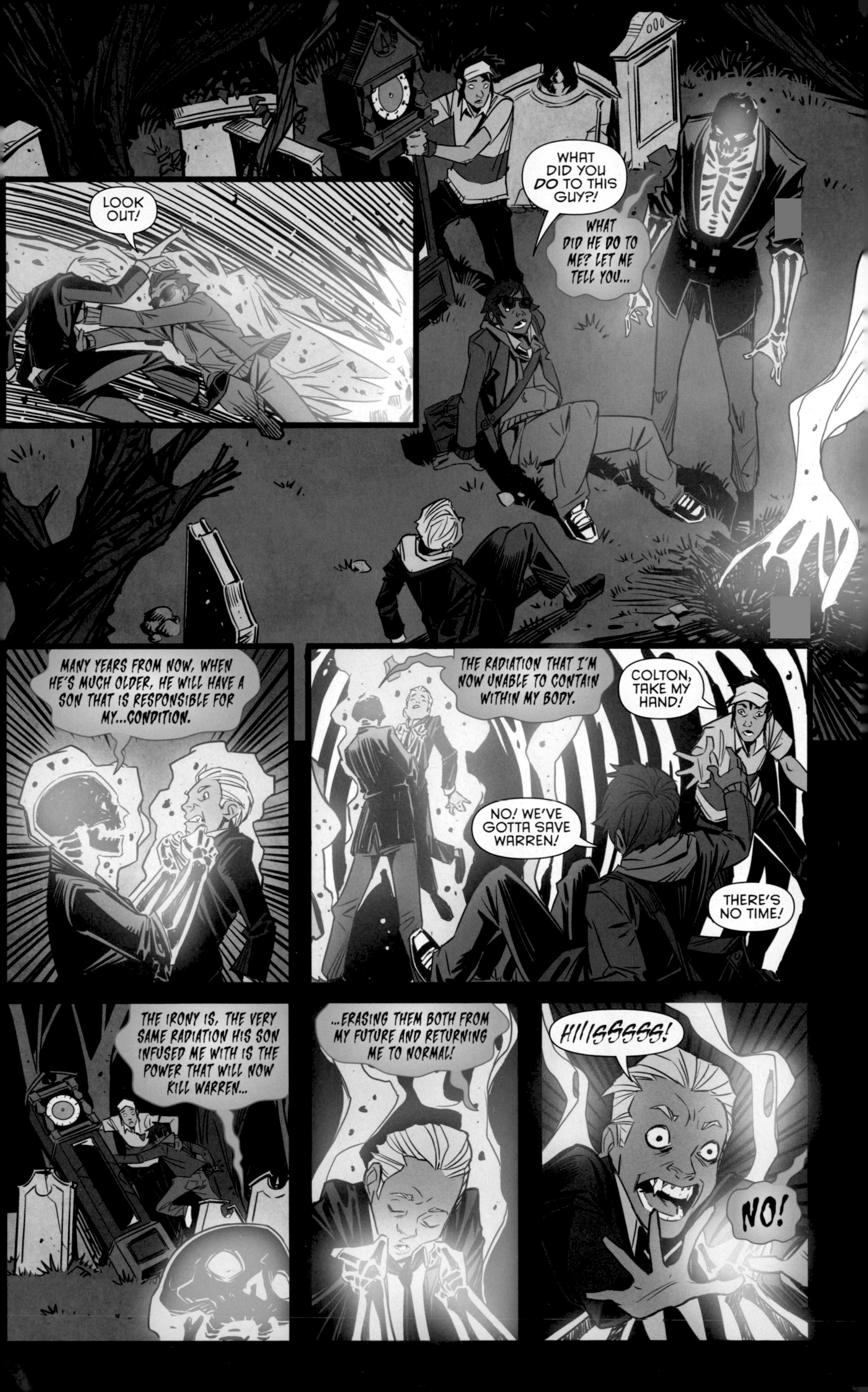
LOOK OUT!
WHAT DID YOU DO TO THIS GUY?!
WHAT DID HE DO TO ME? LET ME TELL YOU...
MANY YEARS FROM NOW, WHEN HE'S MUCH OLDER, HE WILL HAVE A SON THAT IS RESPONSIBLE FOR MY...CONDITION.
THE RADIATION THAT I'M NOW UNABLE TO CONTAIN WITHIN MY BODY.
COLTON, TAKE MY HAND!
NO! WE'VE GOTTA SAVE WARREN!
THERE'S NO TIME!
THE IRONY IS, THE VERY SAME RADIATION HIS SON INFUSED ME WITH IS THE POWER THAT WILL NOW KILL WARREN...
...ERASING THEM BOTH FROM MY FUTURE AND RETURNING ME TO NORMAL!
HIIISSSSS!
NO!

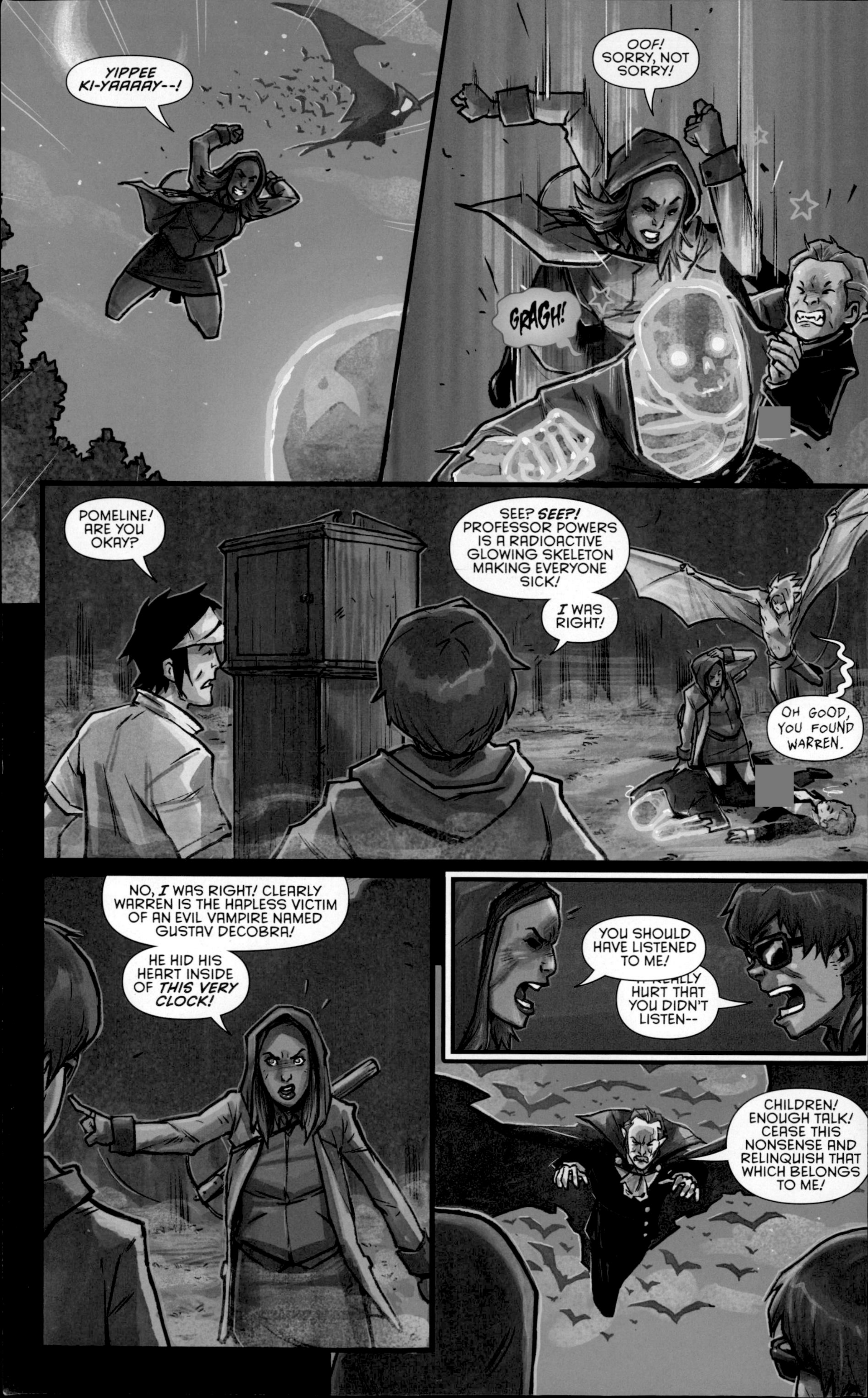
YIPPEE KI-YAAAAY--!
OOF! SORRY, NOT SORRY!
GRAGH!
POMELINE! ARE YOU OKAY?
SEE? SEE?! PROFESSOR POWERS IS A RADIOACTIVE GLOWING SKELETON MAKING EVERYONE SICK!
I WAS RIGHT!
OH GOOD, YOU FOUND WARREN.
NO, I WAS RIGHT! CLEARLY WARREN IS THE HAPLESS VICTIM OF AN EVIL VAMPIRE NAMED GUSTAV DECOBRA!
HE HID HIS HEART INSIDE OF THIS VERY CLOCK!
YOU SHOULD HAVE LISTENED TO ME!
HURT THAT YOU DIDN'T LISTEN--
CHILDREN! ENOUGH TALK! CEASE THIS NONSENSE AND RELINQUISH THAT WHICH BELONGS TO ME!

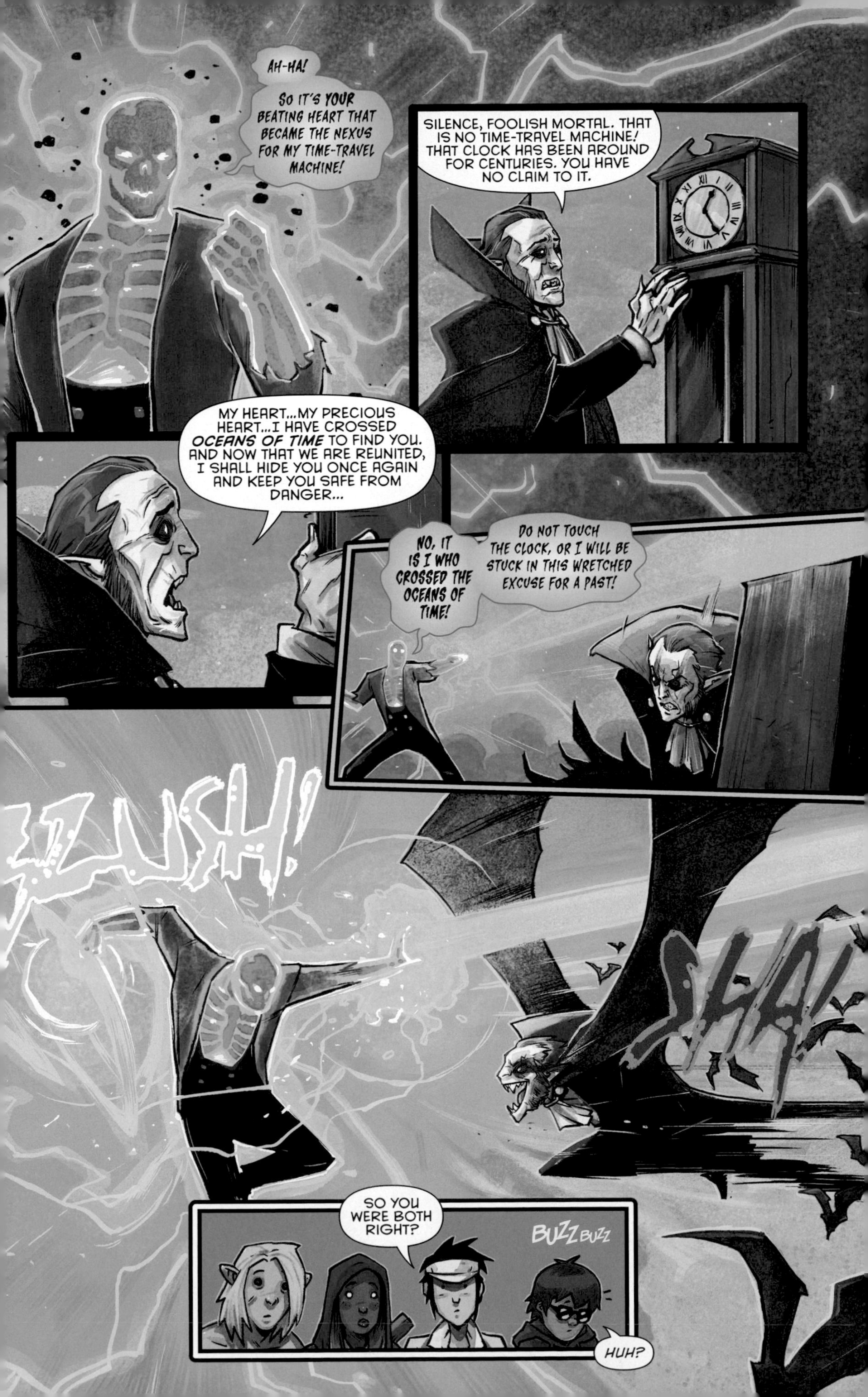
AH-HA!
SO IT'S YOUR BEATING HEART THAT BECAME THE NEXUS FOR MY TIME-TRAVEL MACHINE!
SILENCE, FOOLISH MORTAL. THAT IS NO TIME-TRAVEL MACHINE! THAT CLOCK HAS BEEN AROUND FOR CENTURIES. YOU HAVE NO CLAIM TO IT.
MY HEART...MY PRECIOUS HEART...I HAVE CROSSED OCEANS OF TIME TO FIND YOU. AND NOW THAT WE ARE REUNITED, I SHALL HIDE YOU ONCE AGAIN AND KEEP YOU SAFE FROM DANGER...
NO, IT IS I WHO CROSSED THE OCEANS OF TIME!
DO NOT TOUCH THE CLOCK, OR I WILL BE STUCK IN THIS WRETCHED EXCUSE FOR A PAST!
ZZUSH!
SHA!
SO YOU WERE BOTH RIGHT?
BUZZ BUZZ
HUH?

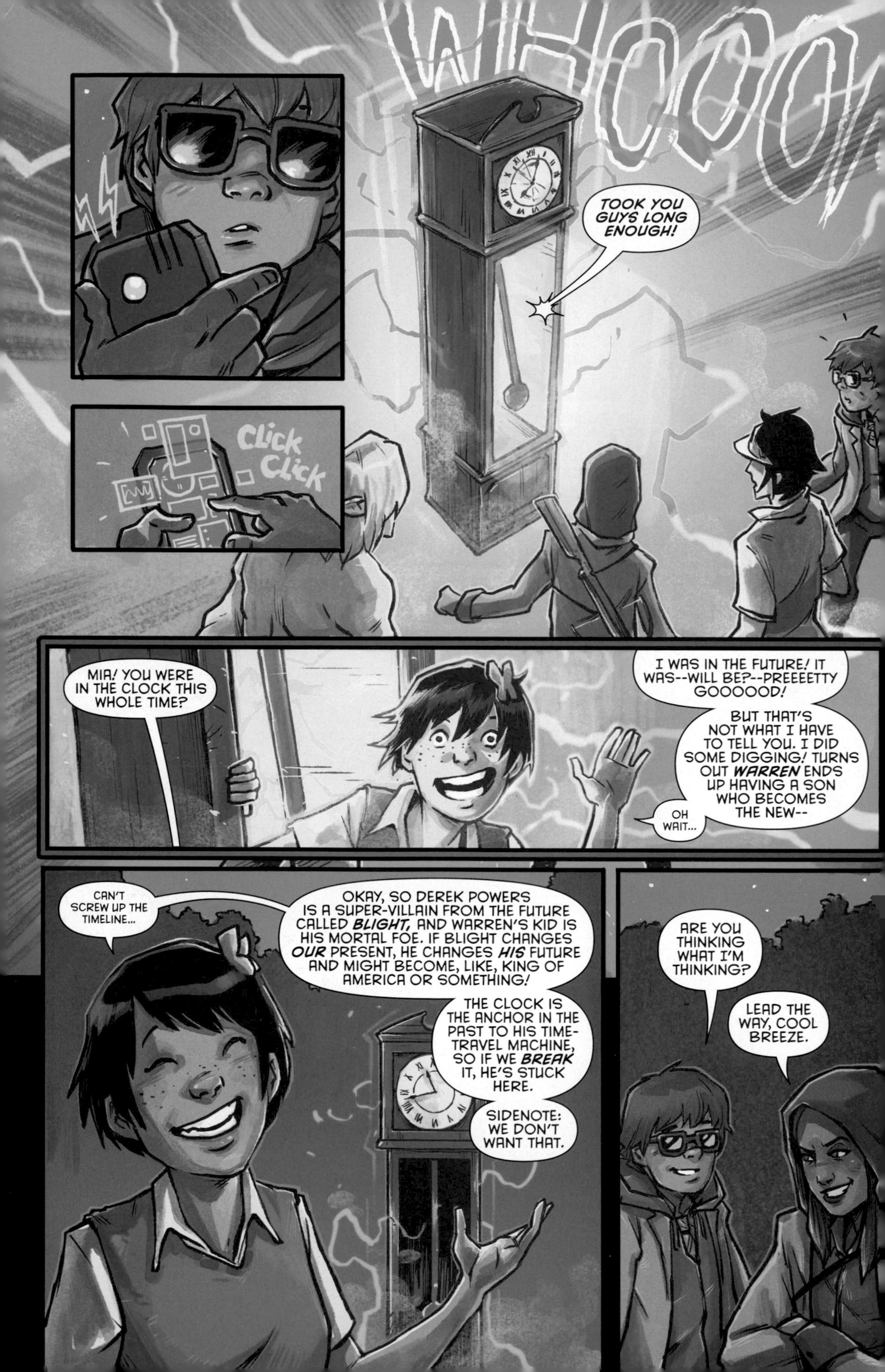
WHOOOO
CLICK CLICK
TOOK YOU GUYS LONG ENOUGH!
MIA! YOU WERE IN THE CLOCK THIS WHOLE TIME?
I WAS IN THE FUTURE! IT WAS--WILL BE?--PREEEETTY GOOOOOD!
BUT THAT'S NOT WHAT I HAVE TO TELL YOU. I DID SOME DIGGING! TURNS OUT WARREN ENDS UP HAVING A SON WHO BECOMES THE NEW--
OH WAIT...
CAN'T SCREW UP THE TIMELINE...
OKAY, SO DEREK POWERS IS A SUPER-VILLAIN FROM THE FUTURE CALLED BLIGHT, AND WARREN'S KID IS HIS MORTAL FOE. IF BLIGHT CHANGES OUR PRESENT, HE CHANGES HIS FUTURE AND MIGHT BECOME, LIKE, KING OF AMERICA OR SOMETHING!
THE CLOCK IS THE ANCHOR IN THE PAST TO HIS TIME-TRAVEL MACHINE, SO IF WE BREAK IT, HE'S STUCK HERE.
SIDENOTE: WE DON'T WANT THAT.
ARE YOU THINKING WHAT I'M THINKING?
LEAD THE WAY, COOL BREEZE.

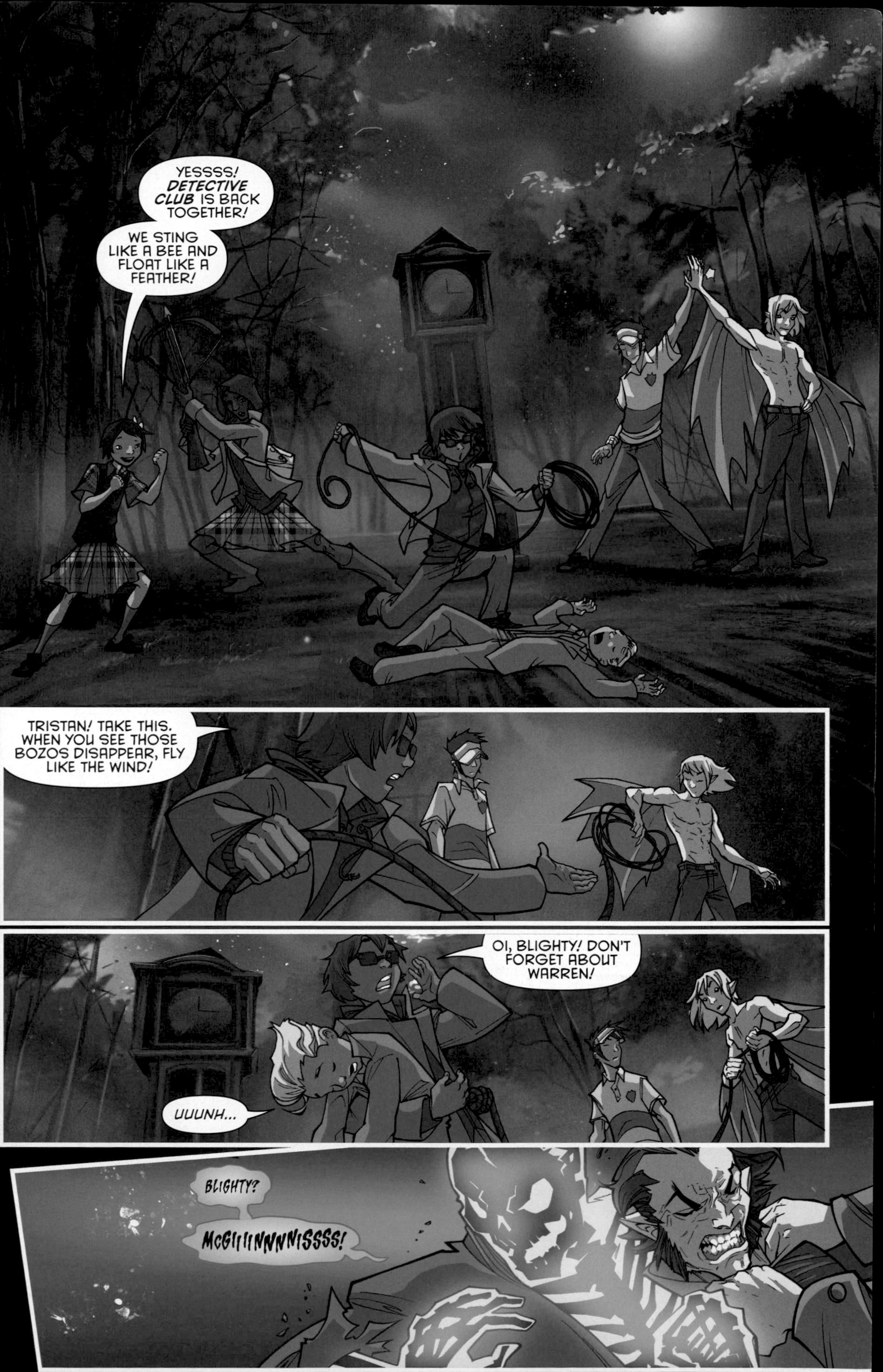
YESSSS! *DETECTIVE CLUB* IS BACK TOGETHER!
WE STING LIKE A BEE AND FLOAT LIKE A FEATHER!
TRISTAN! TAKE THIS. WHEN YOU SEE THOSE BOZOS DISAPPEAR, FLY LIKE THE WIND!
OI, BLIGHTY! DON'T FORGET ABOUT WARREN!
UUUNH...
BLIGHTY?
MCGIIIINNNNISSSS!

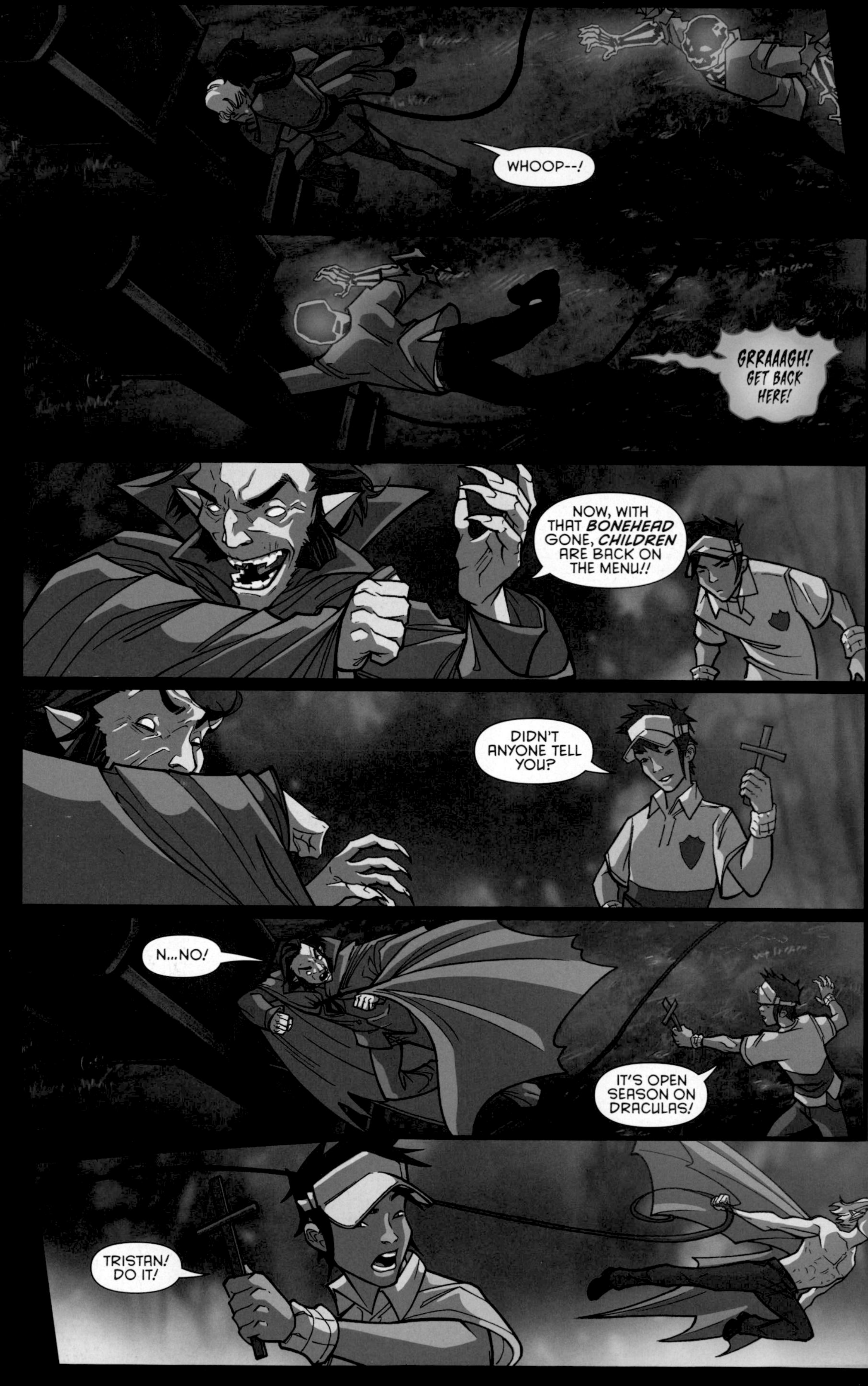
WHOOP--!
GRRAAAGH! GET BACK HERE!
NOW, WITH THAT BONEHEAD GONE, CHILDREN ARE BACK ON THE MENU!!
DIDN'T ANYONE TELL YOU?
N...NO!
IT'S OPEN SEASON ON DRACULAS!
TRISTAN! DO IT!

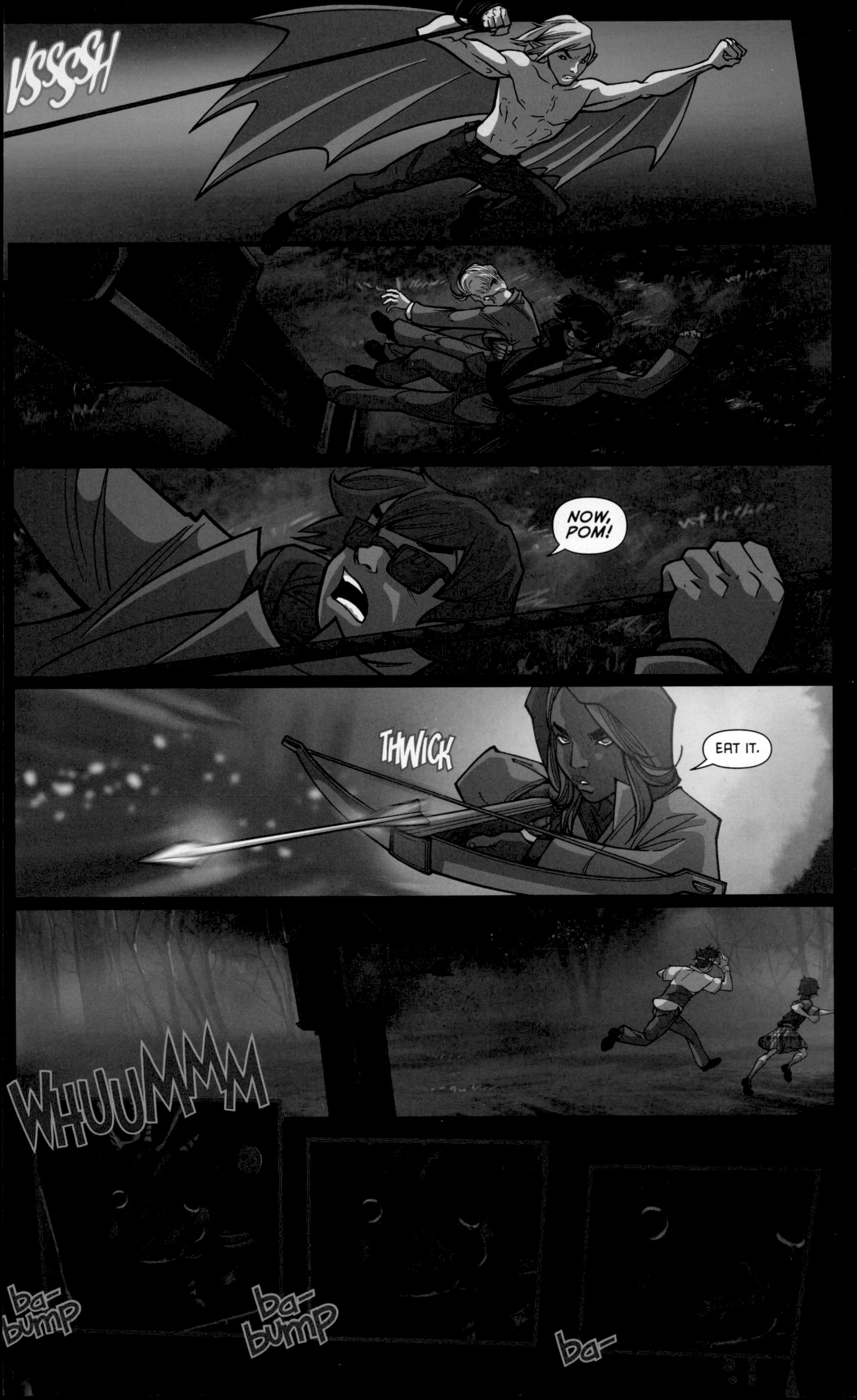
VSSSSH
NOW, POM!
THWICK
EAT IT.
WHUUMMM
ba-bump
ba-bump
ba-

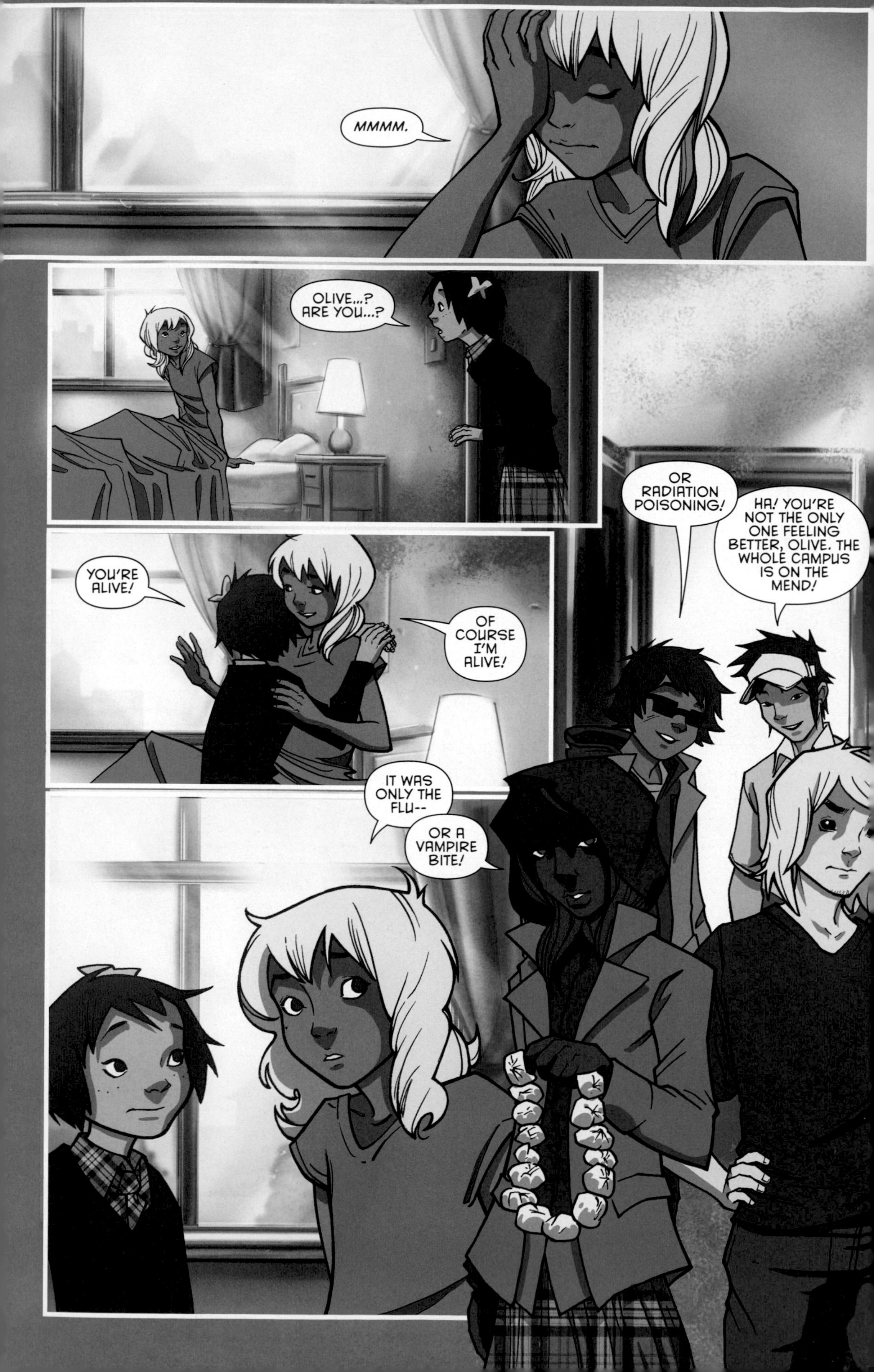
MMMM.
OLIVE...? ARE YOU...?
YOU'RE ALIVE!
OF COURSE I'M ALIVE!
IT WAS ONLY THE FLU--
OR A VAMPIRE BITE!
OR RADIATION POISONING!
HA! YOU'RE NOT THE ONLY ONE FEELING BETTER, OLIVE. THE WHOLE CAMPUS IS ON THE MEND!

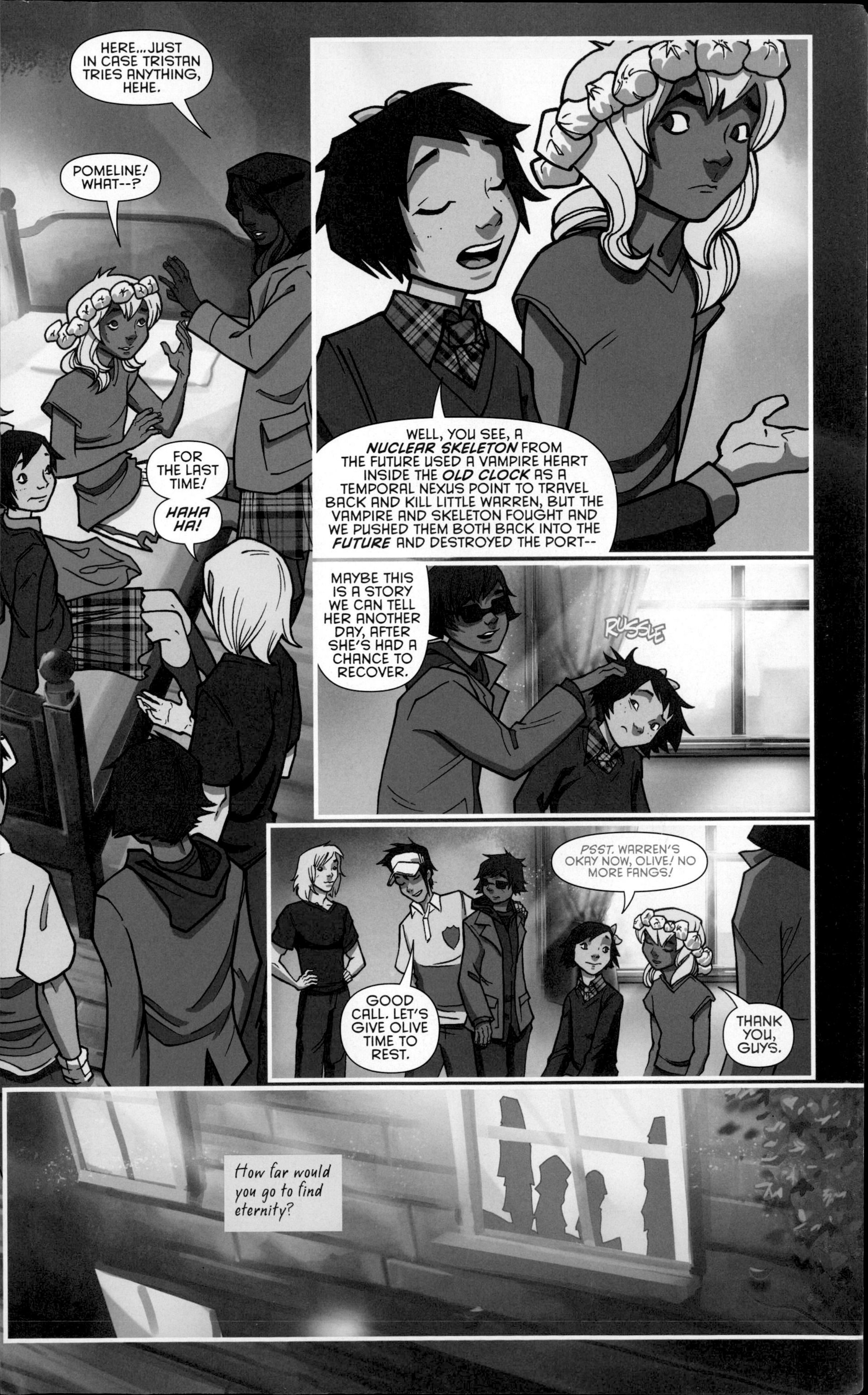
HERE...JUST IN CASE TRISTAN TRIES ANYTHING, HEHE.
POMELINE! WHAT--?
FOR THE LAST TIME!
HAHA HA!
WELL, YOU SEE, A NUCLEAR SKELETON FROM THE FUTURE USED A VAMPIRE HEART INSIDE THE OLD CLOCK AS A TEMPORAL NEXUS POINT TO TRAVEL BACK AND KILL LITTLE WARREN, BUT THE VAMPIRE AND SKELETON FOUGHT AND WE PUSHED THEM BOTH BACK INTO THE FUTURE AND DESTROYED THE PORT--
MAYBE THIS IS A STORY WE CAN TELL HER ANOTHER DAY, AFTER SHE'S HAD A CHANCE TO RECOVER.
RUSSLE
PSST. WARREN'S OKAY NOW, OLIVE! NO MORE FANGS!
GOOD CALL. LET'S GIVE OLIVE TIME TO REST.
THANK YOU, GUYS.
How far would you go to find eternity?

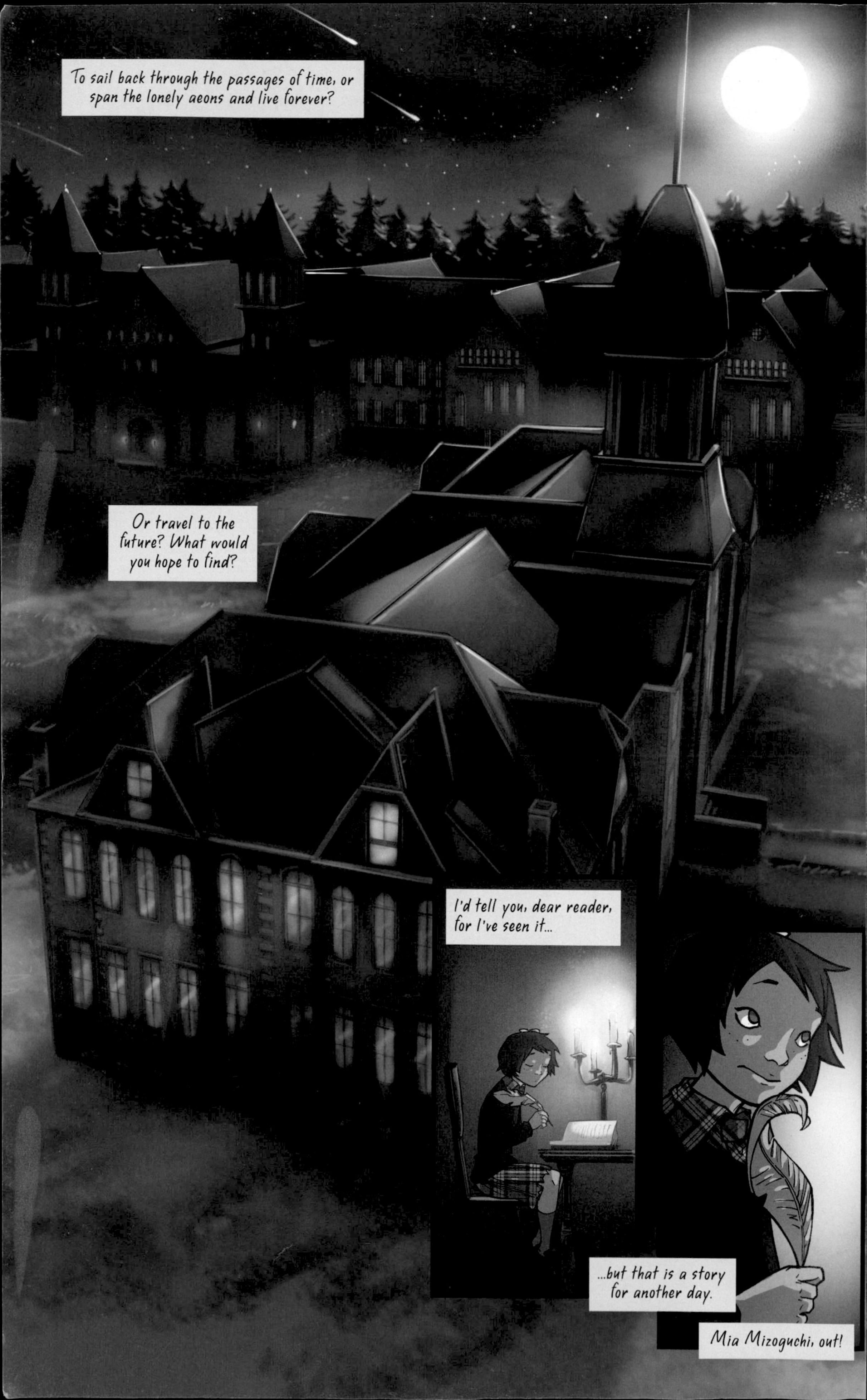
To sail back through the passages of time, or span the lonely aeons and live forever?
Or travel to the future? What would you hope to find?
I'd tell you, dear reader, for I've seen it...
...but that is a story for another day.
Mia Mizoguchi, out!

CHARACTER STUDIES BY **MICHAEL DIALYNAS**

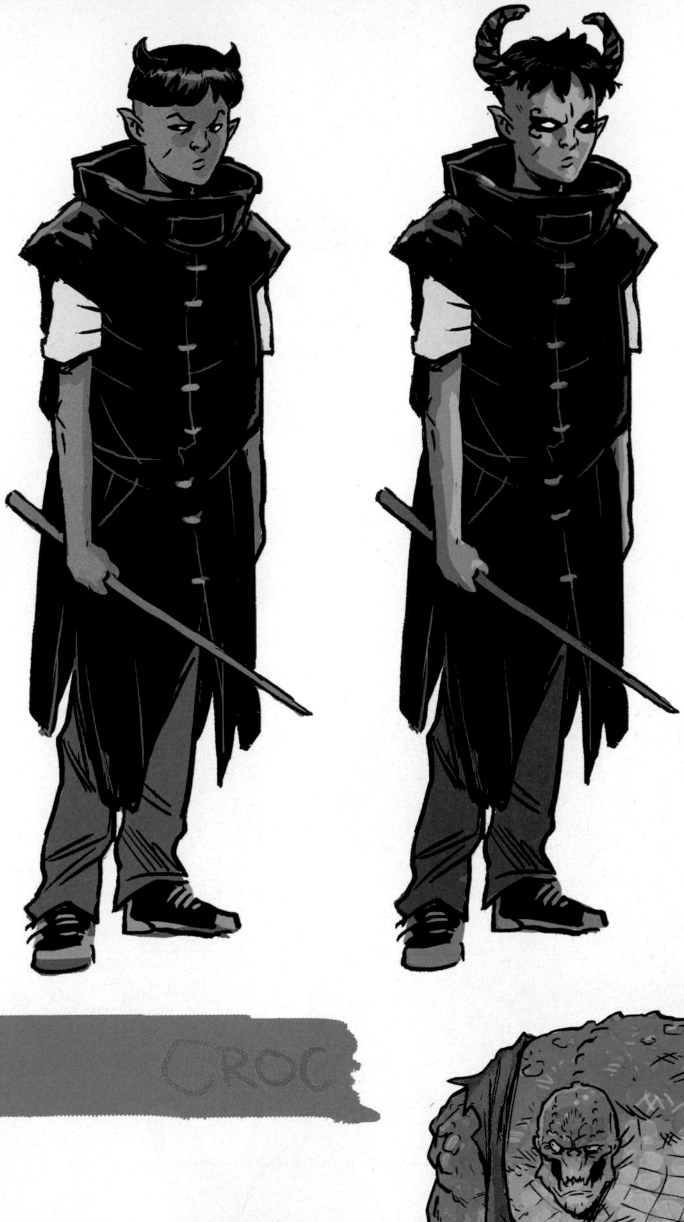

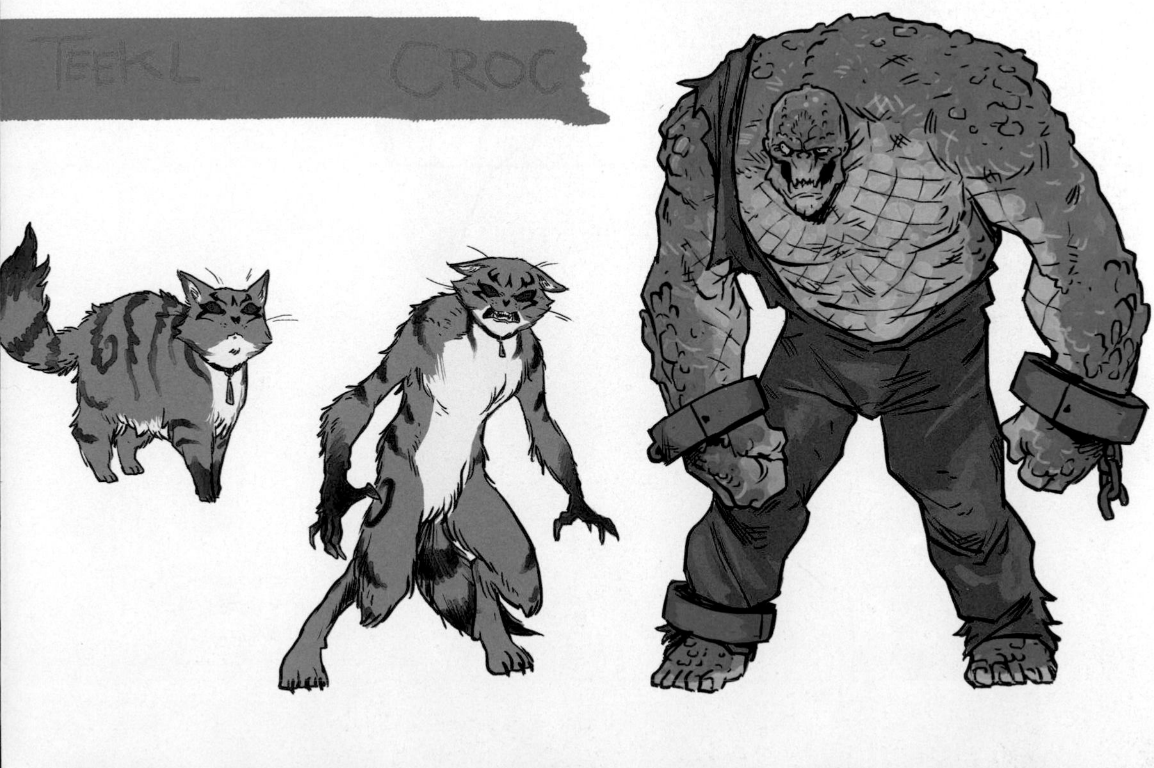
TEEKL
CROC

MAPS AND POMELINE CHARACTER STUDIES BY **NATASHA ALTERICI**

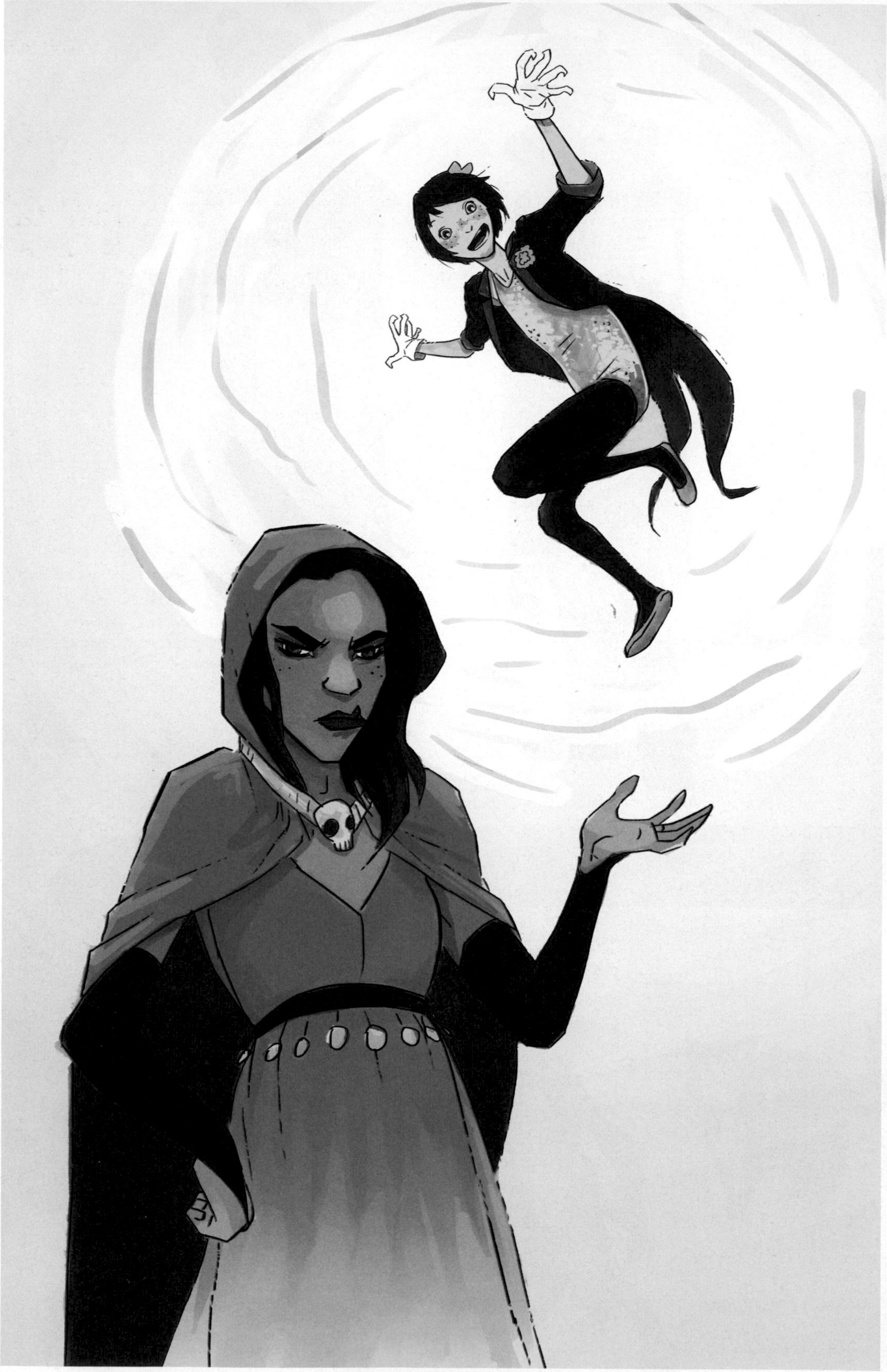

START AT THE BEGINNING!

TEEN TITANS
VOLUME 1: IT'S OUR RIGHT TO FIGHT

TEEN TITANS VOL. 2: THE CULLING

TEEN TITANS VOL. 3: DEATH OF THE FAMILY

THE CULLING: RISE OF THE RAVAGERS

START AT THE BEGINNING!

BATGIRL
VOLUME 1: THE DARKEST REFLECTION

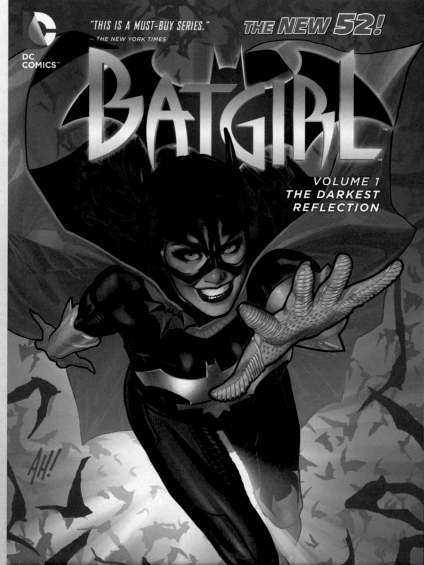

GRANT MORRISON
with FRANK QUITELY & PHILIP TAN

VOL. 2:
BATMAN VS. ROBIN

VOL. 3: BATMAN &
ROBIN MUST DIE!

DARK KNIGHT VS.
WHITE KNIGHT

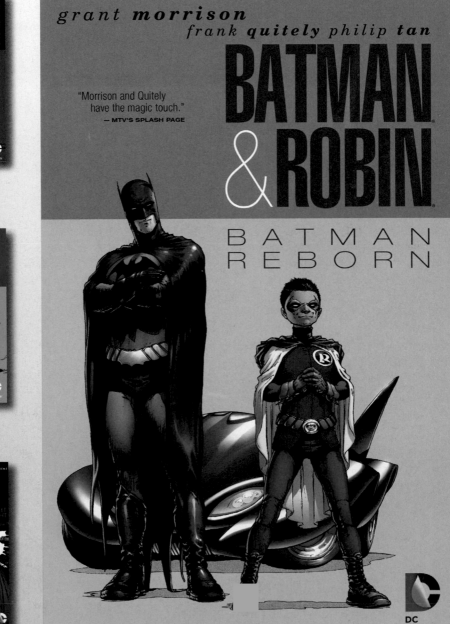